D0150036

Praise for th

GU

"Suspense with a large dollop of romance . . . Done very well." —*USA Today*

"Behre is back with more paranormal romance and danger . . . This story has it all: murder, animal kidnapping, and tender romance." —*RT Book Reviews*

"Behre successfully balances the mystery with the love story." —*Publishers Weekly*

"Fast and satisfying . . . A light detective romance story with a twist of paranormal." —That's What I'm Talking About

"Danger and passion explode in this thrilling paranormal romantic suspense." —Paranormal Haven

"A wonderful story with a little bit of everything . . . A fun, delightful read with a hot romance, mystery, and action-packed suspense." —The Reading Café

"Behre really knows how to write suspense." —Debbie's Book Bag

SPIRITED

"Great! A real page-turner. Once you pick it up, you won't want to put it down until you're done!"
—Lynsay Sands, *New York Times* bestselling author of the Argeneau novels

continued . . .

"[A] sweet, funny, sexy debut!"
—Lena Diaz, author of the Deadly Games series

"No magic crystal ball is needed to foresee this writer is bursting with talent! I can't wait for more from her!"
—Shelby Reed, author of *The Fifth Favor*

"Behre's exuberant debut paranormal romance is lighthearted and easygoing."
—*Publishers Weekly*

"Debut talent Behre quickly proves she will fit into the paranormal romance world very nicely . . . This mix of romance, ghostly visions, and unexpected danger is unbelievably fun and thrilling!"
—*RT Book Reviews*

"Lively, funny, and fresh . . . Just the thing for readers who want their mystery thrillers with a ghostly twist and an offbeat sense of humor."
—*Library Journal*

"A riveting psychic suspense . . . This steady-paced plot keeps the reader on the edge of their seat with lots of suspense, action, and romance . . . The attraction between Seth and Jules radiates heat from every page and the sex scenes sizzle with lots of steamy passion."
—Paranormal Haven

"An exciting story, not to mention also very hot."
—The Reading Café

"An at times humorous, at times suspenseful story . . . [Behre] effectively blends romance with suspense, weaving together stories that work together very well."
—Harlequin Junkie

Berkley Sensation titles by Mary Behre

SPIRITED
GUARDED
HARMONIZED
ENERGIZED

ENERGIZED

Mary Behre

BERKLEY SENSATION, NEW YORK

An imprint of Penguin Random House LLC
375 Hudson Street, New York, New York 10014

ENERGIZED

A Berkley Sensation Book / published by arrangement with the author

Copyright © 2015 by Mary Behre.
Excerpt from *Guarded* by Mary Behre copyright © 2014 by Mary Behre.
Penguin supports copyright. Copyright fuels creativity, encourages diverse voices, promotes free speech, and creates a vibrant culture. Thank you for buying an authorized edition of this book and for complying with copyright laws by not reproducing, scanning, or distributing any part of it in any form without permission. You are supporting writers and allowing Penguin to continue to publish books for every reader.

BERKLEY SENSATION® and the "B" design are registered trademarks of Penguin Random House LLC.
For more information, visit penguin.com.

ISBN: 978-0-425-28200-7

PUBLISHING HISTORY
Berkley Sensation mass-market edition / August 2015

PRINTED IN THE UNITED STATES OF AMERICA

10 9 8 7 6 5 4 3 2 1

Cover art by Tony Mauro.
Cover design by Sarah Oberrender.

This is a work of fiction. Names, characters, places, and incidents either are the product of the author's imagination or are used fictitiously, and any resemblance to actual persons, living or dead, business establishments, events, or locales is entirely coincidental.

If you purchased this book without a cover, you should be aware that this book is stolen property. It was reported as "unsold and destroyed" to the publisher, and neither the author nor the publisher has received any payment for this "stripped book."

For Brian.

ACKNOWLEDGMENTS

Thank you Leis and Nalini for believing in this story.

Now for my big list. Thank you Mike, Susan, Kim, Kevin, Brian, Chris, Scott, and Matt for answering my endless questions about everything from the Marines to tax forms, to becoming an electrician, to keeping it real with police procedures, to various other odd questions that had me zipping out an email at two thirty in the morning. Any mistakes made in this novel were purely my own, and sometimes intentional.

Thank you, my darling husband, for taking the time to teach me how to replace and rewire an outlet as research. I might not be as mechanically inclined as Hannah, but it was so much fun. You're a terrific instructor.

Last but never least, thank you, my brilliant children. You figured out how to make pizza, pancakes, and other delightful, if somewhat unhealthy, dinners while I worked to finish this novel. As always, you are the most important people in my life.

CHAPTER 1

DECEMBER

Fincastle, Ohio

"LOVER, FRIEND, OR family?"

Niall Graham looked from the glass of tepid beer he wasn't drinking and into the golden-hazel eyes of the pretty, young bartender. Her long hair, the same color as her eyes, hung in ringlets to her breasts, except for one long pink braid that trailed from behind her left ear. In jeans and a black T-shirt, she looked young and fresh and hopeful. Everything he wasn't.

Pulling a stained white towel off the black apron tied at her tiny waist, she wiped down the bar. Her voluptuous breasts bounced jauntily in front of him, jiggling the white letters on her shirt.

Keep calm and carry . . .

He couldn't make out the rest of the words on her there-IS-a-God tight shirt. The letters disappeared beneath her curves. He must have stared at her chest too long because she folded her arms on the bar blocking his view. He whipped his gaze to hers.

"That wasn't an invitation." She winked and settled her chin on her hand, giving him a sympathetic smile. "I was asking if it was a lover, friend, or family member on your mind. It's gotta be one of the three. Only they can make someone sit unmoving on a stool for four hours straight in a bar and *not* drink. You've been nursing that same beer since I served it to you at ten. Either you like your barley and hops the temperature and flavor of lukewarm bathwater or something else drove you to sit silently at my bar until past closing."

Niall glanced around. Cheap tinsel and garish colored lights were strewn over every available space of the dark, wood interior until the bar looked like some warped version of a Tim Burton Christmas special. Dreary with a touch of hopeless wistfulness. It suited Niall's mood perfectly.

Another bar, the one attached to the hotel where he was lodged for the night, had been noisy and crowded. For hours, he'd sat trying to drown out the noise of the patrons at Molloy's Pub next door. The locals were throwing an old-fashioned Irish wake. When the noise shifted to depressing songs about fallen heroes, Niall had escaped.

After walking for fifteen minutes on the deserted street, he found himself outside a bar called Heaven's Gate. The door swung open. A stringy man wearing a baggy Santa suit stumbled out and fell into the bushes on the side of the building. He popped back up as if on a spring, puked noisily, then sauntered up the street in the careful way drunks do when trying desperately to prove they're sober.

Despite the inebriated Santa, or maybe because of him, Niall stared at the bar in wonder. It gleamed under a single light post at the town's main intersection. Someone had recently painted a logo on the door. With its tilted golden halo dangling from the tip of a red and black pitchfork, it seemed to beckon him.

Perhaps, this gate will let me in.

Heaven's Gate had been mostly empty. Plenty of room to move. Not that he'd done anything except sit. And sit. And sit more. Around him patrons drank, laughed, paired off, and stumbled out. He was only twenty-eight, but Niall didn't have the energy to talk, to move, to drink.

Christ, he was so fucking tired. Tired of traveling. Tired of the Marines. Tired of life.

"Hey there, where'd you go?" The bartender touched his hand. Her cool fingers whispered across his skin. Something warm and gentle tugged deep in his chest. Her touch, though brief, was a balm to his battered soul. He looked into her eyes and they fucking twinkled. And he felt ancient.

But he didn't want to look away from the first smiling face he'd seen in months that reminded him of home.

"Hiya, I'm Hannah. What's your name, soldier?"

"I'm a Marine, not a soldier," he retorted out of habit, but couldn't stop his grin at her spritely chatter.

"Pardon the insult, Marine." She saluted him quickly, then leaned against the bar again.

Normally, civilians who gave mock salutes annoyed him. He wasn't annoyed by this woman. He was . . . charmed. A surprised chuckle escaped him. "None taken. And it's Niall."

"Niall." She rolled the word on her tongue like she was tasting it. Tasting him.

An odd sexual dip hit him low in the belly. He'd been empty for so long, he'd practically forgotten what arousal felt like. He glanced at her smiling face again. She wasn't classically beautiful. Her eyes were almost too big for her face. Her nose was slightly off center. Her mouth appeared to be smiling, even when she spoke. Certainly not the smoldering, pouty look of a model, yet it all added up to make her remarkably pretty.

"Tell you what, Niall," she said, patting his hand and straightening. "Since you seem to want quiet, I'll give it to you. I'm going to clean up because I'd like to close the bar. You go right on sitting there. Not drinking your beer."

She winked again and went to work. He watched her move around the room, stacking chairs on tables.

The place was completely empty, save the two of them. He should go back to his hotel. But then she'd be here all alone. No doubt she'd closed the bar at night before, but did she often have strange men in there alone with her? Her lack of concern for her own safety had him sliding off the stool and crossing to her.

"Hannah."

"So you do want to talk." She met his gaze, a grin widening her mouth. She flipped over the armless wooden chair and slid it onto the cracked table. "The doctor is in. That'll be five cents, please."

"Five cents?" He froze midstep. With another chair in her hands, she laughed. "Haven't you ever seen Charlie Brown?"

It took him a moment. "So does that make you Lucy?"

"I seem to be tonight. Did you know that Santa has a drinking problem and he's a bit of a horndog too?" She slid the chair onto the tabletop. Her laughter rang through the empty bar like wind chimes. Low and musical.

"Yes. I witnessed his little alcohol issue when I arrived. He stumbled outside and planted face-first into the bushes."

Her smile vanished. "Is Mr. Landsdowne still out there?"

She started for the door, but Niall caught her elbow. Her breasts brushed against his arm, making the hair on his arm stand on end. He had to clear his throat once to make his voice work. "No, he recovered quickly and headed north on the street. No doubt to find his bag and deliver toys."

Hannah blew out a relieved breath, her breasts connecting with Niall's arm again. Christ, it had been a long time since he'd been with a woman if this innocent touch had his balls aching. Releasing her, he stepped back and tucked his hands at the small of his back.

She patted him on the arm. "At ease, Marine."

He laughed at himself. Technically, he was standing at ease and let his arms fall to his sides.

Hannah had already stacked another set of chairs before he remembered his concern. He followed her to one of the dozen small, square laminate tables, spread out in a semicircle around the twin pool tables. "Isn't this dangerous?"

She upended the chair in her hands and slid onto the tabletop. "Not the way I do it."

Niall copied her move with the next chair. Side by side, he towered over her. He was bigger than the average American man, but not by much. He'd bulked up in the Marines. Still, Hannah was a tiny thing that barely reached his shoulder.

"No, ma'am, I can see you can handle a bar chair with the best of 'em."

"That's me all over. Champion bar stool flipper." She lifted the chair in her hands and deftly slid it onto the table. "And seriously, lighten *up* with the *ma'am* thing. This is Fincastle. You only say *ma'am* if you're talking to the minister's wife, bagging groceries, or doing it with a domme."

Niall dropped the chair in his hands. It hit the floor with a clatter.

Hannah laughed. Her body shook and her cheeks were scarlet. "Just seeing if you were listening."

"Yes, ma— Hannah."

She sidled past him to the next table and Niall caught a whiff of her hair. Despite working in a bar that stank of stale beer and old smoke, Hannah smelled like honeysuckles. It reminded him of Tidewater, Virginia, in the spring. A pang of homesickness struck him.

"Isn't it dangerous for you to be alone in the bar with a stranger?" he asked, shoving aside thoughts of home and continuing to help her stack chairs.

"There's always one person left in the bar when I close. Usually, it's a friend or neighbor." She shrugged, finished another table, and moved on. "Besides, you're harmless."

That stopped him. "I'm a Marine. We're not known for being pussies." His cheeks burned. "Excuse my language, ma'am."

"No more *ma'am*. I'm not the minister's wife and you're not bagging my groceries."

His heart tripped in his chest at what she didn't say. Too stunned to do more than stare at the brazen fairylike woman, Niall held the chair aloft.

"I'm not a domme either." She winked and slid the chair from his hands. Setting it aside, she closed the distance between them, and patted his bicep. "Okay, Marine. You're not exactly harmless. But I'm safe with you."

"What makes you so sure of that?" Fuck, this was a small town, when a woman would not worry about being alone with a strange man at two in the morning. "You don't know anything about me. I could be a serial killer or something."

She arched a single brow at him and folded her arms. "Are you a serial killer?"

"No, but that's not the point." Why did he care? Why was he even having this conversation? He should go back to his hotel or just haul ass out of this pissant town. He'd done his duty by attending the funeral of a fellow Marine, now he should just leave. But she was looking at him with such amused defiance on her face he heard himself say, "You seem like a sweet girl and just the type a sick bastard would seek out so he could destroy her innocence."

Her smile faded, but didn't quite vanish. "First, I'm not a girl nor innocent. Hello! Bartender, here. Second, you've got a pretty jaded view of life, even for a Marine." He opened his mouth to reply but she held up her hand and continued talking. "And third, I'm not afraid of you because you dropped your keys a couple hours ago."

"My keys?"

She nodded, her tawny curls bobbing. "Yeah. I handed them back to you right after you didn't drink the beer I set down in front of you."

She grinned again and this time her whole face lit with delight.

Niall tugged his keys out of his pocket. They looked average. His mother's house key, the key to the restaurant his family owned, and a key to the car he'd rented when he'd driven in from Columbus yesterday.

She held out her hand. "Give me your keys."

"I'm not drunk."

"Again, bartender! I know you haven't had a drink all night. It's my job to pay attention to the clientele. I also know you aren't an alcoholic because while you didn't drink, you also didn't stare at the beer with lust or hatred. You wanted to be alone and weren't waiting for anyone because you never once looked at the door tonight. And you aren't married, or if you are, you never wear a ring. No tan line on your ring finger."

"You're very observant. I'm not married. Not dating." Was she digging for information? A little unnerved and a lot flattered by her accurate assessment, he decided to turn the tables on her. "What about you? Boyfriend? Husband? Pet dog?"

"Nope. Single city for me. Not even a Fido to call my own." She wriggled her fingers. "You gonna hand me those keys?"

Intrigued, he surrendered them. She closed her fist around the metal key ring and shut her eyes. Her brows knit as if in concentration. The room went unearthly quiet.

She shivered, then she shoved the keys back at him. He had to grab them quickly or they'd have hit the ground.

For a moment, her tawny-colored eyes were a bit unfocused and her lips moved but no sound came out. Then her eyes cleared and she stepped back.

"Whoa, you've got a lot going on in that noggin of yours, Marine." Tossing her hair back over her shoulders, she tugged at the front of her shirt, holding it out so he could read it. "But to answer your question, it says, Keep Calm and Carry Condoms."

Heat pulsed from his heart to his dick and back again. But a sliver of foreboding cooled his lust.

Ah, Christ, she thinks she's a psychic.

And here he'd assumed he'd left that behind in Tidewater. His hometown seemed full to bursting with people claiming to have some sort of gift or curse or crift or what-the-fuck-ever.

"You trying to tell me you read my mind? I think it's more you saw me trying to read your shirt."

"I don't read minds." Sighing, she moved past him and continued setting chairs on the last two tables. "I figured you were staring at my breasts. It happens a lot in the bar. I mostly ignore ogling, unless some yahoo tries to find out if they're real."

Niall double-timed it after her, his jaw slack. "Are you saying guys ask if you have . . . you know?"

"Implants?" She snorted. "You know, for a Marine who says *pussy*, you probably shouldn't shy away from an innocuous non–curse word like *implants*.

"Yeah, every time some lost tourist looking for Columbus stumbles into the bar, I get asked if my breasts are real. And more. One guy said he needed proof . . . *after* he shoved a twenty down my top and copped a feel along the way."

"I hope you punched the holy shit—um, excuse me. Knocked the holy heck out of him." Again, Niall was struck by her size. She was barely five-foot. Eccentric or not, what was she doing working in a bar by herself at night?

"No, I didn't hit him. However, I did tell him the twenty lodged in my bra was my tip and he still owed me for his beer. He didn't really argue. Granted, he'd sort of tripped over my knee in his crotch at the time." She turned and cast a sly glance over her shoulder. "Then I had my friend the sheriff escort him to jail for assault."

"Outstanding." Niall returned her grin.

"Thanks, I thought so." She shrugged. "My parents, they're totally into nonviolence, weren't too pleased that I'd tried to emasculate the mayor's son."

"I thought he was a tourist."

"Yeah, he was." She stopped Niall from setting the chairs on the next table by whipping out her bar towel and waving it. Wiping the laminate clean, she said, "Turns out, he was from the mayor's first marriage to a stripper from Columbus. Mayor Hobbs didn't even know he had a kid until the sheriff called to tell him I'd racked the guy in self-defense." She tucked the towel back into her apron and shrugged.

"But your parents were angry?"

"Only until I pulled the twenty out of my bra." Her fairy-like face took on a mischievous glint. "Then Daddy had a little chat with him."

"No one hurts Daddy's little girl?"

"Something like that." She flipped another chair, then started wiping down the bar.

They worked in silence for a few minutes. He'd stopped asking himself why he followed her around the bar and simply enjoyed being with her.

"I'm sorry about your friends." Her words were soft, gentle. And startling.

"Pardon?" That sliver of discomfort arrowed up his spine. And the mind-numbing void he'd lived in since their deaths last month in Kandahar threatened to return.

"You asked me why I wasn't afraid to be alone with you, it's because you were thinking about them when you first sat down." She tossed the towel into a receptacle, then returned to her spot behind the bar. While she spoke, she set out two shot glasses and grabbed a bottle of Patron Silver. Pouring the tequila she said, "I knew one of them. Danny Molloy. He was two years ahead of me in high school. I didn't know him well, but when news of his death hit town, we all felt it."

Niall wanted to wrap himself in the nothingness that he'd worn like a shield since the explosion at the barracks. Drift back into the void of emotionless existence. Instead, he dropped onto a seat across from the quirky attractive bartender. "I'm sorry about Danny-boy."

She slid the shot toward him and lifted her own glass, her eyes somber. "I'm sorry for you too. I barely knew him. But you were friends. And you lost another friend too. Iggy, right?"

"How did you know that?" Niall's fingers tightened so fast on the little glass, tequila sloshed over the top and onto the counter.

"I told you, already. Your keys." Without missing a beat, she ripped off a paper towel from a roll standing next to the cash register and blotted up the mess. "I didn't mean to pry. When I picked up the keys the first time, the memory kind of smacked into my brain."

"You some sort of gypsy bartender?" he asked trying to add levity back into their discussion. And hoping the pretty bartender wasn't a nut job. Or worse, that she wasn't really psychic. He already knew one. According to his old friend, being crifted absolutely sucked most of the time. But if Hannah did have some sort of cursed gift, he hoped it wasn't mind reading. Inside his head was the dead last place he'd wish anyone.

"No, I'm really an artist, but I fill in as a bartender during college breaks to help out my parents. They own Heaven's Gate."

"Seriously?"

"Yep, it's my parents' place." She smiled at him, then shook her head. "No, full truth, I'm not really an artist. No money in it. I'm studying to be a journeyman electrician. So I guess you could call me a psychic electrician."

Niall wasn't sure how to respond. Was she joking about the psychic thing? She seemed pretty legitimate when holding his keys. And no one here could have known about Iggy. He'd only arrived in Kandahar the day before the explosion.

Was it worth the stress of wondering if she was crazy or not? She didn't seem like the phonies he'd met over the years. But she also seemed far more comfortable with her gift than his friend back in Tidewater. Then there was the Iggy thing. Hannah had been spot-on about him.

Maybe Niall should just leave the bar and this confusing but fucking attractive woman. He stared into her guileless golden eyes and didn't move.

Hannah lifted her glass and clinked against his. "To the friends that had you sitting in my bar all night."

HANNAH SWALLOWED THE tequila and waited. For a heartbeat, it appeared the hot Marine wouldn't drink. Then he lifted the glass to his lips and swallowed. She'd have to cover the cost of the top-rail alcohol but it would be totally worth it. For him.

She'd sensed more than seen that Niall needed comfort. He'd lost friends in a vicious attack. When she'd held his keys both times, she'd slid into a moment in his memory. Every detail she experienced had been through his senses. The attack had been horrific. The choking stench of sand and blood and death drove her to pouring them each a drink.

She also remembered hearing him talk to someone named Iggy as he lay dying and pinned on top of Niall in the rubble. Niall's gut-wrenching hopelessness at being unable to help his friend had been almost more than she could bear. It was why she'd given him back the keys so quickly. Why she'd immediately sought out the strongest drink in the bar to wash away the vision.

"It's my turn to ask," Niall said, drawing her gaze. "Where'd you go?"

Into your past. But she didn't want to say that. They'd been having a lovely chat before she'd stupidly brought up his friends. She'd only wanted to play a little. Dip into his head and get a reading on him that would make them both laugh. Learn some fun secret, like a *Firefly* or *Buffy* obsession, the kind of energies she tended to pick up in the bar from other patrons.

She hadn't anticipated slipping into the Marine's painful past twice. Certainly not when he'd been showing her what she'd hoped was lustful attention.

Hannah glanced into the Marine's vivid green eyes and saw attraction there. And something more. Something sensual. And strangely peaceful. The sight made her whole body tingle.

"I'm trying to decide if I want to get you drunk and take advantage of you," she said, hoping to throw him off guard.

He rewarded her when his black brows winged up. She didn't miss the way his eyes darkened to the color of summer grass. He poured himself another shot. "Maybe I'm the one who's in danger in this bar."

Interestingly, he didn't immediately pour her one. He lifted the bottle in the air in question and waited for her to nod. Such a gentleman. And so handsome. His blue-black hair was cut high and tight in typical Marine fashion. His jaw was sharp and strong.

Most of the night, he'd nursed his beer, his mouth drawn in a grim line. He hadn't been rude to the few patrons who had braved Heaven's Gate. Instead, he'd been quiet. Reserved. Seated at the end of the bar as if unaware of the world around him.

Most of Fincastle had gone to Molloy's for the wake. No surprise, since Danny's family owned it. Normally, Heaven's Gate and Molloy's competed for business, but tonight Hannah had been relieved to see her parents' bar mostly empty.

"So are you going to get me drunk and stay sober?" Niall asked, sliding her glass closer to her. "Doesn't exactly seem honest."

Could she do something like this? She'd been half-joking when she suggested getting him drunk. She'd only ever had one lover. If she couldn't keep the dull and frankly boring Bryan happy, what did she have to offer the Marine? Then again, Bryan had been dull and boring in bed so perhaps it wasn't her fault. And this man, this wonderfully complex man in front of her, was anything but dull.

She needed a sign that her sudden and unexpected impulse to take the Marine home was the right one. Just one little teensy sign.

He lowered the bottle, the light in his eyes dimmed a bit. And she knew. For tonight, she could give him comfort and give them something they both needed. An escape.

"What if I just offer to take you upstairs to my apartment? I bet if we think about it, we can come up with something to do that would make us both feel good."

The pulse in his neck sped up, otherwise, he didn't move. He eyed her speculatively. "You seem like a nice girl. And I'm not going to lie. Going to bed with you would be the best thing that's happened to me in months. But I feel like I'm taking advantage. I'm a little old for you."

Surprised laughter burst from her. God, she liked this guy. If his words had been a sign they would have been neon green. She was definitely making the right choice. "You're what, twenty-nine?"

"Twenty-eight," he replied almost defensively.

"Six years, Marine." She waved to the space between them. "All that separates us is six years. And I told you. I'm a woman not a girl. But I am nice. Very nice. And I think you could use that tonight. Whadaya say?"

* * *

NIALL STOOD AT parade rest in her tidy bedroom waiting for Hannah to come out of the bathroom. The walls might have been white but there was color everywhere. Tie-dyed curtains. A hand-braided rug straight out of the 1970s covered the faded hardwood floor. Watercolor paintings of sunsets, beaches, and blue owls gave the space a rich personality. Hannah's decorating style was eclectic and eccentric. Niall really liked it. It felt more homey than any place he'd stayed since he'd joined the Marines ten years ago.

The bathroom door opened. The light casting Hannah in silhouette didn't disguise that now she wore only her tight black T-shirt and panties. Hands at her sides, her fingers playing with the hem of her shirt, she said, "So . . ."

Don't change your mind. Oh, please, don't. With his head buzzing from the two shots of tequila—he hadn't had the heart to tell her he really didn't drink—he might just get down on his knees and beg if she changed her mind.

"So," he replied. He wanted to go to her. He hadn't even kissed her before accepting her invitation. And tasting her ranked high on his list of things he'd most like to do.

"Hey, Marine?" She closed the short distance between them. In her bare feet, she had to tip her head way back to look at him. It made him feel too big. Her, too small. "You plan to get undressed anytime soon? Or do you just plan to drop trou and do it with your boots on. 'Cause hot as that sounds, I was kind of hoping for something that would last a little longer than fifteen seconds."

Niall frowned and relaxed his arms, tucking his thumbs in the pockets of his cargo pants. But her words baffled him. "I don't think I've ever had sex end in only fifteen seconds."

"You're so literal. No, I bet you haven't." She laughed while twisting her pink braid between her fingers. "But I bet if we get naked, you could go all night. Wanna find out?"

Her words were brazen but her cheeks glowed red. For all her bravado, she was obviously not in her comfort zone.

Not that Niall was either, but damn, he wanted to be. He wanted her, but not if she was nervous to be with him.

Niall opened his mouth to suggest they slow down—*goddamned moral code*—when she grabbed her shirt by the hem. In one fluid motion, she whipped the shirt over her head, sending it and his resolve sailing to the floor.

Then she stood before him, wearing only panties. Her breasts were perky, lush, and tipped with dusky rose-colored nipples.

Niall's mouth watered for a taste. Reining in his control, he slid his gaze up her body. Her skin had a healthy glow. Freckles dotted her naked shoulders and he wanted to kiss each one. There was a tiny scar on her chin that didn't dim her beauty. If anything, it made her more attractive.

She licked her full lips. They shined in the lamplight.

Niall swallowed hard.

Hannah was a feast and he didn't know where to begin. He wanted to taste her from the backs of her knees to her earlobes. Still, he didn't move.

She shivered and raised her hands to cover her breasts.

"Changed your mind?" Of course she'd fucking changed her mind. She'd been naked and waiting for him to make a move. Instead, he'd turned into Forrest Gump and just stared.

"I'm standing naked in my apartment in the middle of one of the coldest Decembers in history." She shook her head slowly. "I'm chilly and hoping a really sexy Marine will come and sweep me off my feet."

Then she lifted onto her toes, wrapped her cool hands around his neck, and pulled his face to hers. He wasn't sure what to expect. Given her size, he wouldn't have been surprised had she given him the lightest of delicate kisses.

But there was nothing. Nothing. Not one damned thing delicate about what her lips and teeth and tongue did to his. And holy fucking God, he was rock hard for her. He'd had sex before with more women than he probably should have. Never had he felt the fervor in his blood that this woman stoked in him with a single kiss.

And he was just taking it.

Then as suddenly as she started, she stopped and stepped back. She was panting as hard as he. He imagined his eyes were as wild as hers. But there was something else. Some strange emotion flitted across her face, then disappeared. "Hey, Marine?"

"Yes?"

"You gonna just stand at attention or are you going to get naked with me?" she asked, shoving up his shirt. Like before, her cheeks went apple red. This time her hands trembled, but she kept touching him.

He tugged off the shirt, confused at her words. "I'm not standing at attention."

She cupped him right through his cargo pants. "Yeah, you definitely are."

He hissed in pleasure. Without breaking contact, she sat down on her bed, leaned forward, and pressed a kiss to his belly, just below his navel. Her tongue flicked out and drew a wet trail south. He shuddered.

He wanted to rip off his pants and bury himself inside her. Lose himself in the pleasure of her body. Pound into her until the need she created in him was slaked. But she was so fucking tiny, he could hurt her if he rode her the way he wanted.

So he'd be gentle. At least that was his thought until she nipped his belly, and tugged him on top of her.

The moment they were horizontal, her hands were inside his pants, squeezing his ass. She rocked her hips against him. And damn if he didn't grind himself against her. Then his mouth found hers again and there was nothing in the world but this moment. Tasting and touching.

Somehow, his pants were past his hips, bunched at his knees. He was hard as iron and holy fuck! What she was doing with her hands had him damn near ready to explode.

All the sweet hesitancy and blushes were gone. Her touch was out-fucking-standing! His brain clouded and he was awash in sensation. She was squeezing him. Measuring the length of him. Putting the condom on him.

He jerked his head up in surprise. "Where'd you get the condom?"

"From my bathroom. Keep Calm and Carry Condoms." She laughed, then nipped his chin. "Mind if I finish rolling it on you? 'Cause I'm digging your response to my touch."

She didn't wait for him to reply but resumed rolling the rubber down his shaft. Hannah squeezed first his cock, then his balls with enough pressure to make Niall arch his back.

Too much.

He flipped their positions, grabbed her wrists, and held her arms above her head. "You're going to kill me if you keep touching me like that."

She batted her lashes at him. "Guess it's your turn to touch. Because my panties are still on."

Keeping one hand around both of her wrists, he slid the other between her breasts, down her belly, and dipped inside the waistband of her lace panties. She emitted a small noise of pleasure.

Her eyes were hot gold. Her cheeks flushed as he slid two fingers into her. Just short strokes, until he was coated in her moisture, then he rubbed his thumb against the part of her guaranteed to have her hips moving. She spread her legs wider and rocked harder against his hand.

She was beautiful and open and all Niall wanted to do was bury himself inside her. So when she came against his fingers and yelled, "Inside me, Marine!" He didn't hesitate.

Her panties were off and he drove himself into her in one long, hard stroke. They both shuddered and clung to each other. Her short, unpolished nails pricked his back, even as her slender legs wrapped around his hips.

Then her lips found his. Where their first kiss was all excitement and lust, this kiss was passion and more. His breath mingled with hers and Niall felt something shift inside his chest. Unwilling to examine it, he moved his hips and let the excitement wash through them both again. Hotter and harder, but not too hard, he drove into her. She panted, she arched, and when she finally came, he thought his chest might burst.

She reached beneath him and squeezed his balls until he

had no choice but to let go and empty himself in a blinding roar of passion. Panting, slick with sweat, he shifted on top of her and did what he hadn't thought possible only hours before. He relaxed.

In the morning light, Hannah stood over Niall. Her big, tough Marine had needed something last night. If things had been different, she might have thought he could be the one. But he was just passing through town and her final semester started in a couple weeks. All signs definitely said he couldn't be anything but a night of comfort.

Dang it. She should have seen the sign last night. Hadn't she met him at Heaven's Gate after all? But she refused to regret. It had been the most incredible night of her life. And holy schmoley! She hadn't known sex could be like that. Hadn't known the power that came from being the initiator. Why on earth had she ever wasted her time on her ex and his nice-girls-don't-ask-for-sex rules?

Her Marine had been very responsive. And he definitely didn't have a problem with her being the one to get them started. She smiled at the sunlight glinting off his short black hair.

Even in sleep, he seemed rigid and formal. She'd worried the night before that he wouldn't let go of his pain long enough to enjoy himself. And that had been a big reason why she suggested sex in the first place. He was so sad, so buried in the pain of his past that he'd been little more than a vessel of hopelessness when he'd sat down at her bar.

Her phone beeped in reminder. She'd promised her mother she'd meet her for breakfast. Mom and Daddy had something important they wanted to discuss. Probably going to try to talk her into going to grad school again. Not that she would. She had two passions, painting and being an electrician. And grad school wouldn't help with becoming an electrician and she couldn't afford to pay for a master's degree in art.

She cleared the reminder and gave herself one more minute with her Marine. Just a little more time to soak in his quiet, masculine beauty. He lay facedown tangled in her tie-dyed sheets. One leg jutted off the side of the bed, as if he were ready to jump at a moment's notice. She'd have to paint this scene. Later.

Forcing herself away from the bed, she grabbed a sticky note from her desk. Scribbling her phone number and name on a sheet, she stuck it on top of his folded clothes.

She wanted to kiss him good-bye, but then thought better of it. Instead, she ran a hand through his silky short hair and yelped in surprise when he clamped a hand, none too gently, on her wrist.

Niall lifted his head and blinked the hazy look of sleep from his eyes. When his gaze fell on his hand shackling hers, he immediately released her. "Sorry."

"It's all good." She surreptitiously rubbed at the ache. "I gotta go. Feel free to use my shower. Lock up when you leave."

He blinked at her. Confusion in those lovely green eyes. "You're leaving? What time is it?"

"It's six in the morning. And yeah, I'm headed out. I promised my folks I'd help set up breakfast at the church this morning. Maybe I'll see you later?"

Okay, that had been slightly pathetic because she already knew he was leaving. But a girl had to try. And seeing him again would be a great excuse to put off that conversation with her parents.

Niall twisted and sat up. The sheet fell to his waist, affording her another glimpse of his incredible body. And suddenly helping at the church or talking to her parents didn't seem all that important. No. Wait. Those things *were* important. Darn it.

"It sounds cliché and gauche to say thank you for last night," he said, his voice still raspy from sleep. "But thank you."

He lifted her left hand and kissed the inside of her wrist, sending her pulse dancing. And sending messages to nerve endings nowhere near her wrist but much farther south.

Could you orgasm from a guy tonguing your wrist?

Before she could find out, he let go.

With the morning sunlight streaming in through her thin

curtains, Niall appeared bathed in a lovely red light. It made her feel warm and safe. It also made her want to crawl back into bed with him. So she backed to the doorway. "I left my number on the sticky note on top of your clothes. If you make it back to Fincastle, give me a call."

Niall rose from the bed sporting a healthy morning erection that had her seriously rethinking her exit strategy. Then she stopped thinking altogether when he crossed to her. Cupping her face in his hands he pressed a light kiss to her lips. It was gentle and soft and reminiscent of the closeness they'd shared last night.

All too soon, he released her and stepped back. The sadness that had been in his eyes when he had come into the bar last night returned.

Not a good sign.

Despite the knot in her belly, she kept her tone light when she said, "See you around, Marine."

She wasn't surprised when he replied, "Good-bye, Hannah."

CHAPTER 2

THE FOLLOWING JUNE

Tidewater, Virginia

YOU SHOULDN'T DO *this . . . Sinner. Freak. Whore!*

But she wasn't a freak. She wasn't. She was Mercy. And she had to silence the voices in her head that screamed at her. Voices that sounded remarkably like her mother's.

She grabbed her head and sank to the floor. The handle of the chef's knife she clutched in her left hand banged against her temple but did nothing to quiet the storm raging in her mind.

"Be quiet, you bitch. Be quiet, you bitch." She chanted and rocked against the plywood framing of the house under construction. Crickets and spring peepers competed with ocean waves in the distance but even they didn't silence the fucking bitch's words ringing in Mercy's head. The voices, always so full of condemnation and ridicule, like her mother's. God, how she hated that woman.

Even dead and buried beneath the rosebushes she'd adored, the bitch came back to taunt her just when Mercy had found her calling.

"Mercy." Her lover moaned. "What happened?"

His slurred words startled her. And the taunting voices fell blissfully silent.

Mercy smiled her relief. She lowered her hands, tucking the blade behind her back.

Her lover blinked his drug-hazed eyes. Their startling aquamarine color had entranced her when they'd met. Lured her in. But in the moonlight filtering through the open window they appeared bland, less than ordinary. And he looked so much younger than his twenty-six years. The bottle-blond hair that had been roguishly styled at the beginning of their romantic weekend was plastered to the side of his head. His naked chest, ripped and tanned, peeked from the opening of his black button-down shirt.

Mercy wanted to touch him. Again. To taste him one more time, but she couldn't allow herself to be distracted by his deceptive beauty. She loved him too much to go on like this. They'd had two days together, but that was all they could ever have.

"Mercy, darlin'?" He shifted on the plastic sheeting, clearly not quite awake yet. The plastic crinkled beneath him. The drug-hazed expression in his eyes receded and was quickly replaced with fear.

He struggled to move, but Mercy had tied him up while he slept. Panic washed the color from his face. Frantically, he waved his zip-tied wrists and kicked his bound ankles. In his struggle for freedom, he resembled more of a landed fish flopping around than the lover who'd promised her the fuck of a lifetime.

"What the fuck are you up to?" His fear morphed into rage, reddening his cheeks. "I told you. I'm not into that bondage shit. Get these fucking things off me!"

Still she didn't move from her spot. She didn't want to approach him yet. He needed to know. To understand. "I am Mercy. I love you too much—"

"Love me! It was just sex. That's all." His voice rose with fear and fury. "We got drunk, high, and fucked. That's it. You stupid, crazy bitch."

"Don't call me crazy." She pushed to her feet and stomped

over to him. The knife in her hand slapped against her thigh as she towered over him.

"Oh, man! Oh, man! Oh, man. Please. Don't! I didn't mean it." His widened eyes focused on the knife. He struggled more. Blood seeped from beneath the plastic binding his wrists. Then the tears started. He sobbed like a child. "I-I do love you. You're right. It's love. Put down the goddamned knife. Oh, man. Don't kill me."

Poor, pathetic bastard.

"Shhh . . . I know you don't love me. You can't. You don't even love yourself. You've got to be stoned or drunk to feel anything. That's not living. Don't cry. I'll take care of you. I love you too much to let you hurt yourself anymore. Shhh . . . Mercy's here."

She lifted the knife and plunged it into his chest. The blade clipped one of his ribs. Pain radiated from her fingertips to her shoulder. Undaunted, Mercy tilted and thrust harder. The knife resisted momentarily before it slid neatly to the hilt. Death flowed warm and crimson over her hands.

She stared into his eyes until the fear and the life faded from them.

He stared blankly.

Accusingly.

It infuriated her. Embarrassed her. It was the same vapid expression she'd seen too many times before.

Rage burned in her chest and her jarred arm ached more. After all she'd done for him, he had no right to stare at her with condemnation in his eyes.

Stretching out a hand, she closed his lids. Then she pressed a kiss to his forehead. She pulled back and examined the crimson lipstick stain with satisfaction.

There. Much better now.

He looked as he should after being granted her mercy. Peaceful.

Except for the knife protruding from his heart.

She jerked the handle and the body released the knife with a sucking noise. More blood gurgled up and spilled from the hole in the center of his once perfectly chiseled chest.

Shame to have to destroy such a beautiful body. A strange emotion crawled through her as she stared at his handsome face. It poked at her with sharp claws, ripping her apart from the inside. It almost tasted like regret.

Did she have to kill him? Was it truly mercy she granted? Or had she made a mistake? Again.

The questions stole her self-confidence until the urge to plunge the knife into her own chest was almost too powerful to stop.

Mercy turned the bloody knife until the ice-cold tip pricked the bare skin of her exposed chest. She could join him in eternal peace. End her suffering. Grant herself the mercy she gave him.

But what about all the others who needed her? Who would grant them mercy and release them from the evils of this harsh world if she were gone? No one. They'd be all alone and suffering. Like she'd been. So many still needed her.

Mercy should not be denied.

CHAPTER 3

NIALL GRAHAM FISTED his hands at his throbbing temples. The numbers on the ancient computer screen mocked him. They fucking laughed at him. Or they would have, if spreadsheets could laugh.

Unbelievable. He'd nearly died in Afghanistan to come home to a disaster guaranteed to do what the insurgents hadn't. Kill him. Only this death would be painfully slower and it involved his family's money.

His grandmother's restaurant was so far into the red, he wasn't sure he could afford to keep the doors open another month. Sure, the money coming in should have had his business in the black, but the cost of the lease on the new building on the prime piece of Tidewater real estate drained the account faster than it could be replenished. A building his brother had rented at an exorbitant cost without consulting Niall. Now they were locked into a two-year contract in one of the most expensive parts of Tidewater that wasn't even on the beach. Only the luxurious Oceanfront area went for more money.

Niall cleared the cell on the spreadsheet, reentered the figures, then hit sum. The figures were right and seriously jacked up. How in the hell was he going to get the business out of this mess and profitable again?

"Hiya, Niall." His younger brother Ross sauntered into the room. Calm and carefree, as fucking usual. "How're the numbers? Did I tell ya or did I tell ya? This place has been booming since we opened the doors. Location, man. It's all about location. Since we moved, we've been able to double our prices. I admit, it was hard at first because we did it in the off-season, but now, the money's coming. Just like I said it would."

"And we've lost the atmosphere of the old Boxing Cat," Niall couldn't help but point out.

Ross waved a hand dismissively. "You're worried because the Boxing Cat's clientele went from surfers to bankers? That's called progress, my brother."

"Progress? You still dress like a surfer."

Ross tossed a careless glance over his attire and shrugged, a happy expression on his face.

The boy's long blond hair hung in a ponytail trailing over one shoulder of his imported, green Hawaiian shirt. A shirt he left unbuttoned to reveal a white tank top that barely met the board shorts at his bony hips. And he didn't even bother to wear real shoes to work. Instead, he sported his open-toed Birkenstocks that begged for a major toe-amputating accident. He definitely did not fit in with the clientele he claimed improved the business.

Niall's thoughts must have shown on his face because Ross said, "Bro, lighten up. I may dress like a beach bum, but my business mind is sound. The changes we're making are going to rocket the Boxing Cat into being the best in town. Speaking of changes, Virgil's loving this. He's been able to try out some of his more exotic dishes. And it doesn't hurt that we're the only restaurant in town that serves gluten free on a daily basis. I tell ya, once we do a few weddings and the word spreads, we'll be so far into the black we'll need a flashlight to find our way home at night."

Weddings. Yeah, that's just what they needed to do with

their business, cater weddings for the rich and entitled. Which meant spending more money on more expensive products and hiring more people. The thought made Niall's headache ratchet up twelve notches.

"And it's only the beginning of June." Ross, oblivious to the ache burning in Niall's skull, kept right on scheming. "I swear, next weekend's wedding is just the beginning. It's not high society but the bride runs April's Flowers. We make her happy, she'll spread the word, and business will explode so fast we'll have to hire an accountant to come in every week to keep up with all the money we'll be raking in."

That boy always had a boatload of self-esteem and an arsenal of harebrained schemes.

"About that." Niall blanked the screen and pushed to his feet. "Ross, don't you think we might want to wait? Start the catering side of the business after we're a little more settled here."

Ross's smile dimmed briefly, then he shrugged. "Nope, we need this, Bro. Besides, we can't back out now. I've already signed the contract."

Something else the boy had done before Niall had made it back to Tidewater.

Ross wasn't actually a boy. Technically, he was old enough to legally drink. Even had a degree from culinary school. Still, Niall had a difficult time seeing him as a responsible adult and not just because Ross refused to get a decent haircut.

Perhaps it was because they'd spent the last ten years apart. Since Niall had joined the Marines at eighteen, he hadn't seen much of his brother. Ross, who'd been twelve at the time Niall left, spent much of his life more or less like an only child. And acted the part of the stereotype. Impulsive, careless, and sometimes downright thoughtless.

"Relax, Bro. I got this." Ross clapped Niall on the shoulder, then leaned across him to grab an apple from the basket next to the computer. He crowded too close to Niall in the cramped office.

The hair on Niall's neck rose as if trying to widen his

personal space. It didn't work. His heart raced. The walls in the cluttered office shrank. The shelves were suddenly too large. The room dimmed. And God, it was fucking hot. An oven. The tiny space that had once been his office melted away.

Gone was the office and the apple and his brother.

The air grew redolent with the stench of blood and death. Niall was back in Kandahar. Trapped beneath Ignacio and Danny. The two bastards who'd only wanted waffles that morning. They'd stood between Niall and the wall when the insurgents had blown it apart.

Niall shoved to his feet so fast he knocked over his stool. He didn't care.

Christ, he needed air.

Moving to the doorway, he hovered between the office and the kitchen. Not in either room but in both. Two exits, twice as much freedom. And no one buried and dying on top of him beneath the rubble.

Sweat trickled down his temples. He wiped it away, panting. He wouldn't go back to Kandahar. Not in reality and certainly not in a memory. He fucking wouldn't go back. He was home. Stateside. Permanently this time. And the attack had been months ago.

"Niall?" Ross's voice was thin. Distant.

Niall swung his gaze to meet his brother's wide-eyed, worried expression. Ross righted the stool but didn't move closer.

With a calm Niall didn't feel, he grinned and gestured to the computer. "I hate math."

Ross glanced at the darkened screen and back, doubt digging grooves around his mouth. "If you want to talk about it."

"Talk about what?" Niall feigned confusion. The last thing he wanted to do was to discuss his claustrophobia with his younger brother. Or the disaster that had caused it.

The only living person who'd even had a clue what Niall had been through was a bartender who hadn't bothered to give him her correct phone number after a single night of mind-blowing sex.

He wasn't going to think about her. Hadn't he told himself

that twice daily since he'd returned to Tidewater in May and discovered he had the wrong number?

A lesser man might have broken down and called Heaven's Gate trying to find her after he returned stateside. Not that he had. Not that he'd heard she'd left her job shortly after graduation. And certainly not that he'd been told in aggravatingly clear terms that no personal information would be given out on Hannah, since Niall hadn't bothered to learn her last name.

Fuck it.

"Bro?" Ross laid a hand on Niall's shoulder, concern in his light green eyes.

The haven in the doorway evaporated. The walls of the tiny room shrank two sizes again. *Too many people . . . too small a space.*

"Excuse me." Niall sidled out of the room.

Unlike the little dark gray office, the kitchen was large and gleaming white. Granted, there were things both rooms shared, like wire racks lining every available wall space.

But his office shelves were loaded with books, extra bags of flour and sugar, reams of paper, and files. The racks in the oversized kitchen were loaded with dishes, canned goods, pots, pans, plates, and utensils. Two sets of everything. The previous owners had kept to the kashrut, the body of Jewish law dealing with food, when serving kosher meals. While the Boxing Cat didn't need two sets of everything, it came in handy since Niall had added certified gluten-free options to the menu.

On the wall to his right hung a bulletin board littered with schedules, notices, various pictures, notes, and business cards. Next to that was the sink. Over it hung a magnetic knife rack covered in the best cutlery their business could afford.

In the center of the room, between three pillars, were two steel worktables. Two cooks ran the kitchen. The men were dressed in crisp white chef coats and chef pants covered in ugly dancing chili peppers. With the fluidity of dancers, they moved around the kitchen and each other as they prepared meals. The air was rife with the welcoming scents of oregano, caramelized onions, and freshly baked pizza. Niall's stomach rumbled.

"Hey, Paulie," Ross called out to the short, young chef. He spoke around a mouthful of apple. "Wanna hit the clubs tonight?"

That single question had Niall grinding his teeth to stem the flood of words burning his lips. Their business was barely hanging on and his brother wanted to go out drinking. Again. No doubt to get drunk enough to screw some random woman in another pointless attempt to prove to the world that he wasn't gay.

Wish the damn kid would grow up and come out of the closet already.

Ross jabbed a friendly elbow in Niall's side. "You should come too, big brother. You need a night out. Virgil can handle closing after the dinner rush. Right, Virg?"

Niall glanced at the taller chef who'd been on staff for more than thirty years. At sixty, Virgil looked eighty. Skin leathery and bronzed. Hands twisted by arthritis. But his mind was sharper than some recruits fresh out of boot camp. And he was still the best chef in Tidewater.

Virgil lazily shrugged his shoulders and said in a thick southern Tidewater drawl, "Sure can. Y'all go out and have some fun. You boys work too hard, especially you, Niall. Go on out and live a little while you're still young enough to do it. Why, if I was forty years younger, I'd be right there with you."

"Not tonight." Niall shook his head, then noticed a yellow sticky tacked to the bulletin board. He'd put it there yesterday, before he'd left to help his father move his mother into the rehabilitation center. "Ross. You did deposit last night's money at the bank, right?"

Ross screwed up his face in a pained expression. "Ah, crap, Niall. I forgot."

A hot ball formed in Niall's belly. Training warred with breeding. He wanted to give his brother a proper dressing down, but he couldn't do it in front of the staff. Instead, he counted to ten silently.

"Fine," he said, hoping the venom didn't leech into his voice. Two months. Ross had been in charge of the Boxing Cat for two months since their parents had decided to take an early retirement after Pop's heart attack. Their retirement plans took a sharp turn two weeks ago when a drunken jet skier crashed into the kayak Niall's mom had been paddling. Thank God, she hadn't been killed. That could have given Pop a second heart attack.

At this rate, Ross would give the man another one.

Not if Niall could help it. He was here now. He'd handle things, starting with the bank deposit. Turning on his heel, Niall returned to the tomb of an office, beelining straight for the safe.

In under a minute, he'd pulled out the bank deposit bag, relocked the safe, and walked back into the kitchen. Both chefs kept their eyes on their work and their mouths closed. Only Ross had the temerity to try to pick up their conversation.

"So we on for the club tonight, Bro?"

The cooks hustled to their respective stoves, as if trying to blend in with the walls.

Niall's training gave way to his temper. He stepped closer to his brother and dropped his voice to a deadly whisper only Ross could hear.

"I'd worry more about doing your job and less about partying unless you want to see the Boxing Cat go under. Now I'm taking the money to the bank, like *you* should have done last night. Then I am taking the hope chest over to Mom and Pop. Instead of partying tonight, why don't you join us at the rehab center for dinner?"

Ross scrunched his face like a child. "I hate it there. Why don't we bring them over here?"

Niall was pretty sure he was going to break a molar from grinding his teeth. Inhaling a breath for patience he said, "Mom broke her leg. In three places. Doctor says she cannot leave the building, let alone her floor for another six weeks. Whatever. Don't join us. I suggest while I'm out today, you run this business the way I know Pop trained you and less like a spoiled frat boy. The toilet in the men's room is leaking, the light bulbs are burned out in the pantry again, and the walls and floors behind the shelves need cleaning before we get another surprise inspection. Do it."

"We've got staff for all that."

"Wrong." That single word had come out harsher and louder than he'd intended. Counting to ten again, Niall reminded himself that pummeling his brother into the cement floor would only drive their mother to tears. "The people who work for us are waitstaff and cooks. You don't want people fixing the toilet, then handling food. This is why you and I are here. We do the maintenance, the hiring and the firing of staff, and the paperwork. The waitstaff handle the food. Period. Since I'm going to be out for the rest of the day, and there's no one to hire or fire, that leaves you to clean."

Ross's cell phone beeped. He grabbed it from the holster on his hip and checked the message. His face fell. He looked like the sad little boy he'd been the day Niall had told him he was leaving to join the Marines. "Uh, we might have a small problem."

A knot formed in Niall's empty stomach. "What do you mean?"

"That was the client. The guest list just grew." Ross inhaled a deep breath and said quickly, "She's just added twenty more people to the dinner. We're going to need to hire more servers to keep it covered."

Fucking perfect.

HANNAH CLASPED THE heart-shaped sterling silver locket in her hand and allowed the psychometric vision to take over. All around her, present-day Tidewater dulled to gray shadows and muted sounds. Her consciousness spiraled down to the world captured in the metal between her fingers.

Instantly, she was in someone else's body. Thinking someone else's thoughts. Feeling someone else's feelings. It was bittersweet, because for the moment, she was in her mother's body.

Her *first* mother. The woman who'd loved and nurtured her until Hannah had been three years old. Until the breast cancer had snuffed out the woman's life just shy of her thirty-first birthday. And this was the closest Hannah could come to touching her. Dipping into the memory carried by the energy wrapped in the locket.

Clutching the pendant tighter, Hannah let go of the modern world and delved further into her mother's memory. The scent of the magnolias sitting on her mother's table was fragrant and sweet. The hazy watercolor painting of three roses hanging on the wall came into sharp focus. And the connection was complete.

Love overwhelmed Hannah as she watched through her mother's eyes, while the woman carefully cut and glued the picture of three little girls into the pendant's right half and her own picture in the left. "Never forget me, my darlings. Momma loves you."

Less of a participant and more of someone who had no control over the body she temporarily inhabited, Hannah mentally stepped back and just observed. Her mother's consciousness mingled with hers and she temporarily became her mother.

She glanced out the front window. Across the street, a royal blue Geo Metro was parked in front of a pitched-roof brick church. A circular stained glass window depicted Jesus dressed in white robes with arms spread wide, as if beckoning welcome to all who passed by. A pair of three-foot-high Japanese maples stood as proud red-leafed bookends on either side of the front steps. The small patch of neatly trimmed bright green grass lined the walkway to the front door. Someone had even taken care to edge the white public sidewalk.

Pain stabbed from the center of her left breast. She sucked in a breath and held it as she glanced from the pictures of her daughters to the church across the street. Her chest ached and not just where the doctors had stitched her up after the biopsy earlier that week. Slowly, she expelled air and pain. Not much longer now. Two months or two years, the doctors weren't certain. But what hurt most was the knowledge she'd never see her daughters marry in their church.

In the distance, a horn beeped rhythmically five times.

"Two bits," she sang, finishing the seven-note musical couplet out of habit.

Her heart sank as realization set in. Earlier that day she'd learned exactly what kind of selfish bastard he was. Her husband, the father of her children, was a polygamist. And she'd thought the cancer diagnosis was bad.

Sick to her stomach, she watched the old green Chevy truck turn into the driveway and debated her decision. If she did this, her daughters would have no father and, all too soon, no mother either. But she couldn't live a lie and the selfish jerk had hardly been there since Hannah had been born.

The man behind the wheel tugged off his baseball cap, revealing a swath of hair so black it appeared almost blue with the sunlight beating on it through the windshield. He wore large sunglasses, had a bushy black mustache and a weary smile. He hopped out of the truck just below the Woodshire Avenue street sign. He carried a small red-wrapped package with a silver bow.

A gift from his trip. Another lie meant to convince her their life was something it wasn't. The sight of it made her stomach pitch and seemed to ignite the pain in her chest again.

Aching and gasping with redoubled pain, she glanced at the picture of the three smiling siblings and whispered, "I'm sorry, my darling girls, but it's better to be alone than with a liar."

Hannah pulled back from the vision and released the pendant, letting it dangle from the chain around her neck. She took a moment to center herself.

"I'm Hannah Halloran." She slowed her rapid breathing and let go of the last of the lingering pain from her mother's cancer. But it was hard. The only time she could even remember what her first mother sounded like was during a psychometric event.

While she took the pendant with her everywhere, she'd touched it only a few times since her adopted parents had given it to her last winter.

The morning after she'd spent the night with her handsome Marine.

A different sort of pain snuck into the space in her heart he'd somehow claimed in those few hours, but she refused to let it ruin the memory. She'd known he'd leave and not return. She'd seen the signs before their first kiss and still she'd taken him to her bed. Thank God!

The snippet of sorrow at his never calling was worth every second they'd spent together. Not that she'd had much time to grieve that day.

Her parents had surprised her with the news that her birth sisters were searching for her. She'd grown up with the memory of her adoption at the age of three. Still, having a private detective come to Fincastle looking for her was unexpected. Something she'd had little time to process that morning because her parents followed up the big news with something even more amazing. Her mother's locket.

They had expected her to be angry for keeping the chain and pendant from her for almost twenty years, but anger was the last thing she'd felt. She understood their reason for keeping it sealed in a bag in their home safe. Their care of the locket kept her mother's energy undiluted. Had it been handled repeatedly for twenty years, the vision Hannah received would likely have dimmed with time.

She tried explaining this, but it didn't erase the worry from their faces. It was their worry that kept her from returning the call to the private detective of Tidewater Security Specialists. As illogical as it seemed, her wonderful, caring parents feared she'd choose her old family over her current one. Like adoption made their bond somehow less.

Sometimes parents could be so silly. She loved Axel and Rosalind Halloran for giving her a home and a family and better life than she could ever have hoped for in the system. So she'd waited six months before telling them she intended to spend the summer in Tidewater getting to know the sisters she only vaguely remembered. Perhaps it was illogical to want more when she already had so much. But as her father had so often said when she asked why they'd chosen to adopt her and not another child, "The heart wants what the heart wants."

And right now, her heart wanted to find her sisters. But her head buzzed as she fought to withdraw from the vision.

She'd sunk too far into her mother's memory and the present seemed like a faded dream. "I'm Hannah Halloran," she said again, trying to center herself firmly in the current reality.

She tugged off the necklace and dropped it into the small zippered pocket of her tie-dyed backpack. She repeated her name twice more before she broke with the past and was fully herself again.

The Woodshire Avenue from her vision was a bit different from the Woodshire Avenue of present day. The car across the street had changed from a Geo Metro to a Prius. The maple trees were no longer dwarfish but towered at eighteen feet. The pitched-roof church with the stained glass window still stood tall and proud.

Hannah turned on her heel and sought her mother's house. This was the right spot. But it wasn't her mother's cottage. The little house had been torn down. It was now a parking lot for a restaurant.

Hannah stared at the old, two-story, Victorian-style building and something tickled her memory. Laughter and toy dolls at a tea party on a rickety porch came and went quickly like a dream.

There was nothing decrepit about this building. It had clearly been part of the city revitalization project, along with every other building on the street, save the church. Only the church had remained ageless.

The restaurant's mauve walls and dark blue shutters gave it a charming old-world appearance. The front porch was freshly painted with sturdy steps that led to the grassy front yard. At the edge of the short yard, someone had hung a large wooden sign with an orange tabby cat wearing only gloves and boxing with its shadow.

Now that had definitely *not* been there all those years ago.

Hannah couldn't suppress a grin at the whimsical feline drawing. It was a sign to keep fighting. Keep going. Exactly what she needed.

A breeze kicked up, carrying with it the salty scent of ocean on the Tidewater air.

Man, you really can smell the salt in the air, even five miles from the beach.

The wind also carried the delicious smells of cilantro, bacon, and oregano carried from the restaurant's open window. Her stomach rumbled. Okay, maybe she needed a bit of food too.

A tall blond man wearing a garishly bright Hawaiian shirt plopped a Help Wanted sign in the front window of the Boxing Cat.

Hannah couldn't stifle the grin. Another sign that her trip to Tidewater was destined. They needed help and she needed a job for the summer.

Perfect. Absolutely perfect.

"Momma," she whispered into the wind, "I'm home."

CHAPTER 4

"YOUR AURA IS off. Did you have another fight with your brother?"

Hannah sat at the bistro table near the window, toying with the business card of the private detective. She wasn't trying to eavesdrop on the pretty waitress and the man who had posted the Help Wanted sign. Not that she could help it. At three thirty in the afternoon, the place was virtually empty.

Hannah had walked in as eight people, in boring business suits, shuffled out. Only four other people were in there and they sat around the corner in the next room. An empty place wasn't uncommon in Fincastle, but in a city the size of Tidewater with more than a million residents, it seemed strange.

So why weren't more people here? The food was excellent as was the décor.

Whoever had thought to use a Victorian-style house as a restaurant had been a genius. Instead of one large room, the first floor of the building was sectioned off into four eating areas and a kitchen. Glass French doors separated the rooms, making it simple to see all of the customers while still offering a bit of privacy.

The Boxing Cat was as charming inside as it had been outside. Tiny bistro tables draped in antique-style lace tablecloths lined the front windows. The dishes and the cutlery were mismatched. The hodgepodge of pieces appeared intentional and added an old-world feel to the place. Against one of the Nantucket blue walls was a large hutch.

The waitress, with caramel-colored skin, a short cap of curly black hair, and light brown eyes, hitched up her hip and half-stood, half-sat on a lower shelf. The blond man, who looked close to Hannah's age, leaned on the hutch next to her. Neither paid her any attention.

"You know my brother. He's always got a stick up his ass about something when it comes to me," the man said. The smile on his lips didn't quite reach his pale green eyes. "It's nothing. You know I'm really grateful that you got us the catering job, right?" He folded his arms and pressed his thumb against his bottom lip as if contemplating what to say next.

The woman arched one black brow. "Mm-hmm."

"You were right about the bride too. She left a message. She's added more people to the reception."

"Ha! I told you!" The waitress pumped her fist in the air once in obvious triumph. "I told you, Ross. I saw her staring at the guest list and her aura kept shifting between yellow and blue. Auras don't lie. She was indecisive. I told you she'd call back and add more people. But did anyone listen to me? No, they did not. But don't worry. You *can* handle this. All you need to do is hire a couple more servers for the night. You'll be fine and everything will work out."

Ross's cheeks reddened. "I don't need just any servers. I need people who are going to impress the hell out of the bride and groom. If something goes wrong, the catering idea will end before it begins. My brother's already not happy with my new venture." He gave the waitress a calculating look. "Think you could fill in?"

"I'm already filling in. I'd offer suggestions for other servers, but everyone I know in town works here or will be at the wedding as a guest. Except Zig." She shook her head, frowning. "Don't get any ideas about asking him. He won't do it. Trust me, you won't convince my boyfriend to cater no matter how much money you offer him. You're just gonna have to find servers yourself." The waitress patted his shoulder sympathetically.

"I don't know what I'm going to do, Karma." Ross shrugged, then pulled the band from his ponytail, letting his golden-blond hair flow casually around his shoulders. The man had the kind of shiny hair any woman would envy. "What if I offered him an easy two hundred?"

Karma laughed, then scooted until she completely sat on the wooden countertop. "He won't agree. Besides, there is nothing easy about this upcoming gig. Your brother may not be able to see your aura, but I can. And I know despite the show you put on for all the staff here, you are so stressed out about making the right impression that you're going to make yourself sick instead."

Hannah couldn't pretend not to hear anymore. She'd been watching the reflection of the pair in the restaurant's front window. Turning to face them, she met Ross's gaze. "I need a job."

Ross blinked. Then did it again before he closed the distance between them. He settled into the chair across from her while Karma scraped a chair over the polished wood floor. She settled herself next to Ross and stared intently at Hannah.

Maybe speaking up hadn't been such a good idea. But she needed a job if she intended to stay in Tidewater for more than a week. After last night's conversation with her parents, she'd promised herself that she'd find a job of some kind before she contacted them again. They worried.

"Do you have any experience waitressing?" Ross asked, letting his gaze slide over her. The expression in his eyes was assessing but not speculative or even disapproving. Both of the latter happened all too frequently with strangers since she'd arrived in the city yesterday. Perhaps it was her multicolored peasant skirt and white blouse paired with her sandals that made people give her a double take. Or maybe it was her mass of unruly brown hair coupled with a pink braid. Or the new tattoo on her wrist. Okay, so she didn't look like a city girl. She wasn't. But she had the training to be a great server.

"Definitely. My parents own a bar in Ohio. I served food until I was old enough to tend bar. I worked there all through college. I opened, closed, served, and stocked the bar. Not much I didn't do. Being the daughter of the owners meant I got all the grunt work. I even helped out my dad with repairs."

She didn't mention that she'd lived above the bar rather than on campus because her parents had worried the exposure to too many metal objects might overload her system since her visions were brought on by direct contact with all types of metal. Or the fact that her parents had either ripped out metal where they could or simply covered it with plastic or wood where they couldn't to reduce the number of accidental visions she might have had.

Ross clasped his hands together and rested them on the table. Then he turned his head to the waitress and said, "What do you think?"

Karma narrowed her eyes at Hannah, assessing, then smiled wide. "Hire her. I like her aura. It's a vibrant orange. Strong, creative, confident, and detail-oriented. She'll need it if she's going to work with your brother."

Hannah wasn't sure why that compliment sounded so ominous.

FIFTEEN MINUTES LATER, Hannah had been introduced to a half dozen people including two cooks, a shy busboy, and two waitresses, one very tall, one her own height. Both with big hair and bigger attitudes. Hannah had also spoken to a delivery driver with the kind of leer that made her want a decontamination shower after shaking his hand.

And she didn't remember a single name. So much for her aura indicating she was detail-oriented.

Ross filed her past the workers and into a cluttered, cozy

little office. He pressed his hands on her shoulders and gave her a polite push onto a stool that doubled as the desk chair.

"Here, fill out this tax form and the application. You'll also need to provide three references," he said, dropping the papers on the desk.

Hannah stared up at him in surprise. "*Three* references? Is that typical?"

"No, it's not. Most places ask for two but my brother's a little *careful* about who we hire." He paused and muttered under his breath, "He'll trust Karma's opinion but not mine." Louder he added, "It's why I'm scrambling to hire people to work the upcoming wedding. You have experience catering? It's not the same thing as waitressing, you know."

"Nothing as formal as weddings, but we used to rent the bar out for graduation parties." She chuckled. "Can my parents be a reference? No one will give you a more honest assessment of my character than they will."

"Your parents. As a reference." Ross frowned. "The last time someone asked to use parents as a reference, the guy had a criminal history as long as the menu here. Oh God, please tell me you don't have a criminal record. My brother will never go for me hiring another convict. He's a stickler about the staff being reputable. If you even have a pot arrest on your record, we should stop now. I'll never live it down. Even if Karma liked your aura. Hiring you is still my call."

Hannah didn't know whether to laugh or be offended. "No pot arrest. No arrest of any kind. I've never even had a speeding ticket. And I can provide references, besides my parents. They're all out of town though."

"That's fine." The relief on his face was almost comical. The man practically sagged in place. "Still, we have to call all of them. Better to waste the money on long-distance calls than to lose everything to a thief. At least, that's what my brother says."

Ross patted his pockets and pulled out a pen. A very nice, very expensive Cross pen. Made of metal. "Here you go, sweetie."

Hannah hesitated. Given his strong emotional reaction

to learning she didn't have a criminal past, the little writing instrument was probably singing with psychometric energy.

Did she really want to risk delving into a psychic event right in front of a new boss? Then again, he'd find out soon enough. Of course, Ross had been okay with Karma's gift but he knew her. That comfort didn't always translate to a stranger walking in claiming to have a supernatural ability.

While most people in Fincastle accepted her gift as more reliable than the mail, strangers' reactions were unpredictable.

Better to find out now if her potential boss would freak out or be cool with her psychic gift.

"Thanks." She let her fingers close around the cool silver metal.

Yep. Instant connection.

Energy sizzled through her fingertips, up her arm, and straight into her brain. The gray office faded to smoke around her and she was in Ross's body.

"Hey, Paulie, wanna hit the clubs tonight?" he said around a mouthful of crisp, tart apple. His heart fluttered and his pulse raced past his ears.

Paulie turned from his spot at the stove and smiled. The brief curl of those beautiful lips made Ross's heart rate kick up a notch.

He's finally going to say yes. *The urge to dance in place was almost too strong to resist.*

Then Paulie cut a quick glance to Ross's left and the smile died.

So did Ross's hope. He didn't have to look to know Paulie had caught sight of Ross's brother.

Ross's heart sank.

He opened his mouth to say something else to Paulie but the chef had already focused his attention on the mushrooms marinating on the stove.

Dammit! Why did Paulie have to draw that particular line? Didn't he understand that coming out of the closet to the ass-kickingest Marine of them all wasn't something that could just be done? It needed finesse. And Ross needed to give his brother time to get to know him before he messed with the jarhead's narrow way of thinking.

Staring at Paulie's back, the message was clear. Ross had to come out of the closet completely or nothing could happen between them.

His eyes stung but he couldn't show weakness around his brother.

Ross inhaled a breath, then glanced to his left. His brother's mouth was a grim line of disapproval. With a tick working in his cheek, his square jaw looked almost painfully angular. Niall rolled his eyes and scrubbed a hand through his short military-cut black hair.

Hannah dropped the pen.

It rolled off the desk and clattered to the floor. Breathing, always a challenge when withdrawing from a vision, was almost impossible. Her heart pounded so hard against her ribs, it could have been trying to punch its way out of her chest. But holy schmoley, even trapped as she was between Ross's memory and reality, one thing was crystal.

Her Marine was about to become her new boss.

CHAPTER 5

IMAGES OF PAULIE and Niall swirled in Hannah's mind. Her own thoughts blended with Ross's memories, echoing to a crescendo. She fought against the vision. Even with the pen no longer in her hands, residual effects of Ross's memory pulsed through her.

The room swayed around her or maybe she swayed. She wasn't sure. The only thing she knew was that she'd gone into one too many visions today because she was having trouble breaking free of this one.

Propping one hand on the doorjamb, she shut her eyes and repeated the mantra that had always centered her in the past, "I'm Hannah Halloran. Hannah. Halloran."

Somewhere in the distance, Ross sucked in a hissing breath, then muttered, "Oh Christ. You're a nutball, aren't ya, dollface? Niall's gonna kill me." She didn't need to open her eyes to sense he'd moved closer. His breath, tinted with garlic and peppermint, fell against her face. "Come on, sweetie. Open your eyes and look at me."

Slowly, Hannah blinked. Her head felt thick but the vision faded to a misty fog that evaporated beneath the fluorescent bulbs. She blinked again and the room came into focus. Her legs, oddly shaky, still supported her. Carefully she pushed away from the wall, letting her arms drop to her sides. Each breath centered her until the vision was a memory and reality was Ross staring at her with wariness in his too-pretty eyes.

"There you go, sweetie. Welcome back." He glanced out the open door, then slid it closed with the toe of his sandal. He jammed his hands in the pockets of his shorts and looked as lost and innocent as a child. "For a second, I thought you were going to take a swan dive. I know it's not PC to admit, but Niall would probably frown on your little scene here. He likes for the employees to, you know, remain conscious and not mutter their names to themselves in public. Do you have some sort of psychosis I should know about?"

Okay, so not quite so innocent or childlike.

"Sorry about that. Too many trips in one day, I guess." Way too many, if he'd thought she was going to faint. Hannah tugged her pink braid across her shoulder and toyed with it. Glancing around the floor she saw the pen not far from her ankle. "Never felt faint before. Hope to never do it again. I guess the pen's energy was a little more than I was ready for."

Ross arched one perfect eyebrow. He lifted the instrument, and twisting his wrist side to side, he examined it. "The *pen's* energy? I was right here, sweetie, and I promise, it didn't do anything odd. You sure you don't have a mental defect I should know about?"

Hannah managed a smile. The heaviness in her head dulled to a low throb. "No, not a mental defect. Not a psychosis. However, I do get readings from objects."

"Uh-huh." Ross scrunched up his pretty face. "Readings? Like you do tarot cards or something?"

"No." She laughed and waved away the idea. "Nothing quite so technical. I get visions from all sorts of objects but not paper or cards or stuff like that. Metal conducts energy the best. The longer I touch something metal, the stronger the emanation, the harder it is to break out of the vision."

"Okay then. Well . . . Right. No harm. I'm glad you're all back to um . . . *normal* now. Just my pen sending rampant visions your way." Ross retreated two steps. Palms up and out, he waved them at her as if warding off the devil himself. Or a lunatic. "You know, I've made a mistake. We're not really hiring after all. You can just leave all that paperwork and I'll see you out."

Hannah moved toward him and the world dipped threateningly before it leveled out.

Whoa, that was one strong vision.

Sliding to her right, she effectively blocked the closed door and Ross's attempt to escape. "Ross, please wait. I can prove what I say, if you'll give me a chance."

"I'm listening." Ross folded his arms across his chest in the universal move of those who absolutely refuse to hear what's about to be said.

No, he wasn't planning to listen. But he would. She'd make sure of it.

Hannah leaned her back against the door and focused on centering herself.

Ross cleared his throat.

She whipped her gaze to his.

"Any time now." He tapped his foot in an impatient staccato beat. "Wow me with your magic."

"It's not magic, it's psychometry."

"Not magic. Psychic-ometry?"

"No. Yes, I mean I *am* psychic but the gift is called *psychometry*." He stared at her unblinkingly. She kept going. "When you offered me the pen, I hesitated. I knew if I touched it, I'd probably get a vision but I did it anyway. And it did show me something. I was in that kitchen." She hiked a thumb over her shoulder. "You were there eating a really good apple, crisp and tart. Anyway, you were talking to Paulie and your brother about going to a club."

"That was this morning." Ross frowned. "How did you know that? Are you telling me you're a mind reader? Or maybe you were hanging around outside and peeking in through the windows. If you're a mind reader, prove it. Tell me what I'm thinking."

"I'm not a mind reader and I wasn't spying on you." Well, not the way he thought. She waved away his ridiculous demand. "But I can tell you something I couldn't possibly know."

He arched an eyebrow. "What's that?"

She stepped closer and dropped her voice to a whisper, "You're in love with Paulie and you're afraid to tell your brother you're gay."

"I'm not!" Ross paled beneath his golden tan and his eyes went wide and dark. "I-I mean . . . Who told you I'm gay?" He all but whispered the last word.

"You did, when you handed me the pen." She stepped to the side, clearing his way to the door. She wasn't surprised when he didn't move. Except for her college boyfriend, everyone who'd learned of her gift thought it was cool. But Bryan had taught her that it could be a curse.

Ross's color flooded back into his cheeks and his face split into a wide grin. "That is so boss! Can you do it all the time? With everyone? If I give you something of Paulie's, can you tell me if he's in love with me too?"

And again, Ross reminded her more of a happy child than a business owner. And this was the reaction she was used to receiving. Like being with old friends, it warmed her. Once again the universe proved her decision to come to Tidewater had been the right one. Surely, his easy acceptance of her gift meant she was on the right path. Still, she needed to calm him down.

"Wait a sec." She leaned against the closed the door again. "First, I can't do it with everything. Like I said, metal objects work best. Second, don't you want to figure out your relationship on your own? I mean, where's the fun if you already know what's in his head? And I'm not a relationship counselor, but it sounds like you two need to talk."

Ross's smiled dimmed, marginally. "You're right. I know you are. And you totally have the job. Just . . . just don't tell Niall about, well, me being gay."

"Your secret is safe. Besides, that's something you'll want to tell him yourself, isn't it?"

"Right. Of course. When the time is right." He smiled at her. Big. Really, really big. "We've got other things to think about now."

Something in his overly bright expression made her nervous. "Ross, would you mind keeping my little ability to yourself?"

"Oh, sweetie, you're in Tidewater. There are more folks in this city like you than you realize, but sure. No one will hear about your talent from me. It's probably best anyway. We want Niall to get to know you before he hears you can . . . well, you know. He might not take it well. At least not at first. He's very narrow-minded. A great guy, but he has one way of seeing the world and he might not understand this."

Not from her perspective. Niall had seemed lost and lonely when she'd met him six months ago. But not narrow-minded. Sure, he'd been skeptical of her abilities but he had seemed to accept them. Then again, they'd been more interested in getting naked that night.

Honestly, what did she really know about him? He hadn't jumped up and said he believed her when she'd showed him what she could do. He hadn't denied it either. She'd have to consider it. Right now, her biggest concern was his potential reaction to seeing her in his eatery.

"Still, Niall's a great guy. Once he warms up, he'll accept you."

Hannah didn't point out that for all his confidence about Niall accepting her, Ross was still firmly in the closet and showing no signs of coming out anytime soon.

"It'll be a week or two . . . at most a month before he figures out what you can do," Ross said in a rush, color high in his cheeks and his eyes bright with excitement. "Probably less. He's really smart."

Her conscience pricked. She really should say that she knew Niall. But before she could, someone banged on the door. "Ross, we need you out here. The delivery truck arrived and brought organic, whole wheat flour. He says he won't take it back."

"Crap!" Ross replied, yanking open the door. "Paulie, tell him not to unload the truck. I knew we'd have problems when the grocery store fired the old manager. At least she knew the difference between organic and gluten free."

A very flustered-looking Paulie eyed Hannah with obvious suspicion. She retreated to the desk to make it clear she was filling out paperwork. But the effect was sort of lost when she had to search through her bag to pull out her own pen. One that wouldn't send her countless visions.

"Hannah, finish filling out the paperwork and we'll get you started before my brother gets back."

She needed to tell him. He had to know.

"About your brother, I've met him before," she said at the same time Paulie said, "So she's our new server?"

"Well, that'll make it easier introducing you." Ross spared her a quick glance before focusing his attention on the cook who had the look of a jealous lover. But if he could see, Ross didn't react. "Yes, Paulie. I thought you understood that when I introduced her ten minutes ago. She's going to help us work the English wedding this weekend."

A horn beeped outside.

"Crap!" Ross bolted through the door. "Wait a damned minute. Where's my order form?"

Paulie glared at her another second, before chasing after Ross, a white sheet of wrinkled paper crinkling in his hands.

Oh, yeah, Paulie's feelings for Ross were definitely reciprocated. And it made her wonder just how far in the closet Ross was hidden for Paulie to be shooting back-off-my-man looks with his eyes.

Next question. Would Niall be as happy to see her as she would be to see him?

ALL AFTERNOON HANNAH both anticipated and dreaded the idea of seeing Niall again. She'd completed her paperwork, been asked to fill in at the Cat, gone home to change, been assigned to follow around a waitress named Sadie to learn the ropes, and kept a smile on her face doing it, but Hannah's nerves were frazzled.

Somehow, the universe had led her straight to Niall's restaurant. What were the odds? Slim. They had to be slim odds at best. It was a sign. A sign that their night together was destined to be more than a singular, unforgettable event. Right? Or a coincidence.

Nah, no such thing as coincidence.

Perhaps she was here to help the brothers communicate? Clearly, her vision in Ross's head had been fraught with the need the brothers had to seriously talk. Could that really be what she was here to do? Get the men to do the one thing the male of her species hated most . . . express their feelings?

Why couldn't the signs around her be as sharp as the taste of that apple in the blasted vision?

Hannah tugged at the black apron tied and retied around her waist, as if the action could help her figure out what to do. Well, she might not understand what the universe intended for her yet, but at least she'd been smart enough to bring a pair of black slacks and a white shirt with her from Ohio. She'd planned to wear them to interviews to make a good impression. Her folks had been right when they'd told her she'd need the clothes.

One day in Tidewater and she had a job. Not her dream job but one she could do with her eyes closed. One that offered decent money. Yep. One more sign that she was in the right place.

Thank you, universe!

She needed to call her parents and give them an update. Anticipating their pleasure at her news of landing a job so quickly, she tucked her hand in her pocket. Empty. Shoot! She'd left the phone on the charger in the hotel. Oh well, she'd call them after her first shift ended.

"Are you listening to me?" Sadie snapped her fingers in front of Hannah's face, jolting her out of her thoughts. The thirtysomething, faux red-haired waitress's blue eyes narrowed to slits as she tapped one red-tipped nail on the prep table.

"Sure thing. Gold-tipped cooking utensils go in the gluten-free section and the silver-tipped in the regular. The two sets cannot be mixed up because of the risk of cross-contamination. When serving both at a table, bring them out on separate trays and try to serve the gluten-free meals first. Honestly, this is not the first time I've served food. I really do know what I'm doing."

Sadie's overly large nostrils flared. "From what I hear you were a bartender. I'm the only one who tends bar at events so don't try to horn in on my turf."

"Lighten up, Sadie. The girl's only been here three hours." The shy busboy made a sound that was a cross between a snort and a cough. With a gray bin in his hands, he carried in the dishes from the front of the restaurant. His eyes were obscured behind hair that wasn't brown and wasn't blond. His dirty white apron covered his equally dingy white shirt and pants. He might have been sixteen or he might have been Hannah's age. It was hard to tell. But one thing was clear, he was quick to defend Hannah. "It's not like she's applied to take your job. Go easy on her, why don'tcha?"

"Ah, look! The mute has found his voice." Sadie glared at him. "Run along and wash the dishes or clear a table, Mouse. It's all you're good for."

The man seemed to shrink but his white-knuckled grip on the dish bin and the thinning of his lips radiated anger. An anger matched, if Sadie's death ray glare was any indication.

"Is there a problem, Michael?" Karma asked the busboy, stepping into the kitchen through the swinging door separating it from the Master dining room. Her voice took on a slight Hispanic accent that she hadn't had before. Her face was friendly but her eyes assessing. Her gaze bounced from Michael to Sadie and finally to Hannah.

Then one by one, all eyes turned to Hannah, as if expecting her to answer. So she did. "Nope. Just getting the rundown of how the restaurant operates from Sadie and Michael."

"I'll bet." A smile curved Karma's lips and her voice lost

its accent. "Sadie, if you're finished showing Hannah the prep tables, I could use you out front. We have some guests arriving for dinner. Michael, why don't you see about washing the dishes you cleared from lunch? We don't want the boss to come back and find a sink full."

"Fine." Sadie scowled but the moment her palm touched the swinging door between the kitchen and the front room, a believable smile lit her face.

Michael didn't answer, but disappeared around the corner. His expression had blanked to the quiet, introspective one he'd worn when Ross had first introduced her.

"Don't mind them," Karma said when the water started running in the other room. "Sadie and Michael had a fling a few months back."

Oh, ewww.

"But she's old enough to be his mother."

"He's older than he looks. But I suspect the age difference was part of the reason it didn't work out. I think poor Sadie wanted more than a fling but Michael . . ." Karma shrugged. "He's only twenty-five and still trying to find himself. Still young, you know."

"He's older than me. Isn't he older than you?"

"No, I'm twenty-seven." Karma winked. "Women mature faster than men. Besides, you and I are unique. We needed to figure out who we were much younger than most people, don't you agree?"

Hannah wanted to ask what Karma meant by that, but Virgil appeared at the screened-in back door, two grocery bags in his arms. "Can one of y'all pretty ladies get the door?"

At the same time, Sadie appeared in the opposite doorway, the scowl back on her face. "Karma, since you let Dawn go home early, I hope you plan on putting the new girl to work out here. I'm already working with a six-top. We just had two four-tops and an eight-top walk in. I can't do them alone. Not that I've had time to teach her what those references mean."

"A four-top is a table with four customers and an eight-top is eight customers. Or guests, as I suppose you call them here. I told you, I have a background in the service industry."

Hannah glanced at Karma who opened the door with one hand and handed her a pad with the other. "Hannah, are you comfortable doing both of the four-tops? They might be easier than the eight for your first time here, since you don't know the menu yet."

"Sure. I got this." Hannah tucked the pad into her apron, then tightened the strings out of habit. Nope, she might not work in the bar anymore, but food service was food service after all.

Sadie huffed and pushed her way out of the kitchen again, that incredibly realistic smile plastered to her face.

The door swung back before Hannah could reach it. She tossed up a hand to catch it before it hit her in the face. A sizzle of energy slapped her palm where she brushed the metal plate on the door.

She shifted and used her shirt-covered elbow to push on the wooden part of the door. But her arm caught the edge of the metal hand plate and something dark seeped in. She didn't have time for a vision and shoved it away. But couldn't quite shake the quiver in her belly. And this time it had nothing to do with seeing Niall again.

"The Construction Site Killer has struck again. A body of a man was discovered this morning on Arctic Avenue by four teens who had been using the homes under construction in the planned community as a hangout. Police are not releasing details pending notification of family members. But an unidentified source has confirmed that this is likely the fourth victim of Tidewater's first serial killer. We'll have more on this disturbing development on our sister station Channel Nine news tonight at eleven."

Niall rolled his truck into the parking lot behind the Boxing Cat and cut the engine, silencing the news bulletin on the radio.

The Brunswick stew he'd eaten with his mother congealed in his stomach. And that seriously pissed him off. What the hell was this world coming to? A serial killer in Tidewater? It was bad enough he'd faced crazy-ass insurgents overseas defending his country, but to have a psycho in his hometown picking off people like it was his own personal horror movie?

Niall exited his Ford F-250, locking it out of habit and double-checking the lock with the news report still playing through his head. Barely through the door and he spotted a flurry of activity. So much for tonight being a light night as expected.

Virgil loaded a large pizza into the oven while Paulie sautéed mushrooms and spinach in a sizzling garlic butter sauce. Five dinner tickets waited to be filled and six plates loaded and ready to be served littered the counter.

"Boss, Dawn's kid got sick. Sadie's out there but she's in the weeds," Paulie called out over his shoulder. "I can't leave the kitchen and Virgil's not too steady with a trayful."

"Bite your tongue, boy!" Virgil snapped, slamming the oven door closed. He turned to reach for the hot meals only to bang his side into the corner of the metal prep table. "Damn this old hip!"

"You hurt, Virgil?" Niall slid his backpack across the floor, sending it skidding into his office and checked on his oldest family friend.

"Nothing a little ice can't fix." Virgil waved away his concern. "I am old. The boy might be right. I don't seem to be too steady."

"Where's Karma and Ross?" Niall asked, stacking the plates on a tray.

"Ross said he'd be back. We lost an entire tray of food about ten minutes ago. Some Navy guys came in and got fresh with Sadie. Don't know what happened. Karma was calming her down out back. Didn't you see them?" Virgil asked, hobbling over to the freezer and pulling out an ice pack.

"No." Before Niall could say anything else, Paulie spoke up.

"Night's been cray-cray, Boss. Dawn left before the dinner rush started and I do mean rush. Then some sailors from the USS *South Carolina* came in for their first at-home meal in months. Words and Sadie's temper flew. The new girl managed to calm down the guests while Karma hustled

Sadie outside. Then *blam*!" Paulie clapped his hands together. "One minute the new girl's carrying out six meals, and the next, dishes and food all over the kitchen floor. She thought for sure she was going to be fired."

Niall swept his gaze around the kitchen. The only trace of disaster in the room was confined to a few shards of what had likely been a plate in a corner.

"What new girl? Dawn's out sick? Sadie and some sailors? Six meals lost? Sonofa . . ." His string of questions was more of babbled frustration than any real inquiry. Virgil, smart man, just seemed to know it.

"It's fine, Niall," Virgil said, patting his free hand on Niall's shoulder. "Just our way of letting you know we're glad you're here to save us and not halfway around the world."

Count on Virgil to be both poignant and joking in the same breath. Niall exhaled and smiled, since that was clearly what the old guy wanted.

"All right, since I am here, point me in the right direction." Niall hoisted the tray onto his shoulder and turned for the door. "Where are these going?"

Paulie pulled the ticket off the counter. "Table four. Hey, when you get back, can you find Karma? Tell her to hurry up. FYI, that plate by your thumb is gluten free."

Using his foot, Niall gently pushed open the swinging door. The rooms were lit by flickering candlelight on the tables and on the walls. The place was alive with guests at every table in every section. Clinks of silverware on plates, pings of ice cubes in glasses, and the murmur of the patrons' voices added a homey ambience to the Cat.

Moments like these, Niall understood why Ross had wanted this building. There was an atmosphere of comfort and elegance to the place the old Cat never had. The cozy feel certainly, but not this genteel elegance enhanced by the flickering of the candles in the wall sconces in all four of the rooms.

He'd been expecting chaos but everything looked normal. And signs of being a very good night for the business. They almost never had a midweek night this packed in the other store. He'd have to remember to tell Ross . . . whenever his brother showed up again.

Niall made his way through the Master Room, down the narrow hallway separating it from the Three Bells, and through the glass-paneled door separating it from the Quarter Room.

Inside tables had been pulled together to change it from several two-tops to one six-top. The three sets of couples at the long table were surrounded by four more two-tops at each corner of the room, granting every guest the illusion of intimacy and privacy in the busy restaurant.

Pressing the curved handle down, Niall then used his left arm to shoulder open the glass French doors. The chatter at the six-top stopped as all eyes turned to him.

Smiling, he spotted the tray stand set up next to the table and lowered the tray. He lifted the first meal in the air. "Who had the gluten-free linguini with white clam sauce?"

Inexplicably, the patrons erupted in applause.

"Oh, thank you! I was just in the kitchen looking for this." A familiar voice called out from behind him, "See you guys, I told you. The Boxing Cat would get your meal out to you before you knew it."

Niall's fingers, jaw, even his knees went slack as he turned to see Hannah of Heaven's Gate. Her fairylike face alight with joy.

She was here.

His ears buzzed.

She was in his restaurant.

His heartbeat double-timed.

"Let me get that for you . . . uh, Boss," she said, slipping the plate out of his hands.

She called him . . . *Boss*?

Oh, hell no.

CHAPTER 6

"BOSS?" NIALL FORCED the word between clenched teeth. He'd tried for a smile when he'd returned to the kitchen with Hannah, but judging by the way she rolled her pink braid between her fingertips, it wasn't working.

But what the hell? Why was she in his restaurant? Working. For him.

A sliver of alarm rippled through his belly. Was she a psycho stalker?

"Yes, isn't it amazing? Last night when I arrived in Tidewater I needed a job. This afternoon while eating lunch here, I was hired. Really incredible." Hannah dropped the braid, washed her hands in the sink, then walked around the half wall to check over the tickets waiting on the counter. "Anything up for me, guys?"

"Give us three minutes and your pie will be ready." Virgil gave her a wink. "But these are ready to go out to the Half Room, tables six and seven. Can you carry them out for Sadie?"

"Sure thing." Hannah didn't hesitate. She picked up the

tray loaded with four plates and started to reach for the pitchers of sweet and unsweet tea.

"I got the tray," Niall said, sweeping it off her shoulder, leaving her free to grab the pitchers in both hands.

"Thanks." Hannah's face practically glowed. She led the way through the restaurant, smiling radiantly at the customers.

Niall followed her through the restaurant both appalled and amused by how well she'd fit in. The way the guests chatted with her as she refilled drinks, it was like she'd been working here for months, not hours. Hell, several people called her by name but still had no idea who he was or that he owned the place.

After serving the meals, Niall checked on a few tables. Relief swept through him at the sight of Karma and Sadie back at work. A large table of sailors, dressed in their blue fatigues, left. Michael appeared from out of the shadows and bussed the table.

There was no time to talk to Hannah. Why was Niall trying? She didn't seem to have any great impulse to talk to him. Like a social butterfly completely in her element, Hannah flitted from one table to another. Serving food, drinks, and even jokes. It was alarming and disarming. And fuck. He could smell her honeysuckle fragrance every time she strode past him.

The sight of her killer body in the gender neutral white shirt and black pants uniform, the sound of her laughter, hell, even that damned fresh scent of hers was screwing with his head. But the blood pounding through his body was definitely not headed north. He needed to stop staring at her like some horny teenager. So he did.

Around nine thirty, Niall retreated to his office. He kicked his bag under the desk and folded down the step stool into its other shape, that of a ratty office chair. He needed to work. The English wedding was this weekend. There was still work to be done to prepare for it and Ross was still MIA.

As much as Niall hated the idea of expanding the business, he hated failing more. Someone had to do the work, so he'd do it. He'd be damned if he'd let his brother drive the Cat into the ground. With one ear listening for the musical laughter of a certain confusing waitress, Niall set his teeth and focused on the numbers on his computer screen.

Crap! He'd really come full circle today. He'd started the day trying not to think about Hannah while working on this damned spreadsheet. And he'd finish it the same way. Only now, she *worked* for him.

Yep. Fucking perfect day.

"WHAT A NIGHT!" Karma said, locking the front door behind the last couple to leave the Boxing Cat at eleven thirty.

Hannah smiled. She couldn't help it. The job, the fabulous tips, and all the wonderful guests she met tonight had made her feel completely at home. "It was an amazing night."

"You say that now. Wait till Niall docks your pay for those dishes you broke." Sadie tugged off her apron.

"Oh, I forgot about those," Hannah said. So much for her great night. "Will he charge me for meals or just the plates?"

"He won't charge you. Dishes break. She's just teasing. Right, Sadie?" Karma smiled but her brown eyes narrowed and the accent was back in her voice.

"Whatever." Sadie shrugged and glanced around the Master Room, where Hannah had first met Karma and Ross only hours before. "Look, I'm scheduled to open tomorrow. You got the rest of this? I got a date."

"You go on your date. I'll stay and show Hannah how to close up." Karma yawned and stretched. "Zig's on the midnight shift this week, so I'm not in a rush."

"It was nice meeting you, Sadie." Hannah smiled at the older waitress.

Sadie harrumphed, then disappeared through the kitchen doors.

"I think I feel sorry for whoever she's got in her sights," Karma said with a laugh. She hit a switch on the wall, bringing up the overhead lights and started blowing out the candles in the room.

Hannah followed her example and within minutes all four of the dining rooms were lit only by electricity. The stark light made the rooms look more like a museum full of antique furnishings than the bustling restaurant it had been earlier. "Thanks for showing me the ropes tonight."

"You're welcome. You're a fast learner. Besides, I loved how your aura spilled over onto everyone around you all night long. The aura of everyone you spoke with brightened like you were a human torch of goodwill and happiness. Pretty awesome, if you ask me." Karma's large brown eyes were warm. "You really do fit in here. It's like you were always meant to be at the Cat."

Hannah couldn't keep the grin from her face. Karma's assessment made her feel ridiculously happy. "Thanks, but the guests made my first night easy."

"Even when you dropped all those dishes?" Michael's voice preceded him from the shadows. An empty gray bin in his hands. He might have been smiling, but it was difficult to see past the swath of hair hanging in his face.

"You stop. Like you never dropped a dish." Karma swatted Michael on the arm playfully, then wrapped one arm around Hannah's and tugged her toward the kitchen. "Don't listen to him. He's just messing with you. You really were spot-on all night long. I told Ross that orange glow around you would be good for business. You just draw people to you."

They pushed through the kitchen door and found it empty. The back door hung open with only the screened door closed but not latched. But the most interesting door was the office one. It stood ajar with the toe of one of Niall's polished black shoes *tap-tap-tapping* on the concrete floor. He hovered between the office and the kitchen, his attention focused on someone in the office.

"What in the hell is wrong with you? No, don't waste my time lying to me. It pisses me off when you pull shit like this. And don't bother giving me your litany of reasons for hiring someone behind my back. I don't care how much we need another server for the wedding. You had no business hiring someone when I wasn't here. Especially when you didn't bother to do the things I said we needed done. The pantry bulb is still out, the toilet's still jacked up, and I can only assume you didn't clean behind the shelves." Niall's words came out in a series of staccato beats timed in rhythm with his toe taps.

Tension wafted through the air like an overcharged current on a hot summer night. The hair on Hannah's neck rose and she tried to back up but succeeded only in stepping on Karma's toe.

Karma clapped a hand over her mouth and her eyes watered but she didn't make a sound. In fact, she shook her head when Hannah started to apologize. She hiked a thumb over her shoulder in a silent suggestion they head back the way they had come.

No argument there.

Their exit came to a sudden halt when the door didn't move. Michael was on the other side peering through the diamond-shaped opening. Karma motioned for him to move, but he remained still, staring presumably at the office door. Not that Hannah could really see Michael's eyes, but given Niall's volume, it was an easy assumption to make.

"You told me before you left that one of *our* responsibilities was to do the hirings and the firings." Ross's voice, less grave but with considerably more volume, cut through the air. Multiplying the tension by ten. "We had a need, so I hired her. What's the big deal? Or am I no longer qualified to hire people without permission of the great Niall Graham? I'm just some stupid kid who can't do anything right, is that it?"

"I've never called you a stupid anything. Hell, I told you five minutes ago that tonight's receipts were outstanding!" Niall's voice rose to match Ross's decibel.

"And I told you that we needed another server for Saturday. Dawn's kid got sick and she had to leave early. Hannah jumped in to help. You should be thanking me."

"Thanking you for what?" Niall retorted, mockery and disbelief tightening his tone.

"Yes, thanking me." Ross's voice grew marginally louder and the words slurred. "In a single stroke, I got us another trained server for Saturday and Dawn's shift covered for tonight. Not bad for a dumb-ass kid, right? Oh great and powerful Niall."

"Should I also thank you for going out and getting wasted during business hours? Got to get your party on? Or are you going to try to tell me that you weren't at O'Toole's until twenty minutes ago? I should warn you, if you're going to lie to me, that you reek of beer."

"Fuck. You!"

The door swung open, and Niall stumbled backward a few steps as if shoved. He balled his hands into fists at his thighs but didn't raise them. Instead, he turned sideways in the door and let Ross storm past.

Hannah and Karma pushed harder against the door to the Master Room, but Michael didn't budge. Shoot, why couldn't she be endowed with the gift of invisibility? Although, the way Ross ignored them, they might as well have been transparent.

Ross didn't pause, he turned left out of the office and stormed out the back door, nearly knocking over Paulie who must have either been coming in or waiting outside. To his credit, Paulie didn't react. He glanced at Niall who stood red-faced and hands still fisted in the doorway to his office.

Paulie rolled his eyes at the man, then glanced at Karma. "Trash is out and the stoves clean and prepped for tomorrow. Can I—" He nodded toward the exit. "I'm his ride."

"Go on, Paulie," Niall said, turning to the chef. "Goodnight."

Paulie hesitated a moment, then nodded first to Niall, then to Karma, then to Niall again. "See you tomorrow, Karma. Clock me out, Boss."

Hannah's heart pumped like a marathon runner's while she waited for Niall to notice her. Although him not noticing might be a good thing. He'd sounded pretty angry that she'd been hired.

Although what had she really expected?

For him to sweep her into his arms and kiss her the moment they saw each other again? No. But she sure hadn't anticipated him yelling at his brother for hiring her. Maybe if she explained that this was a temporary job. Just something for a few months until she could find a job as an electrician, it would lessen the blow. Reduce the tension.

Niall closed his eyes and his lips moved as if he counted silently. She tried not to stare at him. Tried and hopelessly failed. Because, well, it was Niall.

His very presence filled the room. His hair, although longer than it had been the night they met, was still short. It stood out in odd tufts, as if he'd been tugging at it.

Then his eyes flew open and his gaze zeroed in on hers. She was locked in his sights but not frightened.

Fascinated.

Niall was tall, commanding, and, despite having just participated in a shouting match with his brother, appeared startled rather than angry. And those vivid green eyes. He stared at her with an intensity that made Hannah's cheeks burn. An odd red light surrounded him. She'd seen that light before. The night they'd made love in her apartment. It pulsed and beckoned her. She might have gone to him, touched him, but then he spoke.

"I suppose you heard all that." Niall sighed and shook his head as if resigned, running a hand through his hair. "Of course you did. He shouldn't have hired you. It's nothing personal. Just business."

The words were impersonal, efficient, and had the absolute effect of slicing her in two despite the quiet, beleaguered delivery.

Half of her was devastated by his callous words. The other half just as quickly reminded her that the universe sent her here. He needed her, even if he didn't know it yet.

Now she simply had to convince him of that.

"It's nice to see you too, Niall."

CHAPTER 7

WHAT THE HELL was he saying? Niall finally had Hannah in the same room again after all this time and he was sending her away?

"It's okay." Hannah gave him a winning smile that didn't quite mask the surprise and hurt in her tawny brown eyes. "I'm only in town for a few weeks anyway."

"Niall, we'll be short a server without her on Saturday." Karma stepped between them, but her gaze bounced from Niall to Hannah and back again, like she was watching words volley through the air. "Surely, we can afford to keep her for a few days. The guests loved her. I swear she sold more desserts tonight than we have in a week. And her being here gives me time to train her for Saturday."

He couldn't argue with the logic but Karma didn't know everything he did. A one-night stand showed up unannounced in his restaurant months after their night together. A one-night stand who didn't have the decency to give him her real phone number. Something about the whole thing didn't sit right with him. And not simply because Hannah's presence evoked a sexual response in him.

"Karma, will you excuse us? I'd like to get to know my new employee." He stepped back and gestured to Hannah. "Come into my office."

Hannah's brows knit and she gave Karma a nervous, wary smile. And damn, if that didn't piss him off more. *She* was afraid of him? She showed up in his place of business after giving him a bogus number but was acting as if he frightened her. The woman probably was every bit the nutball he'd suspected she was back in Fincastle. Why in the fuck had he slept with her in the first place?

"Absolutely, Mr. Graham." She gave him a winning smile and strode into his office.

Niall ignored Karma's suspicious stare and closed the door between them. Turning, he found Hannah had claimed the only chair in the room. Sitting cross-legged, with her hands folded primly in her lap, she smiled at him. "Hi, Niall. Or should I call you *Mr. Graham*? Or is it *Boss*?"

He sighed and leaned his back against the door. The doorknob was a lifeline he held on to to keep from crossing the small room and touching her. His head might think she was some kind of wacko stalker but his body certainly didn't seem to care. She was beautiful, ethereal, and damned charming with that mouth that always seemed to be smiling. "What are you doing here, Hannah?"

Her smile widened marginally and she uncrossed her legs, letting her feet dangle in front of her. They didn't quite reach the floor because the chair was set for him.

"If you think I'm some psycho stalker chick, forget it." She shrugged. "I had no idea you even lived in Tidewater. I didn't know you owned a restaurant. I thought you were in the Marines."

"I was. When you met me last winter, I was in the Marines. My enlistment ended in May." He glanced around the cluttered room. "I came home to take over the family business."

"From your brother?"

"*With* my brother," he replied more defensively than he'd

intended. "But you still haven't answered my question. Why are you here, in Tidewater, applying for a job in my restaurant?"

She tilted her chin up and slightly to the left, staring at him with those eyes that seemed to peek into his soul. It was damned unnerving. He almost hoped that she had sought him out, twisted as it sounded in his own head. Then at least this attraction he felt would be mutual. No. Wait. That was wrong. Heinously wrong. He didn't want her to want him because then her presence meant she had to be a stalker.

She's making me fucking crazy and she hasn't even said why she's here yet.

"I'm searching for my sisters. They live here in Tidewater. Or so I've been led to believe." She pushed off the chair. Her shoes scuffled on the floor as she stood. "Relax, Niall. I didn't track you down like some lovesick Marine groupie. My being in this spot wasn't my intention. Well, it was but not because of you. This place," she indicated the space with both hands, "used to be my house when I was a child."

Niall's teeth set at the lie. Christ, he hated liars. Good. If she were a liar, it would be easier to make her go.

He pointed at the floor with a single finger. "This place wasn't habitable until five years ago."

"So suspicious." She crossed the minuscule room, stopping right in front of him. "But you're right. Sort of. This building wasn't habitable five years ago, but an old woman lived here twenty years ago. She was my mother's landlord. My mother's little bungalow sat where the parking lot is now. I came here this morning to see if I could remember anything about living here."

"You *lived* here?" he asked. She shrugged and he clarified, "In a house that used to stand on my parking lot?" It seemed too unbelievable to be true.

"Yes." She pointed at the far wall. "The church across the street was our church. It's where my mother and father were married."

"The parents who own the bar in Fincastle?" She had to be lying. The alternative was too uncomfortable to be true.

"No, they adopted me when I was three." Her ever-smiling

mouth turned down at the corners. "My first mother died when I was three. I was adopted by Axel and Rosalind and we moved to Ohio not long after. I don't really remember much about living in Tidewater. It's why I wanted to come back here and see if I could remember anything before I went to find my sisters."

"And did you?" When confusion wrinkled her brow he added, "Remember anything about living here?"

An odd expression slid across her face. It was so fast, he doubted he'd actually seen anything.

"Sort of. I remembered a day that happened a few months before my mother died but not much else. Anyway, I saw Ross put a placard in the window asking for a waitress. It seemed like a sign."

"A sign?"

That blinding heart-stopping smile was back on her face. "Yes, a sign. No pun intended. I needed a temporary job while I'm in town for the summer. I know it seems like a huge coincidence but I was just as surprised as you to find you here."

"A coincidence?"

"Yeah. Well, a sign. I don't really believe in coincidences. Do you?"

He shook his head. "So you saw the sign and applied for the job?"

"That's what I said." Her eyes sparkled. "Right?"

"Right." He was repeating her but he couldn't seem to stop himself. Something about her made him both want to boot her out the door and go in for another one of her amazing kisses. He did neither but kept talking. "Didn't you just graduate college? Shouldn't you be looking for more permanent work? Or is this what you plan to do while you paint?"

"You remembered that I'm an artist?" Delight made her tawny eyes soften.

"Of course I remember. Your blue owl was unique. Extraordinary." Much to his surprise, her lips were now inches from his. She hadn't moved closer. He had. Somehow he had closed the distance between them without realizing it. His hands, no longer clutching the doorknob, hung limply at his sides. His fingers tingled with the need to touch her. "Are you looking for permanent work or is this a summer break thing?"

"A summer break thing, but shouldn't you be more concerned with, um . . . other matters?" She sucked in her bottom lip, but it did nothing to dim the smile on her face.

"Other matters?" he asked hoarsely.

She folded her arms over her chest, her face solemn. "Firing me, for one. Unless I've passed your not-a-psycho-stalker test."

"Right." Her words dipped him in frigid reality. He had been worried about just that. And clearly, she knew it. Way to look like an ass in front of her.

A stalker wouldn't have given him a bogus number. Therefore, she couldn't be a stalker. An infuriatingly attractive woman he'd slept with once but not a stalker. A woman who had the skills to do the job and do it well. Why not hire her? It was only for a few days.

"Look, what I said out there was true," Niall said. "We cannot afford to keep you on past the wedding but Karma is also right. Since you're not staying in Tidewater indefinitely, this could work out for both of us. You can work this week, while looking for your sisters and another job, and I don't have to find someone else to train." He paused, then added, "Let's just keep what happened back in Fincastle back in Fincastle, if you know what I mean. You work for me, nothing else."

He held his breath.

A vertical crease appeared between her brows and she nodded slowly. "Sure. That's ancient history. You're my boss and I'm your employee. Got it."

Then they stood there.

Unmoving.

Breathing the same air. Honeysuckles.

Christ, the scent made him think of their night together. An incredible night.

She reached out a hand and he might have jumped, if not for his training. It wasn't him she reached for. It was the doorknob.

"Right," he said, reaching past her before she could touch it. He yanked the door harder than he'd intended but it was open. He'd started, so he kept right on going, striding out of the office and to the back door. He didn't trust himself not to touch her when she moved past, so he followed his brother's lead and headed to the exit, calling over his shoulder, "Lock up, Karma. See you tomorrow."

Once outside in his truck, he sat with the key in the ignition.

It would be easy, too easy, to go back inside. Tell her to forget what he said about forgetting Fincastle. Why in the hell had he said that anyway? Like he wouldn't have jumped at the chance to fuck her again.

No, not fuck.

Their night had been more intense than that. More personal than a simple itch that needed scratching. Not the flowery crap that poets write about . . . but something that made a corner of his soul crave the chance to experience it all again.

And that was why he sat in the truck, unmoving. Part of him wanted to leave. The woman was damned unnerving. She affected him in ways he didn't want to think about. She was a stranger. He shouldn't feel this bizarre pull to be around her. Hell, he'd even tried to call her for all the good it did him.

Not to screw her or to touch her or to even see her. Just to talk to her. When had he ever felt that desire before? Never. That cold December night, she managed to reach inside and comfort him on the very night he could have sworn he'd never feel peace again. Then she'd kissed him good-bye and handed him a phone number to nowhere.

And that too kept his ass in the seat of his beloved truck.

Christ, he was a fucking Marine. Marines didn't run from danger, they ran toward it. But he'd bet his left nut that no Marine had ever before gone up against a slip of a woman with a fairylike face and the ability to bring a man to his knees with a simple glance.

Tomorrow, he wouldn't run. He didn't need to. She'd be gone in a few days. But before she left, he'd find out why she'd given him a bogus number.

"ARE YOU ALL right?" Karma asked as soon as Niall left.

"Sure. I still have a job." Hannah smiled and tried to push

away the hurt that had knifed through her at Niall's request to leave what happened between them in Fincastle. She'd already decided she'd have to show him he needed her around. She'd just kind of hoped that he'd *want* to pick up where they'd left off.

Karma pursed her lips, giving her a narrow-eyed stare. "Your au—" She cut herself off as Michael pushed through the door from the Master Room, a bin full of dirty dishes in his hands. Turning to him she said, "Michael, just leave the dishes, I'll get them. We'll see you tomorrow."

Michael's bangs shifted, as if moved by raised eyebrows before he smiled. "Sure. Clock me out?"

Karma nodded, taking the bin from him and disappearing around the demi-wall to the sink area.

Michael removed his apron, tossed it into the laundry basket by the back door, then left. Karma immediately pulled the screened door closed and latched it, then shut and locked the heavy wooden door behind it. Lifting her shoulder in a come-with-me maneuver, she gestured for Hannah to follow her to the sink.

Despite being tired and seriously ready to call it a night, Hannah obeyed.

The big metal dishwasher ran noisily. Steam poured from beneath the grate, wafting through the room like a wet, heavy cloud. But everything, aside from the tub of dirty dishes, gleamed in the kitchen.

"Wow, the cooks don't waste time cleaning their stations at night, do they?"

Karma smirked. "Can you blame them? Virgil wants to get home and spend time with his wife. And Paulie . . . well, he's an enigma. Doesn't really say where he's going at night. But if I had to guess, I'd say he's curled up at home in bed with a book."

"Not an extrovert?"

"Hardly. Our chefs, and we call them chefs here, are more comfortable sorting tomatoes than talking to guests. That's why they have us." Karma set the bin of dishes on the floor next to a white cooler with a blue lid. She lifted off the top, pulled out two bottles of water, and handed one to Hannah.

"Thanks." Hannah twisted off the cap and guzzled half the bottle.

"Worked up a thirst tonight?" Karma asked, grinning when Hannah nodded. She took a pull from her own bottle, then tilted her head to one side as if studying Hannah. "Your aura's looking better. It's a vibrant orange again. Not that sickly yellow it had been when you walked out of Niall's office. And definitely not that hot orange red it was when you two walked into it."

"You really see auras. It's not just an impression of people's characters you get when you talk to them, is it? You see actual colors. All the time?"

The dishwasher made a *shunking* noise, indicating the next wash cycle. Karma eyed it, then lifted herself onto the clean table and sat. Hannah folded her arms over her chest, but didn't join her on the metal table.

"Yep. I literally see colors around living people." Karma lowered her eyes and hunched her shoulders. "Pretty weird, huh?"

"No, not at all. I think that's amazing. I have my own little, um . . . talent." She hesitated briefly, but figured if Karma saw auras, she shouldn't be weirded out by Hannah's gift. "I touch objects and get visions."

"You're a psychometrist!" Karma's expression brightened. "I've heard about people like you but I've never met one in person until now. Now that's a cool gift. How does it work? Is it like mine? Do you do it all the time? Bet that's a great way to weed out loser dates."

Hannah laughed. "It *can* come in handy for spotting the creepy guys but it can be a bit of a pain too. I don't just see visions from objects—metal objects—I mean. I, um, well. Shoot, it's going to sound nuts but I actually live the vision."

Karma frowned. "You mean if I handed you a fork, you'd get into my head and fish around?"

"Nothing quite that diabolical." Hannah twisted her braid in her fingers. "It's more like you hand me something and whatever memory you had when you were handling it will be one I walk through. I'll see it, hear it, smell it, taste it, just like you did. Like a dream, sort of. You know how it's all bright and shiny when you're in the dream and it fades after you wake up? My visions are like that.

"In a way, I am you for a few minutes. But I cannot search for other memories once I'm in there. Usually, I wonder a question, like what's your favorite guilty secret TV show or something before I touch the object. Unless you were really upset when you touched it before me, I'll usually only see the answer to my question.

"I think it's an invasion of privacy to go rooting around in someone else's memories, you know. Anyway, I don't think I can do something like that. I've never tried. And I wouldn't. It's kind of, you know, icky."

The dishwasher emitted a loud hiss, then water ran down the drain. Karma glanced from it to Hannah, then grinned. "We're so going to get along. Tell you what—" Michael Bublé singing "Home" rang out from her pocket. Karma held a finger in the air, then tugged out her cell. "Hey, Ziggy . . . I'm closing up . . . How about I stop by the station in an hour? No, I don't need a ride . . . No, I won't walk there alone in the dark . . . Yes, I can't wait to see you either."

Karma ended the call. Her dark brown eyes were bright with excitement. "Tell you what, I need to finish up in the office and sign the time cards for everyone. Can you do the dishes? You don't need to put away the clean ones, just load the dirty ones into the dishwasher and get it started."

Karma pulled the clean rack of dishes out of the dishwasher and set up another one for the dirty ones.

After receiving a quick demonstration on the machine, Hannah agreed. It wasn't rocket science. And they had a much smaller version of this model dishwasher back in Fincastle. Karma gave her a quick hug and bolted to the office.

Hoping for more time to talk after, Hannah lifted the rubber bin from the floor and started loading the plates. Everything was fine until she grabbed a handful of knives. The world around her went gray.

Then someone screamed.

CHAPTER 8

Everything was dark, but that was perfect. Mercy loved the dark. Besides, the only thing Mercy needed to see was him. And there he sat, trussed up. Naked. Delicious. Dying.

Blood ran black rivers from the left side of his chest. It gurgled and spouted.

The heavy scent of metal clung to the warm, humid night air. And Mercy drank it in. How that smell made her shiver. Excitement danced through her like electricity.

"Mercy, please," her lover begged. His long blond hair hung limply in front of his face. His brown eyes, hollow. The skin beneath them sunken. He radiated pain.

Mercy's joy dimmed.

"You're still here?" She moved closer. He wasn't supposed to be here. Not after everything. He was supposed to be gone. To be free. He shouldn't be clinging to life like this. "That's not right. Not right at all. What do you think you're doing? I set you free. You can't stay."

Her bare feet shuffled across the rough, unfinished floor. He wriggled his legs uselessly. He couldn't fight her. He was tied to the two-by-fours that framed the house's ocean view window. She reached out her free hand to touch his leg and he kicked at her. The weak move sent more blood pumping through the hole in his chest.

Fury exploded through Mercy. This was how he repaid her kindness?

She shifted the knife from hand to hand, slashing the air with each pass.

He screamed again, a long throaty cry of agony.

And she sank the knife into his neck this time.

Blood spurted up into her face. It dripped down her cheeks and lips. "Yes! Yes! Baptize me in your blood. Show me you're grateful for my mercy." Laughter rang out loud and disjointed and she shivered in delight.

He was gone now.

Her mercy had been granted.

"Hannah! Hannah, let go of the knife." Karma's voice filtered in, distant and tinny. Then fingers brushed her damp cheeks. "Hannah, let go of the knife."

Hannah blinked open her eyes. Karma's caramel-colored skin had gone gray and her eyes were wide and frightened.

"Wha?"

"The. Knife." Karma repeated the words, separately, slowly. "Let. It. Go."

Knife?

Hannah glanced down to see her right hand, covered in blood and clutching the blade of one of the dinner knives. She dropped it instantly. Fear and pain rushed in to replace the vision.

"Damn!" She cried out when Karma wrapped her hand in the black apron Hannah had been wearing. "Oh, that hurts! Holy fucking schmoley."

Karma snorted a nervous laugh. "I've never met anyone before who says *holy* and *fucking* like that in the same sentence. Are you back with me?"

"Yeah, I'm here." Hannah nodded. Her palm throbbed and burned. Oh, she was most definitely back in the land of the living. Pain was really good for breaking free from a vision. "Sorry if I frightened you."

"I'm just glad you'd told me about your gift before I found you clutching that thing like you were about to stab someone with the wrong end." Karma gave her a weak smile. "Although, the fact that your aura was no longer any shade of orange but a muddy brownish-black would have clued me into something being really wrong. Are you sure you're okay? Do you think you need stitches?"

"I hope not. No insurance right now." Carefully, Hannah unwrapped her hand and examined the wound. Blood smeared her palm, making it difficult to see the actual damage.

"Come here." Karma gently but firmly pulled her to the sink and ran her hand under a stream.

Hannah's palm burned despite the cool water. "I really think it's fine. A lot of blood, but the wound doesn't look too deep."

"I'll be the judge of that." Karma's voice took on that Spanish accent again. "Do you always whip knives in the air during a vision? Seems like it could be very dangerous to me."

Despite the levity of her tone and the smile on her face, Karma's skin was still gray.

Hannah tried to pull back but gave up when the manager tightened her grip on Hannah's wrist.

"Really, Karma. I'm fine. I'm not sure what happened. I've never done anything like that before."

"How would you know?" Karma pulled Hannah's hand out from the water stream and examined it again. She blotted it dry with a paper towel, only to push it back under the water again. "You didn't seem to know what you were doing when I walked in here."

Hannah pulled free of the woman's grasp and pressed a paper towel to the wound. "Karma, I'm normally very careful about what objects I touch. It was stupid of me to pick up a bunch of silverware bare-skinned. I wasn't thinking. And I certainly couldn't have imagined what I'd see when I did."

Karma shut off the water and handed Hannah another paper towel. "What did you see?"

Hannah focused on stanching the blood from the long, shallow cut and tried to think. She needed to tell someone fast because the vision was already starting to fade.

The name, what did the killer call herself?

Mercedes? Mirabo? Marcy?

Hannah needed to touch the knife again and reconnect with the vision. Her stomach pitched at the idea but maybe she could get something she missed the first time. She held out a shaking hand and said, "Karma, can you hand me the knife?"

"You want it back?" Karma frowned. She held it aloft, wrapped in a hand towel, examining it herself. "Why?"

"Because I need to touch it again to remember what I saw."

"Are you going to stab me with it?"

"Of course not." *I hope.*

Karma slowly lowered it into Hannah's waiting palm.

Instant connection, hot and fierce. A flash was all she needed and Hannah shoved the utensil away.

"You okay?" Karma asked, putting the knife behind her on the table. "What did you see?"

Hannah stared at the gold-handled table knife sitting innocuously on the tabletop. It wasn't the knife from the vision. So why had it sent her world spinning?

"Hannah, what did you see in that vision?"

"A murder."

MERCY SAT AT her mother's vanity and stared at her reflection in the mirror. She wasn't the ugly little nothing she'd once been. So why didn't he notice?

She was a good person. A kind person. She granted peace to all those who suffered around her. Didn't she deserve love?

"You're nothing but a little freak. A whore! Here, freak, let's paint you up like the whore-clown you are. Then I can charge admission. Five dollars a peek at the freak." The bitch's voice cackled with laughter. Her sister's voice joined in the jeering. "What's the matter, sissy baby? Don't like hearing what you are? Freakazoid. Freakazoid. Everybody hates the freakazoid. God, stop that blubbering. If you weren't such a loser, you'd be completely worthless."

Mercy shut her eyes and pounded her fists against her head. Her mother's voice taunted more often. Dead or not, the bitch never let her have a moment's peace. Every time Mercy found a way to be near him, she'd hear her bitch sister's jeers in her head. But that helped. At least then Mercy could remember her purpose on earth was not to be loved but to grant mercy.

Tonight, she'd make him notice her. She'd seen him walking alone earlier tonight. He wasn't like the others she'd set free. He was special. Her one true love. Her dead bitch sister had been wrong.

Mercy wasn't worthless. Wasn't a loser.

Mercy could be loved.

He could love her. He *would* love her. Once she made him notice her.

It was why she was saving him for last. She knew what he didn't. She knew that when he found his peace, Mercy would go with him. Not out of pity or pain but because they were meant to be together.

Not tonight.

Tonight, she'd set another man free.

Mercy selected the tube of Waitress Red lipstick, glossed it over her mouth, blew her reflection a kiss, and imagined it was her true love she kissed.

NIALL WAS A friggin' moron. He'd driven all the way home only to turn around and immediately come back because he'd forgotten to grab the bank deposit. It had been completely by accident. He'd dropped off yesterday's this afternoon, so it had naturally slipped his mind to grab tonight's deposit. Anyone could have made the same mistake.

It had absolutely nothing to do with the fact that the last thing he'd been at the Cat was flustered by Hannah.

Yeah. Right. Tell another, Marine.

That's what she'd called him that night. *Marine.*

She of the fairylike beauty and endless smile.

Hannah. Hannah Halloran. He'd learned her last name when he'd read her application. But he still had no idea where she lived because the address on the form was for the hotel down the street. Okay, he could have gone over there, but hadn't he been the one to make her promise to keep the relationship strictly business?

He was definitely not the kind of boss to screw his employees, figuratively or literally. But damn, she was here. And their one night together had been definitely worth repeating.

Now he was back at the restaurant. Despite the empty parking lot, lights blazed through the high office window. Either he'd left on the office light or someone was still there. The odds that it was Hannah were slim. She was brand new. With his luck, he'd find Sadie in there no doubt writing him a note complaining about Michael or Ross or Virgil . . . again.

Maybe I should take care of the deposit in the morning.

Something crashed inside the kitchen. Hell, it sounded like dozens of dishes breaking.

Niall was out of the truck and banging on the screen door in an instant. "Open up. It's Niall. Hey! Is anyone hurt in there?"

The locks clicked, then the main door pulled back to reveal an ashen-faced Karma. She smiled, a nervous twitch of the lips, then unlocked the screen door. "Hi, Boss. Didn't expect you back tonight."

"Bankroll," he muttered, pushing his way inside.

The kitchen gleamed in the quiet. Only the sound of the dishwasher running around the corner broke the unearthly silence. He glanced around the empty room before turning back to Karma, who'd relocked the doors behind him. "You alone in here? I thought I heard a crash."

"Oh, um." Karma sidled past him, angling for the dishwasher around the half wall. "No, I'm not alone. And nothing's broken."

Niall followed her to find Hannah, pale as death, sitting on the floor. Her back propped against the demi-wall. She alternately sucked in air in gasps and sipped at a water bottle, as if trying to settle her stomach.

Squatting in front of her he asked, "Are you all right?"

"Fine." Her eyes were a bit unfocused but she nodded. Her color was off and she definitely didn't appear fine.

"Did you fall down?" Because that would be his luck. To have her slip on something in his restaurant.

"No," Hannah and Karma replied in unison. They glanced at each other and laughed weakly.

"I had a vision and needed to sit down. I knocked over the clean silverware in my haste." She took another, longer gulp of her drink. "Sorry. I'll clean that up in a few minutes."

Only then did Niall notice the forks, knives, and spoons littering the floor.

"You stay put, I'll get it," Karma said, moving to clean up the mess. "What do you want to do, Hannah?"

"About what?" Niall asked at the same time Hannah said, "Go to the police, I guess."

Hannah and Karma both gave him that infuriating stare that women had when they thought the men they were with were being obtuse. He didn't squirm. If his mother couldn't make him uneasy—well, she could, but only she could do that to him after his life in the Marines—he wouldn't let them.

What did she say?

"What was that about a vision?" he asked. His neck itched at the calm expressions both women wore.

"I was loading up the dishwasher when I had a vision of a murder." Hannah shivered and looked at her hands. "It was gruesome. There was blood everywhere. He struggled and fought, even when the knife was coming down. It was the most awful thing I've ever witnessed. And the smell . . ." She shivered again.

"It was pretty freaky from where I was standing," Karma added, opening the dishwasher as soon as it cut off. "She went pale, and I swear for a minute I didn't think she was going to come out of it. She was saying some creeptastic things."

Despite her deathly pallor, Hannah's eyes went wide. "I spoke? I don't think I've done that before. At least, no one ever mentioned me doing that. What did I say?"

"You kept talking about giving mercy, then you said, 'Baptize me in your blood. Show me you're grateful for my mercy.'" Karma's accent returned, thicker than Niall had ever heard it before. She ran a hand through her short, curly hair and blew out a breath. "You didn't sound like you. Your voice, I mean. It was like someone or something else was talking through you.

If I hadn't known what you can do, if I hadn't already seen your bright, clean aura before, I'd have been hauling butt out of here and calling the cops. You sounded like a psychopath."

Hannah's eyes brimmed with tears in her too-pale face. The sight had his gut twisting even as his mind struggled to wrap itself around this absurd conversation.

"I'm so sorry, Karma. I didn't mean to frighten you. If it makes you feel any better, it scared the dickens out of me too. *Psychopath* is a good word. That vision was definitely seen through the eyes of one crazypants individual." Hannah rolled the open bottle against her cheek, as if needing to cool down. "But I'll be honest, I've never seen anything like that before. I've never been inside a killer's head until now and she was seriously screwed up."

"'She?' The killer was a woman?" Karma asked, her accent gone again. "Do you know anything about her?"

Hannah squinted as if trying to see in the distance or draw up a memory, then shook her head. "Not really. All I can remember is that she called herself Mercy. Wait, there was something else." Hannah squeezed her eyes closed, then shook her head and opened them again. "Something about her hand. Something wrong with it? I can't really remember it clearly."

Karma held up a dirty knife wrapped in a hand towel. "Do you want to try again?"

"Definitely not. Two trips into her crazyland are more than enough for one night. I've never felt so ill after a vision before. Not even when I accidentally stumbled into Mr. Hobson's hidden porn room memory." She paused, grinning. "Although, I'm pretty sure I was blushing when I came out of it."

Niall slowly straightened and just listened to the women talk. He was used to Karma's weird utterances about auras. Hell, she had a gift for reading people and had done more to help him weed out the worst of their staff than Ross and his parents put together. But damn, now he had two women working for him and claiming to be in touch with the other side or some other woo-woo shit.

He should have stayed home.

"Will you drive us?" Karma asked, touching him on the forearm and drawing him from his thoughts.

"Drive you where?"

"To the station. I think someone needs to know about what I saw." Hannah pushed to her feet, finished off the last of the water, then pitched the bottle in the recycling bin. "I have no idea how the cops deal with people like me down here, but I can't do nothing."

"You want me to go with you while you tell the police you imagined you were in a killer's head?"

"No, I want you to drive us to the police station so I can report what I saw in my vision of being in a killer's head." Hannah narrowed her eyes on him. "You'll come with me, won't you, Karma?" When Karma nodded Hannah added, "I need to report a murder. I can give a description of the man who was killed."

"Don't you have a car?" He couldn't help but ask. "How'd you get here from Fincastle?"

"What does that have to do with anything? I took the bus." She gave him a withering sort of smile. The kind of smile that was both adorable and reproachful all at the same time.

He might have laughed if what she was saying hadn't been so serious. And fucked up. She needed to see reason.

"Do you know who did it? Where it happened? *When* it happened? Hannah, how do you know you didn't dream it up? Couldn't this all be in your imagination?"

Hannah's shoulders rolled back and down, as if preparing for a fight. "I didn't dream it up. Nowhere in my imagination would I want to picture some poor young guy getting stabbed to death. And I'd have to work pretty freaking hard to imagine the stench of blood and death that darn near seared the inside of my nostrils during that vision. Whatever! Don't drive me. I'll walk over. Someone just point me in the right direction."

"Hannah, people don't just go to the police to report crimes they haven't actually beared physical witness to."

"I did," Karma interjected. When he turned to glare at his restaurant manager she arched an eyebrow at him and added, "Well, I did."

"As I recall, that wasn't well received, was it?" He remembered the story of what happened when Karma had repeatedly contacted the police to report that a child declared dead was actually alive and kidnapped. No one would listen to her. Well, almost no one. In the end, she'd been right. Something that still floored Niall to think about. "As I recall, that experience was hard on you. Very hard. And people weren't exactly happy with you. Do you want to put Hannah through that?"

"The only people unhappy with me for going to the police were the ones responsible for what happened to that little boy. As I recall, his mother was overjoyed." She turned her back to him and took Hannah by the hands. "Hannah, unlike when I did it, you won't go in there alone. And I'll make sure to introduce you to someone I guarantee will believe you. We'll go see my boyfriend, Zig. He'll know what to do."

The women started past him. Hannah's golden eyes were dull. They'd been vacant when he'd first come into the kitchen but this was different. Hurt swam in them. She paused and glanced up at him. "I'm not crazy. I know what I saw. I thought you would believe me."

"I barely know you. You honestly expect me to tell the cops that I believe you had a psychic vision?" Okay, that was a shitty, vicious lie. He knew her intimately. Niall heard the words come out of his mouth as if someone else spoke them. If ever he wished life had a delete key, this was it. He'd have gone back and erased his thoughtless, rude-ass words from existence.

"I suppose not." She lifted her chin in the air, the dull look in her eyes replaced by golden ice chips and she strode out the back door.

"Very nice, Boss," Karma said, reminding him she'd been standing there.

Crap!

"It's not—"

"You know one of the things I've always respected about you was your brutal honesty. Don't bother to lie now, remember I can see your aura." She was almost to the back door when she turned and added, "You know, if you're trying to drive her away, you're doing a bang-up job."

CHAPTER 9

HANNAH SKETCHED THE image of the victim from her vision on the sketch pad she kept in her backpack. It was hard to stay focused on the image with her squeezed between Niall and Karma in the front seat of Niall's truck. She did her best not to touch him, but it was impossible to avoid his arm considering the truck was a stick shift and her legs were sprawled on either side of the gears.

"Sorry," he muttered when his muscled forearm brushed the top of her left thigh again. She felt the heat of him through her black work slacks.

She held still until he slid the gear into fifth, then she straightened her leg to give them both some much-needed space. She was not going to be attracted to him anymore. Hadn't she been telling herself just that since his comment in the kitchen?

Barely know you. Okay, yes, their time together had been a single, solitary night. But they'd shared something more. At least, she thought they had. Perhaps, she'd been wrong. He hadn't been thrilled to see her today. Except . . .

Except for that single spark she caught in his eyes when he didn't realize she could see him watching her during her shift. No matter his words, he *was* attracted. Even if he had acted like a jerk.

Then Niall had surprised her. He'd followed Karma outside and offered to drive them to the station after all. Hannah hadn't wanted to climb in, much less sit in the middle, but Karma refused to walk in the dark. Not that the city was terribly dark with all the streetlights. But since she didn't exactly know where she was going, she needed Karma.

She glanced at her pad, examining the lines and shading made shaky by the bumps in the road. It wasn't perfect, because she couldn't recall everything. Still, it was good. Good enough to compare to missing persons' photos like she'd seen in TV shows and movies.

Besides, if she kept drawing and erasing, she'd end up drawing Niall instead, since he was foremost in her mind. Tucking the pad and pencil back in her backpack, she stared at the street ahead. Niall radiated an air of quiet brooding that unnerved her. It made her want to strike up a conversation with him, but after his last smackdown, she wasn't sure it was worth the risk.

Hannah inhaled a tired breath. That was really stupid. Now she had to work hard to ignore his delicious masculine scent. That wonderful, earthy, male aroma combined with some light, spicy cologne. She'd first noticed that scent during their night back in December. Sometimes she wished she could draw scents the way she could pictures. She'd capture his and rub it all over her.

Stop it, Hannah!

What was she thinking? She was furious with him, not attracted.

Right. And the sun was a peaceful shade of blue.

The truck bumped and rolled to a stop outside a two-story brick building. Hannah didn't wait for Niall to shift gears again, but flipped her leg over the stick shift, knocking his hand with her knee.

"Sorry," she said, hip-checking Karma, who had the good

sense to get out of the truck so Hannah could follow. "Thank you for the ride, Niall."

He opened his mouth but then closed it again without uttering a sound. A muscle worked in his cheek as if he were chewing on his tongue. The light from the dashboard cast him in an odd, sickly green glow. With a curt nod, he threw the truck into reverse and left.

Hannah stared at the taillights until they disappeared around a corner. An odd sensation pinched in the center of her chest. That was the third time she'd watched him leave. Maybe that was the universe telling her something.

And the temper that had been brewing since the scene at the Cat faded into a cold, withering sense of loss.

"You make him nervous." Karma wrapped an arm around Hannah's shoulder. "Or maybe he's just a coward."

"Yeah, I don't think so. He's anything but a coward." Hannah whipped her head around to gape at her new friend. "He didn't seem nervous to me. He seemed anxious to get as far from me as possible."

"You're right about the not-being-a-coward thing. He's the first to run into danger but you can't see his aura. It was all green when he came in and found you. But just now, it had a nasty yellowish tinge to it. I've never seen his aura so off before. Yep, you make him really, really uncomfortable."

And didn't that just suck to hear?

"I think your gift might be off tonight. I saw that yellowish-green. It was the lights from the dash of the truck."

Karma laughed. A rich, throaty laugh. "Normally, I'd be offended by someone doubting my gift, but since I can see your aura too, I understand. You're under a lot of pressure." She looped her arm through one of Hannah's. "Are you sure you want to go through with this? Niall wasn't altogether wrong about the cops. Not all of them are receptive to the idea of a psychic."

Hannah thought about it for a minute. "I need to tell someone. What if that guy isn't dead yet? No, he is. I know it. I've never had a premonition in my life. I only see what's been. But what if he's still tied up in that building? What if his family is searching for him? He'd want them to know what happened to him. I have to tell someone who can do something about it. The police station is the best place to start."

"All right, let's go inside. Zig is waiting for us. I texted him in the truck." They started up the steps but Karma pulled them to a stop. "Just so you know, I think you and I have more in common than you realize. That wasn't the dashboard lights you saw. Those lights were orange. You saw Niall's aura."

"Orange? You sure?" Hannah asked, then realized she knew the answer. "You're right. So that means what? I'm going to start seeing the auras of everyone around me too?"

"Well—" Karma began but was cut off by Hannah raising one hand.

"Never mind, explain later. Let's just get this over with."

Because somewhere in Tidewater a man's body was rotting in a building under construction.

"TELL US AGAIN." Detective Reynolds crossed his arms over his chest and sat on the corner of his sturdy wooden desk. His partner mirrored the pose on the opposite corner. Both men stared at Hannah with enough skepticism in their eyes, they could have probably written a tome on its definition.

"I told you. All I saw was that guy was my age-ish. Mercy stabbed him once in the chest but must have missed the heart because he didn't die right away. Mercy got really angry and stabbed him in the throat next to make sure he was dead."

"And you say, you got this *vision* from a knife where you work?" the partner asked, his voice oozing disbelief.

"Yes, Detective O'Toole."

"O'Dell. Detective O'Dell," he snapped. "Where's the knife now?"

Karma, who'd been standing against the wall next to Zig, strode forward. "Here it is." She reached into her purse and pulled out the object still wrapped in the hand towel from the Boxing Cat.

"But that's not the *actual* murder weapon," Hannah said as Detective Reynolds examined it. "The blade she used was bigger, sharper. It didn't look like any kind of knife I'd seen before. The one side was curved and the other side was serrated with wide teeth."

"But this knife is what made you go all hooey?" Detective O'Dell asked.

"I wouldn't say *hooey*, but yes, it gave me the vision." Hannah huffed in exasperation, glancing at Karma helplessly. Her friend gave her a small nod. It didn't do much, but it did embolden her to keep going. "Look, the killer must have touched the knife tonight at the restaurant. It's the only thing that makes sense."

"Right. Makes sense," Detective Reynolds scoffed. "You got a vision, saw a murder, but you can't tell us what the killer looks like. You can't tell us where to find the body. And you have no murder weapon."

"Wait, just give me a sec." Hannah pulled her sketch pad out of her backpack and flipped it open to the page she'd been drawing on. "I have a drawing here of the victim. That's got to count for something. Can't you run it through a facial recognition program or something? Find out where the guy lives, who he knows?"

"You watch too many cop shows on television."

The detectives didn't even glance at the drawing. They looked at each other over her head and seemed to share a silent conversation. One that was interrupted by Karma tugging Hannah by the arm. "Let's go, Hannah. They don't believe you."

They were most of the way to the door when one of the detectives muttered loud enough for Hannah to hear, "You need to keep your girlfriend on a tighter leash, Harmon."

Karma must have heard it too because she swung around and hissed out something in Spanish, then spun on her heel and all but pushed Hannah out the door.

Outside on the sidewalk, Karma spoke rapid-fire Spanish under her breath, her cheeks splotchy and her fists clenched.

Hannah patted a hand on Karma's back. "You okay?"

"Yes," her accent thick again. She sounded as if she were choking back tears.

"What did you say to them?"

"I told them their mamas would be disappointed to know that their sons were really little pussies with peanut-sized dicks and no imagination."

Hannah laughed. God, it felt good to laugh. It had been so stressful in the police station. She hadn't really been prepared for it.

Karma laughed too, but her laughter fell away as Officer Zig Harmon stepped outside. By the fierce expression on his face, Hannah expected him to be angry or frustrated. Her jaw went slack when he swept Karma into his arms and kissed her loudly.

"Damn, Karma, you make me so hot," Zig whispered in a deep baritone. "You really pissed them off this time."

"And you just let them talk about me like that?" Karma pushed at his hold, but he didn't release her.

"*Mi amor*, I told them you weren't anyone's bitch, and if they knew what was good for them, they'd hold their tongues around you. You are a McKinnon after all and not all of your cousins operate within the legal system anymore."

Karma laughed and swatted him on the shoulder. Then they stared into each other's eyes as if they were the only people in the world. Their love poured out of them, making Hannah's breath hitch.

Wow, third wheel thy name is Hannah.

She sidled down the steps to the sidewalk, giving them room and a semblance of privacy.

"Hannah, wait!" Karma called out. She whispered something to Zig who nodded, then followed Karma down the steps until they were beside Hannah.

He pulled a card out of his pocket, cast a sheepish look at Karma, then said, "Give these guys a call. If you say there's been a murder, they'll look until they find a body or can prove nothing happened. And unlike the bozo twins," he hiked a thumb toward the police station, "they're more open-minded about visions. They have some experience with that."

Hannah accepted the card and blinked. It was a business card for Tidewater Security Specialists. The same private investigators who'd come to find her in Fincastle. A sign she was doing the right thing. Something she desperately needed after being verbally pummeled by the cops.

Pocketing the card, she nodded. "Thanks, I'll call them when I get back to my hotel room."

"You need a lift?" Niall's voice spoke softly behind her, but that didn't stop her from jumping.

"Hey, Boss, thanks for coming back." Karma smiled warmly at Niall, then gave Zig a kiss on the cheek. "I can definitely use the ride. Zig's got work tonight."

"What about you, Hannah?" Niall asked, his grass-green eyes locked on hers.

Hannah eyed Niall with a mix of lust and distrust. Outrage still pumped through her body at his callous, but all-too-true words but so did the desire to lose herself in those lovely eyes of his.

Who needed Mercy for insanity? Hannah was driving herself crazy without any help.

Niall held out a hand to her and she eyed it suspiciously. It wasn't him she didn't trust, it was herself. She really wanted to invite him back to her hotel room, but she had more self-respect than to throw herself at someone who had already made it clear he didn't want to repeat their time together.

"Sure. I'm at the Blue Owl Hotel."

Niall opened the passenger door. The dome light from the truck cast him in a greenish glow. Not a sickly color but a warm, comforting, soothing light. Hannah nearly sighed until Karma coughed behind her.

"It's him," Karma mouthed to her when Hannah glanced at her friend.

She whipped her gaze back to Niall but the green light had been replaced by the orange glow from the dashboard lights. Before she had time to think, Karma gave her a slight push and Hannah climbed into the cab.

"That's a pretty good hike from the Boxing Cat. How'd you get to work today?" Karma asked once they were all inside and on the road.

"I took a bus. It's an easy line from the hotel to the restaurant. Good sign." Hannah grinned.

"A good sign?" Niall asked. His gaze bounced between the road and Hannah.

Each time he looked her way, her heart did a funny little jump. She played it cool though. "Well, yeah. I needed to go to my mother's house and I just happened to find the Blue Owl in the phone book. Another sign."

"Blue owl like the painting in your apartment?" Niall asked.

"You've been to her apartment?" Karma asked.

Hannah pressed on Karma's toe to silence her friend.

Oh, please don't go there.

Niall might change his mind and fire her after all—even if the slip had been his. He'd been acting so strangely all night, Hannah didn't want to risk annoying him. Yet.

Because whether he liked it or not, she was going to sit down with him and talk this out. He might not think he wanted her around, might even say it in that literal way of his, but his actions sang an entirely different song.

"Long story, Karma," Niall said, his cheeks mottled with color. "Never mind."

Hannah pressed her lips together until the smile that made her mouth itch was firmly restrained. "Right. Anyway, the hotel was perfect." Turning to Karma she explained, "Blue's my favorite color and my favorite animal is the owl. From the moment I decided to leave home, everything lined up perfectly. I sold a painting during the May Day celebration that covered my bus ticket. The electrician I was going to do my apprenticeship with won a cruise and decided to take his wife to Alaska this summer, so that freed me up to come to Tidewater. Then I found the Blue Owl Hotel online and they had a monthly deal that was half the cost of the weekly rentals if I paid up front. The place isn't the Ritz but it's cozy and bright and on the ocean. Altogether, I'd say the universe is practically screaming that I'm on the right path."

Niall snorted his obvious lack of faith at the same time Karma said, "That's really cool."

Hannah turned back to her Marine. "Haven't you ever tried to do something and no matter what you did, it didn't work out?"

"I suppose." He shrugged and adjusted his grip on the steering wheel. "Hasn't everybody?"

"Yes. I know I have but then there's the flip side. Like those times you didn't even have to try but things fell into place. Like every light being green on a day when you should have been late for some important meeting. Only you weren't because of all the green lights. That's the universe telling you that you're on the right path. Doing the right thing. See, that's what the universe is telling me with all those things lining up. I'm on the right path."

"I'm not so sure about that." Niall frowned and slowed his truck as sirens erupted behind them. Hannah tried to see through the back window as Niall pulled to the side of the road. "Looks like the universe is sending you mixed messages."

Four fire engines and an ambulance with their sirens blaring raced past them and directly toward the twenty-foot bright yellow flames licking the night sky. She didn't have to see it to know what was burning.

The Blue Owl.

CHAPTER 10

God, I'm such an asshole.

Niall glanced at Hannah and wished to God he could take back his thoughtless words. But he couldn't and the look of desolation on her face was worse than shrapnel to the gut.

"Maybe it's not as bad as it looks. My room is on the second floor in the back." Hannah seemed to be speaking more to herself than to him or Karma.

An enormous cracking sound splintered the stream of sirens wailings. Then the entire second floor caved in on the first.

"No!" Hannah dove toward Niall's door, trying to climb over him. He grabbed her around the waist, trying to hold her against him but she wriggled like a wet fish in his grasp. "Let me go! Everything I brought is in there. All of my clothes, my money, my art supplies, everything. Even Hootie, the owl my parents gave me on adoption day. I can't let it all burn."

Hannah elbowed his belly in her bid for freedom. She might be tiny but that jab was good enough to make him suck in a breath. She managed to wriggle out of his hands, across his lap, and flung open the door, damn near falling out of the truck. Niall caught her by the back of her shirt and Karma grabbed her legs. Thank Christ he'd pulled off to the side of the road and stopped before the fire brigade came through, otherwise Hannah might have ended up getting her head squashed beneath the tire of a rescue vehicle.

"Chica, escúchame!" Karma tugged Hannah back inside. She rattled off rapid-fire Spanish, then paused as if waiting for a response. The sound of the foreign language was enough to jolt Hannah into listening, at least.

"Karma, you're using your mother's language again," Niall said.

Her mother's Spanish heritage bled through her normal southern Virginia accent, giving her words a rich cross between her Mexican roots and her Virginia ones.

"I was speaking in Spanish?" Karma asked, her accent fading with each word. She shook her head as if to clear it, then faced Hannah. "You can't go running in there. You'll only get in the way. Let's wait until we hear what the damage is."

Hannah made a sound that could have been a chuckle or a heavy sigh. "Sorry. You're right. But I can't ask you two to wait here. It could be hours yet. Look at that." She gestured toward the scene with her hands, then let them flop down.

And yes, that was Hannah's hand on his groin. Oh, holy hell, she was going to kill him.

It was purely physiological, but damn, her touch made him rock hard. And she apparently didn't even realize it, caught up as she was with the flaming scene in front of her. Niall carefully plucked her hand from his lap by her wrist.

"S-sorry." Even in the orange glow of the fire, her cheeks burned red. She rubbed her hands together as if cold.

A firefighter in full turnout gear tapped on the hood of the truck. Niall rolled down his window. "We need to keep this area clear. You need to roll back out of here."

"But my stuff's in the hotel," Hannah called out, once again leaning over Niall's lap. Thankfully, this time she braced her hands on the steering wheel. Still, her honeysuckle fragrance clung to her and for a moment was all Niall could smell. It no longer brought home images of Tidewater but of a certain pretty bartender naked and writhing beneath him.

"Anyone you know of inside?"

Hannah shook her head. "No, I just got to town and I'm here alone."

"Then I'm sorry, miss. The hotel is burning fast. I doubt there's going to be much left. You can call the Red Cross if you need assistance with food, clothing, or shelter but there's nothing you can do here." Something cracked and boomed behind the fireman. The front wall collapsed inward and what had been the roof of the first floor crashed down. The fireman's radio signaled and he tugged the handheld from his shoulder, pressing it to his ear, then talked into it before he returned it to its holder. With one gloved hand, he tapped the open window of Niall's truck. "I need you to clear the road."

Waving them away with one hand, the firefighter jogged back toward the burning building.

With no other hope for it, Niall put the truck in reverse.

"Where are we going?" Hannah asked, her eyes wide with confusion. "I only have fifty in my wallet. Shoot! I left my cell phone charging in the hotel. I don't even have a way to call home."

"You can stay with me tonight." Karma nodded sharply. She pulled out her cell and tapped out a text.

Niall caught the move out of the side of his eye and wondered at the punch of jealousy he felt. He wanted to be the one consoling her. The one to take her home.

He was such a fucking gentleman. He'd get her home and take her right back to bed given half a chance.

"Great idea, Karma," Niall said quickly, turning the corner and heading to Karma's apartment. "You'll be in good hands there, Hannah."

Hannah turned to him, her big golden eyes searching. For what, he wasn't sure, but he hoped it wasn't for him to be her rescuer. That was never going to happen. She was his employee now, and would never again be his lover.

Maybe if he repeated it to himself enough, he'd finally believe it.

* * *

HANNAH RUBBED THE grit from her eyes and blinked. The room slowly took shape. First the portrait of an old woman in a traditional Mexican dress on the far wall came into focus. Beneath that was a plain, olive-colored dresser that looked to be about forty years old and missing handles on a number of drawers. The rug on the floor looked hand-braided in the brilliant shades of orange, yellow, brown, and green.

Sitting up, Hannah glanced at the four-poster bed. A blanket similar in color to the rug covered the bed. It was warm and soft and completely unfamiliar. She remembered arriving at Karma's apartment last night but had no memory of the blanket.

"So she's in the guest room?" Zig's voice filtered through the closed door.

"She needed a place to stay. Her hotel burned down. I thought you understood when you replied to my text last night. Didn't you realize she'd be here this morning?" Karma's voice, filled with humor, lilted through the air.

"Yes, I understood. *Mi amor*, you're always helping the lost, aren't you? Damn, you're so sexy this morning." There was silence for a moment, then the distinct sound of giggling.

Hannah pushed out of bed and stared at her reflection in the floor-length mirror on the bedroom door. She wore a long, thin black Michael Bublé T-shirt and a pair of too-long blue jogging pants. At her reflection she remembered Karma lending the clothing the night before.

"That's not all that burned last night." Zig's voice again, a note of seriousness this time.

Hannah opened the door and followed the voices down the hall.

"Good morning." Hannah made sure to announce her presence before she walked into the room, just in case the couple decided to get smoochy again.

Zig sat at the small, square wooden table in the oversized kitchen. The table, pushed into a corner, made the room seem larger than it was, and that was saying something because it was huge. A mug of steaming coffee sat at his elbow, he had a newspaper open and in his hands, and only the top button of his uniform shirt was unbuttoned. He glanced at her. "Morning. Sleep well?"

"Fine, thanks." She slid into the seat opposite him.

"Coffee or tea?" Karma asked from the stove. Like Hannah, Karma still sported her nightwear. Only hers was matching blue shorts and a tank top with a fluffy pale pink robe belted loosely at her waist.

"Herbal tea, if you have it."

"Yep, I have a cousin who loves this stuff. I keep a box on hand for those times he decides to pop over." Karma smiled and held up a box of chamomile.

In no time, Hannah was sipping the soothing drink.

"What did you mean about the hotel not being the only thing that burned?" Karma asked, taking the seat between Hannah and Zig. She curled her fingers between Zig's. The pair shared a smile that seemed to say so much more than *good morning*.

Hannah sipped her tea and tried not to stare.

"The fire didn't start in the hotel. There was an abandoned house behind it. The arson investigator thinks some kids were playing around back there and started the blaze. It's not the first abandoned building to burn lately. The Blue Owl probably won't open its doors again. I heard the owners defaulted on their insurance." Zig folded the paper and set it aside. "Nothing in the paper this week. Maybe next week, Karma."

Karma gave him a wistful smile, then focused on Hannah. "We're looking for a new place. You know, a place of our own."

"This isn't your place?" Hannah glanced around at the decidedly sparse masculine décor.

"Ah, no. It's Zig's. We want to find an apartment together." Karma looked at him warmly. Zig returned the look and the heat in the room jumped twelve degrees. The love and lust sizzling in the air between them was palpable.

Hannah swallowed hard, averting her gaze. She turned away to stare into the adjacent living room. The faux suede couch was pushed up against the bare wall. A dilapidated coffee table sat in front of it. On the far side of the room was a large flat-screen television nestled perfectly between twin windows. The living room, like the kitchen, held the essentials, plus one small silver-framed picture of Zig and Karma.

Otherwise it was functional and not at all fussy. Definitely not the feminine touch she'd seen in the guest bedroom.

"Did you reach your parents last night?" Karma asked, wandering to the living room and grabbing the remote. She clicked on the television but immediately muted it and faced Hannah.

"Yes, I did. Thank you." Hannah fiddled with the cup in her hands, hating to impose on her new friend again, but couldn't see any way around it. "May I borrow your phone again? I'd like to call my cell service provider and report the phone being destroyed. Oh, and I want to call those investigators Zig recommended."

"You didn't tell her?" Zig stared at Karma curiously when she shook her head.

"I sort of forgot after the craziness with the fire." Karma cast Hannah a sheepish grin. "About Tidewater Security Specialists . . . They're my cousins."

"Small city," Hannah said in surprise.

Zig snorted. "I wish. Be a lot less criminals if it were."

"Good-night, Zig." Karma waved him away with one hand, and sipped the coffee he handed her with the other. She turned her back on her lover and whispered to Hannah, "He's always grumpy after a midnight shift."

"I heard that." Zig slipped between them, pressed a kiss to Karma's forehead, and disappeared into the master bedroom. "Good-night, ladies. I'll see you in eight."

"Not today. We'll be at the restaurant. Boss needs us early to help prep for the wedding and deal with a huge delivery since yesterday's delivery had to be sent back. We're on for a double." Karma gave Hannah a half grin. "Well, I am. Hannah has a choice."

"I'm up for it. After the fire, I could use a few extra dollars in my paycheck."

"Then I'll see you later tonight, *mi amor*." Zig winked at Karma who blew him a kiss.

While Hannah was alternately intrigued and slightly jealous of the byplay between the lovers—she wished someone would look at her the way Zig looked at Karma—she had work to do. She needed to find a killer, some clothes, her sisters, replace what she could, and still make it to the Cat by the start of her shift. How was she going to manage it?

As if reading her thoughts, Karma said, "How about we get showers and I take you out shopping for essentials this morning? You're welcome to borrow my uniform clothes. I have plenty. Although you're probably ready for something of your own to wear right about now. You're welcome to use my phone and tell Ryan or Ian, they own TSS, to meet you this afternoon at the Boxing Cat."

"I don't know. Niall didn't look too pleased last night about my vision of the murder. I doubt he'll be happy to have some private investigators talk to me about it during my shift."

Karma waved her mug as if cleansing the air. "Niall always looks like that. He'll be fine. Besides, he'd be stupid to think we're going to work a double today and not take breaks. And that man is definitely not stupid. Tell my cousins to come before the dinner rush starts at five. I'll put y'all someplace private. The perks of being the manager is that I can decide who takes breaks when. It'll be fine. Trust me. Don't forget, I can see Niall's aura. Despite his words, he's hot for you."

Hannah laughed at the devilish grin on Karma's face. It was hard to believe they had only met yesterday. They were like old friends already. She just hoped when she reunited with her sisters the relationships there would be as easy.

"Yeah, well, don't tell Niall you think he's hot for me. He wants to keep things strictly professional."

"That's what his lips say. His aura tells a whole different story. Trust me, meet with TSS at the restaurant and everything will work out." Karma's smile was big, bright, and a little too optimistic.

Hoping she was making the right decision, Hannah agreed

and tried to ignore the niggle of doubt tickling at the base of her neck.

THE SHOWER POUNDED down. The jets so hot Mercy imagined the pinpricks of water could flay the filth from her skin. Rocking in the shower, she struggled for control.

It should have worked. He should have wanted her last night. She had it all set. The candles. The drugs. The chocolate and roses. But he didn't show. She had dressed for nothing.

Nothing.

Now she needed to rethink her plan.

To truly set him free, she needed three days with him. But the first day was already gone.

Why? Why hadn't he shown last night? He always shows.

Grabbing the bar of soap, Mercy scrubbed her skin the way her mother had taught her. Thoroughly. Roughly. Never leave a speck of dirt behind. No spot missed on the body. And double wash: her face, her hair, and the dirty parts. Always with efficiency.

Mother had given icy showers, but Mercy preferred hot ones. The hotter, the better.

Time to rethink the plan. Perhaps she'd been wrong about him. Maybe he didn't need her mercy after all.

That was fine.

It was a new day. Two days before the weekend.

Plenty of time to find someone else who needed her.

CHAPTER 11

NIALL RUBBED HIS eyes and tried to focus on the computer screen again. The morning sun filtering through the high window of the tiny room highlighted the dust motes floating in the air. They danced in front of his face. He reached for his coffee cup. Empty.

He pushed to his feet and out of the office into the big kitchen of the Cat.

This was the best time of day to be a restaurateur. At barely eight thirty in the morning, the building was silent, except for the distant sounds of traffic outside and the nearby morning song of birds. And he was blessedly alone.

No one to crowd him. No one to clean up after. No one depending on him. He was truly free for a few hours. Normally, this was his best time. He'd get up, go for a morning run, shower, then get paperwork done. Except this morning, he was antsy. His run hadn't helped. Neither had his shower. He was left with the distinct impression he'd left something undone. Sleep.

He hadn't slept much the night before. And when he had, Hannah Halloran of the bewitching eyes had taken center stage. First in her room in Ohio, then in his truck last night, and then in his own bed. The dreams had been so realistic. He woke aching and frustrated. And dammit all, worried for her. She'd looked so lost.

Sure, she was with Karma, queen of the weirdo psychic stuff, but was that really what Hannah needed? She said she'd come to town to find her sisters, not to find him. He might have doubted her but she was guileless and open as she stared at him.

Sonofabitch.

Why couldn't she have come looking for him?

Not that he wanted a stalker in his life.

I'm losing my fucking mind.

The screen door creaked and Ross stumbled in, sunglasses on, hair mussed, wearing yesterday's wrinkled clothes. He stunk like he'd slept in a vat of cheap wine.

"Oh, man, I didn't think you'd be here." Ross groaned and came to a sudden stop. The door swung back and hit him in the ass. "Don't you normally go for like a ten-mile run in the mornings? What're you doing here?"

"I could ask you the same thing." Niall set his mug on the workstation behind him and crossed his arms over his chest. "Are you in last night's clothes? And since when do you show up for work before ten?"

Ross hiked a thumb over his shoulder. "I slept in my car."

"It wasn't out there last night or this morning." Niall leaned to the side to glance past his brother into the still empty parking lot. "Where'd you leave it? At the bar?"

"Ha. Ha. Funny, man. It's where it was yesterday. Parked on the other side of the Dumpster. Since you're too high and mighty to take out the garbage, I took it out last night. Then got in my car."

Niall counted to ten but couldn't quite ignore the heat burning his cheeks. "And what do you mean, I'm too high and mighty? That's bullshit and you know it. You're trying to distract me from your latest screwup."

"What screwup?"

"You smell like you climbed into a case of wine in your car. Do you want to get our license pulled for the Boxing Cat? Because that *will* put us out of business. We cannot compete in Tidewater without a liquor license."

"No! Christ, you're an asshole!" Ross ripped off his sunglasses. He squinted his bloodshot eyes and got up in Niall's face. The stink of stale sweat and staler alcohol had Niall's lip curling. "I went to the bar last night during my shift, okay. I got drunk. Fuck. I got shit-faced. But when I came back you were all up my ass, like you've been since you came home. God, you're such a tight ass. No one is ever good enough for you. Everyone has to be perfect. Except news bulletin: I'm fucking human. I decided to go home instead of trying to prove my worth to the perfect war hero, Niall Graham.

"But I was too fucking drunk to drive. So I slept in my goddamned car. Alone. No drinking. No drugs. Just me asleep in my car behind the Dumpster! I figured I fucked up enough yesterday that I didn't want to get pulled over for drunk driving and tarnish the pristine Graham name. Is that all right with you?"

Niall stared down at his baby brother and saw both fury and hurt in the younger man's eyes. The fury pissed him off, but the hurt had him taking a calmer tack. Something had seriously set off Ross last night beyond their fight. Niall had sensed it then and could still see it now.

"It's fine, Ross. Why don't you go home and get a shower?" Niall reached to pat Ross on the shoulder but his brother shrugged away from the touch.

"That's why I came in here." Ross pushed past Niall and scooped a set of keys from the desk.

Christ, I didn't even notice they were here.

Sunglasses back in place, Ross headed for the back door again.

"Ross, how'd you get in your car if the keys were in here?" The moment he asked the question, Niall knew he'd made a mistake.

Ross cocked his head to the right and said in an almost bored tone, "I leave my car unlocked. It's ancient. There's nothing anyone would want to steal. Unlike you, I can't afford a brand-new truck. I put every dime of my savings into moving into this goddamned building—"

"You really need to lock your car when you're not in it," Niall said, ignoring the remark about the savings. It wasn't like he hadn't invested in the Cat too. Arguing that point wouldn't do a fucking thing to calm his brother right now. "We live in a city filled with criminals. There's a killer on the loose—"

"Yeah, yeah. Can we save the lecture for later? I'm not in the mood for any more brotherly love."

Ross didn't wait for a response. He was outside and roaring out of the parking lot in seconds.

Niall lowered his head and exhaled.

What the hell was he going to do? Maybe Ross was right. Maybe he was a tight ass.

But that didn't mean no one measured up. Well, most people didn't. But some did. As soon as the restaurant was in the black, he'd show his brother how not-a-tight-ass he could be.

Maybe he'd even break a few of his own rules along the way.

Yeah, like taking a certain staff member with a penchant for the weird on a date.

Maybe not something quite so complicated.

Perhaps, just to bed.

One last time.

Who's the tight ass now?

SUNLIGHT GLINTED OFF the steel worktables in the Boxing Cat's kitchen. At ten in the morning, the room, awash in a silvery glow, was as welcoming today as it had been the day before. So why did Hannah hesitate before heading inside? Oh, right. The vision.

Her hand hovered over the wooden frame of the screened-in back door. What if she touched something else? What if she saw another grisly murder? She hadn't told Karma or Zig or even her parents about the nightmares she'd experienced last night. Her stomach pitched at the memory of the terror on the man's face before the knife plunged into his throat. The flecks of blood hitting his cheeks, his nose, his eyes. The way red-black blood burbled from his lips.

"Morning, Hannah."

Hannah jumped at Niall's voice behind her. She whipped around so fast she knocked him over with her backpack. He stumbled backward over something sticking up between the sidewalk and the doorframe. Then he kept falling. Over the curb, over the two milk crates the employees sat on during breaks, and slamming into the front of his truck.

That would have been bad enough but he'd been carrying what had to be four dozen eggs. The cartons flew up, the eggs crashed into each other, and yellow and clear goo slimed Niall from the top of his blue-black hair to the knees of his pressed khaki slacks. Slime dripped from him like he'd been the star contestant on some cable network kids' show.

"No! Oh, crap," Hannah said, tossing her backpack aside and rushing to kneel beside him. "Frackity fracking frack! I'm so sorry, Niall. Are you hurt?"

Niall blinked at her, yolk sliding slowly down his brow between his confused green eyes. "Out. Stand. Ing." He said each syllable as if it were a word he needed to enunciate for her benefit.

She reached for the broken cartons and plucked the cracked shells from his body. He stared at her with such intensity she did the only thing she could think of: retreated into humor. "I'm so sorry. The good news is that it's not tar and I don't have any feathers."

The screen door slammed. The sound was immediately followed by Virgil's voice. "Boy, whatchu doing on the ground? Pretending to be a rooster? Don't you know you're supposed to get the hens to lay the eggs for you, not pelt you with them?"

Hannah closed her eyes, her cheeks flaming.

I'm so fired.

Niall snorted, then chuckled, and finally laughed.

Hannah opened her eyes to see Niall locking his gaze

with the old chef. Both men laughed as if they'd shared some fabulous inside joke.

Virgil extended his hand to Niall, then pulled it back before Niall could take it. "Why don'tcha help him up, Hannah? You're already a sight."

Hannah glanced down at her newly purchased clothes to find she hadn't been spared the egging. She'd been kneeling in the mess and the slime made her knees cold. "Yes, sir."

Virgil headed back inside, leaving the two of them alone in the parking lot.

She offered to help Niall up, but he shook his head and pushed to his feet in one fluid move that made her wonder what his muscles looked like when he did that naked. Niall naked was a sight to behold. Niall naked and doing calisthenics might just set her ovaries on fire.

He turned back and offered her a hand. "No harm." He glanced at the catastrophe. "Well, there's harm, but nothing we can't recover from. Just a cleanup and another run to the store. How about you?"

His gaze zeroed in on her shirt. Yes. Yes, that was egg yolk splattered on the center of her right breast.

Her cheeks flamed even more. *God, I'm such a freak.*

He definitely noticed the splotch but continued to search her body for injury. "Are you sure you aren't hurt? You jumped when I walked up. I thought maybe you stepped on a nail or something."

"Nail?"

He gestured to the one poking up from the frame of the door. Odd, she hadn't noticed it yesterday. Definitely not good construction if it was already pushing out of the wood in a building as recently revitalized as the Boxing Cat's.

Niall frowned. "I told my bro—I mean, I meant to fix that this morning. Serves me right for procrastinating. Egg slop aside, you sure you're okay?"

"No, I'm fine. I didn't trip. I'm really sorry, Ma—" She cut herself short from saying *Marine*. No intimacy. That had been the deal. She was his employee now, nothing more. "It was an accident, Mr. Graham. I can pay for the damages."

Niall's grin faded and his eyes went distant. He swiped a hand roughly down his face, then flung yoke off to the sidewalk. "Hannah. You can call me Niall. Everyone here does. People will start to wonder if you get formal around me."

"Oh, right. Sure." She nodded, stepping back and glanced around. "I can get this cleaned up. If you tell me where to find a hose."

Niall cocked his head as if studying her. "You want to clean up this mess?"

"Well, I made it."

"*I* made it. You were just standing in the doorway, not stepping on a nail." Niall brushed eggshell and slime from his button-down shirt and slacks. "What made you jump anyway?"

"Nothing . . ." she began, then shook her head. "I was looking at all the metal in there and worried that I might get another vision, like last night. I don't think I could handle it right now."

Niall straightened with a grimace. A myriad of expressions crossed his face, all too fast to decipher or catalogue. Finally, he fixed a decidedly flat smile on his face and said, "I'm sure nothing like that will happen again. I don't hire criminals."

Only weirdos. He didn't say the words but the wary expression he gave her was loud enough.

"Look, I need to change and replace the eggs we've lost. The hose is in a storage box behind the hedges on the side of the building. Hose the area down and sweep up the shells while I'm gone, then go home and change." He made a face. "Damn, I forgot to ask how you're doing this morning. Did you get settled in at Karma's last night? You're wearing different clothes, so I assume you were able to borrow some from her. Can you borrow more?"

"I bought these an hour ago before the egg-tastrophe." And now she was going to have to buy another work outfit. Perfect. She was going to run out of money before she received her first paycheck. Maybe she should just go home. Between the vision, losing all of her things in the fire, and needing to buy another work outfit, it seemed as if the universe might have changed its mind about her coming to Tidewater.

Niall put his hands on his hips and surveyed the mess on the ground, then her. A slow smile curled his lips. "Tell you what. We'll call what happened here a draw. Go home and shower. I'll send Karma along with a replacement uniform for you, on me. I'll take care of the sidewalk if you can pick up eggs on your way back. But I need you here in an hour."

"You're replacing my uniform?" Hannah asked in wonder as Niall pulled a fifty out of his wallet and handed it to her. Did he realize how nice he was being?

"Only fair. You've been through some serious sh—uh, stuff the past twenty-four hours." His quick grin gave way to a stern expression as if his next words were meant to convince her of their veracity. "I'd do it for any of my employees."

While he probably would, he was doing it for her. And working hard to convince her it meant nothing. Yeah. Right. Walking backward across the parking lot she called out, "What are you going to do?"

"What I need to." Niall unbuttoned his shirt and tossed it to the sidewalk with a splat. Naked from the waist up, he headed around the side of the building. In seconds, he was back, tugging the long green hose. With a grin, he started the spray. Sunlight glinted off his white teeth and his golden, chiseled chest. "I'm going to shower off and clean the sidewalk. Hurry back."

Hurry back? Oh, yes, she definitely would.

Maybe the universe was telling her to stick around Tidewater a little longer after all?

BY THE TIME Hannah returned with the eggs, the kitchen was bustling. Virgil and Paulie were at their respective stoves. The aroma of oregano, garlic, roasted tomatoes, and caramelized onions wafted from the pizzas, still steaming hot and fresh from the oven.

Niall was gone and the parking lot's only evidence of their earlier collision was the damp pavement.

Hannah shifted her backpack and tried to steady the four crates in her hands. No way was she dropping these. She called through the screened door when Sadie strode past on five-inch spiky heels. "Excuse me, can you get the door please?"

Sadie turned her feline gaze to Hannah. Her makeup fresh and perfect. The short black skirt she wore fit her like a second skin and the button-down white top had a few more buttons open at the top than might have been strictly necessary. The woman oozed sexuality, even at eleven in the morning.

Without a word, Sadie put a manicured hand on the door and slowly let it creak open, barely wide enough for Hannah to fit through. The screen slapped her in the backpack. It might have sent Hannah stumbling forward had she not seen the devilish glint in Sadie's eye a moment before and braced for the impact.

"Thanks. I really appreciate your help." Hannah gave her a sunny smile and enjoyed the way Sadie's eyes narrowed to slits.

It wasn't nice of her to needle the woman so, but there was something about Sadie that made Hannah want to show her own claws.

A small, dark-haired woman with bottle-cap-thick glasses shuffled in from the Master Room, clapping her hands and smiling excitedly. She gestured at the eggs, then at Hannah, then to the back door, but didn't say a word. When Hannah stood unsure what to do, the woman's grin faltered and she tugged Virgil by the sleeve of his chef's coat.

The older man turned to her. A flurry of words danced from their hands as they signed to each other.

Hannah had studied American Sign Language in college, but had only taken one semester, enough to know how to ask for a cookie or directions to the bathroom, but not enough to follow the beautiful way the pair communicated.

Virgil laid a hand on Paulie's shoulder and whispered something. Paulie nodded, then stepped between the two stoves, monitoring both at once.

Taking the older woman, and she had to be at least three

times Hannah's age, by the elbow, Virgil led her over to where Hannah still stood, her arms starting to burn from holding the eggs for so long. "Hannah, I'd like you to meet Miss Renee Gauthier. Miss Renee has been with the Cat almost as long as I have. She makes all the baked goods we sell."

Virgil turned to Miss Renee and signed as he spoke. "This is Miss Hannah Halloran. She joined our little family yesterday. She'll take good care to get those eggs into your car, Miss Renee. Won't you, Miss Hannah?"

There was something so warm and friendly in how Virgil referred to both of them as *miss*. Southern and old school. Hannah couldn't help but reply in kind, "I will do that, Mr. Virgil."

He waved away the title, laughing. "Just call me, Virgil. I call all the pretty young ladies *miss*. Ain't that right, Miss Renee?" Again he signed as he spoke and the old woman blushed.

"Her car's out back," Virgil said, grabbing the top carton of eggs from the stack. "Miss Renee needs those eggs for the cake she's designing for Saturday's wedding." Virgil pivoted left and strode into the large walk-in cooler.

"Lead the way," Hannah said.

"She's deaf." Sadie sneered the last word, practically in Miss Renee's face. "She can't hear you."

To Hannah's surprise, Miss Renee turned a cold eye to Sadie. Color faded from Sadie's cheeks.

"I can read lips," Miss Renee said roughly, signing the words in emphasis.

Sadie picked up the pizza cooling on the workstation and disappeared with it into the main hall.

The old woman watched her go, a toothy grin on her face. With a pat of her hair, she straightened her shoulders and led Hannah out into the sunshine.

BETWEEN THE LUNCH rush, needing to fill in for the mysterious Dawn whose child had her taking another sick day, and helping Miss Renee, who'd returned three separate times for six different ingredients, Hannah was ready to drop from hunger by two in the afternoon.

The Quarter, the Half, and the Master Rooms emptied out all at once. Only the Three Bells still had guests. That room had been occupied by a book club who sat discussing the month's current selection. The single round table held ten women, all dressed in their finest clothes drinking tea and coffee and occasionally ordering an appetizer or a dessert. They were friendly and effervescent and seemed eager to share their love of the latest mystery novel.

Hannah reached for the old glass doorknob to check on the older ladies, but Karma stopped her. "Have you had a break yet?"

Hannah's stomach rumbled. "Uh, no."

Karma laughed. "So I hear. Go grab something from the kitchen. It won't get busy again for a couple of hours. I've got the Killing Them with Mystery book club. I promise, whatever tip they leave, you'll get."

"I'm not worried about that." Hannah waved away the idea. "You've given me a place to stay, clothes to wear, and even got me hired here. I owe you big-time. Especially since you barely know me."

It was Karma's turn to wave away the words. "*Chica*, we are kindred spirits. We were born to be friends, no?"

Hannah studied her for a moment. "Can you do that at will? Turn the accent on and off?"

"Yes, unless I'm mad. Then I can hear my mother coming out of my mouth." Karma shuddered, then winked. "Old habits from having lived in Mexico with her for so long."

"I thought you were from Tidewater?"

Karma grinned, her dark brown eyes shining. "Mama is from Juarez and Daddy's from here. He didn't even know I existed until I was sixteen. I went from being a poor kid practically living on the streets to being part of a huge American family."

"Bet that was amazing to find, huh? A big family?"

"It was. I loved it. I lived with Daddy until I was nineteen when my mama got sick. She needed me back in Mexico."

She frowned and her eyes went distant. Then she shook her head as if to rid herself of a bad memory. "Anyway, I came home a few months ago and I'll never leave here again."

"That's an incredible story." There was something sad in her friend's eyes that made Hannah's chest tighten. She wanted to ask about it but settled on an innocuous question instead. "So are you a US citizen or Mexican?"

"Both. And there's a lot more to the story. I'll have to tell you some other time. Over a very tall glass of wine. Right now, you need a break."

"Thanks, Karma, but I'm so nervous I don't know if I can eat. When I called your cousin Ian this morning, he said he'd be here around three to talk to me." Hannah's stomach rumbled making them both chuckle. "Guess my body wants food after all.

"You know, it's funny. I had their card already in my hotel room. I was going to call them in a day or two anyway. I wanted to get settled into Tidewater first."

Karma's brown eyes widened. "You already had a card from TSS? Why?"

"I have family in the area here. Biological family, I mean. I'm adopted. Anyway, these guys came looking for me. I was supposed to call them when I was ready to meet my sisters."

Laughter erupted from the book club and someone knocked over a glass. It crashed to the floor. Hannah automatically reached for the doorknob.

"I got this. Go eat already." And with that, Karma was gone.

In the kitchen, Hannah spotted Niall through the screen door. Her pulse did a funny little jig at the sight. He was climbing into his truck with a sack of flour.

"Miss Renee's grandson tried to help by carrying the flour into her house. Poor boy spilled it all over her front porch," Virgil said with a shake of his head. "I don't know who's having a tougher day, Miss Renee or our Niall. I don't think he's slowed down since the sun came up."

Paulie snorted. "Virg, you don't give the guy enough credit. I saw him running down the beach before the sun came up. That man hasn't slowed since he came back from the desert."

"Yep. That's my brother. Always a Marine. Faster. Smarter. Better in every way," Ross said, appearing in the office doorway. There was something in his tone that gave Hannah pause. Or maybe it was the way he and Paulie noticeably didn't look at each other. Only Virgil appeared unaware of the tension.

"I don't know about better, Ross. You're a Graham just like he is and just as damned smart."

"Thanks, Virgil." The tension visibly rolled off of Ross's shoulders. He slouched against the doorjamb. "Lunch rush over, Hannah?"

"Yes, Karma sent me back to get a bite to eat." Hannah moved toward the three slices of pizza left on the pizza stone. They were vegetarian, not her favorite.

"Looking for some meat for your meal?" Virgil asked, carrying a plate with a sandwich cut in half. Corned beef, still hot, steamed from between the slices of thick bread.

Hannah's mouth watered. "Actually, yes. Is that a Reuben?"

"Surely is." Virgil's face split into a wide, toothy grin. He grabbed a plate from the rack on the far wall and put half the sandwich on it. "Help yourself."

Ross handed her a napkin.

Hannah took a huge bite and managed not to moan in ecstasy. Sort of. "This is the best Reuben I've ever tasted," she said around a mouthful of food.

"Gluten-free bread too," Virgil said with a wink. "Only the finest ingredients here."

Wow, gluten free never tasted this good when her mother tried to feed it to her back in Ohio. "I've got to send the recipe to my mom. She'd die. And I know her customers at the bar would go nuts."

Virgil just laughed and headed into the walk-in cooler.

Hannah chewed quickly. Since she was taking another break when TSS arrived, she didn't want to risk spending too much time right now. She tried to ignore the way Ross stared at Paulie's back. Hopeless longing in his pretty green eyes before Ross turned his gaze to her.

"Take a real break. Go enjoy the sunshine," Ross said, ushering her out the back.

"I'm going to need to take another one in an hour, so I'm fine."

Ross frowned at her, then glanced around. "Niall doesn't like for staff to eat in the kitchen during a break. Outside would be best." He paused, cocked his head, then winked devilishly. "Besides, dollface, you could use a little color in those cheeks."

Grabbing her plate and another napkin, Hannah slipped past him and stepped into the warm sunshine.

CHAPTER 12

NIALL ROLLED INTO the parking lot of the Cat, surprised to find Hannah sitting on a crate out back. A scraggly dog with a notch missing in one ear sat on its hind legs beside her. With its two front paws in the air, it begged for food. Hannah broke off a piece of the crust from the sandwich in her hands and offered it to the mutt.

She shouldn't waste time feeding strays. Niall should tell her that feeding them only brought more to his door. More to dig around under the Dumpster at night looking for scraps. But there was something so damned charming watching her with the mongrel.

She'd rolled up the white sleeves of her uniform shirt to the elbows. A flash of color on her right wrist had him squinting. Before he could stop himself, he'd cut the engine and was halfway across the parking lot headed straight for her.

The dog yelped and ran between the bushes on the side of the building.

Hannah frowned after it, then up at him. "I think you scared old Snoopy there."

"Maybe Snoopy shouldn't be sniffing around my restaurant for scraps." He stopped beside her, then upended another milk crate and sat down next to her. "How do you know the dog's name is Snoopy?"

"You're always so literal." Hannah laughed, waving away his question. "I don't. But everyone needs a name. And Snoopy fit him. He looks like a live-action, slightly mangy version of the cartoon. Don'tcha think?"

Niall glanced in the direction of where the dog had run and shrugged. "I guess if you squinted one eye and the sun was blinding you."

Hannah laughed, then popped the last bit of sandwich in her mouth. Eyes closed, she chewed and turned her face toward the sky. Sunlight kissed her fairylike face. She seemed to glow in the light. Her tawny hair, even pulled back as it was in a braid, shined bright and coppery in the warm afternoon.

Her ever-present pink braid was the only bit of hair not pulled back with the rest. As if she couldn't stand to yield completely to conformity.

Niall started to finger it, as he'd done all those months ago, but curled his hands together between his knees instead.

"Where did you get the sandwich?" he asked instead.

That got her attention. She whipped her gaze to his. "Virgil made it for me."

"Don't worry. You're not in trouble. It's just the staff usually eats a real meal during breaks."

Tension melted from her face, smoothing out the horizontal worry lines in her forehead. Again, she looked innocent and ethereal. "I love corned beef. I can't get enough of it."

"I would have figured you for a vegetarian."

Hannah fingered her pink braid and gave him a sly look. "What would make you think that?"

"You showed up here in a peasant skirt and your place in Ohio looked like something straight out of the seventies. All tie-dye and peace symbols. You're all artsy and . . .

Don't give me that look. You know what I mean. You have this whole crunchy-granola-funky-earth-dog vibe going on."

"Funky earth dog?" Hannah asked, brushing the crumbs from her slacks. "Wow, I think you're trying to insult me."

"Not dog. Earth woman. Hippie." Niall was fucking this up. He hadn't meant to insult her but if her jerky movements were anything to go by . . .

She returned her milk crate to the stack by the back door, then paced back and forth in front of him, muttering under her breath. It was hard to hear but the words, "asshole" and "show him earth dog" were audible.

"Hannah—" Niall's words were cut off by Hannah spinning around on him.

"I'm not a vegetarian. I might be *funky* but I'm an artist. I'm not afraid to be myself. I'm honest and I'm not going to be called a dog by anyone. Not even by my tight-assed boss, who ought to know better than to go around making assumptions about people. At least I'm not afraid to take risks. Can you say the same?" Color high in her cheeks, Hannah didn't give him a chance to respond before she marched up and pointed a finger in his face. "Now I'm going to take my crunchy-granola-earth-dog self back to work. If you need anything else from me, *Mr. Graham*, you had better figure out a way to address me respectfully."

With that she marched inside, muttering under her breath, "Can't believe he called me a dog."

Niall scratched his head and glanced around the empty parking lot. How in the hell had that happened? He'd been talking to her, then she went nuts on him. Okay, he had called her a dog but he hadn't meant it the way she took it.

And she had yelled at him. No one *ever* yelled at him. Hell, she didn't just raise her voice, she *ordered* him to treat her with respect. Like he would do anything else? Okay, yes, he'd been a slight ass but what the fuck? Who in the hell did she think she was talking to him like that? Her boss.

Well, he'd set her straight about putting her fairy finger in his face and ordering him about. He turned to follow her inside, but realized all the blood in his body had taken up residence in his cock.

Just as soon as his raging hard-on cooled, he'd give her a good talking to. But God alive! She was fucking hot all take-charge like that.

Maybe the rule about leaving Ohio in Ohio could be suspended. He'd have to think about that. Fuck thinking about it. One day in her presence and he was ready to climb into bed with her again. Right, like he hadn't had that exact thought yesterday—which was why he'd declared the Ohio rule in the first place.

His cock ached.

Fuck the rule.

She thought he didn't take risks?

Well, he'd just have to prove her wrong.

"BRAD PITT JUST walked through the front door," Sadie whispered, then pursed her lips and narrowed her eyes at Hannah and Karma. "His table is mine."

Hannah watched as Sadie pushed through the kitchen door, her realistically fake smile in place as she greeted the man who did bear a remarkable resemblance to the movie star. Although, this man looked like a much younger version. She stared through the diamond-shaped window as Sadie shamelessly flirted with the guest.

"You don't think that's really Brad Pitt, do you, Karma?"

"No." Karma laughed. "That's my cousin, Ian. Keep watching Sadie. She's about to be seriously ticked. He's not going to let her wait on him."

"Should I go out there?" Hannah asked.

"Nope, just wait." Karma shook her head, her short crop of brown curls bouncing. "If you try to talk to him before Sadie finishes, she might cause a scene. She's got a temper. It'll be better for everyone if you let him tell her that he's here to see you."

"Why is your cousin here to see Hannah?" Niall asked from behind Hannah.

She jumped at Niall's words and managed not to glare at him. She still couldn't believe he'd called her a dog. A. Dog.

Asshole.

Before Karma could answer, the kitchen door swung open and Sadie strode in. Ooh, she looked angry enough to spit razor-sharp nails. She pointed one of her dagger-like fingernails at Hannah. "You are up. Be warned, he's a jerk. Thinks he's God's gift."

"Sounds like Ian." Karma winked. "He's not that bad. Don't worry, Hannah. I'll introduce you. Boss, we're taking fifteen minutes."

"Karma," Niall said her name like a warning.

"It's important and the dinner rush hasn't started yet. It won't take long. Come on, Hannah."

Hannah could feel the heat of Niall's body against the back of her neck. He stood so close, every breath she took was infiltrated by his spicy aftershave.

"Fine. Fifteen minutes." Niall didn't move or turn his head when he spoke to her, so his breath puffed out against her ear. If she wasn't so angry with him, she might have been turned on. But she was angry.

Not turned on.

Not in the least.

"You coming, Hannah?"

I wish.

Shaking off the totally inappropriate thought, she followed Karma through the Master Room. Ian sat at the same bistro table where Hannah had sat when she had first seen Karma the day before. He had his chair slightly pushed back from the table, one foot tossed lazily over one jean-clad knee. His black T-shirt hugged his muscle-toned chest and accentuated his deep tan. His blond hair was combed back from his face.

Whoa! Up close he looked even more like the movie star. It was startling.

Then he gave her a lazy, knowing smile. The kind of smile a super-hot guy gives when he knows he's being checked out. Not that she was checking him out like that, but Hannah couldn't stop staring. The resemblance was just uncanny.

Karma clapped him in the back of the head. "She's a client. And my friend."

Just like that, the spell was broken. He rubbed his head with one hand and frowned at Karma. "You taking lessons from Ryan? Damn, girl, I think you rattled my teeth."

"Pshaw." Karma waved away his complaint and sat in the chair next to him.

Hannah claimed the chair opposite Ian. "Hi, I'm Hannah."

"Nice to meetcha." Ian grinned again. "My partner is running late. He'll be along shortly. Why don't we get started?"

"Okay." Except she wasn't sure where to start. "I got your card twice. Once in Ohio and again last night."

"Right, Karma's boy toy recommended us last night."

"Don't call Zig that." Karma narrowed her eyes at Ian who only gave her a playful grin.

He turned back to Hannah and continued. "And you got my card in Ohio. Can you tell me who recommended you contact TSS there?"

"Oh, right. I didn't explain that part when I called, did I? Sorry. I'm Hannah Halloran. Someone from your company came to find me in Ohio. One of my sisters hired you guys to find me. I was Hannah Scott at birth."

His eyes lit up. "You're Hannah Scott? Fantastic! Great to meet you." He extended his hand. "Your sisters were hoping we'd get you to Tidewater before this weekend. And here you are."

"Here I am." Although now that she was sitting here talking to the private investigator, she wasn't sure what to say next.

She was saved from having to say anything when the tallest man she'd ever seen in person opened the front door.

"Here comes my partner now," Ian said, waving at the man in the doorway. "Over here, Ryan."

The giant ducked his head and stepped inside. Dressed in black from his T-shirt to his Doc Martens, he was one scary-looking man. Sort of. Like Ian, he had a deep tan, but unlike Ian, the man had a completely bald head. There were a few lines around his dark brown eyes. Eyes the same shade and shape as Karma's.

He moved gracefully into the room, claiming the empty seat next to Hannah.

"Ryan, meet Hannah Halloran. She's the Scott sister from Ohio," Ian said succinctly with an air of professionalism that he hadn't shown with Karma.

"Afternoon," Ryan said in a deep-timbre voice. He shook her hand with the refined gentleness only the very big can pull off without seeming like a limp fish. He might have been huge but he had a calm air that cloaked him like his black clothes. The man was a walking dichotomy.

"She was just telling me about getting our card twice," Ian said. "And why she waited to call us until this morning."

Something about Ian's completely professional transformation made the meeting go smoother for Hannah. She was reporting the facts. She told them about her parents in Ohio, the reason for her delayed response, and her trip to Tidewater two days prior.

Had it only been two days? It seemed so much longer.

"Hannah, now tell them about last night." Karma nodded encouragingly. "They'll believe you."

Hannah worried her smaller braid between her fingers. What if they didn't?

As if she could read Hannah's thoughts, Karma said, "They're my cousins. They've heard of weirder things than psychometry, I promise."

Ryan cocked his head to one side. "Is that when you get visions from objects?"

There was no censure in his question, only curiosity. It settled the butterflies in her belly that she hadn't even realized had taken up residence there. "Metal objects. I get visions from metal things like keys, silverware, hand railings, knives, that sort of thing."

"Does it happen all the time?" Ian asked, pulling out a little black notebook and a pen. He scribbled something in it.

"Not always. I'm usually careful about not touching an object with my skin."

"So, you need the metal to touch your flesh to get a reading?" Ian jotted another note.

"Yes, but it's not a reading. It's more like wandering around in someone else's memory or fantasy. For as long as the vision lasts, I am that person. I feel what they felt. Think what they thought. I can even remember the smells they smelled."

"Tell them about what you saw when you touched this." Karma pulled the gold-handled knife from her apron. At some point between the police station last night and today, she'd placed it in a plastic baggie. The bag crinkled when she set it on the table in front of Hannah.

Hannah sucked in a breath, eyeing it warily. "Have you been carrying that around all day?"

Karma shook her head. "No, it was in my purse until a few minutes ago. I can't get readings from it but knowing what you saw gave me the creeps. I didn't want to touch it any more than I had to."

Hannah wasn't going to touch the knife either. The very sight of it made her stomach pitch. The memory of the vision had kept her awake most of the night. When she had managed to doze off, she'd see the knife, the real one, dripping in blood plunged into the man's neck.

Karma covered Hannah's hand with one of her own. "It's okay. They'll listen and believe you. You're doing the right thing."

Hannah forced her lips to curl into a smile, but given the worry on Karma's face, it must have appeared as forced as it felt. "Okay, here's what I saw."

To their credit, Ryan and Ian sat and listened to her entire tale. They each wrote notes, but neither interrupted. She went over what she had seen in the vision, what had happened at the police station, and even how she'd cut herself during the vision. "That's the strangest part. Usually, I just go into a trance-like state. I sometimes have trouble breaking a psychic link but I've never hurt myself before."

She showed them her right hand. There had been no need to bandage her hand today. The cut on her palm wasn't deep, but the sight of it disturbed her. Because she'd done it during a vision.

"Do you think you were moving during the vision?" Ian

asked, examining her injury. He ran a finger impersonally but gently over the wound. "Or were you seizing or something?"

"She was just standing there in the kitchen," Karma said. "She was so still, I didn't think she was breathing for a moment. But her knuckles were white. That's when I noticed the knife in her hand and the blood. I tried to take it from her but she had a choke hold on it. Her eyes were open and her pupils where huge. I would have tried to shake her awake, but I was afraid she might hurt herself more on the knife, so I started yelling her name."

Hannah didn't miss her friend's accent thickening with each word.

"Guess I'm lucky it was you who found me. Someone else might have called the cops. That would have been really tough to explain to my folks. 'Hi, Mom and Daddy. I'm in jail for stabbing myself with a knife.' Yeah, really tough." Hannah tried to lighten the mood, but her joke failed to evoke more than a quick smile from Karma.

"Not that the cops were any help." Karma turned her gaze to Ryan. "Zig believed her but the homicide detectives treated her like she was a lunatic."

"Reynolds and O'Dell?" Ryan asked. Karma nodded and he shrugged in response.

Ian picked up the baggie-covered knife, briefly examined it, and put it back down. "You were right, Cuz. Those guys are never going to leave. They never could grasp the concept that there's more to solving a case than what the five senses could prove. It's a good thing for Hannah here that we're in business. When others can't, we will."

She'd read that before. On their business card. "You believe me?"

"Sure." They replied with such casual confidence, it sapped the tension from her shoulders.

She sighed with relief until it occurred to her that believing her story was only part of the issue. "But how are you going to find this guy? I only came to Tidewater two days ago, I don't know my way around the city yet. So I can't even begin to guess where his body might be."

"Leave that part to us," Ryan said, running one of his huge hands over his gleaming head.

"We'll find the body and get the cops on the case. But be ready, Reynolds and O'Dell are probably going to want to talk to you when we find the body." Ian's tone was more serious than it had been since she had sat down. "Make sure you have an airtight alibi for the murder. They will grill you hard. They like to close cases, they're not as big into getting the real bad guy."

Ryan growled low in his throat. "Don't scare her."

"You know it's true, Cuz. It's better she knows the facts now." Ian gave his partner a silent stare, then turned back to Hannah. "You said the victim was in an unfinished house and you could hear the ocean, right? I have a pretty good idea where to start looking. Don't worry about it. We'll get on this. While we're working on that, you need to call your sister Jules at this number."

Ian wrote the number on a piece of paper in his notebook, then tore it out and handed it to her. "She's getting married on Saturday."

"Why are you so quick to believe me? Don't get me wrong, I'm thrilled to know you guys don't think I'm lying or crazy or even the killer. But why do you believe me so easily?"

"You're family," Ian, Ryan, and Karma all said at once.

"Come again?"

"Your sister Shelley is married to our cousin Dev," Karma explained. "I didn't know you were the same Hannah when we met. I probably should have put the pieces together but really. What were the odds that the sister-in-law Dev has been searching for would walk into my restaurant and ask for a job?"

"Why didn't you figure that out?" Ian turned a suspicious glare to Karma.

"Because unlike the two of you, I'm not a private detective."

"Security specialists," Ian and Ryan said in unison.

"So all of you know both of my sisters?" Hannah couldn't

explain it but she couldn't stop herself from grinning either. Even as her eyes filled with tears. "And I have this enormous family?"

"Yep." Ian pulled an embroidered blue handkerchief out of his pocket and handed it to her.

Karma laughed and gestured to the hanky. "He thinks he's Cary Grant."

"Shut up." Ian frowned at Karma, then smiled and nodded to Hannah. "Go on. My granddad says gentlemen should always carry them in case of emergencies."

"Like weeping women?" Karma snickered.

"Thank you, Ian." Hannah dabbed her eyes and wiped her cheeks with the soft material. "Sorry. I'm not sad. I'm happy. I knew I'd find them, but this is just, well . . ."

"Overwhelming?"

"Exciting?"

"Perfect." Hannah smiled. "Absolutely perfect. I'm going to call them right now."

"Good, you call your sisters. We'll locate the body."

CHAPTER 13

"HAVE YOU CALLED them yet?" Karma whispered under her breath.

"No time." Hannah shook her head, then loaded up the tray with six hot dinners. "Is it always this busy on a Thursday night?"

Karma picked up a steaming pizza that smelled so good it made Hannah's stomach rumble. "No. There was a benefit at the art museum down the street. I heard the guests talking. The benefit was supposed to go to a local celiac's group but all the food at the benefit had gluten. Bad for that caterer but really good for us—Ross is loving this. He's manning the hostess's station and passing out business cards. Bet we get catering jobs out of it."

"The universe is talking and telling everyone how awesome the Boxing Cat is!" Hannah smiled at her friend, then using her back, pushed open the door to the Master dining room.

There wasn't an available seat in the place. People dressed in cocktail dresses and sharp suits chatted and ate in an almost electrified atmosphere. A line of people waited to get inside the restaurant. Ross carried glasses of tea, and Dawn, of the always sick kid, was finally back. She wasn't much taller than Hannah, but with her hair piled high on her head and her four-inch heels, she towered over her.

"I'm running low on appetizers," she said to Hannah in a thick New York accent. "Tell Paulie to plate up some more while I run these to the guests outside."

Hannah held the door for the woman, then did as she was asked.

The action in the restaurant never slowed. Even Niall worked the floor. He helped Michael clear tables and set them for waiting guests. Niall moved quickly but always took the time to smile and check on guests at neighboring tables. There was a bounce to his step that made Hannah wish she could see him like that more often. He looked nothing like the lost, lonely man he'd been in Fincastle.

As if he could feel her eyes on him, Niall turned and met her gaze. His wicked green eyes sparkled but he nodded his head to her right. Hannah followed his gaze to the table full of gray- and white-haired people waiting anxiously for the tray of food propped on her shoulder.

"Oh, good. Is that for us?" a woman in a dress as white as her short hair asked in a voice that was both elegant and southern. "We are famished."

"That's perfect because you're about to have the best gluten-free meal you've ever tasted." Hannah set the tray on a nearby stand and quickly served the plates of chicken marsala, linguini with red clam sauce, and stuffed peppers. "Enjoy! Do you need anything else?"

They waved her away and Hannah hustled back to the kitchen to pick up the next table's order. It had been like that since seven o'clock. By ten thirty, the crowd had started to thin. By eleven thirty, they were cleaning up and Ross was practically dancing in the office.

"Tell me again, Bro! I know you're dying to say it. I was right. My change was right. Making all the menu items gluten-free options was the smartest thing we could have done. I told you it was worth the investment to have two separate spaces for cooking and preparing food, one for gluten free and one for regular. Tonight proved it! We have three different requests to cater after the wedding. And not just weddings. We've been asked to do an office party, a bar mitzvah, and someone's fiftieth anniversary." Ross pumped his fist in the air. "Am I good or what?"

Niall, who'd been in the tiny office, rose from his seat and moved to stand in the doorway between the office and the kitchen. He patted his brother on the back. "You did good tonight. But you have to admit it was just luck that we got that celiac group tonight. They didn't even know the Cat existed."

"Not luck. Divine intervention." Ross shook his head, the smile in his eyes dimming. "Call it what you want, we're on the map now. Just like I said we would be."

"You said it would be the wedding this weekend that did that."

Ross's smile vanished. "You can't say anything positive to me, can you?" He stormed outside, the screen door bouncing against the frame twice before it slammed shut.

The electric atmosphere was gone. Hannah finished loading the plates into the dishwasher, then came around the half wall to hear Virgil say in a low tone to Niall, "You need to go easier on him. He did a good job tonight."

Niall's lips thinned but he nodded. "*Everyone* did a good job tonight. He wasn't alone out there."

Niall met her gaze and Hannah's heart skipped a beat. It was insane. That visceral reaction. When he turned those vivid green eyes on her, she was as malleable as Play-Doh. And yes, that did make her think of having his hands on her body.

Her cheeks burned and she averted her gaze before he could read the lust in her eyes.

He was her boss.

And he had called her a dog.

Why do I have to be attracted to jerks?

The kitchen door swung open. Sadie and Dawn came through, followed closely by Detectives O'Dell and Reynolds. One look at their faces and Hannah's stomach dropped.

"Miss Halloran," said Detective O'Dell, "we're going to need you to come with us."

BY FOUR IN the morning, Niall had had enough. He'd seen the way those cops had looked at Hannah last night. They hadn't handcuffed her in the Boxing Cat. They had waited until she was in the parking lot, like that concession lessened her humiliation.

Fucking assholes. She had cooperated with them and still they had insisted on the full monty arrest, the entire time saying she wasn't under arrest. Right, like they handcuff witnesses. Sitting in the back of the cruiser, Hannah had hung her head in defeat. And that had seriously pissed him off.

Without so much as a search or arrest warrant, those cops barged into his restaurant and carted her downtown.

Only Karma's promise to call him when Hannah came home kept Niall from following them to the station. And risk getting arrested for kicking some major ass. So he waited. And waited. And fucking waited more.

Four and a half hours later and Karma still hadn't called. The sun would be up in less than two hours and Niall had spent half the night in a restless sleep, waking every hour to check his cell phone.

He couldn't take it anymore and picked up the phone to dial Karma.

His phone rang in his hand. It was Karma calling him.

"Niall, have you heard from Hannah?"

"Crap. That answers my question. She still hasn't come home?" Niall sat on the edge of his bed and pulled on his socks and shoes. He'd slept in his jeans and shirt.

"No. Zig hasn't come home yet either. Wait, there goes my call waiting." An eternity passed in the sixty seconds he sat on hold. Finally she came back, her accent thick. "Damn. Zig says they can hold her all day if they want. Something about waiting for the medical examiner to determine the time of death. They need to rule her out as a suspect since she reported the murder in the first place. God, Niall. I was only trying to help. I didn't think they'd accuse her. But you did, didn't you? It's why you tried to stop us, because you think she's guilty too? She's not. I swear—"

"No, I don't think she's guilty." Niall cut her off. "She's special and unusual and pretty damned scary with her psychic shit, but no, I don't think she killed anyone. But I have seen what happens when cops get their hands on someone who knows things they shouldn't."

"You're talking about when I went to the cops. It wasn't like this when I reported the missing kid to them. They just laughed and ignored me." Karma sniffed into the phone.

"You aren't the only person I know with, um . . . gifts." He could have explained, but honestly, the whole conversation weirded him out and continuing it wouldn't help Hannah. "I worried last night that the cops might accuse her. It's why I drove y'all to the station on Wednesday."

And why he'd picked them up after, to make sure Hannah didn't need an attorney. Now she sat in the station being grilled.

Not on his watch.

"I'll go get her."

"That might not be as easy as you think. Hannah's stuck in an interrogation room with those two jerk detectives from the night before. Zig said he tried to talk to them, but they wouldn't listen and had him sent out on patrol. He's just a kid to them. Never mind that he earned the Silver Star earlier this year. Assholes." She sounded close to tears. "Dev is out of town until this afternoon and I don't know how to reach Seth. He and Jules are supposed to be picking up relatives from the airport today. I know Hannah said she wanted to reach out to them herself, but I couldn't just leave her at the station like that, all alone. God, Niall, this sucks."

"Karma, I need you to get some rest. I'm going to need you to run the Cat for me this morning. Get to the restaurant by eight. After last night we're probably low on stock. Get it checked. Get with Virgil to do the shopping. Make sure Miss Renee is on schedule for the wedding cake for tomorrow. And help Ross prepare for the wedding. I'll go to the station to be with Hannah."

"Sorry, Boss, but what can you do that Zig couldn't?"

"I've got friends in high places. Old Marines buddies." He wouldn't pull those strings unless he had to. "Just do what I said. The next time you see me, I'll have Hannah with me."

"You called her special and unusual but not crazy. Does this mean you believe in her visions?"

"I never said I didn't."

NIALL PULLED HIS truck into a parallel spot on the street in front of the station and cut the engine. Two hours. He'd promised Karma that he'd get Hannah out of the station and he'd damned well do it. He just hadn't dreamed he'd really need to call in a favor from Tommy Parker. Nor had he expected the man to show up at five minutes to six in the morning.

Tommy pulled his silver 1959 Ferrari GT Spider into the spot behind Niall's truck. Dressed in an expensive black suit and red tie, the man looked like what he was, powerful. He was also one of the sharpest Marines Niall had ever known.

On the sidewalk, he extended his hand and Tommy shook it. "Thank you for meeting me."

"No problem. You sure this girl's innocent, Sarge?" Tommy stepped back and stood at parade rest.

"It's just Niall here, Marine. And yes, as soon as you meet her you'll know she couldn't kill anything. Hell, she shares her sandwiches with stray dogs. She's a little unique and was trying to do the right thing. All she did was report a murder. Now she's in over her head."

"Tell me again how she witnessed this murder?"

Niall hesitated then decided to risk the truth. "She had a vision. She touched a knife and saw the murder happen. Sounds nuts, I know, but it's true. I was there right after her vision. You should have seen her. She was pale and shaking. She didn't look like a killer. She looked ready to throw up. Trust me, Lucky Charm," Niall said, using Tommy's nickname from the Marines. "She was telling the truth."

A muscle worked in Tommy's cheek but otherwise he

remained motionless for a moment. Then he blinked his eyes and sighed. "Okay, a vision. Great. How long has she been in town?"

"Less than three days. She arrived by bus on Tuesday. Since then, she's been with Karma or me the whole time."

"Been with you?" Tommy let the words hang in the air.

"At the Cat, dirt brain. She works for me. Nothing else."

"You sure about that?"

Niall didn't glance away from his fellow Marine. He maintained eye contact, trying to ignore the itch at the base of his neck that he got whenever he lied. Not that he was lying now, per se. Hannah was his employee. And there wasn't anything else between them. Anymore.

"Let's say I believe you. You're just a great boss looking out for his pretty server."

"I never said she was pretty," Niall replied defensively, then immediately snapped his mouth shut when Tommy grinned.

"Yeah, that's what I thought . . . Leave the talking to me. We'll get her out of this mess. At least for now."

THE INSIDE OF the police station made Niall's throat close. The faux dark-wood-paneled walls lined a narrow walkway between desks, shoved against one another. Pictures of presidents, sailboats, and the raising of the flag at Ground Zero added what was supposed to be character to the room.

The effect was cramped. Too many desks, chairs, pictures, computers, lamps, and personal crap in the room.

Niall rolled his shoulders to loosen the knots in his neck, scanning for both Hannah and the exit doors.

No way could he stay in this building for long. Right now, it was mostly empty of people. In an hour, the place would be overflowing with cops coming on and getting off shift. There would be discussion of cases, fresh coffee, and if the plates and coffeepot on the folding table in the far corner were any indication, food.

A normal morning.

Just like in the barracks.

Sweat trickled down his back as he fought to shove away the memories and remain in the present. He wasn't overseas. He wasn't under attack. He was in Tidewater. In the police station.

For Hannah.

He exhaled a slow sigh of relief.

Hannah of the tawny-colored eyes and fairy face needed him.

"We're here to see Hannah Halloran. We're her attorneys," Tommy said to the rotund uniformed cop with a badge that read *Spacey*, who came through a side door.

Niall had worked with Tommy enough to know when the man started talking, to let him lead. The Lucky Charm had gotten him out of deadlier situations.

The cop frowned, pulling the door closed behind him. "Who are you?"

"I'm Tom Parker. Her attorney. Now, please take us to her." Tommy stared intensely at the man until he nodded.

Officer Spacey knocked on the door he'd just come through, then opened it a degree. "I got Miss Halloran's attorneys here to see her."

The door pushed open to reveal two men seated on one side of a table nearly as wide as the tiny interrogation room and a very pale Hannah on the other. She turned her red-rimmed eyes to him and Niall wanted to yank her out of the room and run until they reached Fincastle. Go back to the beginning, when she didn't look frightened, or lost, or hopeless.

"Hi, Hannah," Tom said striding into the room, his hand extended. "I'm Tom Parker. You know Niall. We're here to take you home."

Hannah glanced from Tommy to Niall, her expression hopeful.

"You can't take her anywhere. We're questioning her." One of the detectives pushed to his feet. His bushy black mustache quivering and his beady blue eyes snapping fire. "Detective O'Dell, tell Mr. Parker here what Ms. Halloran told us."

The second detective, dressed like the first in a white button-down shirt with the sleeves rolled up, tan pants, and scuffed brown shoes, looked slightly less rumpled than his partner. "She showed up here night before last talking about a murder. Giving us details only the killer could know. And what do you know, a body was found last night. Murdered in the exact manner she'd described."

"Hmmm . . . very interesting." Tommy sat down on the corner of the table with his back to the detectives. "Is this right, Ms. Halloran? Did you describe the murder?"

Hannah glanced at Niall. The question in her eyes and the goddamned trust had his chest aching. He nodded at her.

"Yes, sir. I had a vision of the murder and tried to report it two nights ago."

The two detectives erupted in a show of pounding the table with their fists and declarations of "Bullshit. You killed him. Admit it."

Niall curled his hands into fists and fought to keep his temper in check. As if he knew it, Tommy gave him a reassuring nod. With a dismissive wave of his hand he said, "You don't have to respond, Hannah."

Tommy met Niall's gaze and there was no mistaking the banked fury there. That was something else the Lucky Charm could be counted on for: he hated for the innocent to be even verbally abused.

Niall moved from his anchor in the doorway to stand beside Hannah. He braced a hand on her shoulder and faced his old buddy. "Are we done here?"

"No," the detectives said at the same time Tommy replied, "Yes."

Niall lifted Hannah's tie-dyed backpack from the floor and helped her to her feet. He wanted to put his arm around her. Hold her. Comfort her. She looked so fucking frightened. But those red-rimmed eyes held determination, not tears, so he settled for carrying her bag and following her out the door.

"She requested a lawyer hours ago. Why is it I didn't get a call until thirty minutes ago?" Tommy's voice carried into the main room. "You had no right to interrogate my client without my presence after she asked for me. You're walking a thin line, detectives. Why don't you go out and try to find the real killer instead of wasting time harassing a young woman who wasn't even in the Commonwealth when the murder happened? And yes, I already spoke with the M.E. I know the victim died over the weekend. My client hadn't even arrived in Tidewater until three days ago. The day after, she reported the murder. Had you done just a little checking, you'd have discovered she has an unassailable alibi. We're done here. If you want to speak to her again, you had better call me first."

Then Tommy led the charge out of the building.

On the sidewalk, he resembled the Lucky Charm he'd been in the desert. Happy, carefree, and damned confident that he was always right.

Tommy turned his turquoise eyes on Hannah and a strange pinch of something resembling jealousy had Niall's chest tightening.

"You have quite a story to tell, Hannah. I can't wait to hear it." Tommy paused, glanced at Niall, then back at Hannah. The carefree look was gone again. He was solemn and all too serious. "But I think you could probably use some rest first. Here's my card. Call me when you're ready to talk about what happened. Sooner, if the cops come to find you again. I doubt they will. They know by now that you couldn't have killed their victim. Or any of the others."

"Others?" she squeaked the word.

"Yeah." Again Tommy glanced at Niall.

Recognizing the cue for what it was, Niall stepped up and took Hannah by the hand. Her cool fingers wrapped easily around his rougher ones. "We can talk about that later. Let's get you home."

She smiled, gave Tommy a quick, impersonal hug, then said, "Thank you. I don't know why you're helping me. But thank you."

Tommy opened the truck's door. As Niall helped her inside, Tommy said, "Thank Niall. He's the one who called me."

CHAPTER 14

HANNAH CLUTCHED HER backpack to her chest and willed herself to stop shivering. It didn't work. She wanted to be brave. She wanted to show Niall she wasn't some helpless child but she couldn't quite keep her hands from trembling. Not that he noticed.

He stood on the sidewalk talking to the attorney. Tom? Don? John? Dammit. She couldn't remember. And she really should. He'd somehow talked the cops into letting her go.

Not arresting her. As they had been promising to do for the past six hours.

Her teeth started to chatter and she bit down.

Niall and the attorney shook hands, then Niall climbed into the driver's seat of the truck and started the engine. He pulled a cell phone out of his pocket and handed it to her.

"What's this for?" She stared at the device uncertainly.

"I figure you want to call Karma. She's been really worried." Niall turned left onto the highway, then added softly, "So have I."

Her throat tightened. For a moment her vision blurred with tears. She blinked quickly, sucking in breaths to stop the waterfall. She wouldn't cry. Not now. She was free. She was fine.

So why did she feel like a great big ball of weepiness?

The phone rang in her hands.

"It's Karma. Go ahead and answer it," Niall said, sparing the phone a glance. "I told her I'd call her ten minutes ago, but we were still in there."

Pressing the phone to her ear, Hannah obeyed. "Hi, Karma. It's me, Hannah."

"Oh, thank you, baby Jesus! Niall did it. He told me he'd get you out. I shouldn't have doubted him." The relief in her voice made Hannah's eyes sting all over again. "Tell him I've got it under control at the Cat. Everything will be fine when y'all get in."

Hannah hazarded a glance at her boss. "Does this mean I still have a job?" And a place to live? But she didn't voice that second question aloud.

"Of course," Niall said at the same time Karma replied, "Damn straight. Those assholes have messed with the wrong family. I can't believe they didn't let you go when you told them Dev was your brother-in-law."

"I didn't tell them."

"What? Why not? They probably would have let you go hours ago." Karma paused. "Or maybe not. They're not big fans of Dev. He makes them look bad. 'Cause, you know, they suck at their jobs."

That managed to elicit a laugh, of sorts. Hannah snorted, then shook her head when Niall whipped his gaze to hers.

"Oh, crap. In all the rush, I forgot to leave the door unlocked. Don't worry. Zig's shift just ended. He'll let you in."

"Karma—" Hannah started to protest but was cut off.

"Girl, I gotta go. Delivery guys are finally here. Only a day late. I need to supervise them. Tell Niall I've got it under control and to take care of you. Bye." She didn't wait for Hannah to respond but clicked off.

Niall took the exit off the highway and rolled the truck to

a stoplight. Hannah handed the phone back to him. "Thanks. Um. Niall, you can drop me anywhere."

"Don't you want to get some sleep? You've got to be exhausted." Niall reached out, and for a moment, it seemed like he was going to touch her face but he curled his fingers and pulled back at the last second. "Let me take you to Karma's."

"No. Really, I need to find an ATM. I'm starving and I've been wearing these clothes for twenty-four hours. And . . . I need to rent a room. I can't keep staying at Karma and Zig's. Not after last night." Hannah watched the ocean roll past on her right and added softly, "I don't want to get him into any trouble. Those detectives—"

"Were assholes," Niall snapped. "Pardon my language, ma'am."

"Still not the minister's wife." Hannah surprised them both by quipping back.

Niall's eyes softened and crinkle lines formed around the edges.

Da-yam, the man was hot.

"Zig can deal with the other cops. He'll be fine. You think Karma would tolerate a pussy? Pardon my language. She wouldn't keep Zig around if he couldn't handle himself. But if you're really hungry, let's get food. Then I can take you shopping. Unless, of course, you have a deep-seated need to walk to the store. After that, we'll figure out where you can sleep tonight. Sound good?"

"Not the Boxing Cat, please. I can't face everyone. Not yet. I need a shower and clean clothes first. If that's not okay, then I'll get out at the next light."

Niall glanced ahead, then back at her. He winked. "In case you haven't noticed, we've turned. The ocean is behind us and only the national park is on the right. You'll have a long walk. So sit back, relax. I'll take you to a nice breakfast."

The nice breakfast was at the local family diner. They ate in relative silence. That might have been her fault. Niall had tried to initiate a conversation several times, but she didn't want to talk. Not to him. Not to anyone.

He seemed to take it in stride and when their meal was

over got their coffees to go and ushered her back into his truck. Once inside, she expected him to start the engine but he didn't. He turned to her instead.

"You know, when I was in the desert, I met guys who believed if they kept it locked down, the crap they were facing wouldn't bother them. It's a crock. It still bothered them. And some learned to let off a little steam. Others never did and just blew one day."

Hannah set her coffee in the cup holder and stared at him. "Which one were you?"

He gave her a quick half smile. "Steam guy. I wasn't always. I learned it was better to let a little out than to blow a gasket. So it's okay if you need to vent a little steam right now. You've earned it."

"I'm fine." She let the words hang in the air for a moment, then shook her head. "No, I'm not. I'm all turned around. At least I'm not hungry anymore."

"You look much better than when I picked you up. You've got color back in your cheeks." He sipped his coffee. "So come on, let me have it. You'll feel better. At least, that's what my mom always says."

"Your mom, huh?"

She paused, then decided to trust him. In this moment, he reminded her more of the Marine she'd met all those months ago, except stronger somehow. Not that he'd been weak. But now he appeared ready to offer the ear she had offered him. She took a deep breath and hoped she was doing the right thing, because she really needed him right now.

"Ever have one of those days where you have no idea what the universe is trying to tell you?" She sat back and the seat made an obscene noise. Her cheeks heated but Niall only laughed. She gestured to the seat. "Like that. Everything is going wrong. I thought I was supposed to be here. I really believed the signs were pointing me to Tidewater but from the moment I stepped off the bus everything has gone wrong." She rubbed at the ache in her neck with both hands. "Finding out I work for the guy I had my one and only one-night stand with seemed perfect. I mean, that night had been incredible and finding out you were my boss appeared wonderful for about five seconds.

"Then you showed up and made it clear my presence made you uncomfortable. I mean, come on. You acted like I was some crazed stalker who'd hunted you down with the intention of knocking you over the head and dragging you off to the nearest wedding chapel. Oh, you covered well, but I saw the panic in your eyes.

"Then I had that awful, sickening vision. Honestly, I've never seen anything so monstrous in my life. When Karma told me to report it, it seemed the right thing to do. Again, the universe sent me a resounding, 'uh, no way cupcake' sign. Because what happened when I tried to report it? I was booted out of the station in under twenty minutes. If that wasn't bad enough, my hotel burned down. I lost everything I brought with me including the brand-new art bag that my parents gave me at graduation. It's stupid to be so upset about it, but I really am. It was beautiful. Black leather and large enough to hold my art pads, paints, pencils, brushes. They even had it monogrammed. Yeah, I can get another one, but not like that. Not to mention all my clothes are crispy because as you so deftly pointed out I am an earth dog who wears only cotton."

"Hannah—"

"Then I smashed eggs all over us and you sent me to the grocery store to buy fresh ones. Thank God, you gave me enough money to cover the cost of replacing my ruined uniform, but I don't know how I'm going to repay you if things keep going the way they're going. At this rate, my first check will be in the negative digits. Do you know the best part of my day was when we got slammed with the refugees from the art show fund-raiser? It was the only time I felt relatively normal.

"I mean, yeah, I had to avoid touching silverware and the metal worktables in the kitchen, but no one looked at me as if I was about to jump them or kill them or I don't know . . . burst into flames. And you know what? I *really* like my job. More than I'd ever thought possible. It's more fun than working at a bar. I mean, yeah, I'm supposed to be an electrician because it's safe and I'm good at it but I also don't get to spend much time with other people. So it's lonely. Working at the Boxing Cat was more fun than I've had in months. And until that stupid vision, it was the only time I could be around people and not worry about accidentally getting a vision off them."

A stray tear tickled her cheek in a slow slide but she swiped at it and kept going. She couldn't have stopped talking any more than she could have held back that single escaped tear.

"So there I was at the end of the night thinking the universe wanted me here after all, then those cops showed up. They couldn't pull me aside quietly. No, they had to make a production in front of the whole staff, accusing me of murder. And when they put those metal cuffs on me, I thought I was going to die, right there in the backseat of their car. Do you know the last guy they had in those cuffs murdered some old man because he was jonesing for a fix and needed money? He stabbed the guy for six freaking dollars."

In an instant, Niall had his seat belt off and had unhooked hers. His arms came around her, and still she couldn't stop talking. She gulped air as tears continued to squeeze out from beneath her closed lids. Each breath she drew in smelled like him. Spicy and uniquely Niall.

"Those jerks dragged me out of the only place where I'd felt normal in the whole city and treated me like a criminal." She buried her face in his shoulder. "They spent hours—*hours*—threatening to arrest me. Telling me that I had to be the killer to know everything I did. That I was sick and crazy. If I didn't go to prison they'd make sure I was locked up in a psych ward for the rest of my life. I knew I was telling the truth. I didn't hurt anyone."

"Of course, you didn't."

"But dammit, I started to doubt why the universe had even led me here."

Then, to her horror, the tears she'd been fighting erupted past her control, spilling down her cheeks and onto his shoulder. Her ability to speak gone, she simply wept. Niall crooned softly in her ear. "You're okay now. I won't let them hurt you. You're okay."

He stroked her hair. Gently. So gently. Rocking her, holding her, being so freaking kind.

And that, more than anything, had her weeping harder.

NIALL HELD HER until her tears were spent. She wept silently, her shoulders shaking. She was sunshine and joy personified. It wasn't natural to see her weep. And it ripped him apart.

When she finally pulled back, her cheeks were blotchy, her eyes swollen, her nose running, and she looked so lost. He dug through the glove compartment for tissues, but only came up with napkins. He handed her two. "Sorry. It's all I have."

She gave him a watery smile. "Thank you." Hannah wiped her face and blew her nose, then tucked the used napkin in her pants pocket.

"Feel better?" Niall asked, still stroking her hair. His stupid-ass rule about keeping their relationship strictly professional was seemingly forgotten by her. And he found that suited him fine. When he held her in his arms, he remembered just how perfectly she fit there. How perfectly they fit together.

"Surprisingly, yes." She slid away from his touch. "I guess I needed a meltdown. This is all temporary. Right? I mean, I'm only in town for the summer and *clearly* the universe agrees I shouldn't plan to stay much longer. I won't even have a job past Saturday night. So I need to put aside all the stress and focus on the positive. Like not being at the police station anymore. Thanks for getting me out and for listening, Ma— um, *Boss*."

She used the term to further add distance between them. It left him oddly . . . bereft.

Wasn't that a kick in the balls?

"Hannah, I'm not your boss." A stricken look crossed her face. He backpedaled. "I mean, I *am* your boss, but don't call me that. Just call me Niall. Okay?"

"Right. Just Niall. Nothing else." She nodded but the note in her voice made him want to ask what she wanted to call him. She'd called him *Marine* that night, as if it were a nickname or she was claiming him somehow. But she hadn't done it since she'd arrived in Tidewater. Given the distance she was putting between them now, it didn't look like she was going to do it anytime soon.

Again, that bereft sensation echoed in his chest.

He started the engine of the truck. "So where to now? Clothes? Let me guess, you're not a boutique kind of woman."

"No, I usually shop at thrift stores. Best clothes at the cheapest prices. Considering my body shape, it's too expensive to buy separates retail."

"And it has nothing to do with your hippie ways about reusing things."

"You think you know me so well." There was a note of snark in her voice but the sparkle in her beautiful eyes ignited.

"I've been in your place. Everything was used. Well preserved but secondhand." He pulled back on the road and tried to remember the nearest vintage clothing store.

"Except my art supplies. They were new and top of the line. It's where my money went. Well, that and electrician's school." She cleared her throat. The spark in her eyes had vanished again, replaced with exhaustion.

"How about we do this in a few hours? Let me take you home and you can get some rest."

She shook her head. "I don't feel comfortable. Karma's not there and I don't want to wake Zig."

"Are you afraid of him for some reason?" Niall worried not only for Hannah but for his friend too.

"Oh, no. I don't want to cause him any trouble with those detectives. I heard them talking about him. Saying they'll get him busted down to desk duty permanently when they prove I killed the guy. It wouldn't be nice of me to risk his career when all he and Karma have done is try to help me."

"I think you're not giving him enough credit."

"Or you're not giving those guys enough." She shook her

head and yawned. "If you'll take me to an ATM, I'll rent another hotel room."

"Don't be ridiculous. Stay at my house. I've got room."

She hesitated, twisting her pink braid between her fingers. "I thought you wanted to keep this strictly professional. What would it look like if I slept at your place?"

"Like one of my staff members needed my help again." He paused knowing he was telling her a half-truth. Sure, he'd let staff crash at his place after an event. But that staff was his brother. He never invited the waitstaff, chefs, or busboys to spend the night. But this wasn't the night. And she was exhausted. "You won't be the first staff member to sleep at my place. You don't need to rent a hotel room right now. You *need* sleep. You'll feel better in a few hours. If you're worried about me, I won't be there. I need to head to the Boxing Cat to tend to last-minute details for tomorrow's wedding."

"God, that's tomorrow." She looked like she might break down again, but then pulled herself together with sheer will. "I don't know if Karma told you or not, but the bride, is, um . . . my oldest sister."

CHAPTER 15

WHAT WERE THE odds? Maybe there was something to her faith in signs and the universe.

"Have you called her yet?" Niall asked, turning off the highway and onto his cul-de-sac. His parents' house, well, his house now, stood tall and proud at the center of the turnaround. Pushing the button on the car visor, he raised the garage door.

"No. There was no time. I didn't find out until yesterday afternoon, then we were slammed with guests. Then . . ." She didn't need to explain further.

"Got it. Do you want to call her now?" Niall put the truck in park, closed the garage door, killed the ignition, and started to head inside the house. Hannah followed him.

"No. She's getting married tomorrow. I don't want my first time talking to her in years to happen when I'm confuzzled and weepy. I want her to like me."

"She's going to love you," Niall said automatically, then fell silent. Because, yeah, this wasn't awkward. He held the kitchen door open for her. "Come on in, Hannah."

She stepped inside and stared. Not that he could blame her. "The motif is a little eighties for my taste, but Mom loved it. She picked out the blue rooster wallpaper herself."

Hannah turned a wide-eyed stare in his direction. "Your mother decorated your house?"

"What? You lived over your parents' bar. Don't look at me like that." He waited another beat, then confessed, "I grew up in this house. My parents gave it to me when they moved into their condo. They were going to sell it, but I convinced them to let me fix it up first. Only the kitchen looks like something out of a John Hughes movie. I just couldn't change it yet."

"Too sentimental?" she asked, running her hand over the chipped white enamel stove top.

"Hardly." He laughed. "I was saving this room for last because it's going to cost the most to upgrade. I want top-of-the-line stainless steel appliances and new bamboo flooring. I want to build a center island with a bar. Plus, I need to rewire half the kitchen because whoever did it thirty years ago got a few things backward. Like the light switch over here doesn't work in this room but turns on the fan in the living room."

Hannah swept her gaze around the room with a smile. "I can help with the wiring here. Once I get a few tools replaced. I like your vision for the kitchen. It's gonna be great."

She yawned. Huge. Like he could see her tonsils.

And damn, he'd forgotten why he'd brought her here in the first place.

"Come on." He led her up the stairs to his guest room, then immediately slammed the door closed before she could see it.

Ross, you selfish bastard. Learn to pick up your shit.

He crossed the hall to his room and opened the door. "You can sleep in here."

Hannah stepped inside, a frown on her face. The immaculate room had a framed picture of him in his dress blues hanging on one wall. An extra-wide two-row bookcase was filled with novels by everyone from Tom Clancy to Tess Gerritsen. The tan carpeting was freshly laid, clean, and recently vacuumed. His tan-colored dresser was neat, all of his clothes put away. He'd even dusted this morning when he couldn't sleep. So there was nothing out of place.

Still she frowned.

"Something wrong?" he asked, automatically standing at parade rest.

"This looks like your bedroom." She glanced around. "Not that I mind, but where are you going to sleep?"

"It is my room. Unlike you, I slept last night. I've got errands to do and a business to run. I'm going to help you get settled. Then head out." He strode to the bed and turned down the light blanket and top sheet. Then he pulled his favorite Marines T-shirt out of a drawer and handed it to her. "Here, this will be more comfortable to sleep in."

She took it and hugged it close to her chest.

What he wouldn't give to see her wearing it.

And that evoked a physical reaction that was totally inappropriate since he was only interested in helping her.

Right. Lie some more, dickhead.

She glanced around the spacious room nervously, then up at him. The wariness and exhaustion in her eyes made him want to reach out and hold her again. Help her out of her wrinkled clothes and into his shirt.

The blood in his head flooded south. He had to stop thinking about taking off her clothes.

"There's soda and tea in the fridge. Help yourself." He straightened and backed to the door. "I'll be back tonight."

"My shift starts at three." She followed him to the door.

"You don't need to work it. You've had a hard day." He stopped moving and tried to make her understand. "You need rest. And you don't have any clean uniforms."

She yawned again. Wider this time. "Then what I need to do is to wash my uniform before I take a nap."

"Are you always this stubborn? You're wiped out. You need sleep."

"Yes, I'm always this *determined.* And I need to work more. I have to pay to replace everything I lost. No insurance on the hotel room. I don't even have a cell phone." She smacked herself in the head. "Holy fracking schmoley! I need to call my folks. They'll worry if they don't hear from me today. They were worried enough when I told them about the fire. If they don't hear from me, my dad might just show up at the Boxing Cat."

"Holy fracking schmoley?" Niall tried not to laugh, but failed.

"Yes." Hannah's lips twitched. "Although, I've been known to switch *fracking* for *fucking*, but only when I'm really stressed out."

"*Fracking* for *fucking*?" His cheeks burned, but damn, she was turning him on more and more. "Who says that?"

"I do." Hannah laughed. A full-body, throaty, buoyant, beautiful laugh. Her eyes twinkled. "God, I so needed that. Thank you."

"Oh." Something loosened in his chest at the sight of her smile. He wanted to see her like that forever.

Odd. Two days ago he'd been upset that she'd come to town after giving him a bogus number. Now he didn't want her to leave. But he did want an explanation.

"Hannah?"

She'd been in the process of walking toward his bathroom. She turned to face him. "Yes?"

"About Fincastle—"

"Yeah?"

"Why'd you give me a fake phone number?"

"What?" Hannah blinked and laughed again. "I didn't." Her laughter died as quickly as it started. "I don't think I did. I mean, I was bummed you never called. But . . . Oh my God! Did I write down the 3228 one? It was my number when I was on my parents' phone bill. I got my own cell a few days before I met you. All this time, I thought you hadn't called." Her eyes widened. "And all this time you thought I'd blown you off because you *had* called."

A slow smile spread across her face.

And she yawned again.

"Sorry. I'm really sleepy. I want to continue this conversation. Assuming you do," Hannah quickly added.

"Later." Niall turned her by the shoulders and gave her

a gentle push to the bathroom. "In the meantime, get some sleep. I'll be back tonight."

She turned again. "No, I'll be at the Cat for my shift. I'll wash my uniform, assuming you don't mind me using your washer and dryer. Then I can call a cab."

"I could stand here and argue with you about coming to work—"

"Please don't. It's the one place I don't feel quite so freakish."

"—But I won't." Niall fingered her pink braid. "I'll pick you up in time for your shift. Get some sleep. Don't worry about the clothes. If you take them off, I'll put them in the wash for you."

There was no missing the heat that flared in her eyes. And oh, yeah, he wanted to get her naked in more ways than one. But she needed her rest.

"I'll be just a minute." She stepped into the bathroom and shut the door.

True to her word, she was back in under sixty seconds wearing only his T-shirt. He'd never looked that good in that shirt. He might have it framed and hang it on his wall after today.

Accepting her laundry, he left the room. What he wanted to do was tuck her into bed.

No, what he really wanted was to tuck himself into her in his bed. And dammit, he would. Later.

But he'd seen that smile on her face when she realized he'd tried to call her. She wanted him. And he wanted to give her a reason to keep smiling.

Suddenly, he had a mission.

MERCY KEPT HER head down. She did her job. She was friendly when she needed to be. A bitch when warranted. And completely in-fucking-visible. No one knew her. Not the real her.

She'd worried last night when the cops showed up. How? How had they tied the death to the restaurant? She'd been careful. Meticulous. No one she selected had any reason to associate with the Boxing Cat. But those cops had known. Or thought they had.

They'd taken that stupid out-of-towner hippie into custody.

A smile tormented the corners of her mouth, but Mercy knew better than to let any real emotion show. Not here. Not where others might see. And mock.

But the question wriggled in her brain like a feasting worm.

How had they known about the Boxing Cat? Had it just been dumb luck?

Around her, the place was abuzz with excitement about catering tomorrow's wedding. Wondering why the boss had decided to take off today, when he hadn't taken a single day off since he'd been back. The news of the dead body on the television. The whispers that the hippie might have done it.

The back door swung open. Sunlight poured in, temporarily blinding Mercy. Then he was there.

Smiling as usual. This time his long blond hair hung loose around his shoulders. He wore a green Hawaiian shirt that brought out the green in his sexy eyes. He tucked his hands in his cargo pants and audibly jangled his keys.

Something he did when he was nervous or excited.

Mercy averted her gaze and pretended to work. No one could know of her attraction to him. No one could guess that one day very soon, she would make him hers.

She would grant him a bliss-filled weekend.

Then she would set them both free.

Forever.

NIALL OPENED THE garage door out of habit, then cursed himself. If Hannah had still been asleep, the noisy creaking door would have definitely put an end to that. With no hope of surprising her now, he collected the bags from the truck and headed into the kitchen.

He was greeted by the sound of the shower running.

Images of her naked and soapy under the steaming water sprang to mind. He wanted to join her. So bad he had actually walked halfway down the hall with the bags in his hands before he caught himself.

Sure, she'd confessed that she hadn't intentionally given him the wrong number. But that wasn't a blatant invitation to come get sexy, slathery naked in the shower.

Dammit!

Making a U-turn, he arrowed for the kitchen table, dropped the bags on it, then headed toward the living room. Pushing the coffee table aside, he dropped to the floor and started a rep of push-ups. Maybe he could get through fifty and get the blood flowing to other parts of his body before she came out.

He did fifty and fifty more before she appeared with a bath towel wrapped around her voluptuous body and a second one around her head. Niall straightened and she jumped.

"Oh God!" Hannah said, clutching the towel. "What were you doing there, Marine? Push-ups?"

"As a matter of fact."

"Oh. Really?" She took another step toward him, her hand still holding firmly to the bath towel. "You do that a lot?"

Niall glanced at her body, her face, and the floor again. "Uh, yeah."

Hannah cocked her head to one side. "Are you embarrassed? It's not like you haven't seen me naked. And I'm covered. I'm not going to drop the towel and jump you or anything. Well, unless you call me *ma'am*."

Niall whipped his gaze to her twinkling eyes. "Feeling better after your nap?"

"I feel like a new woman." She glanced at the bags on the table. "Uh, you shop at Victoria's Secret a lot, Marine?"

"Wha—? No. That's for you." He strode to the kitchen table. "Actually, all the bags are for you. You said you needed clothes. I had to guess your size. There are two uniforms in there. I also bought you two pairs of gloves. One white and one black. You can wear them when serving, so you don't have to touch the silverware."

"You bought me gloves?"

"I figured you didn't need any more visions today. I thought you'd had enough. I also picked up a pair of rubber gloves for when you do the dishes. I know they're not recyclable, but you said skin contact with the metal caused visions. These should help prevent that, right?"

"Y-yes." The look on her face was a cross between astonishment and adoration.

Niall kept going through the bags. "There are also jeans, tees, shorts, some pajamas, and a couple bras. You should have seen the look on the woman's face at the store when I tried to describe your—well, you know."

Hannah blinked. She glanced at the bags, then back at Niall. "You bought me clothes *and* gloves?"

"You needed them." Niall shrugged. "Oh, and here. Use this until your cell is replaced. It's got a month of pre-paid minutes on it. The instructions are in one of the bags." He handed her the burner phone.

"What happened to earth dog and we're just employer and employee?" She delivered the question with wonder in her voice.

Niall closed the distance between them. "Hannah, I didn't mean the earth dog comment the way you took it. You're a tree hugger. Is that better?"

Hannah stared up at him, her eyes round with surprise. "Yes. And the other thing?"

Goddamn, he wanted to kiss her. To sink into her and lose himself.

So he stepped back instead.

"You've had it rough for a few days. You needed clothes. I have the money. It's no big deal. It's nothing I wouldn't have done for any of my employees."

Damn his lying ass.

"Oh." Hannah sighed and shrugged. "Well, then I'll pay you back, Mar—Niall."

She'd been about to call him *Marine*. Her pet name for him. But she stopped herself. How many times had he thought she was trying not to call him Mr. Graham? She hadn't been forcing herself to sound casual, she'd been distancing herself.

Fuck. He just gave her another reason.

"Hannah—"

"I'll be ready to go to the Cat in fifteen minutes." She collected the bags. "Thank you for these. I promise, I'll pay you back."

Then she was out of the room and racing up the stairs.

"You don't need to," he said in the silent room.

Truth was, he owed her so much more than she had ever owed him.

And he just kept fucking it up.

CHAPTER 16

THE CLOSED SIGN was up. Finally.

Hannah helped Michael and Karma clear the last of the dishes from the front while Dawn and Sadie set the tables for the next day.

"Why are we wasting our time setting the tables in the restaurant? We need to be getting ready for tomorrow night's wedding," Dawn said, her Brooklyn accent pitched and whiny. The mascara she'd put on this morning was smudged under her eyes. She looked tired and a decade older than her twenty-eight years.

"Because we're still serving brunch in the Master Room in the morning. Get over it, Dawn. It's not like you have to work on Saturdays." Sadie slammed plates down on the table hard enough that it seemed to defy the laws of physics because they didn't break. "Doesn't your kid have basketball or something tomorrow?"

"Soccer." Dawn blew her pink-tipped bangs out of her eyes. She appeared ready to continue the argument the two waitresses had been having for hours. "What's your problem?

Aren't you getting like double time or something to work the wedding? Why do you always have to be such a—"

Hannah didn't wait to hear the argument escalate but pushed the dishpan full of dirty dishes through the swinging door into the kitchen.

"Will you trust me for once in your miserable existence?" Ross hissed out the last word.

Hannah stepped back from the doorway to the office. The whole night had been busy. While the Cat had been markedly slower than the night before, everyone was hustling to make sure all of the arrangements for the wedding were in place.

Several times she caught Ross going over a list or signing off on a document only to find Niall double-checking him. Yikes, the Marine was a major control freak.

A control freak who had bought her lightweight cloth gloves to wear while working so she wouldn't accidentally get another vision. A control freak who spent his own money to buy her clothes. Nice ones in her size. A control freak so bent on keeping their past relationship a secret from the staff that he held her close with one arm and pushed her away with the other.

Well, that wasn't going to happen.

Yes, she'd lost her way after spending the night at the police station. She shivered at the memory. But then she'd slept in his house. In his bed. His headboard was a very nice black metal. That she purposely did not touch. She came to understand the universe brought her into his life to help him connect with his brother. Why else would she have had the vision about Ross if not to help them?

She might have originally come to Tidewater to find Jules and Shelley but the universe had bigger plans for her. Bigger even than helping Niall and Ross. She needed to find the killer.

It had come to her in the shower this afternoon.

The cops didn't believe her. They didn't know how. But she had already established a connection with the killer. If she could reconnect, she might be able to glean enough details to get TSS on Mercy's trail. The question remained, was there anything left in the restaurant that the killer had touched?

Probably not. But maybe the other silverware Mercy had

touched hadn't been touched by anyone else. Odds were slim that the customer who did the murder would come back. Hannah considered asking Karma for the knife that had sent her into the vision, then changed her mind. Her friend would likely try to talk her out of searching for another vision, especially while they were working.

Hannah had spent most of her shift surreptitiously touching every piece of metal she could. Both wishing she would and wouldn't see anything. Oh, she got visions all right, just none related to the cruel Mercy.

"This isn't about trust." Niall's words were calm, cold, and lowering with each syllable. "If you'd actually listen to me, you'd know that."

Ross's response dropped to a muffle but the tension in the air was palpable.

Virgil and Paulie cleaned their stoves for the night, both glancing intermittently at the door. Neither spoke.

Hannah carried the tub of dishes to the dishwasher around the corner and slipped off her gloves. This was the last set of dishes left to be washed for the night.

With a deep breath for courage, Hannah reached into the tub and grabbed the silverware propped up in a glass. A myriad of images slipped through her mind. Images of sunsets, flashing lights at a nightclub, a perfect golf swing, a sick baby cuddling as it nursed, a handsome young man with laughing eyes, and more zipped through her mind. Scents of magnolia perfume, menthol cigarettes, baby powder, and cigars floated through her senses. There wasn't a single image stronger than another. Nothing to mentally grab on to. Too many to decipher but there was a distinct lack of violence in the overlapping visions.

No blood.

No death.

No Mercy.

"Hannah? I thought Niall gave you gloves," Karma said from behind.

Hannah jumped, dropping the cutlery. Forks, knives, and spoons clattered against the concrete floor. Her breath whooshed out as the tenuous connections snapped in an instant.

"Whoa! Sorry. I didn't mean to sneak up on you." Karma bent to retrieve the flatware.

"He did. I, uh, just forgot to put them on." Hannah tugged the rubber gloves from the sink counter and jammed her hands in them before helping Karma pick up the scattered utensils.

"You know your aura is this brilliant shade of orange," Karma said conversationally, after they cleaned up the mess. She laid a hand on Hannah's forearm. "Except when you lie. It turns a funky brownish color. Not very pretty."

Hannah glanced at the demi-wall to make sure no one was nearby. "Sorry about that. I was trying to see if I could get another reading on . . . you know, *Mercy*." She whispered the name.

Karma pulled her by the arm into the corner, fear on her face. "Are you nuts? After everything that's happened, why would you do that? I saw what it did to your aura. You weren't you. Not when you had the vision."

"I never am." Hannah tugged the gloves back on her hands and shrugged. Big mistake. Karma's face drained of color. "This is why I didn't tell you what I was doing. Don't worry, I'm fine. When the visions happen, I am the person who sent me the vision. I usually come through it unscathed."

"Usually?" Karma looked around the kitchen, then lowered her voice again. "And how many times have you been inside a serial killer's head?"

"Just the one time. Stop looking at me like you expect me to go all Norman Bates on you. I won't. My plan to find something else *she* touched didn't work anyway." Hannah raised her glove-covered hands helplessly.

"You still didn't explain why." Karma folded her arms over her chest. "Why would you go looking?"

"Because a killer is out there. We served her a meal. Frick, I could have talked to her and not even known it. Then I spent all night in a room with two cops trying to convince them that I'm neither a killer nor crazy. They didn't believe me. They're so focused on proving it's me, I'm afraid the real killer is going to do it again. I don't want someone to die because of me."

"No one is going to die because of you," Niall said, startling Hannah and Karma.

"Way to go all panther-like, Boss." Karma blew out a nervous breath. She waved at Hannah. "Maybe you can talk some sense into her."

"Hey!" Hannah wheeled around. "I'm not a child. And I'm not a fool. You weren't there last night. Those cops wouldn't listen to me."

"And you think digging around for more *evidence* will help your case? If they didn't listen last night, what makes you think they'll be any more willing tonight or tomorrow or if you *do* find the right thing to touch?" Karma's cheeks were mottled with color, but it wasn't rage in her eyes, it was fear.

Hannah touched her friend's shoulder. "You introduced me to your cousins. They listened. If I get anything, I swear I'll give it to them. I won't go back to the station."

Karma sighed, stepped closer, and lowered her voice. "What about the other thing?"

"What other thing?" Niall's black brows drew together.

"It's nothing." Hannah shrugged and tried for an it's-all-good smile.

"Your aura's getting brownish again." Karma looked from Hannah to Niall. "She had trouble breaking the connection with the killer during the vision last night. It's how she cut her hand."

Niall's green gaze swung to hers. "Is that true, Hannah? You never mentioned this before."

In the bar.

He didn't say it but that had to be what he meant. And yeah, that sent her mind spinning in a whole different direction. One that had nothing to do with serial killers or kitchen knives.

"Your aura is, um . . . getting kind of red," Karma whispered to her.

Hannah tore her gaze from Niall's and back to Karma's. But her friend was staring quizzically at Niall. Hannah hazarded a glance back at him. He was bathed in a lovely red light.

"Hannah," Niall said sharply. The red light zapped out of

existence. "What did she mean about trouble breaking the connection?"

"I was sort of stuck. Karma called my name and helped ground me." Okay, that was an oversimplification but it was the gist.

"See why I'm worried, Boss? She was looking to see if she could get a vision on the killer again."

"In my restaurant?" His eyes widened and his cheeks reddened with obvious anger. "You think the killer works here?"

"No, no. I don't. I think the killer ate here. I didn't get a vision from something back here. I got it from the knife that someone ate with."

Niall exhaled his relief, then glanced at Karma. "Why would you let her try to do something like this?"

"Hey!" Hannah clapped her hands. The sound was muffled by the gloves but it did the trick: they both looked at her. "Don't talk about me like I'm not here. Or like I'm an errant child."

"Then don't act like one," Niall snapped.

"Are you kidding me?" Hannah whipped off her gloves and stood toe-to-toe with her handsome, frustrating, egotistical boss. "I'm not a child. And I have every right to do whatever it takes to keep from being wrongly questioned or arrested for something I didn't do."

"Yeah, I'm going to, uh . . . go in the other room. Zig'll be here in fifteen to pick us up, Hannah." Karma started to sidle out of the room. She paused next to Niall and said, "Boss, blowing it."

Hannah and Niall both glared at Karma's retreating back.

Niall glowered intensely for several long seconds, his lips moving as if he were counting to ten. "Hannah, you are not a child. I know that better than anyone. I don't want you questioned again either. But I don't see how looking for another vision is going to help your case. If you do see something, then what are you going to do?"

"I already said I'd call the TSS guys. They believed me. They didn't think I was crazy or lying or doing a bar trick."

"That's not fair." Niall lowered his face until they were

nearly nose to nose and whispered, "You were the one who acted like it was a bar trick."

"Only because it so clearly freaked you out."

"I never said I didn't believe you. I drove you to the station to report what you witnessed, didn't I?"

"After trying to talk me out of it." Hannah rolled her eyes. Why was she fighting? What did it matter?

Niall put his hands on her upper arms. She sensed the control in him snapping but his touch was gentle. His thumbs rubbed against her shoulders. Goose bumps ran down her arms.

"I was afraid something like last night would happen. I'd seen it before. You're not the only psychic I've met." He gave her a half grin. "Hell, Karma works for me. I've known others. And I've also seen what happens when people don't believe them. I didn't want you hurt."

The absolute truth shining in his eyes made her knees weak. He was worried about her.

"Oh." Her mind blanked. She wanted to thank him.

She wanted to jump him, if she was really being honest with herself.

But even though he cared about her, he didn't want her. Not the way she wanted him. And it wouldn't work anyway. She was only here for the summer.

But he simply stood there. Holding her by the shoulders. His lips close enough to kiss. Just a few inches and she could taste him again.

His eyes darkened to the color of summer grass. God, it was so sexy how they did that.

He licked his lips, and yes, seeing him do it had her licking her own lips.

Somehow they'd moved closer. Less than an inch now.

"You ready, Han—? Oops! Sorry!" Karma appeared beside the wall, only to whip around and head back the way she came. "Don't mind me. I'll be waiting, outside. Uh, with Zig. Come . . . oh, shit, I can't believe I just said that. See you when you're ready."

Niall pulled back from her and scratched his neck. "You'd better go."

"Now? But—"

"This is my place of business, remember?" His back went ramrod straight. He pivoted on his heel and disappeared into his office.

Yeah, his place of business. She remembered.

It was where she'd witnessed a murder in a vision.

Where her boss had nearly kissed her.

The universe was definitely sending her mixed messages.

"I WASN'T SURE you'd be staying here tonight," Karma said, standing in the doorway of the guest bedroom.

Hannah looked up from one of the many bags that Niall had bought her earlier in the day.

"Do I need to go to a hotel? It's totally fine."

"That's not what I meant." Karma waved her hand in the air as if shooing away the idea. "I saw the way you and Niall looked at each other. Woo!" She fanned herself with one hand.

"It's not what you think."

"Right. And you two didn't have matching flaming-hot red auras earlier." Karma cocked her head to the left and a wicked grin spread across her face. "And don't try to deny it. Your aura might be orange now but your face is as red as your aura was back at the café. Don't be embarrassed, clearly Niall is hot for you too."

Hannah stopped digging in the bag and crossed to the doorway. "Please don't say anything to Niall. He doesn't want me as anything more than a temporary employee."

Karma snorted. "Yeah, that's what he thinks. It's not true. Even if I hadn't seen the little aura-iffic display, I'd have guessed he wants you more than he's letting on when I saw this."

She straightened from the doorjamb and pulled a huge black artist's case from the other room. It had to be an artist's case. It was big enough to hold her supplies. If she'd had any left. The shoulder strap was padded and the case was black leather. A small bronze plate was affixed in the middle of the flap on the front. He had had it engraved with her first name.

"Holy frack! Niall did this?" Hannah had to swallow past

a lump in her throat. She accepted the case and traced the nameplate with a finger. "How? When? Why?"

"He must have dropped it off when he dropped off the bags of clothes. Zig had everything on the couch but this must have fallen behind it." Karma followed her into the bedroom, shoved the clothing bags aside, and sat down on the bed. "Aren't you going to open it?"

A part of her didn't want to open it yet. She wanted to call Niall. Okay, she wanted to go to his place and thank him in person. All night. But that wasn't an option. If he'd wanted her to open it when he was there, he would have given it to her in person. So why did he buy it for her?

"Hannah, you okay? Your aura's doing a weird jumbly thing." Karma started to rise but Hannah gestured for her to remain seated.

"I'm fine. Overwhelmed. Amazed. He's so hard to read. One minute he's acting all proper and distant. The next he's buying me clothes and art supplies. I just don't know what to think."

Hannah sank onto the bed and popped the clasp on the leather case. Inside were pastels, chalks, ten different art pencils, paints, a pad of excellent drawing paper, a pad of watercolor paper, gum erasers, and even a tiny little sharpener. Tucked into one pocket was a folded sheet of paper with her name on it.

Hannah reached for it, then glanced at Karma. Instead of reading the message, Hannah closed the case with it still inside.

Karma whistled. "In all the time I've known him, I've never heard of Niall doing anything so romantic. Girlfriend, you've got him wrapped around your finger. Hope you plan to do right by him."

"Me do right by him?" Hannah shook her head. "Karma, I think you're confused. He's the one who isn't sure what to do with me. Every time I get too close, he pushes me away. Then he does something like this and . . ." She let her words trail away. "I swear, in the dictionary under *mixed signals* is a picture of Niall Graham."

Karma clucked her tongue. "He's got a thing about space. Ross says Niall changed after he survived an attack in Afghanistan. All I know is, the man hovers in doorways.

The one time I saw someone block his exit out of the office, his aura went crazy. As dark as outer space."

Hannah nodded. "I didn't realize you knew about the attack."

"That makes two of us." Karma leaned her upper body closer. "Who told you?"

"Niall."

Karma gave her a wide, toothy grin. "Yep. That man might have an issue with space, but I'm telling you. He wants you. As far as I know, he doesn't talk about Afghanistan. With anyone. But you're here two days and he talks to you."

Hannah didn't correct Karma's assumption. She couldn't if she was going to follow Niall's rule about keeping their night together a secret.

Karma pushed to her feet and started for the door. "We've got an epically long day tomorrow. Get some rest. Oh, and Hannah, those mixed signals Niall's sending. I think it's claustrophobia. It's not that he doesn't want you. I think he does. I think he's afraid of getting too close to you."

THEY WERE FIGHTING again. The pair of them.

Mercy watched from the shadows as Niall and Ross argued in the parking lot, riveted by them in all their male beauty.

"You can't keep doing this, Ross." Niall didn't shout but his voice cut across the empty parking lot. At two in the morning, sound carried through the quiet night like waves crashing on the shore. Sometimes a soft, rolling noise, other times a clapping crescendo.

"Doing what? My job!" Ross's voice, passionate and echoing fury, smashed through space. "I seem to recall your ass definitely *not* here for hours today. So before you go pissing on me because I was checking on a potential client, you better check yourself, *Sarge*."

"Checking on a potential client, my left nut. You are so full of shit. You were at the bar. Again. Getting drunk. Again. Do you really want to go down that road? Dad's lucky Mom didn't toss his ass out years ago." Niall hiked a thumb over a shoulder as if to emphasize the point. "The only thing that saved him, their marriage, and the restaurant was that he was man enough to admit he had a problem before it ruined everything."

"I'm not an alcoholic." Ross's denial was a little too rehearsed. "There's nothing wrong with getting a beer with a client now and then."

"Sure." Niall nodded. "Now and then. But you're drunk so damned much you forget details like depositing money. What the hell, Ross? If we don't put that money in the bank, our employees don't get paid."

"It was one fucking time, asshole!" Ross shoved at Niall's shoulders, but Niall was immovable. "You may have never made a fucking mistake, but the rest of us plebeian humans have. So get off my case."

Niall inhaled a deep breath. His chest seemed to expand with the added oxygen. He appeared to get bigger. Wider. Taller, even.

Mercy licked her suddenly dry lips, waiting. God, had she ever been more aroused? If she tried, she could pretend they were fighting about her. One declaring his undying devotion to her. The other defining her as something to be given up. Which one would win? Her lover, of course, but that was fantasy. In reality, she had no idea if they would truly come to blows.

"I'm not on your case, little brother. But if you fuck up tomorrow's catering event—"

"I know how to do my job. I set it up. Arranged all the details. I've double-checked and triple-checked everything. Nothing will go wrong." With a sneer Ross clapped Niall on the bicep. "Thanks for the vote of confidence though. Gets me right here." He thumped his fist against his heart.

Niall shook his head. "Just promise me you won't drink until after the event ends. Not a drop. I need you clearheaded for tomorrow."

"If that'll get you off my case. I promise not to drink all weekend. Hell, if I thought you'd actually believe me, I'd swear never to drink again." Ross raised three fingers in a scout salute.

"Don't make promises you can't keep."

"Yeah, that's what I thought." Ross pulled keys from his pocket and crossed to the driver's side door of his beat-up blue Pontiac. "You know, everyone else at the Cat sees me as a good boss, a solid leader, a fucking decent person. Why can't you?"

"Ross, I do see all those things. But you've got a problem. One that can't be solved by an argument in a parking lot at two in the morning." Niall followed his brother, who strode away from his car and to the bus stop at the end of the parking lot. "Where the hell are you going?"

"I'm drunk, as you pointed out. I'm taking the bus."

"Ross, wait. I'll give you a ride." Niall quickened his steps to reach his brother but Ross kept his back to him.

"So I can listen to you lecture me all the way home? Thanks but no thanks." A Tidewater Transit Bus lumbered to a stop in front of Ross. He climbed aboard, then turned and faced his brother. "Whatevs, Niall. I'm done with tonight's brotherly chat. I'll be here tomorrow. I promise, no drinking. Good enough for you?"

He didn't wait for a reply. He gave Niall the one-fingered salute and the doors closed between them.

Niall stood watching until the taillights faded, then he simply lowered his head and closed his eyes.

Mercy's heart pounded. Fury and pity pumped through her. She should grant them both her mercy. They each needed it in their own way. But Niall wasn't her problem. His issue was self-induced. He made himself miserable through his own actions.

Ross, now, he couldn't help who and what he was.

It was Ross who truly needed her. She wanted to go to him tonight, but that bus could take him anywhere in the city. So she'd wait until tomorrow.

After the reception he'd be ready for her.

And she'd set him free.

CHAPTER 17

NIALL DIDN'T SEE Hannah all day. There hadn't been time to talk to her, even if he had. Dawn had called out again, having caught her kid's bug. The Boxing Cat was still booming thanks to the museum's mix-up two nights before. People were talking and a blogger for a gluten-free site had come in to sample the cuisine.

Niall split his time between serving the Saturday afternoon clients and coordinating the catering event by phone with Ross. He clicked off the cell phone and stared in silent wonder. His little brother actually seemed to be getting his shit together.

Ross had arrived at the Cat early in the morning, ready to work. No telltale signs of a night spent drinking and partying. His eyes were bright, his color healthy, and his energy up. He'd helped Michael load the dishes into the van. Helped Virgil and Paulie load the food. He'd even offered to cover the restaurant and let Niall go to the site to set up for the wedding reception.

It was the most together Ross had ever been.

Niall had almost accepted the offer but Ross had worked

hard to get the catering gig. Taking it from him at the last minute would have been cruel.

"Boss, it's four. I've put up the Closed sign," Karma said, poking her head into the pantry where he'd been emptying boxes. "Paulie's already on site and Virgil's waiting for me to head over. You ready to go?"

"What about the cleanup here?" Niall broke down the last of the cardboard, adding it to the stack. He picked up the lot and turned to Karma. Her cap of dark brown curls was slicked back from her face into tighter ringlets than usual. Perhaps it was the black cummerbund that made her look more professional or the way she carried herself. But it was a little too formal.

"Hannah swept the kitchen, vacuumed the front, and loaded the last set of dishes before she rode with Paulie to the site." Karma cocked her head to one side. "Didn't you see her leave? She went to your office looking for you."

"No, I didn't see her." He wished he had. He wanted to know if she'd liked the art supplies. Niall opened his mouth to ask Karma, then closed it again wordlessly. Karma already noticed too much, no need to give her more information. "Go on ahead. I'll be at the site shortly."

"Meet ya there." Karma nodded, then withdrew.

Niall followed her out the back door and tossed the flattened boxes into the recycling bin, then headed back inside. He'd barely flipped the lock when someone knocked. He opened the door to find Dawn. She looked exhausted and too ill to be at the restaurant.

"What are you doing here?" Niall asked, hurrying to where she swayed in the doorway.

"I forgot to give this to Miss Renee." She lifted a bag in the air.

One glance inside and Niall understood. The cake topper and cake cutter were nestled inside. He took the bag from her hands and put an arm around her waist. "I'll get them to the site. You need to get home and back in bed. Did you drive here?"

She nodded and swayed more. Niall tightened his hold on her, then brushed his cheek against her hot forehead.

"Well, leave your car. I'll take you home. You shouldn't be driving. You're burning up." He helped her outside and into his truck. "Stay here, I need to lock up."

He dashed inside to grab his tuxedo shirt, tie, and cummerbund from his office. On his desk sat a watercolor portrait of him in his Marines uniform. The note next to it read, "Thank you for the art supplies. I love them—Hannah."

The painting was curled at the edges, but otherwise flawless. Hannah had drawn the portrait of him his mother kept in his bedroom. It was incredible. An almost exact copy except for the tiny blue owl in the lower right corner next to her signature.

Niall grinned, then carefully laid the painting back down. He'd take it to his mother in the rehabilitation center tomorrow before he introduced her to Hannah.

After locking up, Niall returned to his car to find Dawn fast asleep, her head propped against the passenger side window. He drove her home and managed to get her to the front door. It swung open and her mother appeared wearing a bright red track suit, Dawn's son wrapped around his grandmother's right leg.

"Momma tick?" the child asked around a mouthful of thumb.

"Yes, she is. Can I bring her in, Mrs. Mays?"

"Her room's at the end of the hall." The woman swept the preschooler into her arms and followed Niall down the hallway. She skirted past him and opened a door on the right. Two twin beds were pushed to opposite sides of the room. One bedspread was decorated in cartoon planes and covered with toy cars, bears, and stuffed trucks that matched the comforter. The other bed was more sedate. All yellow sheets and blankets.

Niall set Dawn down on the yellow bed, then turned to her mother. "I'm sorry but I can't stay."

"The wedding reception." The older woman nodded. She stroked the little boy's brown curls. "She was really counting on that money today."

Dawn was a good employee. She hadn't missed a day of work until this week. "We'll work it out. Is there something she needs today?"

The woman glanced at her daughter, then shook her head. "No. What she needs is rest. I'll take care of her. Thank you for bringing her home. I was so worried when she got in the car this afternoon. But she said she had a job to do and didn't want to let you down."

"She did a great job." Niall turned to Dawn, who'd already drifted back into a fitful sleep. "Get some rest. I'll see you when you're feeling better."

Niall ruffled the boy's hair and made him giggle, then headed to the site. He hoped whatever Dawn had wasn't catching. He couldn't afford to lose another server tonight.

HANNAH KEPT HER gloves on while she helped set up the twelve circular tables and the metal folding chairs. No one noticed, or if they did, they kept the questions to themselves. Thank goodness.

She'd expected hard work setting up for a wedding reception and wasn't disappointed. What surprised her was how much fun she was having. The catering staff laughed and joked the whole time. And as each table was decorated on the grassy knoll overlooking the ocean, the place became more ethereal.

The tables were arranged beneath a large, white, canopied tent. White lights were strung around the edges of the tent, then crisscrossed under it, so it would resemble stars in the sky when the sun went down. White taper candles in hurricane glasses were centerpieces. Each glass was surrounded by a wreath of purple, red, and yellow roses.

Hannah smiled. The flowers reminded her of her tattoo. She suspected that was not an accident. She may have only remembered about the triumvirate of roses because of the locket, but her sisters had probably always known.

She headed past the three-tier wedding cake, elegantly decorated in white roses with tiny silver bells and balls cascading down what appeared to be a long veil from the top of the cake. It would have been stunning, except the cake topper was noticeably absent. By design?

Even in her artistic brain, the piece looked unfinished. But some people liked that style.

A crash erupted in another tent. The food tent was set up behind the huge three-story house everyone called a cottage. The tent shared a wall and part of the roof with the cottage. It was probably used as a patio when caterers weren't there.

Hannah hurried away from the cake table, across the dance floor, and into the portable kitchen. Paulie and Ross were struggling to right the toppled baking rack of trays. One wheel had slid off the puzzle-piece flooring and sunk into the sandy grass. One long tray of bruschetta lay splattered on the ground.

Hannah jumped in and tried to move the wheel from the sand, but couldn't lift it.

"Switch with me," Paulie called out.

They changed spots, and in moments, the wheel was out of the sand and back on the flooring again. The rest of the appetizers had slid on their trays, but otherwise remained unscathed. Except for the two dozen on the floor.

"What happened?" Ross panted, his hands on his knees.

"I don't know. I went to put the last tray on the shelf and I bumped into the pillar. Something shocked me." Paulie rubbed his left elbow and gestured to the white wall of the house. A thick orange extension cord trailed from the house to the portable refrigeration unit.

Hannah trailed her hand down the wall and across the box. Both were cool to the touch. Then she followed the orange and black cord from the spot where it was plugged into the wall, and back to the refrigeration unit. She was nearly there when she found it.

"I see the problem." She gestured to the cord's frayed and exposed wiring near the base of the fridge. "The cord's damaged. You need to unplug it before it starts a fire. Do you have a spare one?"

"Not with me. Dammit," Ross said, yanking it from the wall roughly.

"I'm not trying to be picky but that might be part of the problem. You shouldn't yank cords out of the outlet like that.

Look at this." She held up the power cord to show where the wiring was exposed near the head. "This happens when people don't pull it by the base."

"I don't need a lesson, I need a damned working cord," Paulie snapped. "My food is going to spoil in this heat before we can serve the salads."

"It'll be fine, Paulie." Ross patted him on the back reassuringly. "I'll go buy another. Won't take me more than a few minutes. You think you can handle the setup until I get back?"

The question was posed to her and Hannah blinked in surprise. "Me?"

"You're the only server on site that I've worked with before. Sadie's not here yet. Karma is on her way with Virgil. Who knows where Niall is. And all the rest of the staff were hired for this weekend only."

Seemed like a lot of responsibility to put on the shoulders of someone he'd only met a few days earlier, but she could see how important a successful event was to him. Plus, it was her sister's wedding reception. Not that Jules or Shelley knew she was here. Yet.

"Sure, go ahead."

"Thanks, Hannah. You're the best." Ross's eyes sparkled. "Paulie, I'll be back fast."

"I can go, Ross," Paulie said, putting a hand on the other man's arm, holding him in place. "Really, I need to get this up and running in under ten minutes. If the food goes bad, that'll be the end of the catering business."

The men seemed to be talking in some sort of code. As if they weren't really discussing the need to replace a broken power cord.

"I promise you. I *will* be back in ten minutes." Ross smiled but the spark of hope and joy in his eyes had dimmed. "Trust me."

Again, there seemed to be a silent code going on between them. Paulie released his hold and nodded. "See you in ten."

Ross didn't smile, didn't nod, but turned and strode out.

Paulie watched him leave, then turned a sharp look her way. "Next time you notice a problem, can you please take it to Niall or fix it yourself? Ross shouldn't have to deal with everything."

Hannah started to ask what he meant, but Virgil walked in with Karma. Niall appeared right behind them.

"Shit," Paulie muttered.

Niall glanced around. His gaze collided with hers. Her pulse and her breathing kicked up as if she'd just run a half marathon. What little breath she managed to suck in was sapped out when he smiled at her.

"Hi, Hannah," Niall said, pulling her aside. In a lowered voice only she could hear, he said, "Thank you for the painting."

Warmth spread through her at his touch. At his words. "You like it?"

He nodded. "I was thinking, if it's all right with you, I'd give it to my mom. She always loved the picture of me in uniform."

She wasn't sure what to say. He liked the painting enough to give it to his mother? A ridiculous bubble of hope rose in her chest. "Sure. That-that'd be great."

Niall glanced at the others who appeared to pay them no mind. He stepped closer until he was practically close enough to kiss, then asked in an even quieter voice, "Did you paint that from memory?"

She tapped her finger against her temple. "Almost photographic. Sometimes I can see an image and it just sticks." Like his face during their night together. "I'm glad you liked it."

"Where's Ross?" Virgil asked, his voice cutting through the intimacy of their moment.

"He, uh . . . will be right back," Paulie replied.

Niall's grin transformed into a scowl. He stepped back and whipped his gaze to Paulie. "He's not here? It's nearly five o'clock. The reception starts in an hour. And he decided to take off *now*?"

"We had a problem, Niall." Hannah picked up the damaged cord and held it out for Niall's inspection. "The wires are frayed. Paulie got shocked when the exposed wires came into contact with the tray stand. Ross went to pick up a new power cord. He'll be right back."

Niall put his hands on his hips and glared at Paulie. Then he shook his head. He appeared to be counting if the fingers tapping against his tuxedo-clad thigh were any indication.

"Boss, I'll check the tent and see what needs finishing," Karma said, taking Hannah by the elbow.

"It's all set up." Hannah let herself be pulled out of the food tent but rounded on Karma before they went into the reception area. "What's going on? Ross said he'll be right back."

Karma glanced around. They stood between the two tents in the late afternoon sunshine. Yards away sunlight sparkled on the ocean and waves crashed against the shore. Unlike the touristy area of the beach, this section was private and virtually empty.

"I don't know if you've noticed it or not, but Ross has been leaving the restaurant during work hours and getting drunk. All of us, Virgil, Paulie, and me, know about his drinking problem but no one's saying anything to Niall. There's enough crap between them right now. Only, Ross is gone again before our first catering event. Niall's pissed and really worried. I am too. I don't know what's gotten into Ross lately, but he can't keep doing this." Karma exhaled a hard breath. "Look, don't say anything to Niall about this. He hates gossip and I don't need him pissed at me."

Hannah's neck prickled and she had the distinct impression someone was watching her. She glanced back at the food tent. The flap closed. Whoever had been there must have heard Karma. Hannah hoped it wasn't Niall.

"Come on, I promised Niall I'd make sure everything is ready to go." Karma pushed through the door flap and disappeared inside the reception area.

Hannah followed after her but came to a halt at the large portrait of Jules and Seth, the bride and groom, sitting on an easel in the corner of the room near the cake table. They were posed on a fire escape. He was leaning out a window kissing her. It was fun and flirty and romantic.

"They make a great couple, don't they?" Karma stepped up beside her. "Have you called her yet?"

"No, I thought I'd surprise her today." Hannah took in the

beautiful area, then looked down at her tuxedo-style uniform and started to rethink her plan. "Or maybe I'll leave her a message tomorrow. I don't want to take away from her day."

"You won't take away from her day. Stop worrying." Karma rolled her eyes but grinned. "It's killing me keeping this secret from Dev. And I can't tell him because there's no way he'd keep it from Shelley, who'd tell Jules. So hurry up and call them already."

Karma's happy chatter brought to light another serious question. "Ryan and Ian haven't said anything yet, have they?"

"Not a chance." Karma shrugged. "They wouldn't tell your sisters because you said you wanted to contact them yourself. Those two know how to keep a secret. Trust me on this."

"Oh, good." Hannah glanced around the pretty setting.

"Hey, did you replace your cell phone?" Karma asked, rearranging a table setting at the head table. She straightened with a frown. "Crap, I forgot you haven't had a chance to go shopping. Do you want to use mine?"

"Actually." She tugged it from her pocket. The bright and shiny phone didn't have the pretty silicone case her other one did, but it was hers. Bought and paid for by the ever-confusing Niall. "I'm all set, thanks."

"When did you do that?" Karma narrowed her eyes in that assessing way of hers.

Hannah needed a subject change and quick. Niall didn't like gossip, and no matter what he said, she suspected he didn't regularly replace his employees' phones.

"You're certain Zig won't mind if I stay one more night? I promise to find another hotel room in the morning. I ran out of time before my shift started."

Karma waved away the concern. "I think Zig likes telling the guys at work he's living with two women. Don't be in a rush. Besides, once your sisters know you're here, they'll probably open up their homes to you. So save your money."

Hannah doubted that Jules, who was getting married today, and Shelley, a newlywed with a child, would want or need another person living in their homes. Even temporarily. Certainly not someone they probably barely remembered.

* * *

Ross strode into the food tent, a brand-new power cord draped over his shoulder and grin on his face. "Got it. Told you I'd be less than ten minutes."

Niall didn't miss the relief in Paulie's eyes. Clearly the chef had been as convinced as he that Ross wouldn't make it back in time, if at all. Paulie closed the distance and took the extension cord. He mumbled something to Ross, but Niall couldn't make it out. Then he hooked up the refrigeration unit.

"Don't everyone thank me at once." Ross's lips thinned. "Problem, big Bro?"

"Nope." Niall paused, then added, "Thank you for getting the cord."

"It's my job, isn't it?" Ross gave Niall his back. "I do know how to do it. Checking up on me again?"

"No. Dawn couldn't make it. I came in her place."

"You could've called. I don't need you here breathing down my neck."

"I also came to bring you these." He opened the bag containing the cake cutter and cake topper. "Miss Renee left them with Dawn. Dawn gave them to me. Do you want to set them out or do you want me to do it?"

"Give 'em here." Ross took the bag, then muttered, "Thanks. But you don't need to be here. I swear I can do this. Without you."

"Niall, can you come help me, son?" Virgil called from the stove. He waved a spatula in the air in a come-here gesture.

"Yeah, go help Virg," Ross intoned, then disappeared through the tent flap.

Niall couldn't win. Ross wanted someone to show gratitude, but when Niall did, all he received from Ross was sarcasm. Fucking outstanding. Niall drove Dawn home, then hustled over here to bring Ross the topper and the cake knife but did he get an ounce of gratitude?

The night had damn well better improve. Or this would be the last one the Boxing Cat would cater. Niall might hate tight places but he fucking despised drama more.

Hannah hurried into the kitchen tent. Her tawny hair was again pulled back in a braid except for the length of pink plaited over one shoulder. She laughed at something Karma said until she saw Niall. When he met her gaze, he swore an arrow went straight into his chest. It was sharp and burning and decidedly not painful. No, he could experience it a thousand times more and still want to feel it again.

"Excuse me," she said to Karma before she crossed the room to him.

"Niall, you gonna help me—?" Virgil began but Karma cut him off.

"I can help, Virg. Tell me what you need." Karma strode over to the stove and, using one arm, turned Virgil back to the stove again. She peeked back over their shoulders and winked at Hannah.

Hannah's cheeks flamed. "Can we talk someplace private?"

Niall led the way out of the tent and around the side of the house. Hannah followed, her face turned up to the sun. Her tawny hair blazed golden red in the late afternoon rays. They stopped a few feet from the driveway. Where they stood, they could see the kitchen tent, but not much else.

"I wanted to thank you for everything you've done for me since I arrived in the city. As promised, here." She pulled a wad of twenties out of her pocket and tried to hand them to him.

Niall tucked his hands behind his back. "I don't want your money, Hannah. They were a gift."

"You always give your staff such extravagant presents?" Hannah countered, again trying to hand him the money. "Those art supplies were high-end. I know supplies and what you gave me cost more than what I lost."

"You and I both know you're not just a staff member." Niall stepped forward and did the one thing he'd promised them both he wouldn't do.

He lowered his head and kissed her.

CHAPTER 18

HANNAH SAW THE move. She knew he was going to kiss her, and she could have waited for him to close the distance. Instead, she lifted onto her toes and brushed her lips against his. And yes, this. This was what she'd been craving since that cold morning last December.

His taste. The feel of his mouth on hers. She inhaled him. She didn't question why or how this moment finally arrived. She didn't worry about what would happen when it ended. She simply reveled in the heady sensation of Niall's mouth on hers.

His hands gripped her hips, pulled her tight against him. She moaned or maybe he did. Or maybe they both did. Who cared? He was kissing her again. Finally.

She drove her hands into his soft hair, pulling him tighter against her. She couldn't get close enough. Air was unnecessary. Breathing inconsequential. All she wanted for the rest of her life was to go on kissing him. Feeling him hard and hot and heavy against her.

And holy schmoley, the man was an encyclopedia of control.

She tugged at his hair, and he growled, kissed her harder, then gentled his touch. The restraint was barely in place. Oh God, what she wouldn't give to see him lose his control. To feel him lose it because of her touch.

"Niall? You out here?" Virgil's voice was better than a bucket of ice water.

Hannah and Niall broke apart like two kids caught doing . . . well, *exactly* what they were doing. She started to giggle. Niall pressed a finger to his lips.

"Yeah, just a sec, Virg," he called out in a roughened throaty voice. His lips swollen with her kisses. His hair mussed. His eyes wild and unfocused. "Sorry," he mouthed. "Shhh."

She clapped a hand over her mouth but couldn't quite stifle the laugh. God, that had been fun. So much better than the first time he'd kissed her and that had been smoldering, rock-your-socks-off hot. This was better. Different. Sexier and more sensual somehow. But Niall's wide-eyed panicked expression kept her giggling.

He pulled her tight against his chest and she laughed into his shoulder.

"Go on in, Virg. This might take a minute," Niall called out, his voice distinctly more in control than before.

"All right. Meet ya back in the tent." Virgil's voice faded.

"Do you think he knew what we were doing?" Hannah asked between snickers.

"If he hadn't before you started cackling, he definitely knew then." Niall's words were clipped, but his eyes were twinkling. "Damn, I've wanted to do that since I found you in my restaurant on Wednesday."

"Yeah?"

"Yes, ma'am." Niall kissed her again.

"Not bagging your groceries." Hannah was pleased when Niall laughed.

Then he had to ruin it by getting serious. He stepped back and kept an arm's length between them. "Hannah, we can't do this here. We can't . . . This is my business."

She nodded. She understood. She really did. But, man, did it suck. "I get it. That was just a one-time thing."

"Oh, hell no." Niall pulled her against him and kissed her again. More power and more passion and even less control than before. Then he put her at arm's length again. "I meant we can't do it here. My staff needs to respect my authority. I can't get that if they think there's any hanky-panky going on."

"Hanky-panky? Marine, you say I have weird expressions." Hannah laughed. "So does this mean you want to . . . ?"

"Yes, ma'am." He put his finger over her lips to stop her from speaking. "And if you make any more references to sex, I'm going to break all my rules and take you right here."

She shivered, grinned, then lightly nipped his finger.

Niall shuddered. "After the reception." He shook his head. "After the cleanup after the reception, I'll take you back to my place. Tell Karma you're sleeping somewhere else tonight."

She tried to ignore the niggle of doubt that he hadn't said *Tell Karma you're sleeping at* my *place tonight*. Instead, she nodded. "Okay. Just remember my rule. Keep calm and carry cond—"

He kissed her again, cutting off her words. When he'd sufficiently kissed her breathless, he whispered, "I've got two boxes."

DURING THE TOAST, Hannah snuck into the reception hall. Shelley and Jules were seated at the head table with their husbands, Dev and Seth. Her sisters looked like they could have been twins despite the three years that separated them. Shelley had blue eyes and was curvier. Jules had green eyes and was an inch taller than Shelley. Otherwise, they were identical. It was uncanny. And a bit unnerving.

They looked like a perfect blend of their parents. Hannah only slightly resembled them. She had the same nose and chin, but otherwise, she looked more like their mother than either of her sisters.

Twice, she started to go to the head table to surprise them. Twice, something got in her way. First it was Sadie demanding that Hannah take drinks to one of the back tables. Then it was Michael dropping a tub full of dishes in the prep tent. She hurried to help him, and by the time she returned, her sisters were on the dance floor.

There never seemed to be the right moment to approach them. And she was enjoying watching them laugh. Soon, she'd introduce herself. But for now, she'd just listen. Maybe learn a little more about them.

"We need you in the food tent. Got to plate up the cake and get it served." Ross was positively glowing. He appeared to be enjoying himself as much as the guests.

"Sure thing, Ross." Hannah headed for the kitchen tent.

"Hannah, you really should think about sticking around. You're a big reason tonight went so well," Ross said, then surprised her with a quick hug. "Think about it. I know Niall said tonight was your last night, but really, you should think about joining the staff permanently."

"When did Niall say that?" Hannah stopped moving, suddenly understanding why Niall had been so *affectionate.*

"Five minutes ago."

Of course he had.

Hannah wasn't sure what to think. Or how to respond. Of course Niall assumed she was still leaving. Maybe that was why he suddenly decided to act on the attraction.

God. Men are so stupid.

"I'll think about it, Ross." Hannah patted him on the arm. She didn't wait for him to respond, there was no need. He'd already told her everything she needed to know anyway.

Hannah strode into the prep tent. Virgil cut the cake while Paulie, Sadie, Karma, and two more servers that had been hired for the night set the pieces on plates. The plates were then loaded onto large serving trays. Hannah joined the line and added plate after plate.

She'd been rolling right along when Sadie bumped into her. Hannah went to catch herself before she fell and ended up throwing out her hands to stop the fall. Her hands fell into two different slices of cake. Chocolate and white icing coated her white gloves.

"Sorry," Sadie said in a completely unapologetic tone before she hefted her tray of desserts onto her shoulder and headed through the tent flap.

The icing was sticky and cold and seeping through the cotton gloves. Hannah yanked them off. She might pity Sadie if the woman didn't try so hard to be unlikable. Ah, well, no sense letting her ruin Hannah's good mood.

Hannah tossed the gloves into the collapsible towel bin near the back of the tent. Then she reached for her tray of desserts. She crossed into the reception tent again. In those few minutes, the sun had gone down and the tent was lit by the hundreds of tiny lights strung from the canopy. It was whimsical and beautiful. And dark.

The flickering candles on the tables didn't lend much light. The lighting was perfect for romance and ambience. Not so great for serving food. But she managed to find her table.

Most of the guests were on the dance floor shaking it to Maroon 5's "Moves Like Jagger." Hannah tapped her toe to the music as she quickly set the desserts at the appropriate places. Flipping her tray under her arm, she half-danced back to the kitchen.

"You're not here to dance. You're here to serve the guests," Sadie snapped in her ear. "No wonder you're only a temp."

Hannah turned to her. "Sadie, what have I ever done to you? Or is your life so incomplete that the only time you feel good about yourself is when you're tearing someone else down?" Hannah put her hand on Sadie's arm. "I'm no threat to you. I think if you spent a little time getting to know me, you might really like me."

"Fat chance, bitch." Sadie had two wide rings on her fingers that connected with Hannah's skin when Sadie tried to pluck Hannah's hand from her sleeve. The instant the metal touched Hannah's skin, she was zapped into Sadie's reality.

The tent and the reception faded to gray smoke around her and Sadie's memory came into raging color.

The tiny apartment was clean, if sparse. But she'd taken the time to prepare a special dinner tonight. They'd been having problems for a while but she could fix it. He'd promised he'd be home right after work. He'd lied. Again. Instead, he'd sent divorce papers.

She propped her elbows on the table and stared at the blue-and-white candles, now burned down nearly to the nubs, flickering in the center of the dining room table. The delicate antique white tablecloth she had picked out hid the scarred secondhand table and added an air of elegance to the space. It looked perfect.

It should have been perfect. She'd even taken the time to make his favorite meal, sirloin tips in sherry. The dinner sat cold and untouched.

Tears tracked down her face. She swiped her cheeks, then wept freely into her hands. When she finally had cried herself out, she scrubbed her face. Her vision still blurry from the crying jag, she stared at the papers in front of her. Divorce papers. He hadn't even had the courtesy to tell her in person. He'd filed for divorce and sent the papers by courier. That bastard. That fucking bastard. He promised nothing would ever change his feelings. Why didn't he love her?

The connection snapped free as Sadie broke the contact.

Hannah stared in her eyes. Eyes filled with so much hate. So much pain.

She wanted to hug her. To promise not all men were like that bastard ex-husband. Two things held her still, the images still swirling through her mind, clouding her sense of self. And the utter disgust on Sadie's face.

"Hannah?" Karma touched her sleeve. "I need your help."

Karma didn't wait, but pulled Hannah out of the tent and into the fresh air.

"I'm Hannah Halloran," Hannah said, trying to ground herself. She wasn't sure how many times she said it before Karma answered her.

"Yes, you are. Are you back now?" Karma pursed her lips and stared intently in Hannah's eyes. "You don't look like you did the other night. What happened? I thought you only got visions from metal."

"She was wearing rings."

"Ah." Karma nodded.

Hannah sucked in a deep breath and blew it out slowly. "Was it really obvious?"

"Only to me." Karma pulled a bottle of water from her apron, twisted off the lid, and handed it to Hannah. "I walked up just as you gave her that awesome come-to-Jesus speech. At first, I thought she'd hurt you because you went very still. It wasn't until I saw your aura shift from orange to muddy red that I realized what was going on. It happened fast. I don't think Sadie would have had a clue even if she knew what you can do."

Hannah sipped the cool water. It washed down her throat, taking with it the remaining strains of Sadie's painful memories. "God, she's had a rough time. So much pain. No wonder she's angry all the time."

Karma shrugged. "Maybe. And maybe some people are just mean and bring meanness on themselves."

Hannah wasn't sure about that. But the universe had given her a glimpse of Sadie's life. There had to be a reason. Question was, what was she supposed to do about it?

She didn't have time to wonder long. The night was wrapping up fast. Jules and Seth were sharing the last dance of the night.

Hannah watched from the tent flap again. She'd just do it. She'd cross the floor, put out her hand, and introduce herself to her sister. It was late enough that she could finally surprise her sisters without taking anything away from Jules's special day.

"We're supposed to be cleaning up, not gawking." Sadie shoved an empty tub at Hannah and stalked off.

Poor lonely, grumpy Sadie. Hannah couldn't muster up the energy to be annoyed. She was too nervous. Too excited about talking to her sisters.

The song ended and Shelley moved to hug Jules.

Hannah started toward them when Sadie was back, grabbing her elbow. "Over here."

Before she could stop her, Sadie had tugged her to the nearest table and started tossing silverware into the tub. A fork bounced out and Hannah caught it out of reflex.

If she'd been thinking, she'd have let it hit the ground. She'd have pulled on her spare gloves. But she hadn't.

The world around her faded to gray again. Like smoke in a glass the present swirled and clouded. Unprepared to have another vision so close to the last one, Hannah could do little more than sink into someone else's consciousness. All the light in the world sucked down to a single flicker of flame.

Red candles were spread around the room. Some large, some small. Some old, some so new the wicks had trouble lighting.

The bed in the center of the room was covered in red satin. Red for passion. Satin for romance. Rose petals were strewn on the bed, the floor, the new IKEA dresser. The stench of roses clung to the thick, hot air. It nearly masked the scent of sex on the rumpled sheets.

A toilet flushed in the other room.

Her heart pounded.

With surprisingly steady hands, she poured another glass of wine. The alcohol masked the drug in his glass. He never asked. Of course he didn't. He didn't care about the drug. She was setting him free. Giving him this one weekend of indulgence, of a glimpse of the life he could never have to be who and what he truly was.

The clock in the bedroom chirped the time. Four in the afternoon.

Mercy sighed. Despair washed through her. Their time was nearly up. In a few hours, she'd suggest they go someplace exciting. A house under construction. One she planned to buy for him. They always liked knowing she wanted to give them things. They always took everything she offered.

Including their freedom.

The bathroom door opened. Brandt sauntered through in that way only a sexy man could. All prowess and power in his sleek, naked body. He rubbed his head as if it pained him.

That simply wouldn't do. No pain. Not yet.

"Here, lover," Mercy said, handing him the wine.

He gulped it greedily.

"Thirsty?" she asked, knowing the answer. Waiting for the change.

He nodded.

She took his manicured hand in hers and led him to the bed. "What you need is a good massage."

He lay on his stomach and Mercy climbed on top of him.

The room vanished, replaced by the image at the construction site.

Brandt sat bound and dead.

Blood ran in rivulets from the wound in his neck, in his chest.

Mercy climbed onto his naked lap and pressed a kiss to his forehead.

Red lipstick stained his skin.

NIALL AVOIDED HANNAH most of the night. Not because he didn't want her. He had a job to do. Respect to maintain. And he didn't trust himself not to haul her back to his place, forsaking his duty. He had to be crazy to even think about spending the night with her again.

This was supposed to be her last night at the Cat. Could he really take her walking out of his life again? He'd survived it the first time because they'd been virtual strangers.

Now he knew more about her. He knew her hopes and dreams. He'd seen her in high temper when she thought he'd insulted her. He'd seen her afraid at the station. He'd seen her in the throes of ecstasy and in moments when her unshakable faith in the universe made her fairy eyes sparkle.

He started to break down the portable kitchen shortly after the cake was served. The sooner they finished, the sooner he could start his night with her.

"Niall!" Ross rushed up behind him, panting for breath. "Come quick. Something's wrong with Hannah."

The stove was half-in and half-out of the truck, he struggled to slide it in but the rubber floor mat kept snagging it. Niall shoved it, only half-caring when he heard the flooring rip. But the stove slid inside.

He followed Ross around the house. He expected to find Hannah in the kitchen tent and was stunned to find her heaving on the grass at the side of the cottage. She was surrounded by Karma, Sadie, Virgil, Paulie, and Michael.

"What happened?" Niall asked Karma, dropping to Hannah's side.

"I'm fine," Hannah managed before retching again. Thank God, someone had the sense to put a five-gallon bucket in front of her or they'd be cleaning up more than usual tonight.

"Right, she sure looks fine," Sadie said under her breath. She leaned her head close to Michael's and whispered, "She probably got into the champagne."

"Everybody back to work," Niall snapped. Sadie didn't want to start tonight. "Karma, you stay put."

"I wasn't going anywhere." Karma knelt beside Hannah and rubbed her back.

"For her head." Virgil handed him a damp dishcloth before he returned to work.

Hannah shook violently but after a few minutes the retching subsided. She sat back, her face pale and shadows smudged beneath her eyes. She took the cloth from him and dabbed her face and mouth.

"What happened?" Niall asked again. "Are you sick?"

"I think she had another vision. Didn't you, Hannah?" Karma moved the bucket away and put her arm around Hannah's waist. "What does that make, two visions inside of ten minutes?"

"Yeah, it was so much worse than the last time." Hannah started to shake. "Mercy was here tonight. She . . . she . . . Mercy was thinking about that guy she killed. God, it was awful. She kept him for days before killing him. Doing things to him."

She clapped a hand over her mouth and lunged for the bucket again.

Karma and Niall exchanged glances over her head. Then looked around.

"I'll take her home," Niall said, forgetting who he was talking to.

"Your place?" Karma quirked an eyebrow. "Niall, I—"

"To rest, Karma. Only rest. Unless you want her puking in your apartment all night." When it looked like Karma might argue with him, Niall slashed a hand through the air. "I'm taking her to my place. End of discussion."

"And if she doesn't want to go with you? You gonna make her, Boss?" Karma's accent got thick and color rose in her cheeks. "She's my friend and family. I should take care of her."

"She's still here," Hannah said weakly. She lifted her head. With her arms draped over the rim of the white container, she looked nearly too exhausted to move, let alone argue. But she wouldn't be ignored. "Karma, I'll be fine."

"Yeah, but—" Karma's words cut off. She cocked her head, then swung her gaze between Hannah and Niall as if connecting something. "Oh."

"Yeah," Hannah said, then dropped her head back on her arms again.

"That settles it," Niall said, pushing to his feet. "Hannah, will you be okay for a few minutes while I get things squared away?"

Hannah nodded against her arms but didn't speak.

Niall left her alone long enough to ensure that Ross and Karma could handle the breakdown and cleanup back at the Boxing Cat.

"She's okay?" Ross asked. "You think she's got what Dawn has?"

Niall shared a glance with Karma. He wasn't sure what Ross knew and didn't want to lie to him, but it wasn't his place to tell the truth either. Niall was saved when Karma answered for him. "It's possible. All we know is that she's sick and needs a ride home."

"I can take her," Ross said, surprising him with the offer. "I promise to take her home and come right back. No stops along the way."

It was a test. Niall knew it. He wanted to let Ross prove he could do what he promised. But not with Hannah.

"I'm driving her, but thanks for the offer."

Ross rolled his tongue over his teeth. "Niall, she's a great employee and a sweet person. You ought to consider letting her stay. Okay, she got sick tonight, but she busted her ass all night right to the end. None of the guests had a clue anything was wrong."

"They never saw a thing," Karma interjected. Niall got her message. No one but the two of them knew why Hannah was really sick.

Niall nodded. "Ross, she said she was only in town for a little while." And damn if that didn't suck. Maybe he could convince her to stay longer.

"Whatevs." Ross shrugged but the look of disgust on his face belied his casual facade. "Look, if you're hell-bent on driving her, then do it. She shouldn't be out there all night. The guests haven't seen her yet, but someone might if she keeps doing vomit-o-rama in the yard."

Crap. He'd failed Ross's test.

"We've got this, Boss." Karma said, confidently. "Ross, if you can give me a ride back, I'll stay until it's all done tonight."

Ross brightened at her offer. "Maybe we can celebrate after?"

"Definitely." Karma grinned. "Let's see if Paulie and the others want to join us. Zig's off tonight. You name the place and we'll be there."

"Later, Bro," Ross said, his voice cooler than it had been only seconds before. "Better take Hannah home."

"Right." Niall started to walk away, then paused. "I can open tomorrow if you want to sleep in, Ross. Good job tonight."

Ross's scowl melted into a surprised smile. "Thanks, man."

"That was nice," Karma said after Ross walked away. She pressed her lips together the way women did after applying lipstick, then she said quietly, so only Niall could hear, "Boss, you know I love you like family, right?"

Niall nodded, uncertain where this conversation was going.

"About Hannah . . . if you fuck with her heart, I'll kick your ass."

CHAPTER 19

NIALL BOLTED UPRIGHT on the couch. He hadn't had time to clean up his guest room since he'd discovered yesterday that hurricane Ross had trashed it. A scream pierced the silence. His heart slammed against his ribs as he stumbled down his darkened hallway to where Hannah slept in his bed.

She lay, curled in the fetal position, her hair a wild tangle of light brown curls around her damp face. Her entire body twitched. She cried out again.

Goddamn. She was still asleep.

Carefully crawling onto the bed, Niall pulled her into his arms. "Shhh . . . You're all right, Hannah. Wake up now."

She stiffened in his embrace, then went limp but she stopped screaming. Silent tears dripped down her cheeks and onto his bare chest.

This was the fourth time in the past two hours she'd woken him with her nightmares. He hadn't pushed her to talk about her vision or the nightmares, but this couldn't continue.

"Hannah? You awake now?" He stroked his hand up and down her back.

"If I say yes, will you let go?"

"Do you want me to?"

"No."

He rested his cheek on the top of her head and smiled. "Then no, I won't let go."

To emphasize the point, he pulled her onto his lap and held her closer. She still trembled from the nightmare, even as she burrowed closer to him.

"Better?"

She nodded.

The scent of honeysuckle invaded his senses. He'd assumed it was a shampoo or a perfume she wore, but it seemed to be her natural scent. She'd showered, brushed her teeth, and donned one of his T-shirts before bed. She shouldn't smell so damned sweet, but she did.

"Sorry I woke you." Her words were muffled with her face pressed against his shoulder.

"I'm not complaining." He rocked her gently. "It might help if you talked about it."

He expected her to say no. To pull away. She was silent so long, he wondered if she had fallen back to sleep. Then she spoke, quietly. Slowly.

"His name was Brandt Branko." Hannah shifted on Niall's lap, resting her head against his shoulder. Her breath warm against his skin. "Mercy didn't just kill him. She drugged and raped him first. It was awful. She has some sort of clock she goes by. She watched him. Hunted him. Stalked him. Then she picked him up at a bar. She promised him paradise. The fuck of a lifetime."

Niall had heard her curse before but not like this. Hannah seemed unaware she'd even said the word.

"She took him back to her place and that's when she drugged him again. God, I wish I had vision bleach to erase the memory. Even though it's faded like the others, I can still see him dead. There are some things you should never see. But her memories were all jumbled. And off, somehow. Like maybe the whole thing wasn't real?"

"What do you mean wasn't real? You think Mercy didn't kill this Branko guy?"

Hannah straightened. Her golden eyes bloodshot from lack of sleep and too much stress. "No, she definitely killed him. But just as the knife came down, there were other faces. A half dozen different men. Some blond, some brunette, one guy had a tattoo of a pentagram on his chest. It was like she was killing them all over and over again. The vision had a surreal effect that made it seem both like a nightmare and a memory smashed together. Like all the guys she killed were the same man, but not. Wait, that doesn't make sense. The only thing that tied everything together were her hands. I could see them gripping the same knife in every kill. But . . ."

"But what?"

"But her hands were wrong."

"How?"

"I don't know. They were just wrong. It's hard to describe." She shuddered. "And there were all of these vicious voices in Mercy's head. Two women kept calling her horrible things. Made her beg for a leniency they never gave. It was like having people screaming inside her mind all the time, except when she plunged the knife. Only then did the voices get quiet. She's really sick and twisted. And I thought I was going to go crazy with her, stuck in that vision. I thought the first time was bad. This was so much worse. I think whoever Mercy is, she needs to be locked up before anyone else gets hurt."

Hannah's eyes brimmed with unshed tears. She worried her braid between her fingers hard enough that strands pulled free.

"You're safe, Hannah. You'll never have to see those visions again." Niall pulled her back into his arms.

"You can't know that, Niall." Hannah stiffened and fought against his hold. "Just because I don't work for you anymore doesn't mean I won't be forced to face Mercy again. There's a reason the universe has put her in my path."

The last thing he wanted was her afraid. "Maybe we should call Tommy. Get his take on it. See if he wants us to take this information to the police?"

"What 'us'?" Hannah slid off the bed and stood several feet away. "You fired me, remember. You told me I could work the wedding and then I needed to find a different job. There's no *us* here, Marine."

He warmed at her pet name for him.

"Yes, there is, Hannah." Niall rose and crossed to her. "You want to have this discussion now and avoid the Mercy topic, that's fine with me."

"I'm not avoiding anything." She folded her arms and stared at him defiantly. "I don't work for you. We both know that's the only reason you wanted to sleep with me tonight. Because you like me. Too much. And it scares the crap out of you. You think you can screw me out of your system. Well, try. It won't work."

"Screw you out of my system?" Niall counted to ten in his head. Still his words came out sharper than he'd have liked. "You're the one who gave me a bogus number."

She waved away his ire. "I already explained that. It wasn't intentional. I wouldn't have written anything down if I hadn't wanted you to call. Think about it, Marine. I could have snuck out and said nothing. You'd have never known the difference. Or I could have kicked you out without anything more than, *well, that happened* but I didn't. I wanted you to call and I was pretty miserable that you didn't."

"Why didn't you try to find me?" Niall wasn't sure what pissed him off more: her blithely dismissing his feelings or the fact that she hadn't ever sought him out. Because he'd sure as hell looked for her.

"Hello! I'm not stupid. You said, 'Good-bye, Hannah,' not *see you around* or *catch you next time I'm in town*. Good. Bye. I do have some dignity. I left it up to you to find me. Then I left it up to the universe. I guess the universe figured I should have a second chance to get to know you. And do you know what I learned? You *don't* want me around because I scare you. And not for the same reason I scared my last boyfriend. You actually seem okay with the whole vision thing. You are afraid because you actually like me! I freak you out because when you're with me, life doesn't suck."

Her cheeks were red and her hands clenched. She panted her fury but her eyes were sparkling. He wasn't sure if he was pissed that she was basically calling him a coward or relieved to hear she was miserable without him too. It made him laugh.

Big mistake.

She uttered a muffled scream of frustration and threw her hands in the air. "You're enjoying this! You like arguing with me."

"Not exactly." But she was right, on both counts. He was enjoying being with her, even now. It sure as hell beat the alternative of not being with her. "But I'm not unhappy to be talking to you like this at this hour."

"Yeah?"

"Yeah!" he shot back.

For a moment she was silent. Then she grinned and said, "I like you. I like talking to you. When I'm around you, I feel free and alive. On the right path. So yes, I am enjoying this too. Don't think I haven't noticed the fact that every time I say you want me, you move a step closer to me. Just like you did right there. If I say it a few more times, you'll be inside me." She laughed. "Ooh, you like that idea too. Your whole body went rigid and not in the offended kind of way. You're turned on. Hard and ready and turned on. Well, guess what, Marine? So am I." She pointed to herself. "I'm right here. If one night is all you want to share with me. Take it. Take me. I want more, but I'll settle for tonight."

He stared in wonder at the tiny spitfire of a woman wearing only his Brown Coats Unite shirt and swallowed hard. He didn't want only one night. He wanted everything. And damn, she was right, he was afraid.

Fuck that.

He was a Marine. Marines don't run from danger. They don't run from fear.

"You gonna do it, Marine? Save me from my nightmares, if only for tonight?" Her eyes were suddenly vulnerable. She needed him. "You gonna spend the night with me?"

Niall slid his hands around her waist, brought her flush against him. Just before he closed his mouth over hers he whispered against her lips, "Yes, ma'am."

NIALL'S NAKED CHEST was hot and smooth beneath her fingers. Hannah could feel his heart pounding against her palm. It raced in time with hers.

He'd called her ma'am again. Judging by the way his grass-green eyes were twinkling, it hadn't been a slip of the tongue.

For all her bold words about being okay with the idea of one night with him, she wanted more. Needed more. But she needed his mouth on hers. His hands on her body. In his arms, she felt safe. Something she was desperate to feel tonight.

He shifted his position, his lips brushing hers but not initiating the kiss.

"Niall, what are you waiting for?" Hannah asked, moving with him. Closer and closer but still not crossing that one line.

"For you, ma'am."

"I'm not a domme," Hannah said with a giggle. "But if I told you to kiss me—"

That was all she managed before he silenced her with a kiss that stole her words, her breath, her freaking mind.

God, yes! Yes!

This had been what she'd wanted. His kiss earlier at the cottage had been nothing compared to the heat and passion of now. He didn't just kiss her, his hands were on her, lifting her in the air.

She wrapped her legs around his waist and he groaned against her lips. His control was splintered. She tasted the way he was trying to rein himself in. Not gonna happen.

Driving her fingers into his hair, she pulled back enough to whisper, "The wall. Take me against the wall."

Niall stumbled. His fingers gripped her hips and thighs hard, but it didn't hurt. "Hannah, you're going to kill me."

"Not tonight." Hannah bit his chin, then his earlobe. "Niall, we're closer to the wall. Take me here. Now."

She rocked her hips against his abdomen. All of her clothes were in his washing machine. The only clothing she had on was his shirt that fell to her knees. Or fell to her knees when she wasn't wrapped around his waist.

Hannah reached between them and patted his rather large bulge. "You're ready, I'm ready."

He made a sound deep in his throat, then kissed her again.

She would have gone on rubbing his impressive erection through his sleep pants, but he tugged her by the wrist. Then they were moving across the room. Toward the bed.

Hannah wasn't exactly disappointed, after all she was going to make love with Niall. Something she had thought she might never do again.

He managed to surprise her when he stopped at his nightstand and yanked open the drawer. Two unopened boxes of condoms were shoved inside. He grabbed one and ripped it open with his teeth.

She started to laugh. She couldn't help it. He'd mangled the box but the accordion of condoms was still inside. "Let me help."

She reached for it and started to tear one off when he said, "Grab the lot."

Then they were moving again. He didn't go far, but he did find some wall space.

"You like it when I tell you what I want?"

"Fuck yes!" He kissed her again with such unrestrained passion that she nearly dropped the condoms. When he pulled back from the kiss, his cheeks were mottled with color and he breathed heavily. "Um . . . excuse me. I meant, I think it's fucking outstanding. Damn." He shook his head.

"If you're apologizing for saying *fuck*, don't." She managed to shove his pants and boxers past his hips. His erection sprang free between them. She quickly unrolled the condom, loving the way his eyes closed and his head lolled back as she gripped him. Squeezing her legs together for leverage, she lifted her hips and held there until his eyes opened. "Just do me."

"Yes. Ma'am," he said, then with excruciating slowness, he slid her down onto his shaft.

Hannah wanted to go faster. To take him in but when she wriggled, the grip on her hips tightened and held her still.

"I don't want to hurt you," he said.

"So not worried." She laughed and tried to move faster.

"Hannah, I'm on the edge here." Niall's eyes were wide and dark. Most of the green had been swallowed by his pupils. "I want you so fucking bad."

"I'm right here, Marine." She kissed his shoulder, his neck, his chin. "Take me now. Hard and fast. I want you. All of you. Don't hold back."

She felt his cock jerk at her words. His eyes went darker.

"You won't hurt me," she whispered. "Do me, Marine."

Love me. But she didn't dare utter those words aloud. They might just make him come to his senses and erect the walls she'd fought hard to bring down.

"Hannah." His eyes softened, some of the green edging back. He let go of her right hip to touch his fingertips to her face. "I never want to hurt you. I-I care about you."

He was in control again. Slowing down, being gentle with her.

She didn't want gentle. She didn't want control. She wanted him, all of him.

Hannah lifted her hips, then let herself drop onto his shaft.

"God!" she cried out at the same time he said, "Fuuahhh."

Then she lifted her hips and slid down on him again. Niall gripped her hips and ass with both of his big hands and controlled her speed.

Or at least, he controlled her speed until she kissed him with all the love and passion she felt for him. He kissed her back with matched intensity. His thrusts quickened. Harder and faster until her head banged against the wall. Somewhere nearby, something fell and shattered.

If Niall heard it, he didn't react. He kissed her mouth, her neck, her shoulder.

Hannah was with him one minute, then flying with such an intense orgasm it sucked the air from her lungs. She'd barely recovered from the first when the second started to build. She wanted to share this amazing feeling with Niall. Leaning forward, she bit his earlobe. Like before, she witnessed his control splinter.

"Hannah!" He cried out her name only moments before she was flying again.

This time was so much better because he was right there with her.

As she sank back to herself, one thing became abundantly clear. They'd been against the wall for quite a while. The muscles in Niall's arms bulged and his knees shook.

Slowly, Niall slid her off of him and lowered her to the floor. He pressed his fists against the wall, panting for breath. Hannah was breathing heavy too but she hadn't been holding another person in the air all that time.

"You're naked," Hannah managed between gasps of air.

"You're not," Niall replied with a sexy half smile.

She glanced down. She still had on his shirt. "Kind of like a love slave fantasy."

"Yes, ma'am," Niall said, pulling off the condom and disposing of it. He kicked his boxers and pajama bottoms into a corner, and gathered the unused condoms from the floor. He dropped them on the nightstand. Then he turned to her. "You know, it's hot the way you boss me around in bed."

"We're not in bed. Yet. But I think that's where you should take me next."

"You think so?" He loped toward her. The sexiness and raw masculinity in his gait made her shiver.

"Oh, yeah," she said, breathily. "Judging by your fast-rising erection, you like that. A lot."

"Oh, yeah," he echoed before gripping her shirt by the hem. "May I?"

She lifted her arms and the shirt was off.

Niall then dropped to his knees in front of her and whispered, "You stole my control."

"You loved it. And so did I." She ran her fingers through his hair.

"It was outstanding." Niall nodded, then leaned forward.

He ran his tongue on the underside of her breast and up across her nipple. He slid two fingers back and forth teasingly across the center of her before sliding them deep inside.

Hannah gasped at the sensation. Her nerve endings were still sensitized from their rigorous lovemaking. She shivered. Her knees went weak, but he cupped her thighs, holding her in place in front of the bed. "Niall, we haven't made it to the bed yet."

He blew warm air across her core and licked her from navel to nub before pulling back. "I see that. I'm not ready for bed."

"Wh-what are you doing?"

Niall lightly nipped her right hip, then her left. All the while letting his fingers slide in and out of her. His thumb circled and pressed against her core in a rhythm so languorous it was driving her mad with desire. When she whimpered in need he chuckled devilishly and said, "Isn't it obvious? You stole my control. It's my turn to steal yours."

CHAPTER 20

HANNAH CURLED AGAINST Niall's back with her arm draped over his waist. She'd tried to sleep but ended up listening to him breathe instead. Reveling in the sensation of him relaxing in her arms. He didn't exactly snore, but he made an adorable little noise. Something she could really get used to hearing.

Holy frack! She couldn't do this to herself. She'd offered him one night, knowing he'd take it. Knowing she had enough self-esteem not to beg for more. But she wanted more. So much more.

Who was she kidding? She didn't have time for more. Her life was in shambles. She'd come to Tidewater to find her sisters. Sisters she had been mere feet from earlier tonight.

Her chest ached. She'd been so close to talking to them. If only Sadie and her freaking visions hadn't gotten in the way. Visions of a murder so vicious that Hannah was afraid to sleep. She let herself grieve for a moment more, then shoved away the disappointment. She was still in town.

There was still time to meet Shelley and Jules. Hannah would make certain nothing interfered again.

Niall shifted in bed, his breath falling on her arm.

Hannah couldn't keep the smile off her face. No, she hadn't accomplished everything yet, but she had found her Marine. And made love to him again, and again. And again.

She ached in places she never had before and yet she still wanted him. She wished he'd wake up and love her again.

"When did you get this?" Niall stroked a finger over the tattoo on her right wrist.

Hannah swallowed back the yelp of surprise. "I thought you were out."

Niall yawned, rolled onto his side, and propped his head on one hand. "I'm a Marine. We sleep light. It's ingrained."

"You're not in the service anymore. Shouldn't you get out of the habit?" She mirrored his pose, then pulled the sheet up to cover her breasts.

"Once a Marine, always a Marine." He tugged the sheet down exposing her nipple again. He fingered it, sending ribbons of shivers through her body. "When did you get inked? You didn't have this last time. I'd remember."

"Oh, uh . . ." she managed when Niall shifted and took the nipple into his mouth. "I-I can't think with you doing that."

He let go with a resounding pop.

"Hey! I didn't say you should stop."

"I'll get back to that. Promise." He danced his fingers over her sensitized skin, then pulled the sheet up. "Let's put those away for now. Too distracting. I want to know about the tattoo."

Hannah tugged the sheet down, teasingly. "Sure you wouldn't rather?"

Niall groaned and lifted her wrist to his mouth. He kissed it lightly, then stared at the three roses. A peculiar look crossed his face. Quietly he asked, "Who's Scott?"

"Jealous?" she teased, then decided it might be better to allay his fears quickly. "It's me. I was born Hannah Eleanor Scott. I didn't become a Halloran until I was three and a half."

He tugged her wrist closer, then rolled away to switch on

the light. In an instant he was back in bed and examining the roses that decorated her skin. "Are there names in the roses?"

"Yes. Mine and my sisters'."

"I thought my tat was detailed but yours . . ." He shook his head. "You didn't ink yourself but did you design it? It looks like a one of a kind."

She smiled in spite of the sadness that always crept inside at the thought of her first mother. "No, my mother did. Remember I said my mother's house was where the Boxing Cat is today? Well, I know that because of a vision I had. In that vision, she had a painting on the wall. Three roses, one yellow, one red, and one purple, all wrapped in a green ribbon. It hung on the wall in her kitchen. That's where the tat came from. Until I had that vision, I didn't even remember the painting. I never wanted to forget it, so I drew it and had it tattooed."

He stroked a thumb down her cheek, his green eyes warm and soft. "Maybe you did it in honor of her too?"

The tide of sadness washed away and she grinned. "Very astute of you, Marine. Is that why you got inked? In honor of Iggy and Danny?"

A tick worked in Niall's jaw. He released her wrist and ran a hand over the large Marines tattoo covering most of his left upper arm. The eagle had a banner in his mouth that read *Semper Fidelis*. The initials D.M. and R.I. were etched on an axis above and below the anchored earth.

Niall was quiet for so long, Hannah feared she'd blown the intimacy and their night together. She struggled to think of a topic change when Niall met her gaze again. In his eyes was a pain so profound, she physically ached for him. "Yes, I did it for them. Do you know what *Semper Fidelis* means?"

She shook her head.

"Always faithful. Like you, I never wanted to forget."

And that was Niall to the core. He'd brought Danny home, had probably done the same for Iggy. Then he'd returned to the Marines to finish out his tour. When that was done, he came home to Tidewater to help his family's business. And somewhere in there, he'd kept his word about calling her. Always faithful.

Now he lay naked, barely covered by a thin sheet, and looking as lost as she'd ever seen him.

Well, she could fix that.

"Hey, Marine, I think I'm done talking for a while." She tugged the sheet down to her waist and crooked her finger. The light in his eyes returned. It was heady, this power she had to turn him on. Although, if she were being honest with herself, he turned her on just as much. "Want to see how fast I can make you come this time?"

"Yes, ma'am." Niall lowered his head and took her breast in his mouth.

"Still not the minister's wife," she managed on a groan. "But I can run to the kitchen and bag your groceries if you prefer."

Niall laughed around her nipple, then rolled his tongue around it.

Her heart hammered, her mind blanked, and her core went wet.

He rolled her onto her back, and nestled himself between her legs. With a loud pop, he let go of her nipple and reached across her body for the condoms. "Clearly I haven't done my job if you're still able to talk. I'll just have to try harder to wear you out. You need your rest."

"You're doing this for me?" she said as he rolled on a fresh condom.

"Yes, ma'am." He thrust into her all the way to the hilt. "I could sleep now but what kind of man would I be to leave you hanging? It's a hard job," he said, sliding out, then back in. "But I'm the right man for the job."

"You're truly an altruist." Hannah gasped as that incredible build started in her midsection. She wanted more. She'd learned their first night together that if she cupped him, he went crazy.

Hannah reached to touch him, but he stopped her by shackling her hands above her head. "Not fast this time, Hannah, let me . . ."

What was he going to say? Let me shag you, ride you, love you? Frack it, she needed to stop analyzing this relationship. She never planned. Never begged. She always waited for the universe to send her a sign. But Niall made her want more.

His rocking hips slowed. He released her wrists and touched her face with his fingertips. "Hey, where'd you go?"

"I'm here." She smiled at him. When he didn't move, she kissed him, then cupped him.

His back arched, and he growled a laugh. "That's dirty pool."

"Show me how you use your cue stick."

He nipped her shoulder, making her laugh. Then he moved again, slow with long, deep strokes. Sensation built higher and higher in her midsection. He had her strung so tight, she thought she might explode from the impending climax. Still, she wanted more. He was so right. While she loved it when he rode her hard and fast, this languid pace of his kept her spinning until finally . . . finally . . . she snapped free. Like the faithful Marine he was, Niall drew out her orgasm, only giving into his own when she was well and completely spent.

His roar of her name was the sweetest music she'd ever heard. Despite their short time together, her heart belonged to a man with a tattoo of fallen Marines, a soul scarred by war, and a heart so guarded, she doubted he even knew how to give it away.

Sinking into sleep she grinned when his arms wrapped around her. He pressed a kiss to her hair. "Sleep now, Hannah. I've got you. Don't worry about the nightmares. I'm right here. I won't let you go."

If only that could last a lifetime.

NIALL HAD ALREADY been up for an hour, showered, dressed, and had made it to the donut shop and back before Hannah opened her eyes. He'd wanted to surprise her with coffee and breakfast in bed, then maybe have another lovemaking session before he had to open the restaurant.

But the damned floor creaked near the end table. She rolled over. He all but threw the food and drinks down as he tried to strip off his shirt before she opened her eyes.

"Where'd you go?" she asked, stretching like a cat. Naked

and unabashed, she let the sheet fall to her waist as she smiled up at him.

"Got breakfast." He gestured to the end table, then toed off his sneakers and climbed onto the bed wearing only his jeans. "Wasn't sure what you'd like so I got a little bit of everything. There's coffee, herbal tea, donuts, hash browns, sausage, eggs, ham, and biscuits."

She blinked at him. Her face alight with pleasure. "You really did think of everything."

Hannah grinned but then glanced around the bed, rolled to her side, and bent over it to peer at the floor, giving him a glimpse of her glorious naked ass. Images of what he could do with her in the position arrowed straight to his cock.

His jeans grew uncomfortably tight. "What're you doing?" His voice cracked like an untried teen's.

"Looking for my shirt," she said, pushing to a sitting position, only to crawl across the bed and bend over it on the other side. This time her ass was close enough to nibble.

He might have gone in for a bite, but she sat back, waving the shirt triumphantly in the air. "Here it is."

The naked goddess disappeared beneath the brown tee. Damn.

"You hungry?" She held out a sausage biscuit.

"Yes, for you." When she laughed, he accepted the food. Okay, new plan. Eat as fast as possible without choking. Then love her all over again. He quickly opened all the food and spread it out on the bed.

"Thank you for last night," Hannah said, then took a bite of the egg sandwich.

Niall didn't know how to respond. He wasn't ready for their time to be over.

"You were right, talking did help." She paused a moment before adding with a grin, "So did the incredible sex."

"Any time." With a start, it occurred to him that he meant it.

Clearly, she didn't believe him, if the doubt on her face was anything to go by. "Well, I do feel better. Not sure what I'm going to do today."

"Stay in bed with me." The words were out of his mouth before he'd even realized he'd given voice to his wish.

"Ooh, don't tempt me." She took another bite of her sandwich. "But I meant, do I go to the police again?"

"No. The last thing you do is go back to the cops." Niall's stomach turned over at the thought of Hannah possibly being arrested. "Hannah, those cops thought you knew too much before. Now you know even more. What can you do, really? The guy's already dead. They've probably identified the body by now. You can't help him."

"What if Mercy kills someone else?" Color washed out of Hannah's cheeks. "If I don't do something, tell someone, it'll be my fault."

"No, it won't. It'll be that psycho's fault." Niall set aside their food and took Hannah's cold hands into his. "You told me last night that you know that Mercy is crazy. Crazy and a killer. What if Mercy finds out you're going to the cops with information? Right now, you can't identify her. That psycho could come after you. And I wouldn't know how to protect you."

"Protect me? I do a pretty good job of that all by myself, thanks. So, what? I'm supposed to do nothing? Pretend I didn't have those visions?" She tugged free of his grasp and shrugged. "I don't know what I'm doing. The signs are all messed up. I have no place to live, no job, and I still haven't managed to meet the sisters who I came to find. I need time to think. Time to get my head on straight."

"Come with me to the Boxing Cat," Niall said, surprising them both. But it made sense. If she were with him, she'd be safe-ish.

"You fired me," she reminded him, then sighed. "Crap! This isn't even my shirt. It's yours."

"I didn't fire you."

Hannah arched an eyebrow and stared at him silently.

"Okay, yes, I thought your last day would be yesterday. When I said that I wouldn't need you past Saturday—"

"You thought I was a stalker who'd given you a fake phone number, then hunted you down." She rolled her eyes.

"Doesn't say much for your opinion of me, does it? And still I slept with you."

Niall pulled her into his arms and kissed her until she melted against him. "Doesn't say much for my logic. You baffle me, Hannah. You're all about signs and visions. I'm not like you. I'm serious and grim. You're sunshine and paintings of blue owls. It seemed impossible to me that you were real. The bogus phone number made sense in a twisted way. Like that one night together was all that was meant to be. Then you showed up and sent my world spinning. I was wrong to push you away. I know that now."

Hannah reclined back on her elbows and grinned up at him. "I told you, you like me. A lot."

She managed to surprise a short laugh out of him. "Yes, I suppose I do."

"Ouch, must have hurt to admit that." Her eyes twinkled for a moment, then she sighed. "That still doesn't fix my problems. Mercy. A place to live. A job."

Niall shoved the food wrappers off the bed, then crawled toward Hannah. He straddled her naked thighs and pressed a kiss against her neck. "Come back to the Cat. I know it's not an electrician's job, but it's a steady paycheck for as long as you're in Tidewater."

She worried her pink braid between her fingers, then nodded. "Okay, that's one problem down. Now I need to figure out the Mercy problem and a place to live. Oh, and my sisters. I still need to get in touch with them."

He didn't even want to think about Hannah going near anything associated with a psychopath, and skipped to the next problem. "You've got a phone, you can call your sisters later today. As for a place to live, stay with Karma a few more days. Or . . . Or you can stay here. With me."

"Stay here?" she said breathily. He wasn't sure if her heightened response was due to his words or his fingers gliding inside her hot, slick body. And he was quickly losing interest in the conversation. Not that it wasn't important, but he'd already settled the discussion in his head.

"Yes," he said, then lowered his head to suck on her breast

through the cotton shirt. "Now say you'll do it, so we can get back to more important things."

She arched her back, and moaned.

It wasn't exactly a resounding note of agreement, but it worked for him.

MERCY SLIPPED QUIETLY from the bed. She crouched down and tugged her box from beneath the bed. Inside were all of her prized possessions. Her mother's wedding rings, her father's signed Babe Ruth baseball, her first driver's license, the red silk scarf she'd taken from her sister's dead body, her police-issue handcuffs, syringes filled with morphine, and the pictures of all the lovers she'd set free. Soon, she'd add another picture to the collection.

Carefully, she removed the cuffs, and crept back to the bed where he lay naked on his stomach. Sunlight peeked through the dark red curtains and cut a swath across his perfect golden back. His face buried in the pillow he clutched with both hands. Swiftly, she closed one metal bracelet on his right wrist.

He exhaled a loud snore and turned his head.

Mercy's heart hammered. She froze. One cuff on him, one still loose in her fingers. Had she not given him enough of the drug? Was it already wearing off? She knew he drank to excess; would that affect his body's metabolism with her love potion?

Time stretched on. She lived and died a hundred times over, waiting for him to wake and fight her. She was too far away from the syringes. Her breath caught and held on to an inhale until her chest ached.

He didn't wake.

She exhaled slowly.

He still didn't wake.

With steady hands, she locked his other wrist. When he didn't move, she grabbed a syringe and plunged it into his thigh. He did wake then. His eyes wide and filled with terror briefly before he blinked once, twice, three times. His eyes glazed over . . . Closed.

Now she was safe. She pushed up the wooden headboard until it revealed the hook and length of chain in the wall. Mercy wasted no time padlocking the cuffs to the wall chain, then lowered the headboard again.

Sliding her Italian scarf from the box, she wrapped it around his head and across his mouth. On the off chance he woke before she returned, he wouldn't be able to scream.

She made quick work of binding his ankles, then stretched out on the bed facing her sleeping lover.

"I'll be back soon, then we'll have our first official date tonight." She stroked a hand down his face. "Tomorrow night, we'll both be free."

CHAPTER 21

"YOU COMING?" NIALL asked her, as he held open the Cat's back door.

"Go on in. I need to make a couple phone calls." Hannah tugged the phone he'd given her along with the wad of twenties from her pocket. "Thank you again for this, Niall. I wish you'd take the money for the phone and clothes."

"Don't worry about it." He pushed the bills back at her. His black brows drew together and he hunched his shoulders. "I didn't do it so you could pay me back. You said yourself you don't have much money right now. I've got plenty. Giving it to you isn't that big of a deal."

"It is to me." She tucked the phone away again.

He shrugged and drove his hands into his pockets. "You're so damned stubborn."

"Yeah, it's one of the things you like about me." She waited until he grinned back at her, then said, "You've gone out of your way to help me the past couple of days. I don't see you getting much out of it."

"Last night was worth it." The flare of desire in his eyes made her cheeks heat. "And tonight. And as long as you want to stay with me."

"Stay with you?" she repeated in wonder. Sure, they'd talked about it, but that was before they were at the restaurant. "Somehow I thought you'd have changed your mind by now."

"What would make you think that?" He kissed her again. Kissed her like he had last night. Like he had this morning. It was a kiss of promise. If only that could last. But it couldn't. All too soon, he ended their embrace.

Karma appeared at the screen door. Niall wouldn't be happy to know they'd been seen.

Hannah stepped back and gestured to the back door. "Employer and employee, remember."

Niall tossed a glance over his shoulder, as if considering. He turned back and rested his hands on her shoulders. "I have never dated one of my employees." He winked. "Before you."

Then he kissed her. Slow and deep.

Hannah swore the strength of that kissed turned her knees to jelly.

It was a kiss filled with passion.

When he finally pulled back, his cheeks were mottled and he was panting as hard as she. "You make me want to break all of my rules."

She arched an eyebrow. "Oh, really? Is there another rule you're thinking of breaking?"

"The one about no sex in the parking lot." He paused, then frowned. "But it's too early to do that. We should wait until it's dark outside."

She shivered at the heated promise twinkling in his eyes.

"Protecting my honor?" she teased.

"Always," he replied, caressing her cheek with the backs of his fingers.

Her heart skipped a beat. "Broad daylight or not, that could be a lot of fun."

He groaned. "Go make your calls. I'll be inside if you need me." He started to walk away, then pivoted on his heel, tugging something from the pocket of his navy slacks. "I washed your gloves last night."

"You know, for a Marine, you're more like an Eagle Scout. Always prepared." She slipped the soft cotton onto her hands.

"I was an Eagle Scout too." He winked, then headed inside.

Hannah couldn't stop smiling. Niall wanted her to stay. At the restaurant. With him. Maybe not with him forever but the signs were there that he would eventually want her to stay longer. Not that she'd slip and tell him that. It might just have him retreating and that would break her heart. Or break his. Because she had a life back in Ohio. One she needed to get back to at the end of the summer.

Although with each passing day, it was getting harder to picture living in Fincastle again.

For now, she needed to focus on the present. The present involved getting in touch with her sisters and solving the Mercy problem.

She'd figured out who to talk to about Mercy while Niall had been in the shower this morning. It came to her in a flash: Ryan and Ian. They'd believed her and located the body. Maybe they'd believe her again, but this time talk to her before they went to the police.

She dug their business card out of her pocket and dialed the number.

"Tidewater Security Specialists, this is Ian."

"Hi, Ian. It's Hannah Halloran—" Hannah began but was cut off.

"Hannah, are you all right?" Ian asked in a rush. "We came to the kitchen tent to find you last night but the staff said you were ill and had to leave. Are you better today?"

"Yes, I'm fine. It's not what you think. Actually, it's the reason I'm calling. I need to talk to you and Ryan. I had another vision." Hannah glanced up as Sadie drove into the parking lot.

The gray compact car had so many scratches and dents, it looked like it was held together by paint and sheer will alone. Michael sat hunched in the passenger seat, while Sadie appeared to be talking rapidly in the driver's seat.

Hannah turned her back on the couple and continued her

conversation. "Can you guys meet me at the Boxing Cat this afternoon? I might have more information. I don't want to get into it on the phone."

"Definitely." His tone had changed from friendly to serious in a single word. "I have an appointment in an hour but I can grab Ryan and be at the restaurant by three. Will that work?"

"Yes, thank you." Hannah was aware of three voices filtering through the air behind her. She glanced over her shoulder to see Dawn lumbering out of the back of Sadie's car. Hannah faced the back door again. "And, Ian, promise me you won't take this to the cops without talking to me first. I don't want to spend another night at the station."

"My word on that." Ian got quiet for a moment, then added, "I apologize for that. We . . . *I* forgot that Dev wouldn't be at the station that day. You can count on us, Hannah."

She smiled at the sincerity in his words. "I know that. Thank you."

Hannah ended the conversation seconds before Dawn spoke to her. "Feeling better? I hope I didn't give you my kid's stomach bug. I heard you had to leave the reception last night."

"Not before she left us a mess to clean up," Sadie sneered.

"Lighten up, Sadie." Michael's hair hung in front of his eyes as usual, so it was difficult to know where he was looking, but he seemed to be looking at Hannah. "It's not like she planned to be ill. You look better today. Got color back in your face."

"I feel better, Michael. Thanks."

He gave her a brief smile, then filed into the kitchen behind Sadie and Dawn.

Hannah waited for them to go inside before she called her parents. She hadn't talked to them since before her interrogation by the police. As expected, her mother was thrilled with the call. Her father was worried about her safety. At one point, he sounded ready to board a plane and fly down to bring her home. With her mother's help, she managed to convince him she was fine. She wasn't in danger. She had a safe place to sleep, a job, and clothes to wear. When they asked about her sisters—her actual reason for coming to Tidewater—she had to admit she hadn't met them yet.

Hannah almost confessed about last night's vision when she had the strangest sensation she was being watched. She glanced around the parking lot. She was the only one there. But the feeling wouldn't go away.

A very real fear that perhaps Mercy might be somewhere close had her ending the conversation with a promise to call again soon. She hurried to the back door, thankful that Niall had taken the time to wash her gloves for her. And doubly thankful that he waited only a few feet away.

"NIALL?"

He glanced down from the ladder where he was replacing a light bulb in the pantry to find his manager looking fresh and bright. "What can I do for you, Karma?"

"I need to borrow your office for a few minutes. My cousins are on their way and we have a surprise for Hannah. I don't want to spring this on her in the middle of the Master Room. Think you can cover the front for a few minutes?"

Niall twisted the bulb into place and climbed down. He tossed the bad bulb into the trash, then collapsed the ladder. He moved a little more quickly than he normally would have but she was blocking the exit. The walls were closing in. Leaning the ladder against the wall, he sidled past her and into the kitchen.

Inhaling deeply, his body relaxed even as the aromas of spices mingled with waffles around him. "Are these the same cousins who were here the other day?"

"Yes." She glanced around, then stepped closer to him, lowering her voice to a whisper. "They're bringing her sister Shelley with them."

Niall understood the importance of the event for Hannah. He wanted to be in the room with her when she saw Shelley again, but there's no way he could squeeze into his office with five other people. His head might explode. Still, he could watch from the doorway.

"And you need me to cover your station because . . . ?"

"She's family." When Niall stared at Karma in confusion she continued, "Shelley's married to my cousin Dev."

"Karma, you have so many cousins, I can't really keep track." He was only half-kidding. "Which cousin is this?"

"Very funny, Boss." She made a face at him. "Can I help it if the McKinnon clan are really fertile? Well, yes, I can help it in my case." She waved a hand through the air. "Anyway, Dev's the detective who helped solve the Diamond Gang case and those murders last fall in Elkridge."

"So where was he the other night when Hannah was being grilled for hours?" Niall hadn't meant for his tone to sound so sharp, but dammit, he'd seen how shaken Hannah had been the next morning.

"That wasn't my fault. We forgot that Dev had taken vacation days and was out of town that night." Karma paused and cocked her head to one side as if noticing mustard on his tie.

Niall glanced down to make sure his shirt was clean and that he was not in fact wearing a tie. "What?"

"Your aura is all green." She whistled. "Ooh, you've got it bad for her, don't you? You've got the whole protective thing going for Hannah." She squinted her eyes and stepped closer. "Oh my God! You're—"

He didn't get to find out what she thought he was because someone knocked on the back door.

"That's them. So can you cover the front for me, Boss? Won't take long, I just want to make sure my cousin's all set."

"Dev?"

She laughed and hurried to the back door. "No, Hannah."

He followed her out of the pantry, slightly startled by the revelation. If Hannah was Dev's sister-in-law, Niall supposed the McKinnon clan would claim her. For a powerful family, they had a habit of collecting kin.

Karma threw her arms around a bear of a man who stood next to a curvaceous redhead. Behind them the giant and the actor look-alike waited.

"Karma, waffles are up," Virgil said over his shoulder.

"I got it, Karma." Niall loaded the plates on a tray for table six. "I'll send Hannah to the office."

"Thanks, Boss!"

For the past two days, Niall had believed Hannah had needed him. That she was alone in the city searching for sisters she hardly remembered. Instead, she was part of a huge family, whether she knew it or not.

He searched for the relief he expected to feel and found only a vague sense of unease. If she didn't need him to help her get on her feet in this city, what did a too-serious Marine have to offer a free-spirited fairy?

HANNAH HADN'T KNOWN what to expect when Niall had sent her to his office. At first, she hoped her Marine might be looking to break another rule. One that involved his office chair. But was quickly disabused of the notion when he didn't follow her.

Virgil was at his station in the kitchen.

"Paulie still hasn't come into work this morning, Virgil?" Hannah asked, glancing at Karma standing in the doorway of the office.

"No. I hope he didn't get that virus y'all had yesterday. He's all alone, with no woman to take care of him." Virgil shook his head, then flipped the pancakes on the griddle. He glanced at her and winked. "Go on in, Hannah. They're waiting for ya."

Karma crossed the kitchen and took Hannah by the arm. "Ian and Ryan called me. They came early to see you."

"Oh, but shouldn't we cover the front?"

"Nah, Sadie and Dawn are out there plus Niall's got it covered. He said we could use his office. Come on."

Hannah let Karma pull her across the room. There was something downright giddy in Karma's demeanor. "You seem awfully happy this morning."

"You have no idea." Karma pulled Hannah's gloves off her hands and tucked them in Hannah's apron. "You won't need these."

Before Hannah could ask why, Karma pushed her through the office doorway.

Hannah swallowed.

A familiar redhead sat in the only chair, surrounded shoulder to shoulder by three very tall men. All of whom Hannah recognized instantly. The woman fiddled with the hem of her pencil skirt, a nervous smile on her face.

Before Hannah could move, Shelley leapt to her feet, her hand extended. "Hi, Hannah. You might not remember me, but I'm your sister—"

"Shelley." Hannah closed the distance and took the proffered hand. It was awkward shaking hands with the first blood relative she'd met in almost twenty years, but Hannah sensed the other woman's unease. "I saw you last night at Jules's wedding. I wanted to come introduce myself then, but well, that didn't happen."

Then in an instant, the awkward handshake became a psychic link forged by the wedding rings on Shelley's hands.

The room faded to smoky gray.

Shelley stood behind Jules, staring into a full-length mirror.

Jules's wedding gown sparkled in the reflection. Shelley wrapped her arms around Jules's waist and rested her chin on her sister's shoulder. "You're so beautiful."

"You only say that because I look like you," Jules teased, then ruined the joke by sniffling.

"Momma would have loved to have been here." Shelley stared in amazement at the reflection staring back at her. She was with Jules again. She had a family of her own now thanks to Dev and Beau. And thanks to Dev she had Jules back in her life.

"I just wish they could have found Hannah," Jules said, her wide emerald eyes misted with unshed tears. "Listen to me getting all weepy wishing for things. It's my wedding day. I should be thrilled. Overjoyed. Not wishing for more."

Shelley debated telling Jules about what Beau's newfound dog had shown her in a telepathic link earlier that day. That Hannah was somewhere in Tidewater. She opened her mouth but Jules cut her off.

"No, don't say it. I'm happy. Really happy. You're here.

Seth is waiting to marry me in a few minutes. And they found you, they'll find Hannah too. Just not today."

The connection snapped.

Hannah watched the scene in the bridal room fade away and the office come back to full color. The men and Shelley were all staring at her. And she still had her hand hanging in the air.

She dropped her arm and tried to center herself. The people around her spoke but their words were garbled like words spoken underwater. Hannah closed her eyes and whispered to herself, "I'm Hannah Halloran. Hannah. Halloran."

It took another moment for her to realize the chatter around her had stopped. She could hear bacon sizzling on the grill, smell the frying meat, waffles, and cinnamon in the air. Finally, she opened her eyes to find herself alone in the office with Shelley.

"You back with me?" Shelley asked, offering Hannah the chair.

Hannah gestured for her to take the seat. "I'm fine standing. Sorry, I didn't mean to startle you."

"You didn't. But I figured you'd like some privacy. I think we freak out Ian and Ryan," Shelley said with a grin.

"Oh, not as much as you'd believe. Did you know that many of the women in their family have some sort of psychic gift?" Hannah nodded at her sister's stunned expression. Her. Sister. It hardly seemed real. "Yeah, Karma sees auras and she told me about an aunt they have who reads fortunes in bowls of vodka. But I'm not sure I believe that story."

Shelley laughed, her blue eyes shining.

A lump formed in Hannah's throat, making speaking and laughing suddenly difficult. "You both really wanted to find me? I thought when I came in that you didn't. You seemed so nervous. Then that handshake."

Shelley's eyes brimmed with tears but she swatted the air. "God, don't pay attention to me. I'm the serious one in the family. I tend to retreat to formal mode when I'm nervous."

"No," Hannah said, moving closer to her. She sat on the desk next to Shelley's chair. "You don't understand. When you shook my hand, I got a vision. I saw you staring in a mirror at Jules's wedding. I heard you two talking about me." Hannah had to pause to collect herself. "I didn't just see you, I was you for a moment. I felt everything you did in that vision. And wow! I'm going to get all watery and wishy-washy, because on the one hand I don't know you guys, and yet, after being in your head, I feel like I do. Sounds nuts, right?"

Shelley gaped. "You can read my mind? Do you do that with everyone you meet?"

"Whoa. No, I'm not a mind reader." Hannah quickly explained her abilities and pulled out the gloves Niall had bought for her.

Shelley visibly relaxed. "Jules is never going to believe this. We've wondered for years what form of the Scott crift you had."

"Crift?"

Her sister's blue eyes twinkled. "It's what Jules and I called our abilities. You probably don't remember that."

"Not really." Hannah shook her head. "I remember coloring in a coloring book. The Little Mermaid. She had red hair just like you. But even that memory is hazy."

"What else do you remember?" Shelley crossed one knee over the other, then frowned. "I forgot I got dressed up to meet you. I usually wear jeans and button-downs."

Hannah gestured to her uniform. "I know what you mean. This is so not me. I'm more your peasant skirt and blouse kind of girl."

"Just like Momma."

And in that single sentence, Hannah found what she'd been looking for. A link to her past and to her future.

CHAPTER 22

NOT LONG AFTER Hannah disappeared into the back, Karma reappeared.

"She's talking to her sister, so my cousins are going to get a bite to eat." She gestured to the men seated at table four. "I'll serve them."

With nothing else to do, Niall returned to the kitchen. He manned Paulie's stove and helped Virgil with the orders.

"Where is that boy?" Virgil asked, agitation in his tone. "Ain't like Paulie to be late and not call."

Niall split his attention between his head chef and the closed office door. "Has anyone called him?"

"Karma's done it twice. No answer. No answer from Ross neither. Hope those boys didn't get the bug that's going around."

"Uh-huh," Niall agreed, not really listening to the old man. Then Virgil's word sank in.

Niall *hadn't* seen Ross all day either. Hell, he hadn't even noticed his brother's absence. At first, he'd been riding high after last night's lovemaking with Hannah.

Not that he was his brother's keeper but he sure as hell should have noticed the fact he wasn't around all day on a Sunday. Did that make him eligible for brother of the year or employer of the year?

No, it made him a fucking tired human.

Dragging a hand down his face, he sighed. "I'll go give Paulie and Ross a call, Virgil."

"Flip them jacks over first," Virgil said, a note of humor in his voice.

He turned the pancakes on the stove, then took two steps toward the office and remembered why he hadn't gone in already. Hannah was in there with her sister.

Niall might have felt guilty for eavesdropping if he'd actually heard anything. But the door was closed and their muffled conversation barely filtered through the wood.

Earlier, he'd worried that Hannah might be hurt or disappointed if the meeting didn't go as she hoped. What if she found she didn't get along with her sister? What if Hannah took that as a sign to leave?

A foreign pain pinched in the center of his chest.

It was crazy to want her to stay, but hadn't he said that very thing this morning in bed? He did want her to stay. Not only in Tidewater. Not only at the Boxing Cat. Not only in his bed.

In his life.

He shot a look at the still closed door and willed it to open. It remained firmly shut.

"You're burning the pancakes." Virgil took the spatula out of Niall's hand and removed the inedible circles of charred rock from the stove. "Go on in there, Niall."

Niall whipped his gaze to the old man's leathery face. "What?"

"You're burning a hole through the door as wide as these dead flapjacks." Virgil waved the spatula at the office. "Go on, boy. I'm sure she won't mind. And don't look at me like that. A blind man, dead for forty years, could see the way you two kids look at each other." He laughed.

Niall started to deny it but why bother? Virgil was right.

Niall was no good out here when what he really wanted was to be with Hannah. He crossed the short distance to the door in three long strides and rapped his knuckles lightly. "Hannah? May I come in?"

He waited for her response. Instead, the door swung open.

Eyes dancing, Hannah started to reach for his hand, then seemed to think better of it. "Come on in, M—Niall."

He took her hand in his. Her cool fingers were delicate against his large rougher ones, but she squeezed with a grip that would have made a wrestler proud. Bouncing on her toes, she gestured to the redhead from last night's reception. "Niall, this is Dr. Shelley Morgan-Jones. My sister."

Shelley rose from the chair. The statuesque redhead wore a light blue top and dark blue skirt that showcased her body in a way that was both elegant and tasteful. She offered her hand to him. "Pleased to meet you, Mr. Niall."

"Just Niall." He cut a silent gaze at Hannah when she snickered.

Shelley's smile stayed in place as she released his hand but confusion clouded her blue eyes. "Am I missing something?"

"I'll explain later," Hannah promised. She turned to Niall. "Did you know she was coming this morning?"

"Karma told me a few minutes before you found out." Niall barely got the words out when Hannah threw her arms around him in a fierce hug that ended entirely too soon.

"We've been having the most amazing conversation. Did you know my sisters each have abilities like me, only not like me? They call it a crift. Isn't that such a cool word? Crift. Shelley talks to animals. Which makes her the perfect vet. And remember Snoopy? The stray I fed a few days back? He's her dog! Although, he's not too fond of her ferret, Lucy. Gosh, I love ferrets. I can't wait to meet her. And Jules! Guess what she does? She communicates with ghosts. We all have a psychic ability but each one is different. How amazing is that?"

Honestly, he wasn't so sure he agreed, but Hannah was beaming. "Very."

"Best of all, Dev and Seth are detectives at the police

station. Shelley was telling me how they solved murders in two of Tidewater's biggest cases. She thinks if I tell Dev and his cousins about my latest Mercy vision, they might be able to use the information to find the killer."

Niall's gut shriveled. "Hannah, I thought you were going to focus on *other* things after what happened last time."

"Last time?" Shelley said, turning to her sister. "What happened last time?"

THANKS SO MUCH.

Hannah stared at the curious expression on Niall's face. He'd appeared anxious, eager even, when she'd opened the door, now he looked worried. Worried with a touch of severely pissed off.

"I-I got brought in for questioning," Hannah said, turning to Shelley. "Two homicide detectives took me to the station. They didn't believe I had a vision. They thought I must've committed the murder or knew who did."

Hannah didn't like the way her sister's eyes narrowed to slits.

"*Who* brought you in for questioning?" Shelley asked Hannah but was looking at Niall.

"A couple of jerks by the names of—"

"Reynolds and O'Dell," Dev said from the doorway.

He had returned with Ryan and Ian. The three men looked a like a human mountain range squeezing into the doorway. The trio formed a human talking wall as Dev and Ian spoke over each other updating Shelley on the situation.

Hannah shot her gaze to Niall. His face hadn't changed. He still appeared worried and angry but now a bead of sweat trickled down his right temple. His hands were balled into fists and his eyes were going vacant.

Silently, she moved to his side and took his left hand into her right one. For a moment, his hand remained fisted, then his fingers loosened and curled around hers.

This close, Niall's face had a light sheen of perspiration. He swallowed but gave her a weak smile. "Thanks," he said, squeezing her hand lightly.

It wasn't enough.

Niall's eyes darted to the doorway and away again.

He needed his space.

Hannah tugged him by the hand to where the three other men stood. She gestured with her free hand into the office. "I'd feel better if you guys came in."

Ryan didn't wait, but stepped through and crossed the room until his back was against the rack on the far wall. Ian and Dev followed. While they moved to flank Ryan, Hannah led Niall to the open doorway. As usual, he stood with one foot in the office and one foot in the kitchen.

When he exhaled softly, Hannah let go of his hand. She wanted to check on him, ask if he felt better, but didn't dare in front of others. He hid his claustrophobia, and she wouldn't risk calling attention to it. Instead, she started to move away to give him as much space as was possible.

Niall wrapped an arm around her waist and held her back to his front, holding her in place. He lowered his head and whispered a single word, "Thanks."

When he lifted his head again, he addressed the men. "You know the assholes?"

Dev glanced at Ian, who didn't bother to hide his grin, then Dev said, "Yes. They pride themselves on being pricks. They're not bad detectives but toss in anything paranormal and they're useless. They think all psychics are charlatans or crackpots looking to make a dime." Dev leveled his gaze on Hannah. "Did you ask for anything when you spoke to them?"

"No." Hannah was appalled at the idea. "I went on Wednesday night when I had the first vision. I told them about Mercy. What she did. I told them about the knife. About how my visions work. I tried to give them as much information as possible." When no one spoke, Hannah added a bit defensively, "Ask Karma if you don't believe me."

"They believe you. Don't you, Dev?" Shelley said, pushing to her feet and rounding on her husband. "You know she's not making this up."

Hannah hadn't expected her sister to leap to her defense so quickly. She also hadn't expected the sensation of love sweeping through her within minutes of being reunited. But she'd really hoped for it.

The universe wants us back together.

"Shells, I'm not doubting a word she says. I need to make sure I have all the facts," Dev said, then gave his wife a gentle kiss on the cheek.

The love between them was palpable. It warmed her to see it. And warmed her more when Niall gave her a gentle squeeze. She tilted her head back and glanced at his face.

He was bathed in a soft green glow. It flowed from all around him but especially from his eyes. It was beautiful. Hypnotic. Alluring. And pretty seductive.

The kind of seductive that made her want to kick everyone out of the office and show Niall how much fun they could have in a small space. Maybe find a creative way to help him get over his claustrophobia.

His aura, she realized with a start. It was what Karma told her she'd seen. But what did it mean?

"Excuse me," Ian said. "Hannah, what did you mean, your *first* vision?"

Hannah tore her gaze away from Niall of the sexy aura, and focused on Ian. "Oh, I had another one last night at the reception." She glanced at Shelley, who stood in front of Dev, mirroring Hannah and Niall's position. "It's why I didn't get to introduce myself like I had planned." She glanced at her sister. "See, I was going to do it right after the cake was served. I was going to show you our mother's locket, so you'd know it was me."

"Hannah, you look just like Momma," Shelley said, her voice thick with unshed tears. "We'd have known you anywhere."

Hannah's own eyes misted. "Really?"

Shelley nodded.

"Not to break up the reunion scene, but can we focus a minute?" Ian said. Ryan swatted him in the back of the head, ruffling the man's perfect hair. "Cut it out, Cuz."

"Give them their moment." Ryan's voice was so deep, it sounded like it originated from his toes.

“They had their moment. Ow! Stop that.” Ian rubbed the back of his head.

“Don’t mind them,” Dev said, a smile on his face. “They’re more like brothers than cousins. Comes from their moms being twins.”

“Not the point,” Ryan said. He turned his dark brown eyes on Hannah. “Ian is right. Can you tell us about the second vision?”

Hannah opened her mouth to speak, but Niall cut her off. “That depends on you two. The last time she trusted you, she ended up hauled downtown. How do we know that won’t happen again?”

Hannah tensed in Niall’s arms. If he noticed, he didn’t show it. He held on to her as he spoke, as if he were afraid she might run away. Ha! Like that would happen.

She wasn’t going anywhere. Not when life was getting interesting.

Well, except for the whole crazed psycho killing men with carving knives thing. *That* she could definitely live without.

“They grilled her for hours on the little bit she did see before.” Niall’s voice was sharp and impatient. “She and Karma believed you two would help her. Instead, Hannah spent a night at the station, with men you yourselves describe as pricks.”

“Niall, it’s all right,” Hannah said, moving out of his arms and turning to face him. She kept hold of one of his hands, or maybe he hung on to hers.

“No, he’s right.” Ryan’s voice rumbled like thunder through the room. When she turned to face him he added, “We should have anticipated them. I’m sorry.”

“Cuz, it’s not like we had any idea that the assholes would go after a civilian.”

“We should’ve, Ian. *I* should have. I was a cop. I know how cops think. Especially those two. I should have expected it.” Ryan ran a hand over his bald head and turned to Hannah. “I promise you, we will do whatever it takes to keep you out of it this time.”

“And I’m back at work tomorrow,” Dev said, stepping between his cousins. “I’ll keep my eyes and ears open.

Anything that comes in on the case that looks like it might affect you in any way, Hannah, I'll let you know. My cousins are the best PIs—"

"Security specialists," Ryan and Ian said in unison.

"Security specialists," Dev amended with a shake of his head. "In the business. They'll be working around the clock until this case is put to bed."

"Now," Ian clapped his hands together once. "Tell us what you know. So we can catch a killer."

BY THE TIME Ian and Ryan left, Hannah clearly needed five minutes to herself. Niall couldn't deny her a little privacy and offered up his office. After checking to make sure everything was running smoothly out front, he decided to check on her.

"I thought you could use a cup of tea." Niall set the drink on the desk and knocked off a couple of pens in the process.

"Very coordinated." Hannah laughed and bent to collect the pens.

"Maybe it was all part of my plan to get you bent over like that." Humor threaded through Niall's voice, making Hannah laugh.

"Niall, come down here." Her arm stuck up from beneath the desk, waving him closer. "I need you to look at this."

He squatted to her right and peered into the little black hole she'd squeezed into. Sweat trickled down his back. He might be okay locked in the office with her, but not under the desk. "What do you need?"

"Hang on. Is your computer off?"

He glanced at the darkened monitor. "Yes. Why?"

She shuffled out of the space, then sat on her legs holding up an orange plug that had been in the wall. "This is not up to code. If the inspector spotted this, you could be in trouble. If it caught fire, the whole place could go up."

Niall plucked the outlet from her hand. "Ross said the Cat had been rewired and passed inspection. Dammit. I'm gonna kick his ass."

"Wait a sec." She took the piece into her hand again with a gentle smile. "What was this room before? I might have lived next door, but I don't remember much about this place except the rickety front porch that isn't here anymore."

"This used to be a closet, then a pantry or maybe the other way around." He gestured to the area. "Until I came home last month. When I said I needed an office, Ross spent a weekend turning it over."

"That was nice of him."

"Yes, I suppose it was." Why had Niall never thought of it before? Had he ever thanked Ross? Shit, probably not. He should probably call him. Niall nearly pulled out his cell to check on him when Hannah distracted him.

"I think I get what happened. Sometimes when old buildings are rewired, rooms that aren't used for more than closets or pantries get forgotten or ignored." She tossed the adapter in the air and caught it again. "This is a bad shortcut that people take when they don't know better or how to do it properly. I can fix it. I just need to run to the hardware store and grab a few things."

"You want to rewire my office?" He stared at her, amazed and pretty damned impressed with her skills. "Right now?"

"Sure." She beamed at him, then narrowed her gaze at him. "That is unless you'd rather hire a local guy to do it. I mean, I'd understand since you don't know—"

"Go for it," he said, cutting her off and was rewarded with another one of her heart-stopping smiles. "Let me tell Karma where we're going and I'll drive you."

"Don't you need to be here?"

It was his turn to beam. "Lucky coincidence. Sundays are short days. We serve brunch from ten to three, then we're closed until Monday. It's a tradition left over from when my grandparents ran the first Boxing Cat. Plus, Virgil likes to have Sunday dinner with his wife."

"Coincidence, huh?" She grinned at him. "I don't believe in them."

"I know. You're all about signs from the universe. You're even starting to convince me." He clapped his hands together.

"If I'm going to have you rewire my office, the least I can do is buy the supplies. And before you try to shove those twenties at me again, I'll remind you that we paid for the replacement parts when we hired the electricians who rewired the kitchen and the dining rooms."

Hannah traced her tongue over her lips in a move that was far more sensual than she probably realized. "Fair enough. You buy the replacement parts, I'll rewire the office. By six o'clock tonight you'll have an office that's up to code."

Niall helped her to her feet, then slid his arms around her waist. "Hannah Halloran, when you say things like that, you get me so hot."

And since his office door was closed, he decided to show her just how hot.

CHAPTER 23

HANNAH TWISTED THE screwdriver one last time on the cover plate of the newly installed outlet in the office. It hadn't been as quick of a job as it would have been if she'd had her tools from home, but it was complete. And this time done correctly.

She smiled at the shiny new outlet, then shoved out from under the desk. One quick test with the new multimeter she had refused to let Niall pay for, and it was official. But before she could tell Niall his office was up to code, she needed to turn the power to the office back on to run the test.

Hannah stepped over the battery-powered lantern and opened the office door, surprised to find the staff standing around the cleaned kitchen yelling at one another.

"No one took your purse, Sadie." Virgil stepped between Sadie and Michael.

Sadie rounded on the old man. "You calling me a liar? That little bastard asked to borrow my keys to get his precious jacket. I don't see a jacket on his skinny ass, do you?"

"I didn't take your purse. I borrowed the keys you left on the counter and put them back there." Michael's voice was low and raspy. He pointed a shaking finger to the counter beneath the corkboard where a pink poodle key chain sat. "I put them back where I found them. I'm *not* a thief. My jacket is right there." He pointed to a light green raincoat hanging on the wall hook by the back door.

"I didn't see you bring in your purse today," Dawn said, helpfully. "Could it still be in the car?"

"Of course not. I'd never be that stupid. Why are you defending him?" Sadie let out a growl, then pointed a finger at Hannah. "Maybe the new bitch took it. You did. Didn't you? Admit it."

Sadie marched over and poked Hannah in the shoulder. "You took my purse and my money. Everyone knows you've been humping the boss for extra pay."

"Enough!" Virgil yelled, stepping between them. "Sadie, I don't know what's gotten into your brain today, but you'd better pipe down. You're spouting things you know ain't true. This young gal's been working on the wiring in the office. She ain't come out all afternoon. Now whatever you got that's making you so angry, you better'd take it home before you find yourself out of a job."

Sadie narrowed her eyes. "You can't fire me, you rumpled, stupid old man—"

"But I can." Niall's words sliced through the air, cutting off Sadie. He held a small red clutch in the air. "I found this in the bathroom. I think it's yours."

Sadie's face drained of color. "Shit. I took it in there this morning."

"So I guessed." Niall crossed the room and handed her the bag, disappointment and fury warring in his eyes. "Go. Home."

Sadie whipped her gaze around the room, her eyes brimming. "I need this job, Niall."

Niall folded his arms over his chest and sighed. "Everyone go home."

Virgil was the first to obey. He strode to the back door. "Good-night, everybody."

Dawn and Michael followed after him. Neither looking at Sadie. "Come on, Michael. We can catch the bus."

Sadie sniffed but didn't let a single tear fall. The woman was made of iron will. If Hannah hadn't seen Sadie weep in a vision, she'd have thought the woman incapable of it.

"Go home, Sadie," Niall said, holding the back door for her. "You can pick up your check next Friday."

Sadie lifted her chin and was almost through the door when she stopped. "I was wrong to lose my temper."

"Yes. You were," Niall agreed. The resignation in his eyes made Hannah's chest hurt. "I warned you before not to go on the attack with my staff. I've lost too many people to your bad temper. I can't keep you here. No matter how much I might like you."

"Fine." Sadie cleared her throat. "Well, we'll see what Ross has to say. He hired me. I'll only accept being fired by him."

A tick worked in Niall's jaw and his lips thinned. "You want to go to Ross? Fine. Have you seen him today? Neither have I. He's not here, so it's my call. Don't bother picking up your check. I'll have it mailed to you."

Niall gestured for Sadie to continue her exit. When she passed through the door, he tugged it closed and locked it. His movements were quick and jerky. Fury radiated from him.

"You okay, Marine?" Hannah wanted to go to him, but kept her spot.

Niall closed the distance. His eyes softened as he looked at her. Gently he pulled her against him and kissed her. The control and the gentleness of his touch amazed her. She let herself be swept away in the moment. All too soon, he pulled back.

"I'm much better now," he said with a grin. He set his chin on her head and stared at the wall behind her. "Sadie's been here a long time."

Hannah turned in his arms until she faced the corkboard. Aside from the work schedule and various notes posted, there were a dozen pictures. A few faces were unknown to her, but most of the people on the wall were the staff she'd met since coming to work for the Boxing Cat. Some pictures were from holiday parties, some were from what had to be the old restaurant, and there were a couple photos of people smiling outside the current restaurant. Niall plucked one off the wall and held it out to her. "That's from opening day here."

"Ross looks pretty happy." Ross had his arm slung around the necks of Paulie on his left and Michael on his right. Sadie and Dawn had their arms thrown wide and Virgil pretended to box with the cartoon cat on the front lawn. "They all do."

Niall nodded. "Crap. Ross and Paulie didn't show for work today. Now I've fired Sadie. This keeps up and I'll be the only one showing up for work on Monday."

Hannah set the picture on the counter and squeezed Niall into a tight hug. "It'll be okay."

"Is that the universe talking?" He kissed the top of her head.

"Nope. That's all me." She released him. "I'm all finished in your office. Just need to turn the power back on."

"Let me do that." He started away, then pivoted on his heel. "Hannah, thank you."

"Hey, being a waitress is fun, but I get this little rush when I work on wires. All that energy, I guess. So I should be thanking you."

Niall opened his mouth as if to say something, then closed it again. He pivoted once more and left the room.

Hannah returned to the office. The lights flickered on overhead. She grabbed the lantern from the ground and switched it off. Earlier, Niall had pulled it down from a shelf in the office for her. The least she could do was return it.

Now that Niall had explained his office had once been a closet, Hannah could see it. In some ways it still was. A closet with a computer.

She pushed the lantern onto the shelf and had only a moment to regret not donning her gloves. The instant her skin connected with the metal, the world faded to smoke around her.

LIGHT PEEKED FROM under the closet door. The black closet wasn't nearly as scary as the black shadows that moved and blocked the sunshine.

The shadows meant she was back.

She always brought pain with her.

The door swung open. Sunlight poured in blinding streams. Then came the shadow and a vicious shove.

Mercy tripped over the shoes in the closet and banged against the wall hard enough to see stars.

"Stupid, clumsy freak!" Mona cackled. Tall and mean, Mona was supposed to be in charge when Mother was out. Instead, Mona did things. Bad things. Things with matches and pins and the bottoms of Mercy's feet.

If Mercy tried to tell, Mona made up a story. Mercy learned long ago it was better to be silent than to be beaten twice.

"Little freak! Get out of my shoes." Mona snatched up a sparkly blue heel and swung it in the air.

Mercy ducked. Tried not to shake. In the dark, waiting for the blows to begin. Nothing happened.

"Whatcha got in there?" A man's voice spoke.

Mercy looked up to see a beautiful man. He was maybe six years older than Mercy and Mona. His long blond hair was shiny and golden in the sunlight, like a halo. He wore a ratty biker shirt, blue jeans, and cowboy boots. He looked like a fallen angel. Rugged and rough but kind.

"No one, Gray. Let's go back to bed. I can do that thing you like me to do with my mouth." Mona stepped between Mercy and the angel.

"You got a kid in the closet, Mona?" Placing his hands on her shoulders, he pushed her aside, then squatted until he was eye to eye with Mercy. "Well, lookie here. It's not a kid. Why didn't you tell me you had a twin, Moaning Mona."

"Eww, don't call me that. Besides, what do you care what I keep in my closet? That's the freak. Just ignore it. It doesn't understand you anyway. You know, it's not all there." Mona made the cuckoo sign, circling her finger next to her empty head.

Mercy was a lot smarter than Mona or their mother knew. Smart enough to keep quiet and avoid some of the beatings their mother was so fond of giving.

"Shut your bitch mouth. You can't go locking people up in a closet. What is wrong with you?" Gray turned back to Mercy and extended his hand. "Wanna come out?"

His face was mostly shadowed but his voice was gentle.

Mercy started to say yes, but if this was a friend of Mona's he could be trouble. She shook her head.

"You're all tied up. Did Mona do that to you?"

Mercy nodded hesitantly.

"Gra-ay! Come on. I'm horny. Leave the freak alone. My mom'll be back soon and if she finds out I had a guy here, she'll tie me *up in the closet. And you don't want to know what she'll do to you."*

The gray angel ignored her. He did something with his shirt, but it was hard to see, because squatting as he was, the sunshine poured in around him. His hair glowed in the light but his face and his front were hidden in shadows. Mercy squinted but then didn't need to. The scent of chocolate filled the air.

He stretched out his hand. "Come on out and I'll give you something sweet."

Mercy moved into the light. God, he was an angel. Gently, he unwrapped the binding and Mercy's hands were free. Then he even rubbed the ache out of them."There. That feels better, doesn't it?" he asked. "Want a brownie?"

Mercy nodded.

What was he doing with Mona? He was nice.

Mercy was so hungry. She ate the brownie in two bites. It was sweet with a strange aftertaste. Maybe all brownies tasted like that. She couldn't remember the last time she'd had one.

"Good, isn't it?" he asked.

Mercy nodded again. More would have been nice or some water. That stupid closet had been her home since Mona had locked the door at five this morning after Mother had left for work.

"Come with me," he said with a warm smile. "A closet's no place to live. And you're so pretty."

"No! You're mine! You came here with me! Get away from him, you freak!" Mona raged and slapped Mercy again and again until the angel threw her to the floor.

"Stay down or I'll whip your ass. Damn bitch. Don't you ever put your hands on me." With his shoulders hunched and his hands fisted, he looked like an avenging angel. All rage and glory. "You are one fucked-up bitch!"

Mercy loved seeing Mona beaten. Bitch deserved worse. The gray angel was beautiful and terrifying. Something quivered in Mercy's belly. It wasn't fear.

And when he led Mercy to the bed, with Mona still crying on the ground, Mercy tasted love for the first time.

"LET GO," NIALL said, prying the fingers of Hannah's right hand off the vertical pole of the metal rack. He'd heard her scream and come running. He hadn't expected to find her dangling like a seizing doll from his shelving unit.

His heart hammered as he tugged her hand free. She slumped against him, her eyes wide and vacant. "Hannah. Talk to me. Hannah."

What could have sent her into a vision in here? And why had she touched something without wearing her gloves?

Hannah moaned and shifted away from him. She drew her knees to her chest and mumbled her name. "I'm Hannah. Halloran. Hannah. Halloran."

Niall sat down beside her, rubbing her cold hands between his. "Yes. You are. Hannah Halloran." Wishing he could shake her free of the vision that she seemed trapped in, he curled his body around hers. The scent of honeysuckle invaded his senses. Linking his arms around her waist, he rocked her. "Hannah. I'm right here. Wake up now."

She shuddered once, then exhaled a long breath. Leaning against him she whispered, "I'm okay. I'm back."

"You sure?" He pressed a kiss to her hair, faintly surprised by the uptick of his blood pressure when she finally spoke. "Want to talk about it?"

She nodded, then shook her head.

"Not exactly. Gimme a minute. I need to catch my breath. No, don't let go. Please," she said when he started to pull away.

"I'm right here, my fairy queen," he said, hoping to make her laugh.

She turned in his arms to face him. "Your what?"

"My fairy queen." He winked at her. "Hannah of the fairy face and the queen of optimism."

"You're an odd one, Marine." Color was returning to her cheeks. "Anyone ever tell you that?"

He laughed. "Right. You have visions but *I'm* the odd one."

"Got me there." She closed her eyes and rested her forehead on his shoulder. "I need to talk to Ian and Ryan again about Mercy."

"You had another Mercy vision?" Niall's stomach shrank as understanding crept in. He swung his gaze around the tiny office. "In here? You can't honestly think someone at the Cat is a killer?"

Niall's mind wanted to rebel at the idea. He knew these people. Had hired most of them. Worked with some for years.

And yet . . .

Hannah pushed shakily to her feet, then climbed onto the chair. With her head between her knees she gulped air audibly. Finally, she spoke.

"Niall, I know you don't want to believe it but I don't know what else to think. Every vision I've had of Mercy has been in the Boxing Cat. Until now, I thought she was a guest. But you don't let guests in here, do you?"

Niall waited until she lifted her head, her golden-brown eyes huge and shadowed with fear. "No, I don't."

"That's what I thought." Her eyes went vacant again.

"Hannah? Hannah, are you still with me?" He squatted in front of her. As if his hand had a will of its own, he stroked her cheek. When she met his gaze, he breathed easier. She might be frightened, but she was still with him. "There you are."

"Why'd you close the door?"

He glanced at the shut door. "It must have happened when I ran in. I hadn't even noticed." Honestly, he was a bit startled by the revelation. He was in an enclosed space but it didn't evoke the usual bout of suffocating claustrophobia. "Must be because I'm with you. Don't worry about me. I'm fine, love. It's you I'm worried about. Can you tell me about the vision?"

"I can't. Not yet. I don't think I can talk about it more than once. I want to do it with Ryan and Ian here." She turned green. "I think . . . I think I'm going to be sick."

* * *

NIALL HADN'T TAKEN her vision well. Not that Hannah could blame him. But he had agreed to call Ryan and Ian for her. That gave her time to wash her face.

And sent her into a third vision in the bathroom. She was getting pretty tired of seeing scenes through a lunatic's eyes.

Hannah kept rinsing her face in the hopes the cold water could wash away the icky feeling in her chest. The newest vision clung to her with razor-sharp talons. Sliced through her reality. Touching the faucet had been stupid of her, clumsy. It had sent her spiraling further into the vision. Showing her things her brain could never unsee.

Then she did get sick. Horribly, viciously sick.

This time, when she went near the sink, she used a wad of paper towels to avoid touching the metal knobs as she shut off the water.

She stared at her reflection, still seeing the gray angel from Mercy's memory.

"Hannah?" Niall knocked on the door again. "Are you okay? The guys are here."

"I'm better," she said, opening the door. "I think I need some fresh air."

"I thought you might." The worry lines in Niall's face stood out in stark relief. "They're out back waiting for us."

Niall wrapped a hand around hers and led her outside.

Ryan sat on the grass beneath a pink crepe myrtle tree. Ian and Dev shared space on the hood of an expensive-looking Lexus, talking.

"I'd be good to her," Ian said, bumping shoulders with Dev. They made an odd pair on the car. Dev wore a dark three-piece suit with shoes polished to a shine. Ian, nearly his polar opposite, had on a white T-shirt, blue jeans, and sneakers.

"I'm not selling my dad's Charger." Dev pulled the sunglasses off his face and rose to his feet.

"But I helped you rebuild her." Ian hopped off the car, but clearly had not finished arguing his case. "I'm a good driver."

"He said no, rain man," Ryan called out from beneath the tree, then spotting Hannah, pushed to his feet.

Dev laughed and clapped a hand on Ian's shoulder. "Rain man? I thought you were Robin?"

Ian pointed at Ryan. "He's Robin. I'm Batman."

Ryan turned an aggravated glare to Dev. "You had to start that again?"

"I win," Ian said with a grin, turning to Hannah.

"You still don't get the Charger."

He shrugged good-naturedly, then greeted Hannah. "As pretty as you are to look at, Hannah, I'm not sure I understand why we're back so soon. We don't have any information for you yet."

Ian's head snapped forward as if Ryan or Dev had popped him in the back of it. It was impossible to tell which one had done it, since both men stood quietly with their hands in front of them.

Hannah liked these guys. A lot.

"This might take a few minutes. Can we sit down? I'm not feeling my best."

Niall swept his arm wide, gesturing to a picnic table. "Let's sit down over there."

On the far side of the lot, beside the shed, was a wooden table-and-bench set. They each claimed a seat, Niall holding Hannah's hand on one side of the table, Dev, Ryan, and Ian on the other.

Hannah told them about her vision in the office.

"How old was Mercy in the dream?" Ian asked. Like before, he and Ryan wrote notes in separate books. This time, Dev did too.

"It wasn't a dream. It was a vision," Hannah corrected. "I don't have prophetic dreams."

"Sounds like you did this time." All of Ian's playfulness had been replaced by an air of professionalism.

"I guess you're right." Hannah rubbed at the base of her neck, trying to soothe the ache. Niall reached over and rubbed it for her. His touch was a balm to her aching flesh. She tried to think. "Eighteen. Mercy is one of a set of twins. Her sister's name was

Mona. She didn't think of her age but she thought the gray angel was probably six years older than Mona, who was eighteen."

"About how tall were they?" Ian stood up and held up a hand to show height against his ribs. "This tall? Shorter? Taller?"

"Definitely taller, maybe to your shoulders, I think." Hannah closed her eyes, willing herself to remember but it was hard. "Sorry, it's all fuzzy. When I first come out of a vision, it's crystal. Then it gets like a photograph left in the sun. It bleaches out the clarity and the sharpness. If I had to guess, I'd say despite her physical age, Mercy was pretty naive about sex. Old enough to know her sister had a lot of it with different men but Mercy was a virgin when she met the gray angel. It's weird but I think despite being drugged, and she was definitely drugged, she thought she loved him." She shivered. "She really confuses sex and violence with love. The gray angel beat her sister and Mercy was okay with that. Mona was crying on the floor when he took Mercy to bed."

Niall dropped his hand from her neck and interlaced his fingers with hers. "You're okay now."

"There's more," she said with a shake of her head. "I had another vision in the bathroom."

Nothing in Niall's tone or his face showed his annoyance, but his hand tensed in hers.

Ian asked, "Can you tell us about the vision in the bathroom?"

"Okay, give me a sec." She closed her eyes and tried to concentrate. "In that vision Mercy was older. I think it was recent. Like last week or this week. Or maybe even today. She was looking at the man she had taken the night before. He's asleep—drugged, I think—on her bed. She was really mad. Her thoughts were jumbled but something about taking too long to get him into her place. No time to . . ." Hannah widened her eyes intentionally.

"She hasn't raped him yet?" Dev guessed.

"Yeah. And let me tell you, there's something different to her about this one." Hannah bit her lip trying to understand what she'd felt as Mercy. "With the gray angel she thought she loved him. I think in her warped way she's loved everyone she's killed. But this guy, he's really special to her. I think she believes they're soul mates or something. She expects him to love her in return. She actually believes he will love her. Will want to be with her. It's really freaky in her head."

"Can you tell us more about what you saw in the room?" Ian interjected.

"Let's see, uh . . . There's red everywhere. Red sheets, red candles, red curtains. They're drawn by the way. Only a sliver of sunlight gets through between the drapes. Mercy was going for the whole psycho-romantic thing, I think. There are red rose petals all over the bed and the floor." She shivered. "Really never want to see rose petals all over a bed after this."

"Can you see anything else? Any ticket stubs or receipts lying around? Anything to indicate where they are? Did you hear any noises?" Dev kept the questions coming.

Hannah tried to focus on the room again, but without a direct connection, the images were fading. "Okay, windows were covered. Nothing on two walls. On the wall over his head is this month's calendar with today's date circled in red. She's really got a thing for red. Even the poster on the bedroom door is of some band called Red Reedus Live at the NorVa is red."

"There's a poster of Red Reedus on the wall?" Ryan asked, an odd note in his deep, rumbling voice.

Hannah nodded. He glanced at his cousins, but no one spoke, so Hannah continued describing the vision. "Mercy's staring at him from a doorway and she says, "Tonight, we'll both be free."

"Do you think she's going to let him go?" Dev stilled his pen and met her gaze.

"No. No, free is what Mercy thinks she's doing when she kills her victims. Setting them free from life," Hannah said, then watched Dev's expression change. His eyes went flat. Scary flat. The same look she'd seen in the eyes of the two cops who'd questioned her.

"What can you tell me about the victim?" Dev asked in a brisk tone.

"Not much." Hannah shrugged. "I didn't see his face."

Dev and Ian started firing off questions in tandem.

“What was he wearing?”

“What’s his hair color?”

“How tall was he?”

“What’s his race?”

“Did he have any distinguishing marks?”

Hannah bounced her gaze from one man to the other as the questions flew at her. With each question she felt more useless. They needed to find this guy. Fast. And she didn’t feel like she was helping.

“Hannah?” Ian reached across the table and gently cupped his hand over hers. “You still with us?”

She nodded.

Niall put his hand on hers. Ian pulled his back.

Hannah hid the smile that tugged at her lips. Now was not the time to get all marshmallowy over Niall all but claiming her as his.

“Hannah, it’s very important that you tell us everything you can about the victim. That poster you saw is only a week old. So the victim is likely still alive.”

“How do you know that?” Hope tasted like warm caramel in her mouth.

“Because I play drums for Red Reedus,” Ryan said. That was about the last thing she expected to hear from the security specialist who dressed like a rogue biker. “And we only played the NorVa once. Last Saturday.”

“And I read the case reports at the office,” Dev interjected. “There have been eight murders committed by the Construction Site Killer over the past three years. They were all white men, ranging in age from eighteen to thirty-five, and they were all blond. Some had their hair dyed, but they were all blond at TOD. Uh, time of death. So any detail you can give about the victim might save his life.”

“Okay, okay, let me think.” Hannah closed her eyes and tried to remember the room. It came but it was fuzzy, faded. “I can’t tell you more. Unless . . .”

“Unless what?” Niall said, his voice sharp.

“Unless, I go back to the bathroom and try to get the vision again.”

CHAPTER 24

THEY WERE OUTSIDE and yet the walls were closing in. Sweat rolled down Niall's back despite the unseasonably cool, late afternoon breeze. She'd just *offered* to go back into the vision of a serial killer? Was she out of her ever-loving mind?

"Hell no." The words were out of his mouth before he'd even realized he'd spoken aloud.

All eyes turned to him.

Hannah rose from her seat and placed a gentle, cool hand on his cheek. "I need to do this. What if they're right? What if the guy I saw is still alive?"

Dev's cell phone rang out with the Righteous Brothers, "You've Lost That Lovin' Feeling."

The man jumped to his feet. "Sorry, I gotta take this." He turned his back and said, "Hi, Shells."

Hannah still had that sweet, pitying smile on her face. The sight of it seriously twisted his insides when she followed up with, "Niall, can I talk to you for a minute?"

She pulled him by the hand across the parking lot to the crepe myrtle tree. In the late afternoon sunshine her hair looked like flames aglow with a pink braid over one shoulder. "Niall, I can do this. I really can."

"Hannah, you screamed like the hounds of hell were after you." Niall wanted to pull her close, hold her. He crossed his arms instead.

"I'm sorry about scaring you last night but—"

"Not last night. Today. In my office. You screamed and I thought—" He scrubbed his hands through his hair. "I don't know what I thought. But it wasn't good. Now you want to go back in?"

"No, I don't want to go back in. Not ever." Hannah grabbed one of his hands with both of hers. "But I need to. If I saw anything that could help them find this guy before she kills him, I need to. I couldn't live with myself if he died and I didn't even try to help. Could you?"

Ah, Christ.

"No, I suppose I couldn't either." Niall hated this. All of this. "I wish you didn't have to put yourself through this. You should have seen your face when I found you this afternoon. You were terrified. You looked traumatized. I can't tell you how happy I am to hear that your memory of the vision fades after a while."

Hannah's gaze cut to Dev still speaking quietly into his cell.

"Hannah, it does fade, right? You don't remember everything?"

"We should get back to this." She started to walk away but Niall grabbed her arm.

"Don't walk away from me. Talk to me. Tell me the truth." Niall wished with everything he had he could save her from this curse she called a gift. "It does fade?"

She exhaled a breath on a tired sigh. "Once I'm out, yes, it does fade. But while I'm in it. I feel like *I* am fading away. Becoming her . . . Mercy."

"You mean getting the sudden inexplicable urge to slice up men?" Niall said, only half-joking.

She didn't smile.

His gut cramped and the tree they were under seemed to suddenly loom instead of merely providing shade from the harsh late afternoon light.

"Not exactly. More like I'm losing . . . me." She shrugged. "It happens if I stay too long in a vision or if I go into the same one too many times. I have this locket that used to belong to my mother. When I hold it I get a vision of her right after she found out she had cancer. I felt everything she felt from the pain in her chest because of the disease that would eventually kill her to the pain in her chest at finding out my father was a polygamist. I remember that vision clearly because I've gone into it probably twenty times. I can't keep going into it, because one day, I might not come back."

"And you think going into the head of a serial killer is a *good* idea?" Niall paced away from her only to pace back. "You're a smart woman. What happens if you go in and don't come back? Huh? Do you die? Do you go catatonic? Or maybe you just go stark raving fucking mad!"

A few startled birds in the tree above took flight at his words.

Hannah's eyes shimmered with unshed tears. She opened her mouth and Niall waited for her to blast him right back. It would have been well deserved. He made a point never to yell at anyone now that he was out of the service. Five days in her presence and he was already raising his voice.

She lifted a hand and placed it against his heated cheek. "You're so sweet to worry. I'm not foolish. Despite what you think, I'm not naive either. I know the risks. If you don't want to be here when I go back in, then I understand. You don't owe me anything, Marine."

Don't owe her anything?

"Hannah, you couldn't make me leave if you called in shore patrol. My ass is here to protect yours."

"Actually, that's why we're here," Ian said from right behind Niall.

Niall whipped around to find the pair of TSS guys standing close enough to kiss him. Or to try to kick his ass. Dev was farther away, an intense look on his face as he ended his call.

He strode over, tapping the phone against his chin.

"Everything okay with the little woman?" Ian asked with a shit-eating grin. "Need ya to bring home some milk?"

Dev didn't speak until he stood, literally, on Ian's foot. "We've got . . . a concern, you might say."

If his puckered lips were any indication, the concern was going to be a pisser of an issue.

"What?" Ian asked, sliding his foot from beneath his cousin's. He appeared to snap to attention.

Dev turned to Hannah. "That was Shelley on the phone. She got a call from Jules, who had a visitor early this morning. A young man by the name of Brandt. Seems he's worried about a friend yours, Hannah."

"Wh-which one? All my friends are in Ohio." All the color drained from her face. "Except for the ones who work here."

"Do you know someone named Ross?"

"YOU'RE WRONG," NIALL snapped. "Ross is at home."

Hannah reached to touch him, to calm him, but he acted as if she wasn't there. As if he didn't need her.

"When was the last time you saw him?" Dev asked as Ryan and Ian stepped up to flank Niall.

"Last night, at the reception. He was supposed to clean up and meet me here. This morning. He didn't show. But that's not surprising. I told him to sleep in, that I'd cover opening the Cat this morning."

"Did he show up late? Call? Has anybody seen him since the reception?" Ian asked, notebook and pen at the ready.

"No. I-I don't know. That is we, uh . . ." Niall tossed a confused glance at Hannah.

"We didn't get here until late this morning. Virgil opened the restaurant," Hannah answered for him. She wanted to reassure him, but with each passing second the fear mounted. She took his hand in hers. "And Niall and I left around noon to get supplies for a wiring issue."

"Did you call him when he didn't show?" Dev kept the questions coming.

"No, shit. I promised Virgil I'd call Ross and Paulie.

Neither of them showed today, but I got distracted." Niall pulled his hand free of Hannah's and began to pace. "I'll call him now. You'll see, he's sleeping off his latest hangover. He is *not* in fucking danger."

Niall tugged his cell phone from his pocket and pressed it to his ear.

Answer the phone, Ross. Please God. Answer your brother's call.

"It's ringing," Niall said and hope sparked in Hannah's chest. Then he rolled his eyes and her heart sank. "Voice mail. Ross, it's Niall. Call me back."

Niall's green eyes were dull and his face had turned pasty white. "I had to leave him a message . . . Are you sure Jules's visitor was right? I thought the Brandt guy was the name of the dead guy Hannah had a vision about earlier in the week. Maybe Jules got it wrong."

"Niall, I told you earlier about Jules's crift." Hannah forced the words out around the tears clogging her throat. "She talks to ghosts. I doubt she'd get the names wrong. Would she, Dev?"

Niall turned a vacant gaze her way. She opened her mouth to say more but the words wouldn't come.

"You're right, Hannah. She's never wrong when it comes to names. Jules and her ghostly visitors have helped us solve two murders and put us on the path to solving two others," Dev said. "Why don't we go back to the picnic table and have a seat, Niall? You look like you could use it."

Dev reach for Niall but was shrugged away. "I don't want to sit down. I want to find my brother, now."

"We're going to do everything we can—" Ian began but Niall cut him off.

"Fuck that! I'm a Marine. I was an MP. I want in. I want to find this bitch holding my brother."

"We need Hannah to do it," Dev said, nodding to her. "She's given us our best lead yet."

"What about Jules? Does her ghost have any more information?" Niall clapped a hand to his head. "Fuck me. I can't believe I just said that."

"Jules is driving back from her honeymoon right now."

Dev's words surprised Hannah. "She and Seth were supposed to board a plane to Greece this morning from DC but only got as far as Jamestown before the ghostly visits started. As soon as Jules heard the ghost mention your name, she called Shelley, who told her you were in town. Jules made Seth turn around. They'll be here in about two hours."

"We're not going to wait two hours, are we?" Hannah cast a wary glance at Niall, who was steadily pacing a groove into the parking lot.

"No," Ryan said. "We're going to do it now."

CHAPTER 25

HANNAH TRIED NOT to be nervous stepping back into the bathroom. But being followed into a restroom by four big guys, even big guys whose job was to protect you, was intimidating. She flipped on the light and said, "You know, Niall, I could install an energy-saver switch and bulb here. Wouldn't take much time."

"Hannah—" Niall started but Dev cut him off.

"I know you're nervous, Han. You don't need to be. We won't let anything happen to you." He patted her gently on the shoulder.

She couldn't quite suppress the smile. "I haven't been call Han since I was little."

"Oh, sorry. It's what Jules and Shells call you when they talk about the past." Dev glanced at his cousins as if for help, but Ryan's impassive expression never changed and Ian looked mischievous, as usual. "Ready, Hannah?"

"Han's fine. I kind of missed the nickname," she admitted. "Yeah, I'm ready."

At her words, Ian's face hardened. It was unnerving and fascinating. And just a little scary.

She blew out a breath. "Come on, universe. Show me a sign," she said, stretching out her hand toward the faucet.

Before her fingers contacted the metal, Niall put a hand on her wrist, arresting the movement. "You don't have to do this. We can find another way."

"Yes, I do." She met his gaze. A war of emotions raged in his eyes. Fear, anticipation, hope, and despair were all there playing across his face. Then that beautiful green aura began to glow around him. It made her heart swell to the point it nearly choked her. He was afraid for his brother and wanted to protect her. God, she loved this man.

She'd suspected it the night they had met, impossible as it sounded. In this moment, suspicion gave way to truth. She loved him. She'd do anything to erase the loss he'd experienced over the last year. She might not be able to save his friends, but she might be able to save his brother.

"Niall, you need to let me do this. I need to. It's why the universe brought you to me." She moved his hand from her wrist. Before he could stop her, she clamped a hand onto the faucet as she had done earlier.

The world around her faded to light gray smoke.

Behind her came the faint scuffling of shoes on tile. Muffled male voices faded with the room. And she was no longer herself.

Ross sat at the bar sipping his scotch. Mercy couldn't stop her heart from racing. He was beautiful, kind, and so damned lonely. He didn't know what he was. She would show him.

She moved through the crowd at the pub. No one noticed her. No one ever did. Tonight, she counted on it. The only person who needed to see her was Ross. Sliding onto a stool next to him, she palmed the drug in her purse. Just a little in his scotch and he'd go anywhere she suggested. He only needed a little help to be the man he truly was.

Just like her first time. The brownie had helped her to see what she was.

She'd be gentle with Ross, as she'd been with the others. Wait for him to come to her. Show him he could be loved. Show him they were soul mates. After they made love, she'd set them both free.

She signaled the bartender. He strutted over and leaned on the bar.

"What'll it be tonight?" he asked. He might have been cut with that tight powder-blue shirt with O'Reilly's Pub emblazoned across the center of his chest, but he wasn't her type.

"Stoli Martini, extra dirty with three olives," Mercy said.

She felt more than saw Ross shift on the seat and face her. Pretending not to notice, she waited for her drink, setting the cash on the bar. Mr. T-shirt returned with her drink and swept up the money in one deft move. She held the drink with one hand, being careful to keep the other one with the drug out of view. No one could see what she held there and she needed the distraction.

She hated the costume but it was a necessary evil. Anyone who bothered to remember seeing Ross tonight would only remember a woman leaving with him.

Sipping her drink, she glanced at Ross.

He nodded at her, an impersonal smile on his face. The grin gave way to surprise. He opened his mouth to speak, but she put her finger to his lips. "Shhh . . . our secret, okay?"

Ross glanced around the pub.

Mercy didn't hesitate. She dropped the drug into his scotch. It had already dissolved by the time he'd glanced back at her.

She sipped her martini again, giving him her most innocent face.

"I had no idea I'd see you here tonight," Ross said, lifting his own glass to his lips. "You're the dead last person I ever expected to find in the pub dressed like that."

Mercy shrugged, pretending his words didn't hurt. How could he not have known? She'd known him the moment he'd hired her at the Boxing Cat.

Her mother's awful voice screamed through her mind, "Stupid freak! I should have had an abortion."

Go away! Go away!

Then her sister's voice rang out, "You stole my boyfriend. I told you, Mom. The freak's a whore!"

I killed you once you fucking bitch. Why won't you die?

"Hey? You okay?" Ross covered her hand with his. His touch silenced the voices in her head until she only heard him. "You look a little ill. Do you want to get out of here? Go somewhere and talk?"

Mercy's heart leapt.

Maybe she hadn't needed to drug him after all. He was already offering to leave with her. She didn't trust her voice not to crack and simply nodded.

During the short walk from the pub to her first-floor apartment on Arctic Circle, Mercy let Ross do most of the talking. He was still riding high from the success of the catering event. "The bride loved everything. We've got to remember to hire an extra couple of servers if the next wedding we cater is that big."

He swayed and cradled his head in his hands.

"You all right?" Mercy asked, fishing her key from her purse.

"Yeah, too much celebrating, I guess." He reached for her, missed, and face-planted into the sidewalk. Rolling onto his back, he laughed. "Crap. Niall's going to kick my ass if I show up hungover tomorrow."

Mercy bent to help him up and into her apartment when someone called out.

"Ross?" Paulie came around the corner. "What are you doing?"

Mercy gave him her back. She couldn't risk him seeing her face. One look and he'd know.

Stupid interfering bastard.

"I've got him," Mercy whispered, letting her blond hair fall in front of her face. "Thank you, sir," she said, pretending not to know Paulie.

"Hey, Paulie!" Ross threw his arms around the man. When he kissed Paulie on the lips, Mercy's vision went bloodred. She'd planned to let Paulie go. Not anymore.

"Actually, if you could hold him while I open the door," Mercy said, using a sugary tone that made her own teeth ache.

"You're going in there? With her?" Paulie's tone was incredulous. "Who the hell are *you? You don't live here."*

Mercy ground her back teeth as she jammed the key into the lock. Without looking back, she flung the door wide and reached for the bat she kept just inside. Without hesitation, she grabbed and swung wide.

Paulie threw up an arm to block the swing. There was a satisfying crack as the bat broke his arm. Ross, who'd been leaning on Paulie, crashed to the sidewalk. His eyes rolled up.

Mercy smiled at her sleeping lover, then glared at Paulie.

"What? Why?" He gaped in recognition and his eyes widened in horror. "God, please! Don't!"

He tried to crawl away, only making it as far as the mouth of the alley before Mercy hit him twice more. Blood poured from his ears and his head. His body didn't even twitch.

Satisfied with a job well done, Mercy turned to where Ross lay on the ground. She lifted him into her arms and carried him inside. Once he was secured on the bed, she returned to the alley.

Had Paulie moved?

Her mind was playing tricks on her again. He couldn't have moved. Snatching up his wrist, she felt for the familiar thump, thump, thump. *Nothing. With a sigh of relief, she dragged his body deeper into the alley. She considered putting him in the Dumpster, but didn't want to risk it. No, she'd leave him buried beneath the empty boxes tossed out by the Save-N-Go. If he was still here tomorrow night, she'd cut him into manageable pieces and toss him into the ocean. If someone found him sooner, they'd assume it was a mugging gone bad.*

Whistling "Mercy" by OneRepublic, she headed home.

CHAPTER 26

HANNAH LOOKED AS if she were being electrocuted. Her body trembled and jittered. Her eyes rolled back in her head but she remained upright.

"We've got to stop her," Niall said, reaching for her. Someone, probably that Hollywood wannabe, shoved him back. He swung around to face a human wall of McKinnons. "You ever put your hands on me again, I'll fucking feed you your own dick."

Ian laughed. "Try it, asshole."

Dev jabbed an elbow into the cocky bastard's ribs. "Not helping, Ian."

Ryan stared at them all with his fucking impassive expression. The man was a human cyborg. "I know this is hard, but she wanted to do this."

"Yeah, she did. Now it's time to stop it." Niall reached behind him and grabbed a fistful of her shirt. He yanked her free of the sink, breaking the connection. With an inhuman cry, she collapsed. Niall pivoted in time to catch her.

The scent of honeysuckle and fear-soaked sweat permeated the air. Her head lolled back and her eyes remained closed. He shook her gently in his arms. "Hannah. Hannah, wake up and talk to me."

"Give her a second," Dev said, squatting down and taking her pulse at her neck. "She's alive. Probably just fainted. She'll come around."

"What makes you such a fucking expert?" Niall couldn't—wouldn't—disguise the venom.

"Her sister Jules has done this a few times," Ian said, all humor gone from his face. "First time she did it, scared the piss out of me."

"Dev." Ryan handed him the small white trash can that was usually under the sink.

"Right. Thanks," Dev said. "In case she needs to vomit. Happens with Ju—"

"Happens with Jules. Got it." Niall shifted, trying to reach the paper towels.

"Here." Ian pulled out a handkerchief from his pocket, ran it under the sink, then handed it to Niall.

"Thanks." Niall dabbed her forehead, willing her to open her eyes. It didn't work. "Tell me something, since y'all seem to know so much, when this happens to her sisters, do they risk their sanity too?"

The trio wore matching expressions of surprise on their faces. Niall's heart sank. "Yeah, I didn't think so."

"What makes you think her sanity is in danger?" Dev asked, tugging his cell from his pocket and glancing at the lit screen.

"Hannah warned me. It's why I was trying to break the connection when she started to convulse. She'd been connected too long. She told me she becomes the person sending her the vision when she's there. The more she visits, the harder it is for her to come back to herself." Niall stared into her blanched face, regret eating a hole in his stomach. "Come back, Hannah. Come on, love. I need you to open your eyes."

"Did you know about this part of her crift?" Dev asked his cousins. "Her sister's going to kill me if something happens to her."

"She was only touching it a few seconds," Ian argued, but there was no heat and no humor in his voice.

"St-stop talking about me like I'm not here," Hannah said, weakly. Her eyes fluttered twice but didn't completely open. She licked her lips as if thirsty. "Mercy is one cray-cray woman . . . or not."

"What does that mean?" Ian knelt beside Hannah. "What did you see?"

"I know who's not the killer. It's not Paulie. He's bleeding to death. I beat him with a baseball bat because he knows who I am. He's dying behind my . . . no. Her, *her* apartment building." Tears leaked from Hannah's closed lids. "I'm Hannah Ha—Halloran. I'm Hannah." She repeated her name several more times.

The men glanced at Niall in confusion.

"She's still connected. She's trying to break free." Niall took her hand in his free one and squeezed gently. "Come back to me, Hannah. You're safe now. Hannah Halloran. Say it with me. All safe now."

"All safe now," she replied dutifully, then fell silent again.

"What's Paulie's last name?" Ryan asked, nodding to Ian who rose and pulled out his cell.

"Hurst."

Ryan and Ian didn't answer but exited the bathroom, like men on a mission.

"Check the hospitals and morgues," Dev said. He gestured with his chin. "Looks like she's coming around again. Welcome back, Hannah."

Those golden eyes opened. Niall's heart actually ached in relief. "It's the fairy queen," he said and got what he wanted. A smile. It was weak, brief but there.

"Oh, Niall, I'm so sorry. It is Ross. Mercy has Ross."

NIALL HELPED HER move from the bathroom to the office. Hannah settled into the chair and watched with some dismay as he took up his post in the doorway. Ryan, Ian, and Dev squeezed into the room with her.

Carefully, she explained everything she'd seen. She told them about Paulie, the drugs, even the whistled tune. Everything she could remember.

"Nothing at the morgue," Ryan reported.

"I have two John Does at Tidewater General," Ian said, scratching the side of his chin. "Hannah, can you remember anything else about the apartment complex. You said she lived on the first floor. How many doors did she pass on the first floor before she opened hers?"

"One," Hannah answered after a moment. "Well, from the street. From the alley side, she was right there."

"Do you remember the name of the street? Did you see a sign, a business, anything that could tell us where to locate her?" Dev asked, tugging out his phone. He frowned at it. "Ian, go to the back door, Shelley's pulling up."

Ian obeyed.

"I told you everything I remember." Frustration made Hannah's eyes burn. "They walked two blocks from O'Reilly's Pub to get to the apartment. Mercy was looking at Ross most of the time, not where she was going. Her apartment was behind a store, that's why she didn't go in the first door. And she left Paulie's body beneath some boxes."

"You don't remember what was on those boxes?" Dev asked again.

"No! I told you, they all said different things. Some were marked eggs, candy, wait!" Hannah shut her eyes and tried to remember the label on the egg carton. "Arctic Avenue. The address was number 55 Arctic Circle."

"Avenue or Circle?" Niall's voice was tense.

"Uh, let me think again." Hannah searched the fading vision for the label again. "Circle. Definitely Arctic Circle.

"Holy shit!" Niall strode into the office, all but pushing Ryan away from the filing cabinet. He yanked open a drawer, thumbed quickly through files, then pulled out a manila folder. "Paulie lives on Arctic Circle. Next to . . ."

His face blanched.

Hannah didn't think, just rushed to his side. "Who, Niall?"

"Hannah," he said, his voice as hollow as his eyes. "You said something was wrong with Mercy's hands, remember?"

"Yes." A pit opened in her belly.

"Michael lives next door to Paulie."

"The busboy?" Hannah nearly laughed until she remembered his hands. The way his fingers curled around the gray tub were identical to the way Mercy's fingers curled around the bat. With the pinky permanently facing the wrong direction. "Oh God. Mercy is Michael."

EVERYTHING HAPPENED SO fast. Hannah could do little more than watch as the men sprang into action around her. She wanted to go with them to Mercy's apartment but she was still shaky. And she didn't relish the idea of touching anything else that might send her into more of Mercy/Michael's horrible memories.

"You've done everything you can to help them," Shelley said, putting her arm around Hannah's shoulders. "Now you need to let them do their jobs."

"But Niall's not a cop," Hannah argued, watching the men pull out of the parking lot in a caravan of speeding cars. "He owns a restaurant."

"It's okay, Han. He's with Dev." Shelley squeezed her shoulder. "Didn't you say when you met Niall he was in the Marines?"

"Yes."

"Aren't the Marines tough?"

Hannah shrugged in defeat. "Yes. Okay, he wasn't just in the Marines. He was military police. But that was before. He doesn't carry a gun now."

"Are you sure?"

She rolled her eyes. "Of course I'm sure. I've seen him naked."

"No one carries a gun naked." Shelley paused, then added with an arched eyebrow, "Well, not the kind that fires bullets anyway."

"You are so wrong. Aren't you a mom now? Isn't there

some rule about moms not making sexual innuendos or something?" Hannah closed the back door and locked it.

"Most moms get that way through sex. I'm the exception. Though we're definitely trying the traditional route. A lot."

Hannah covered her ears. "Eww. Stop. I don't want to know about you and Dev."

Shelley laughed, then cocked her head as if listening to the wind. "Someone's coming in the back door."

"How do you know that?" Hannah asked, hurrying to the door.

"The birds outside . . . Hannah, wait, don't open the door!"

Hannah had already flipped the lock. She froze when Michael eased it open.

CHAPTER 27

"WAIT IN THE car," Dev said to Niall.

"Fuck that."

"What's with the salty verbiage?" Dev asked with a shake of his head. "Is it a Marine thing?"

"It's a some-psycho-has-my-brother-chained-up-like-an-animal thing." Niall reached for the sidearm he no longer carried. Crap. "I can't sit out here. It's my brother in there."

Dev pulled into a spot on the street, blocking the alley. He called Detective Reynolds. Again. "Reynolds, where are you and O'Dell? I'm outside the suspect's apartment."

Niall could make out the angry male voice on the other end of the line, but not the words. The meaning was clear. Stay put.

"Understood. I'll await your arrival," he said into the cell, then clicked off. "Fuckers."

Niall might have smiled at Dev's response had the situation been any less dire. "So we're going to what? Just sit with our thumbs up our asses and wait for the Dudley Do-Wrong Detectives to show up?"

"Yes, we wait. I follow protocol. Until I have a reason to go inside, we don't move." Dev turned his gray eyes on Niall, his expression serene. He sent a text that read, "Plan B."

"Who are you texting and what's Plan B?"

Dev's placid smile didn't waiver. "That was to TSS. And Plan B is—"

"Help!" The scream was loud and male and sounded like Ian. It also appeared to be coming from inside the building. "Help! Police!"

"Now we have a reason." Dev was out of the car and at the door in seconds.

"WHAT ARE YOU doing here?" Michael asked, frowning at Hannah. He glanced around as if searching for other people, but Shelley had been smart enough to duck into the Master dining room. "Alone?"

"I could ask you the same," Hannah retorted. Okay, not the brightest thing to say to a psycho killer, but it was all she had.

"I, uh, forgot something." He turned and locked the back door.

With his back to her, Hannah turned to Shelley who appeared in the diamond-shaped window of the swinging door. Waving at her sister to stay hidden in the front room, she mouthed, "Tell Dev Mercy's here."

Shelley didn't wait.

Hannah spun back in time to catch Michael staring quizzically at the corkboard.

In two fast strides, Michael grabbed her by the arm and hauled her over to the board. "Where is it?" he demanded.

"Where's what?" Hannah asked, tugging free of his hold.

Michael glanced from his misshapen pinky to her arm, then whispered, "Here."

He lifted the picture from the counter. The same one Niall had shown her earlier. Michael tucked it into his pocket and headed toward the back door. He had his hand on the lock when he turned back and asked, "Why are you here?"

"Waiting for Niall." She kept the table between them this

time. Michael took a slow circuit of the room. When he pressed his nose to the window of the swinging door, Hannah's heart beat so loud, she worried he'd hear it.

Michael stared at her. His eyes remained mostly hidden but the weight of his stare was choking. She coughed, raised her voice hoping her sister could hear her.

"Michael, how-how'd you even know someone would still be here?" She inched her way toward the back door, keeping the prep table between them.

"I didn't." He matched her step for step. Each time she lifted a foot to move to her right, he did too. Only the table kept her out of arm's reach, but it wouldn't last much longer. "Ross keeps a Hide-A-Key in a rock by the back door."

At the mention of Ross's name, Hannah jerked to a halt.

Stupid, stupid, stupid!

His lips curled into a slow, sinister smile. The kind that had her knees turning to rubber and her heart trying to leap into her throat.

"I know all about you, you know. Ross told me." Michael took one of Virgil's skillets from the hook on the wall over the stove. He twirled it like a baton.

"Nope, I don't know what you mean." She nodded toward the back door, keeping her eyes on Michael. "You got your picture, don't you want to head out?"

"Wouldn't be right to leave you here alone." Michael shook his head. "Nah, I can wait for Niall with you. Want me to fix you something to eat?"

The pan arced through the air with a swish.

She swallowed hard. "No, I'm not hungry, thanks."

Like she'd eat anything he offered.

"Huh." He set down the wooden-handled skillet on the table between them and put his hands on either side of it. "Why do you look scared?"

"No reason. Psh-pah. I'm not scared." She tried her brightest this-is-just-a-drunk-customer smile. "Why do you ask?"

"Because when I said Ross, you jumped." He pointed at her. "Just like you did that time. You know, don't you?"

"Know what?" She feigned ignorance and gauged how long it would take to get to the back door and unlock it before Michael caught up to her. Too long.

Michael leaned his face forward and gave her a sinister smile. "Mercy," he whispered.

Hannah grabbed for the skillet and swung at his head. And missed. She did clip his shoulder. Michael slammed into Virgil's stove and crashed to the floor.

Thank you, Buffy reruns!

"Run, Shelley!" she yelled, bolting for the back door, only to swing around at a thunderous crack behind her.

Michael was on his feet again, slamming the swinging door against Shelley's unmoving body. She must have been waiting on the other side of the door and rushed into the kitchen, only to have Michael catch her with the door.

Rage flowed through Hannah like a landslide. The skillet still clutched in her hands, she charged around the table and swung at his head before he'd looked up.

Hannah swung twice, knocking him away from her sister's unmoving body. He fell against the wall and the lights went out.

SEVERAL ALARMS BLARED at once. People rushed out of the surrounding apartment buildings from all directions. Niall raced past the confused citizens stumbling into the street, staying on Dev's six.

Like in combat, he catalogued the outside noises—a baby crying, questions being volleyed, sirens in the distance moving closer, and silence coming from inside Michael's apartment. Catalogued and ignored all but the most important.

Glock in hand, Dev used his free fist to pound on the door. "Tidewater Police, open up!"

Nothing. Not a sound. Not a movement. Utter silence.

He did it again.

This time, Dev asked, "Did you hear that? Sounds like someone calling for help."

Dev didn't wait for a response but kicked in the door. It

took two vicious attempts, but he broke open the door. The cracked frame went with it in a crunch. Despite the glow of the sunset outside, the inside of the apartment was dark, cavernous. Cramped.

A sickly sweet stench of roses hung in the air, like someone had plugged in one too many air fresheners. The smell was overpowering. Blackout curtains hung over the windows in the living room; only a red night-light in the hallway offered a glimmer of relief from the oppressive dark.

Dev turned his head and mouthed, "Stay here."

Niall wanted to fight that command and search for his brother, but Ian and Ryan had arrived behind him. Like Dev, they had weapons at the ready. Each member of the three-man team began to clear the apartment.

Now this Niall understood. He'd been in combat zones long enough to know how to clear a room. Unarmed as he was, he couldn't do much more than get shot if he opened the wrong door. As much as it chafed, he remained on guard by the closed front door.

"Clear."

"Clear."

"Got something," Ian called from the back of the apartment. "We've got a live one."

Niall didn't think, didn't wonder, simply bolted to the room. His brother lay exactly as Hannah had described, facedown, naked, and chained to the wall. Ian was at his side, checking his vitals.

Niall reached for the hook, holding Ross's chains, but Ian stopped him by placing a hand on his wrist. "Don't touch him yet. He's alive but unconscious. He's okay for now. We don't want to disturb the scene. You're not supposed to be here, remember. Neither are we."

Staring at the blond hair plastered to the side of his little brother's face, Niall's insides twisted. He wanted to set him free. Not wait and leave him chained like an animal. But that bastard, Michael, needed to pay for what he'd done to Ross. At least his baby brother slept through this part. Perhaps he'd sleep until he reached the hospital.

Ian pushed to his feet and moved to the doorway. "It was a cursory check but his vitals seem stable."

"I take it you two are Plan B?" Niall asked, switching places with Ian. He couldn't set his brother free so settled for kneeling next to the bed.

"That's us," Ian said, but his tone lacked its normal humor.

"Time." Ryan appeared in the doorway. His monosyllabic word had Ian hustling to his side.

"Got this, Dev?" Ian asked.

"Go," he said to his cousins, then picked up his cell and placed a call. "This is Detective Devon Jones, Tidewater PD. I need an ambulance for an unconscious white male, early twenties. He's been kidnapped and appears to have been drugged. We're located at . . ."

While Dev spoke with EMS, Niall turned to the doorway saying, "Thank you—"

Ian and Ryan were gone. They'd left the same way they'd arrived, silent as wraiths.

CHAPTER 28

COPS SWARMED INTO the apartment around Niall. The group included the two homicide detectives who had given Hannah such a hard time. One glare from them and Niall realized she'd probably like to know all of her visions hadn't been for nothing. He stepped out of the bedroom as the paramedics hurried in.

"I need to call Hannah," Niall said, pulling Dev aside. "Where's Michael?"

"We've got a BOLO for him. Right now, let's focus on the positive. We've found your brother and he's alive."

"Right, good point." Niall scrubbed a hand down his face as the detective headed toward the homicide cops. "Dev, I'm going to ride to the hospital with Ross."

"Good idea."

Leaving Dev to deal with the cops and medics, Niall stepped out into the warm evening air. He took his first deep breath since Hannah's visions had started earlier that night. He needed to call his parents, not that they could go to the hospital, but they'd need to know. In a few minutes. Right now . . .

He dialed Hannah's number. It went to voice mail. She was probably talking to her sister. Or in the bathroom. Or . . .

Ryan's blue Ford Ranger screeched to a stop at the curb. Ian opened the passenger side and jumped out. He raced past Niall, into the apartment. Niall turned to follow but Ryan called out, "Niall, get in the truck. Hannah's in trouble."

He moved as ordered. Jumped in. Closed the door. Fastened his seat belt. All without feeling a damned thing. His mind had spiraled down to one thought, *Hannah's in trouble.*

Fuck.

That.

Not one to mince words, Ryan said, "Hang on," and peeled out, tires squealing.

IN THE DARK, Hannah nearly tripped over Shelley's hand. Her arm was bent at an unnatural angle around the swinging door. With the skillet still in one hand, Hannah pushed on the door until she squeezed through. Then as gently as she could, she tugged Shelley fully into the Master Room.

The last rays of sunshine filtered through the room's giant windows, casting the bruise on Shelley's head in stark relief. Hannah kept her back against the door. Using her foot, she pulled a chair across the floor.

It squeaked on the hardwood, but she had to do something. Out in the open they were in danger. The chair wouldn't keep him out, but it would slow him down.

She needed time to get her unconscious sister to safety. Carefully, Hannah inched her way toward the front door, dragging Shelley with her.

Michael must have awoken because there was the distinct sound of things crashing in the kitchen. For a heart-stopping minute, she thought he'd left. The back door closed and the silence that came after had Hannah holding her breath.

She held her sister's limp body close in the shadows and started to inch toward the front door again, when the back door banged a second time. Something else crashed, this time against the door separating the kitchen from the Master Room.

Certain Michael was going to burst from the kitchen at any moment, Hannah moved as quickly as possible, trying not to jostle Shelley too much. She'd just managed to get her sister outside when Michael started cursing at her.

"This is all your fault! He needs me to set him free. But am I with him? No! I'm wasting my time with you!" Michael grabbed Hannah by the hair.

Her scalp burned as he wrenched her backward, off her feet, and dragged her back into the restaurant. Hannah twisted and dug her fingernails into his right wrist.

Michael shouted in pain and dropped her.

Hannah's heart pumping at a frantic pace, she shoved to the balls of her feet. They'd shifted positions. Now Michael blocked her path to Shelley. She stepped to her right, he followed. She jumped to the left, so did he. He wasn't touching her anymore but his arms were spread wide and his fingers flexed.

She had two choices: try to go through him or go into the kitchen. Hoping he'd follow, she darted toward the back of the restaurant.

The slaps of his sneakers against the floor told her he'd followed.

Hannah nearly tripped over the chair he must have tossed aside when he'd come through the kitchen. Jumping over it, she threw her hands up and shoved the door wide.

The stench of gas hit her in the face before her feet touched the ground. She choked on a cough and covered her mouth with her hand. The burners hissed, flameless.

Michael must have turned them on when he arrived and since broken off the knobs. They lay scattered in pieces on the floor. Terror had her feet turning to cement when he said, "I don't want to hurt you, Hannah."

He stalked through the door and drew a knife from the magnetic rack near Paulie's stove. It sang sinisterly. The sight of the large silver blade shattered whatever mental block had her frozen. Hannah backed up, determined to survive. Her lungs burning and her eyes watering from the gas filling the room, she searched for something to help her.

She spotted a wooden-handled frying pan that Michael must have thrown on the prep table during his temper tantrum. Grabbing it, she held it aloft. "Back off!"

"You're going to hit me? Why?" His voice took on a high-pitched quality. Younger somehow. "I liked you. You were nice to me. You never called me names. You didn't make me do things. You were a good person."

Hannah swallowed hard. He'd switched from present tense to past tense mid-rant. As if she were already dead.

"But I have a destiny. A mission." His voice hardened, deepened. "I save people."

"Seriously? You just bashed my sister's head in and you're planning to kill me. That's not saving people!"

Michael's face contorted with rage. He arced the knife up and came for her.

Hannah didn't think, just swung the pan hard. It connected with Michael's damaged hand. He howled in pain. The knife clattered to the floor and slid under one of the prep tables. She thought he might dive for it, instead he charged her again.

He tackled her. The pan skidded across the floor and under one of the metal racks, out of reach. Hannah's head slammed against the floor hard enough to make her see stars but she refused to die like this. She brought her knee up, driving it between his legs.

Michael emitted a high-pitched scream and rolled off her. She flipped to her belly and started to push to her feet but he grabbed one of her ankles with both hands.

Hannah's face slapped against the floor before she rolled onto her back. She kicked Michael, pummeling his face, head, hands, shoulders, and any other part of him she could reach. She kicked until long after he'd stopped moving.

In the stillness, she lay listening to her heart thunder in her ears. The air in the room was heavy with the weight of gas. Coughing, she started to crawl on sweaty hands and shaky knees. Her eyes, lungs, and ankle burned, and her whole body ached. But she was freaking alive. *Thank you, universe!*

She pushed to her feet in front of Niall's office. Michael groaned and she glanced back. She choked on a scream. He was digging a match out of one of the matchboxes the Boxing Cat kept for lighting candles.

Hannah's pulse hammered in her throat. She'd never make it to the back door. She ran into the office, slamming the door shut and diving under the sturdy wooden desk. The door blew apart in the explosion. Heat and debris slapped at her back. It sounded like bombs dropping as storage supplies crashed down from the shelves onto the workstation above her. The desk shimmied but didn't collapse.

In the silence that followed, all Hannah could hear was a grotesque ringing in her ears. Was she dead? Not if the tinny sound in her ears and the pain singing through her body were any indication. *Thank you, God!* Somehow, she was alive. Aching but definitely breathing and in one piece, amazingly enough.

She started to crawl through the smoky room. She had to get out of the building and find Shelley.

Hannah hadn't made it far when her shirt snagged on a metal rack. She tugged herself free, then crawled toward what remained of the kitchen.

The back door had blown off its hinges. Water rained down from the sprinklers in what was left of the ceiling. Metal racks, pans and pots, and pieces of ceiling fell like hail in a summer storm. Funny, she would have expected everything to have already been on the ground. It was stupid, but she found herself staring around in morbid fascination. The shelves were twisted and bent. The workstations had taken most of the blast and were little more than shards of shrapnel embedded in what was left of the walls.

Nearby, Michael groaned and the racks shifted. She threw up her hands to shield her face from any more falling objects and had only a nanosecond to realize she'd made a fatal mistake.

Michael lay dying, his face and left arm horribly black

and burned. His right arm had been ripped off in the blast. There was an oozing bloody stump where his elbow had been. His clothing had been burned away along with most of the skin on his chest. He was gurgling in agony and touching the same rack she was.

And she'd just formed a psychic link to a madman.

"YOU BETTER HIDE in there, you freak. If you ever go near another one of my boyfriends, I'll cut off your dick," Mona screamed as Michael hid in the bathtub.

He'd scrubbed his naked body until it was raw. He couldn't get the blood off his skin. His gray angel was dead.

Still, Mona kept screaming, "He was my boyfriend. She killed him because of you!"

The vision swirled from the grungy white-tiled walls to his mother's pristine little bedroom decorated in forget-me-not wallpaper. His mother's angry, disgusted face so close to his, it resembled an evil clown with crazy eyes.

"He was mine! Mine! You had no right to take him away from me, Mother!" Mona yelled. Fat tears poured down her ugly face. She clutched at the dead body on the floor. Black blood pooled beneath the body on the once immaculate green carpeting. "It wasn't his fault. The little freak demanded the fuck. Begged for it. And today wasn't the first time."

Their mother let out a howl of fury. With arms like windmills, she beat his back until he couldn't draw breath without agony. The strikes weren't as torturous as the vicious words pouring from her mouth, "You're a good-for-nothing little shit. Just like your useless prick of a father. Nothing but a whore with a dick. That's all you freaks want to do, fuck anything that moves. Now look at my carpet. It's ruined and it's all your fault!"

Michael was spun around. His mother held him painfully by the scruff of the neck. Her fingernails digging into his flesh as she forced him to stare into the vacant eyes of his dead lover.

He wouldn't weep for his gray angel. Mother would only

punish him more. Michael wished he could have gone with him. But not the way he'd died. The sight of the knife sticking out of the angel's stomach was sickening. He'd suffered for hours before he finally exhaled his last breath.

His mother kept spitting vitriol at him. "You're so foul, no one could love you. I should have had an abortion the moment I found out about you but then I would have destroyed my real baby too." She threw him hard against her aging dresser. Michael tripped, his pinky finger catching in a broken drawer. It caught and bent backward.

Blinding pain ripped through him as the bone snapped in two places.

"Quit your squalling!" Mother said, hauling him to his feet. One look at Michael's broken finger, and she paled. "Now look what you made me do! I killed for you and now you made me break your finger. You piece of shit."

Mother wrung her hands together.

"I'm sorry, Mother," Michael said through tears he couldn't fight any longer.

"You're right, you're sorry. A sorry excuse for a human being!" His mother paced back and forth, hands shaking. She swung around and slapped Michael across the face hard enough to split his lip. "Stop making all that noise! I can't think."

Then he begged using the only word that had ever seemed to affect her in the past, "Mercy."

Michael bit down, blood pooled in his mouth and dribbled down his chin. Finally, the wild animal look in his mother's eyes faded and she exhaled a long breath. Gently, she tugged Michael to her side. "You liked that boy?"

"He was mine, Mom! Do you hear me? Mine! And the whore stole him from me. Now he's dead!" Mona yelled, leaping to her feet. She was backhanded as Michael had been and crashed to the floor. Like Michael, his sister had taken a beating when Mother had found him in bed with the gray angel and Mona still crying on the floor. Then Mother had killed his love.

For a moment Michael had thought perhaps she had

done it out of a misguided need to protect her children. Until she'd gone berserk and beaten him until he couldn't see clearly through his swollen eyes.

Mona whimpered as she crawled back to the angel's body. One day, he'd make that bitch beg for all those times she'd locked him up and tortured him when he'd been too weak to fight back. And he'd make her suffer for taking away his love.

"Come here." Michael's mother pulled him close and roughly bound the finger with a piece of torn T-shirt without bothering to straighten the damaged bone. The agony had his stomach twisting with the repressed need to vomit.

"You are never to do that nasty thing again. Not with any boy. Do you hear me? You'll help me clean up the mess." Mother gestured to the dead body. "Then we'll never talk about this again. Don't look at me like that. I did him a favor. He wasn't right. I was merciful. I set him free from his torturous life."

She bent over and kissed Michael between the brows. "Go and get a shovel, Michael."

Mona still wept in the corner. Maybe their mother should have set his bitch sister free too. Pausing beside the mirrored closet, Michael stared down at her.

"What are you looking at, freak?" Mona wailed and pressed a kiss to the angel's forehead. Red lipstick stained his skin.

And just like that, Michael knew who he really was.

Oh, he was still Michael to the world, even mostly to himself.

But somewhere inside a small part of his heart, Mercy had just been born.

And she had a mission.

CHAPTER 29

NIALL HELD ON to the chicken bar with one hand. Ryan took the corner to the restaurant so fast, Niall swore two wheels left the ground. The giant barely uttered a word, but he could've probably given race car driver Jimmie Johnson a run for his money.

The truck slid into the parking lot of the Cat. His place looked like it had been bombed. Niall didn't wait for the complete stop but was out and running.

"Hannah!" he called out, racing to what had been the kitchen entrance.

Her scream pierced the parking lot and arrowed straight into his chest.

Ryan the giant grabbed him in a bear hug and pulled him to a stop. "You can't go in there."

"Hannah's in there. Call the paramedics, she's alive in there right now." He pushed the giant away. "I've been in combat. Survived bombings, you can't keep me out."

"Where's the gas line?" Ryan asked.

"Around the side."

Ryan nodded, then dialed 911 and ran to shut off the gas. In seconds, Ryan was back and talking to EMS.

Niall dug his way through what had once been his back door.

The kitchen was in shambles. Black smoke poured out and floated to the sky. Somewhere nearby, sirens erupted. He had to hurry. Digging away pieces of building, soot, and debris, he called out to Hannah. She didn't answer.

"Do you hear anything?" Ryan asked.

"No, but Hannah's in there somewhere." And she'd better fucking be alive. There was no *or else.* No alternative. She had to be alive or he might as well have died with her.

"Fuck me," Ryan said in what had to be the most emotional response the giant had ever uttered.

Niall turned to see what had elicited such a reaction. Shelley, her skirt torn, and holding her arm at an odd angle, stumbled into view.

"Where's Hannah?" she asked, sliding to the ground.

As if to answer the universal question, Hannah emitted a long, piercing scream.

Niall dug faster. Ryan dropped to his knees and joined in. When they'd dug out a hole barely big enough to squeeze through, Niall stuck his head in.

Thick smoke clouded the room. Metal racks had twisted and bent at odd angles, virtually blocking entry to the kitchen.

Hannah's pink braid stuck out from the office door. She lay on her back. "Hannah!" Niall called out, but if she heard him, she didn't respond.

"Dig faster!" Niall said, shoving his shoulders into the tunnel they'd created. "I can see her."

He pulled out of the hole. Together with Ryan and Shelley, who only used one arm, they dug until the space was wide enough for him to squeeze through.

Niall wriggled into the hole, keeping his eyes on Hannah. "Fuck! She's going into a seizure. Help me get this shit out of the way!"

Niall spotted an opening in the twisted metal barely big

enough to squeeze into, but it would get him straight to Hannah.

"Ryan, can you hold this up?" Niall pointed to the snaking wire rack.

Around him, metal shifted over, then up, giving him room to army crawl toward her. Ash and debris floated around him like sooty snowflakes, but he kept going.

At the edges of his mind, Afghanistan resurfaced. Other screams. Other walls caving in. Others dying around him.

Not this fucking time. Hannah was right in front of him. Right there. He'd be goddamned fucked if he let her die now.

The opening swam in his vision. His throat tightened. His heart pounded painfully against his ribs, but he kept going. Shards of broken metal snagged his clothes, scraped his shoulders, his skin. The metal enclosure seemed to grow tighter and still he kept going deeper into the tunnel toward her. With each inch gained, more of Hannah's face came into view. She was awake. Her eyes were wide, vacant. Her mouth open in a silent cry. Tears tracked down the sides of her face, saturating her hair.

"Hannah, I'm coming," he said, gaining another two inches. "Hold on, love. Just hold on. Do you hear me?"

The metal overhead shook and screeched as if about to tumble. Niall kept his gaze focused on Hannah and held his breath.

"Got it. Keep going," Ryan called from somewhere above.

Niall wriggled a hand forward and touched Hannah's cold, clammy hand. "I'm here, love. Can you hear me?"

She didn't answer. Her body vibrated as if she were being shocked.

The metal. Ryan was touching it. God, it had to be sending her into sensory overload.

"Ryan, prop up the shelf with your shoulder but don't let your skin touch it. You're connected to her. Break the connection." Niall searched for injury. Her ankle bled freely. A few inches above that a thin spike speared her pant leg. He wanted to yank it but was afraid of causing more damage.

"I'm out," Ryan called back.

Behind him sirens roared, signaling the arrival of EMS.

Hannah still shook and wept, her eyes still vacant.

"Do you see Michael?" Niall swiveled his head, but only saw crisscrossing metal. "Is he touching the racks?"

"I don't know. I can't search for him without letting go here," Ryan answered.

Dev's voice boomed. "Status."

An explosion of voices and sirens filled the air, drowning out Ryan and Dev's conversation. Niall was alone with Hannah beneath the twisted metal. Both of them were trapped, but she was lost. Lost in visions and he couldn't help her.

Or could he?

"Hang on, Hannah, I'm coming for you." Niall clutched her hand in one of his, then reached for the metal bar piercing her leg. "God, let this work. Hear me, my fairy queen. Hear me. I love you."

Mercy's screams were relentless. Her whole life alone. Locked in one closet or another. Forced to be nothing. Forced to live in a world that was too cruel to notice the weak. She'd shown them all. Mom, Mona, everyone. It had taken years, but she'd shown them she wasn't worthless. She was Mercy.

"Hannah! Hear me, my fairy queen!"

Mercy spun around in the mist that clung to her like a silken dress.

Niall lay on the ground, pinned beneath Iggy and Danny. Their broken bodies bloodied and Iggy's lips moving.

The world tilted. She wasn't Mercy. She was looking at Mercy.

She was Niall.

But that didn't make sense. Niall was still talking to her. How could she be Niall?

"Hannah! You've got to come back. Fight the vision, dammit! Where's my stubborn fairy queen right now?" Niall said.

He lay on the floor of the destroyed kitchen. Twisted racks coiled with black soot bent around him. Ash and pieces of ceiling tiles falling.

The image changed and he was back under the dead bodies again. Blood fell on his face like teardrops.

Back in the cage that had once been a kitchen. Sirens screaming.

"Goddamnit, woman! Fight the vision. Take mine instead. See me loving you. See us in the Cat. See me marrying you. See me looking at you. Fight the vision. You're Hannah Halloran. Say it! Say it, damn you."

Mercy screamed and the faces of every man she'd killed filled her mind. Mother killing the gray angel. Then a parade of men Mother had killed starting with Father.

She was Mercy again. Dying. Dying. God, the awful, unrelenting pain. The loneliness. She'd show them all. Kill them all. Everyone who had ever hurt her. She'd save the ones she loved. Set them free.

"No!" Niall's voice cut through the cries like a claymore striking stone. He squeezed her hand hard enough to jolt her out of Mercy's head until she was a shadow in the mist surrounded by his voice alone. "You are Hannah Halloran. Hannah Eleanor Halloran. Say it! Come on and say it! Hannah Halloran. Don't forget who you are. A psychic artist and electrician. With a family you're only just getting to know. You love me. I love you. You're Hannah Halloran. Stay here. Stay with me."

Hannah blinked in confusion as the cool, white mist gave way to gray darkness. She called out weakly, "Niall?"

HANNAH BLINKED OPENED her eyes. Reality filtered in around her like the smoke that rose up to whisk her away into a vision. The first thing she heard was Niall's raspy voice.

"Hannah, come back, sweetheart. I'm right here. Tell me you hear me." He brushed a thumb over the back of her hand. Gently, reassuringly. "A big wedding, if that's what you want. We can go anywhere you want for the honeymoon. Where do you want to go? Name the place and I'll make it happen."

She tried to turn her head, only to realize she couldn't. Panic ballooned inside her. "Niall? What's happening?"

"Hey there, Hannah. Welcome back. Don't move, I don't want you to hurt yourself." She couldn't see his face, but could hear the smile in his voice and feel the steady stroke of his thumb on her hand. "She's back. Someone get us the fuck out of here."

Hannah blinked twice more before the room came into focus, even if she didn't completely understand it. "Ohmigod! Michael blew up the kitchen. Where's Shelley? She was hurt. Did you find her? How did you get in here?"

She coughed as ash and dust stirred in the air.

"It's okay. She's outside. She made it out." He kissed her hand. "You saved her by putting her on the front porch. The kitchen took the brunt of the explosion. You'll be out of here soon. Just don't try to move." He laughed but it sounded like he was choking back tears. That couldn't be right. "The paramedics are outside waiting to take you to the hospital. Shelley won't go without you, she said."

"Yeah?" Her eyes misted.

"Yes." He kissed her hand again. "How are you in here?"

"It's where you needed me. I'm here." Niall squeezed her hand, then let go.

"No!"

"I'm right here, I won't leave you." He squeezed her hand again, then said something she couldn't quite understand. Another reassuring kiss on her palm, then he said, "Get ready. They're going to start cutting away the racks."

She slid her gaze down her left arm to see Niall squeezed into the cage of shelves with her. His broad shoulders pressed against the tunnel of metal. His white shirt was torn and there were bloodstains on the sleeves. "Oh, Niall, you're hurt."

She tried to crawl to him but something held her leg. The moment she moved, pain sliced up her left leg. She screamed.

"Don't move! Just wait until they get in here." Niall inched forward until his face pressed against her hand. "There's a wire embedded in your calf. Hold still."

Pain was its own life force pulsing below her knee. It sucked the air from her lungs and made her eyes well with tears. "Okay. Okay. Stay put. I got it. But you should go. I know you hate tight places. Don't torture yourself."

"God, you really are like some fairy queen." Niall laughed again, managed to move another inch toward her, close enough he trailed his fingers up her arm to her face. "You squared off with a serial killer, were damn near killed in an explosion, went into some psycho's head, and it's me you're worried about."

"Oh, the restaurant, it's destroyed. Isn't it?"

"That's what I have insurance for." His fingers brushed her lips, and he laughed again. "God, I love you."

"I know," she said with more than a little relief.

"Of course you do." Tracing her jawline with two fingers he said, "Is that all I get for crawling through what's left of my kitchen for you?"

"Ah, Marine, I love you too."

CHAPTER 30

NIALL HESITATED OUTSIDE of the pristine hospital room. He'd already checked on Hannah, but she was in X-ray at the moment, making sure the pole that had pierced her leg hadn't broken any bones. She didn't need him right now, and Ross did.

His brother sat with his back to the door at Paulie's bedside. Ross's shoulders shook in his hospital gown and robe as he sobbed, clutching Paulie's hand.

"I swear if you wake up, I'll stop drinking. I'll tell the whole world. I'll do anything you want. Please, please don't leave me." Ross sniffled. "Paulie, they told me you tried to save me. That has to mean something, right? It has to mean that no matter how much I disappointed you, you still love me. Oh God, please don't leave me."

Niall's chest ached for his brother. He couldn't imagine how hard this must be for Ross. Clearly, Ross's feelings for Paulie had gone deeper than even Niall had guessed. He only hoped Paulie knew how much he was loved.

"Please don't leave me," Ross whispered to Paulie again.

And Niall's heart squeezed more. He'd uttered those same words hours earlier to Hannah. He wanted to go to Ross and tell him it would be okay, but truth was, the doctors weren't sure Paulie would ever wake up. Maybe it would be best to give them some privacy.

He started to back up and bumped into a pretty platinum blond nurse who'd been headed into the room. "Sorry," he said at the same time she said, "Excuse me."

Ross turned his bloodshot eyes to Niall. He scrubbed his wet cheeks with one hand, still clutching Paulie's hand with the other. "So now you know. What are you going to do?"

The anger in his eyes didn't mask the fear or the despair. Before Niall could respond the nurse spoke.

"Paulie's looking much better." She checked the various machines that beeped rhythmically in the room.

The young chef lay unconscious in the bed. The white room, sheets, and blanket gave his normally Mediterranean look a sallow complexion. If this was better, Niall hated to imagine what he'd looked like when he'd been brought in.

The nurse took Paulie's pulse, and stared at her wrist to time it. Without glancing away from her task, she said, "I'm coming to your room in five minutes to take your vitals, Ross."

"Can't you do it in here, Erin? I don't want to leave. What if Paulie wakes up while I'm gone? He'll be all alone." Ross reclaimed his seat and pressed a kiss to his lover's hand. The move was tender and intimate. So natural. Why hadn't he seen Ross do that before? Why hadn't he noticed his brother's feelings for Paulie went deeper than friendship?

Erin tossed a calculating look Niall's way, then nodded. "I'll make you a deal. You can stay in here if you promise not to go on a walkabout. We need to make sure all those nasty drugs are out of your system, okay?"

Ross nodded, then ran a finger down Paulie's cheek. "I promise. I won't leave."

Erin nodded and left.

Niall doubted Ross's promise had been made to her. Ross hadn't taken his eyes off Paulie when he spoke. He seemed as unable to leave him as Niall had been to leave Hannah trapped in the kitchen.

He crossed the room and took Paulie's free hand, then waited until his brother looked at him. With a deep breath, Niall said, "Nothing."

Ross screwed up his face. "Nothing? What are you talking about?"

"You asked me what I was going to do about you finally admitting you're gay." Niall shrugged. "Nothing. I've always known."

Ross's jaw went slack, and he slowly shook his head. "You couldn't have."

"Do you remember when I came home from boot camp with Angelo?" Niall asked, then grinned at Ross's expression. "You were twelve and you got that same look on your face the first time you saw him."

"You can't tell me you knew. I heard you telling him to stay away from me—"

"Yeah, you were *twelve*. I'd have kicked his ass if he'd touched you. You were a kid." Niall conceded the point. "Gay, yes, but still a child. I didn't want anyone to take advantage of my kid brother. You deserved someone who'd love you. And trust me, Angelo was not that guy."

Ross lowered his head, resting it on Paulie's hand. "Why didn't you tell me?"

"I figured when you wanted to talk about it, you would. It's not like I walked up to you and said, 'Hey, I'm straight.' It didn't matter to me who you loved, as long as they loved you and treated you with respect." Niall frowned because Ross's shoulders shook again. Ah, crap. He hadn't meant to make him cry.

"So does that mean you're out of the closet?" Paulie's words were weak but clear.

Ross's head snapped up.

The chef's eyes fluttered several times before they finally opened to slits. "Does this mean I'll finally get invited to dinner with your parents?"

"Yes!" Ross popped out of his chair and rained kisses

down on Paulie's face. "Yes. Yes. If you still want me, then definitely, yes."

The machines in the room beeped and popped. In seconds, Erin was back. The spitfire blonde shooed Niall and Ross into the hallway. "Welcome back, Paulie. Great to see you."

Niall clapped his brother on the shoulder and was stunned when Ross threw his arms around him. His brother hadn't willingly hugged him since he'd joined the Marines. Until this moment, he hadn't realized how much he'd missed him.

"Thank you," Ross said when he pulled away. He used his open robe to wipe the tears from his cheeks. "Paulie had broken it off with me a few weeks ago because I wouldn't tell you about us. He said he wouldn't be shamed into silence."

"Ah, the drinking binge."

"Yes." Ross lifted his shoulders, then let them sag again. "He called me a coward. Guess I was."

"You're not a coward and you're not a kid anymore." Niall took his baby brother by both shoulders and stared into his eyes. "You faced down a serial killer. No, don't look away from me. Michael would have killed you. He damn near killed Paulie. You both survived it.

"It would be cowardly to sink into a bottle and pretend this didn't happen. But you're not doing that. You've been by his bed when you should have been resting. You can make it through this together."

Ross's eyes brimmed but he lifted his chin. "If I'm not a kid anymore does that mean you're going to stop coming down on me?"

Niall winced at a truth that didn't sit well with him. "I promise to try. And I'll start by handing you the reins to the catering side of the business when the Boxing Cat is back up and running again. I'll keep my nose out of it, unless you ask for my help."

"Seriously?" Ross's face lit up. "And Paulie?"

"What about him? He still works for the Cat. He can cater with you if that's what you both want." Niall patted his brother's shoulder. "He was badly beaten. It won't be an easy road for him. Given what I just saw in there, I think he'll recover faster with you at his side. I think you both will. I heard you promise not to leave him. So don't."

"I won't. Not ever again." The fierce determination in Ross's eyes reminded him of Hannah.

"Good." He clapped his brother on the shoulders again. "Now go back in there and be with the one you love."

"Where are you headed?" Ross called out when Niall was halfway to the elevator.

"To kiss the one I love."

HANNAH HOBBLED ON crutches to the door of Shelley's hospital room. She paused at the conversation inside.

"You should be on your honeymoon, Jules," Shelley said, then grunted. "I'm fine."

"Right. You have a broken arm and severe concussion, but you're fine. Good thing for you, I'm here. Who would fluff your pillow for you if I wasn't?" Jules asked, her tone teasing. Shuffling noises indicated she moved from her chair next to the bed to do exactly that.

"I have a husband and a son, you know."

"And where are they?" Jules asked.

"Beau is back home with Karma and hopefully getting some sleep. Dev is at the station finishing paperwork," Shelley replied with a note of amusement in her tone. "I hope Hannah gets here soon. Dev said the doctor wasn't going to admit her. Just wanted to run a few X-rays. I still can't believe we both survived that explosion."

"I'm glad that psycho didn't survive." Jules's words cut a swath of uncomfortable silence and kept Hannah hovering by the door.

"That's a little vicious for you, isn't it?" Shelley briefly met Hannah's gaze. A white bandage wrapped around her bruised head. Her right eye was swollen and discolored from the blow she'd received at the restaurant. The sight had Hannah's stomach jittering.

"Maybe, but he tried to kill my sisters. Both of them." Her words came out as if she choked back tears. "I couldn't imagine losing you again after getting to know you. And I haven't even had a chance to talk to Hannah. He could have stolen her from me before I ever heard her voice."

"I'm here," Hannah said, hoisting herself awkwardly across the threshold. "The X-rays are all clear. No broken bones."

Jules pushed to her feet. Her straight red hair was pulled up in a ponytail that swung to the collar of her blue sundress. A huge smile on her face, she crossed the room with her arms wide. "Hannah!"

In seconds, Hannah was engulfed in a huge hug. The scent of strawberries wrapped around her. There was something so familiar about being hugged and smelling strawberries. Some faint memory of dolls and sunshine on green grass. And laughter.

"I remember you," Hannah said, tears clogging her throat. "We used to play with something in the backyard. Dolls?" She glanced from Jules to where Shelley lay in the bed with her arm trussed up in a cast. "And you used to bandage a stray dog's paw, then give it treats for being a good patient."

Shelley nodded, her lips quivering but smiling. "Sounds like us."

"I remember that," Hannah said again in delighted surprise. "I thought the only things I would remember would be the memories I lifted when I touched something that belonged to you. But I remember that."

Jules burst into tears. Big, loud, noisy sobs that had Shelley rolling her eyes. "Don't mind her. She got all weepy the first time she saw me too. Sit here and let her get it out of her system."

"I did not. I helped you get a kitten out of your bra," Jules replied with a scowl and sniffed. "But sit, Hannah. You should have your leg up, right? That's what Dev said."

"Wow, Dev really stayed on top of the doctors here."

"Had to. He needed it for the paperwork." Shelley winked. "This is the biggest case to hit Tidewater in fifteen years. And Dev got the collar."

Shelley pumped her good fist twice in the air.

"A little proud?" Hannah asked.

"Super proud."

Hannah took the chair next to the bed and allowed a very weepy Jules to fuss over her for a few minutes. Finally, Jules dragged over a second chair and sat.

"I wanted to surprise you at the wedding reception," Hannah admitted. She circled a finger in the air to indicate the sterile walls. "This wasn't exactly the place I had in mind for a family reunion."

"Could be worse," Shelley said, handing Jules the box of tissues. "At least you're here. If, uh, you're going to be in town for a while, we'd like to spend a little time with you."

"Yes, no pressure though." Jules nodded, then pitched the used tissue into the wastepaper basket. "Oh, who am I kidding? I don't care about pressure. You could've died at the hands of a psycho tonight. So, I intend to spend every second I can getting to know you. I can't believe I found you and almost lost you all in the same day."

Jules dissolved into tears again.

Shelley rolled her eyes and shrugged. "Give her a little more time. It's been a long day for her. She supposed to be on her *honeymoon* and not sitting in a hospital room."

Jules gave her a watery glare, then blew her nose. "Seth understands that I need to be here. Do you really think he's complaining? He's at the station with Dev closing the case on that psycho Mercy-Michael."

Hannah shivered at the mention of Mercy's name.

Shelley rubbed a consoling hand on Hannah's arm. "You okay, Han?"

"I guess. It's just—" Hannah cut herself off and gave her head a sharp shake. "Never mind."

"No, talk to us." Jules sat on the bed facing Hannah and Shelley. "We're family. We want to know."

Hannah considered changing the subject. Had planned to do exactly that but when she opened her mouth the words spilled out. "Being in Michael's head was terrifying. He wasn't always damaged. He was tortured by his mother and his sister for years. His mother had some twisted hatred of men. She killed them in front of him. I don't think he ever understood why she didn't kill him too. She and his sister tortured a confused little boy until he snapped."

"You think they're why he went after men?" Shelley's red brows narrowed. "Like they made him gay or a transvestite or something."

"No." Hannah shook her head slowly. "Michael was always gay. They turned him into a murderer. They twisted love in his mind until he confused it with sex and violent death. When his mother killed the man he thought of as his gray angel, he disconnected. Mercy was created from that loss. Ironic really. Mercy was created by the very women she later killed."

"He," Jules corrected.

Hannah shook her head. "No. Michael was a he. That part of him that became Mercy was a woman."

They sat there in silence for a long time. So long, Hannah regretted even talking about what she'd seen in the visions. This wasn't who she was. She wasn't morbid and dark. "Can we please talk about anything else?"

"I have a ferret." Shelley's eyes rounded. "What? She said she wanted to talk about something else. I could talk about Lucy all day."

"Don't tell Dev that." Jules grinned, then she leaned over and said in a stage whisper, "He still cups himself if Lucy gets too close."

"Stop that!" Shelley laughed. "Don't let Dev hear you. He'll be calling her a man-eater again."

And just like that, the spell was broken. Laughter filled the hospital room. Even Shelley's singed hair from the explosion became a source of entertainment with Jules offering to trim it.

"Oh, no, you stay away from my hair. No one touches this but Niko. He'll fix it up." Shelley shooed away Jules's touch. She turned to Hannah. "He could probably help you too."

Hannah ran a hand through her hair, dismayed at the crunchy feeling. "Great, now I really *am* a crunchy earth dog."

"I'm never going to live that down," Niall called from the doorway.

She met his gaze and her heart bounced into her throat. "Hi, Marine."

"Aww, they're so cute. Ow!" Jules said when Shelley elbowed her. "What? They are."

"Pay no mind to our eldest sister, Hannah. You should see her watch Hallmark movies. She always gets misty when the credits start to roll."

"Like you don't." Jules shrugged. "I like the music."

"Speaking of music, did I tell you?" Shelley said to Jules. "I got Ian to score us backstage passes to Savannah Storms's next concert. Wanna go with us, Hannah? You can come too, Niall."

"When is it?" Niall said, coming through the door. He carried a vase of flowers and a box of cookies. He set the cookies on Shelley's tray table.

"You didn't have to bring me cookies, Niall," Shelley said, smiling.

"I didn't. These are from Karma. She told me to tell you not to worry about Beau. Your son is gorging on popcorn and they're on their second Transformers movie." He laughed when Shelley groaned.

Jules popped up, stepping aside to give him room.

"These are from me." He handed the flowers to Hannah, then brushed his lips over hers. "Hi."

"Hi," she said back. Warmth spread through her like sunshine. The lovely green glow bloomed from the center of his chest and pulsed around him. It was a sign.

She was home.

At last.

EPILOGUE

THE LATE AUGUST afternoon was hot and sweat dripped down her back, soaking her Savannah Storms concert T-shirt. Hannah didn't care. Music pumped through the air. Concertgoers danced on the grassy hill all around her. She'd danced too until she thought her feet would fall off. Then she and Karma headed to the concession stand to get drinks for her sisters, their husbands, Zig, and Niall.

"Hey, Karma, come here!" Ian called to her friend. "I need to talk to ya."

Karma frowned, but collected her tray of drinks. "Better go see what he wants. Meet you at the blanket. If you see Zig up there, tell him where I went."

Hannah nodded and carried the other four drinks up the hill, dodging dancers, volleying beach balls, and people lying on the grass. The summer had been a dream and it was only getting better. Next week, she'd start working for one of Dev's many cousins. Dustin was a master electrician who needed—yeah, right—an apprentice. While Hannah doubted he needed her, she was grateful for the salary and the experience.

"Over here!" Shelley called out, waving her arms in the air. Hannah grinned and made her way over. She handed the tray of drinks to her sister and then plopped down on the blanket next to her. "Where'd everybody go?"

Shelley sipped her beer. "Jules and Seth went to get his daughter a T-shirt. Dev got a call from Ryan about an arson case TSS has been looking into. And Niall—"

"Is right here, love." His body cast a long shadow over them. "Miss me?"

"Definitely." Hannah patted the space beside her but he made no move to join her on the blanket. Instead, he glanced at Shelley.

"Well, that's my cue." Shelley hopped up and disappeared into the crowd without another word.

"Am I supposed to believe it's a coincidence that she needed to run?" Hannah asked, turning back to Niall.

He knelt on the blanket, a black velvet box in his hands. "You don't believe in coincidences."

Her heart beat faster than the drums in the song pounding through the air. "Niall?"

"Hannah, I love you more than I've ever loved anyone in my life. More than I ever dreamed possible. I want to wake up with you, go to sleep next to you, and know when I'm old and my hair's fallen out you'll still be there keeping my life interesting. I know you can touch this ring and see into my head. So put it on and see what I have in mind for the rest of our lives. Hannah Eleanor Halloran, will you marry me?"

Hannah stared at the box, at the Marine who'd stolen her heart, and said, "Of course I'll marry you, Marine."

Read on for a sneak peek at the second Tidewater novel from Mary Behre

GUARDED

Available now from Berkley Sensation!

"SOMETHING'S WRONG WITH Mr. Fuzzbutt." Beau's angelic voice rang out seconds before the backside of his long-haired black guinea pig bounced before Dr. Shelley Morgan's eyes. At almost the same moment, a cry went up from the back room of the small veterinary clinic.

"Shelley, I need you!" Feet pounded quickly down the short hall before Jacob, the veterinary clinic's too-excitable intern, burst into the room yelling, "Lucy is trying to turn Hercules into her Thanksgiving dinner. And this time I think she might just chew his balls off."

"Language! And Thanksgiving's four weeks away. At most, she wants a light snack," Shelley said, pushing to her feet and sweeping the fur ball known as Mr. Fuzzbutt into her hands.

But Jacob hadn't heard her attempt to lighten the moment. The intern/groomer/assistant had already spun around and disappeared into the back room. His cries of, "Stop that, Lucy. Get up, Herc," were nearly drowned out by the cacophony of dogs barking.

Ah, it *was* a Wednesday. Most people hated Mondays because they believed the first day of the workweek was full of insanity, but Shelley knew otherwise. In her twenty-four years of life, every major catastrophe occurred on the day most folks referred to as "hump day." Today was shaping up to be as invariably crazy as every other weekday that started with the letter *W*.

"Doc, can you help him?" Beau's voice, still high-pitched from youth, wobbled as he spoke.

She turned to the worried ten-year-old who was small for his age. His large, luminous, brown eyes were framed by thick, black glasses. His clothes, although threadbare and clearly hand-me-downs, were clean as were his faded blue sneakers.

"Don't worry, Beau. I'm sure he'll be fine. Just have a seat in the waiting area and I'll be back shortly. I'll bring Mr. . . ." she couldn't bring herself to say the word *Fuzzbutt* to the child, and settled with "your little buddy back after I've examined him."

"Okay, Doc. I trust you." Beau nodded. His words so mature for one so young. "But I can't just sit and wait. How about I bring in the bags of dog food from outside?"

"That would be a big help, Beau. You remember where the storeroom is? Just stack the ones you can carry in there. And don't try to lift the big ones."

Not that the little guy would be able to do much. The last time the clinic received donations, the dog food had come in fifty-pound bags. Beau likely didn't weigh more than sixty-five pounds himself. Plus, it had rained late last night and the town handyman she'd hired hadn't had a chance to fix the hole in the shed's roof. So chances were good several of the bags were sodden and useless.

Still, he beamed as if she'd just handed him a hundred-dollar bill. "You know it! I'll have the bags all put away before you can bring Mr. Fuzzbutt back. Just you wait and see."

Then Beau was out the front door. The length of bells hanging from the handle jangled and banged against the glass as he took off around the corner to the storage shed.

Gotta love small towns. Shelley couldn't suppress the grin, even as good ole Mr. F made a soft *whoop, whoop* noise in her hands. She glanced into his little black eyes and asked, "So are you really sick?"

The eye contact formed an instant telepathic connection. Shelley's world swirled to gray. Still vaguely aware of her surroundings, she focused her attention inward on the movielike scenes sent from the little boar in her hands.

An image of Beau's anxious face peering between the bars of the cage, filling and refilling the bowl with pellets, sprang into her mind. At first she thought the guinea pig was repeating the same image over and over, but quickly she realized what was happening.

"Oh, so you've been eating," she said. "But Beau doesn't realize it because he's been topping off the food bowl."

Mr. F. *whooped* again.

She chuckled. "Well, you're a pretty wise pig not to eat everything you've been given. Many others wouldn't have such restraint. I'm not sure I would. You sure you don't feel sick?"

The little pig winged an image of Beau snuggling him close and occasionally kissing him on the head as they watched *Scooby-Doo.* The image was so sweet she let herself get lost in the moment and almost forgot she was at the clinic.

"*Shell-ley,*" Jacob wailed.

She jumped and turned in time to see Jacob burst through the swinging door separating the back hallway from the reception area of the clinic. "Jeez! Jacob. You'll freak out the animals."

"Come *on.* I can't stop her and he's just lying there!" Jacob gestured wildly with both hands.

Right. Lucy attacking Hercules. Although Lucy was all of three pounds and a *ferret*, to Hercules, a ninety-pound dog. How much damage could she do?

"It's Wednesday," Shelley said on a sigh. "Although, at least if it started out like this, it can't get any crazier."

Mr. Fuzzbutt whooped again. *I swear, the little pig's laughing at me.*

"Jacob, take Mr. F and put him in examination room

one." She hurried through the swinging white door, which led to the back, stopping briefly to hand Beau's pet to her intern. "There's a small cage in the cabinet under the sink. Pull it out and put him in it, then meet me in the doggie spa."

Without waiting for a response, she hustled to the back room. She usually avoided this area. She'd spent a weekend painting murals of fields, dog bones, blue skies, and fire hydrants on the walls to give dogs and their owners the impression of luxury accommodations. According to Jacob and their boss, Dr. Kessler, her hard work paid off. Unless she was in the room with the canines.

Today, six dogs were there for the Thanksgiving Special, a deluxe grooming, complete with a complimentary toy turkey. Metal cages lined one wall, each with a plush foam bed. The occupants waited in doggy paradise for their turn at the day's scheduled deluxe treatment by Jacob. Soft strains of Bach filtered through the air, barely audible over the ruckus of barks, yips, and howls as the canines commented on the show in the middle of the floor.

That was, until one of them caught her scent. Mrs. Hoffstedder's beagle noticed her first. He let out a single high-pitched yowl, then lowered his head and covered his eyes with his paws. One by one, the other five dogs did the same.

Shelley didn't bother to wonder why they feared her. She'd given up asking that question years ago. It's not as if she'd ever beaten an animal. Jeez, she didn't even raise her voice. But almost every dog she'd come into contact with for the past seven years either hid from her or tried to attack her.

Thank God, Jacob had remembered to lock their cages before he called for her, or it would have been dog-maggedon as the pooches ran for freedom.

She had to be the world's weirdest vet. Telepathic, she could talk to any animal alive, including snakes, hedgehogs, and naked mole rats. Any animal, that is, except for the canine variety. She hadn't spoken to a single dog since Barty, her Bay retriever, died in the car crash with her parents all those years ago. Just the thought of them made her chest tight. She shoved away the memories and focused on the clinic's current crisis.

Dr. Kessler's extremely valuable St. Bernard, Hercules, lay stretched out in the middle of the floor. The six-month-old puppy remained still. No small feat, considering Lucy, her beautiful cinnamon-colored sable ferret, was steadily chewing on his upper thigh, incredibly close to his testicles.

"You okay, Hercules?" she asked, gingerly kneeling down beside the pair and making eye contact with the dog.

Lifting only his head, he looked at her.

The telepathic connection zapped into place. An image of her prying her ferret off his body followed by him licking his dangly bits in relief flashed through her mind. She had to put her hand to her mouth to stifle a chuckle. Herc let out a loud sigh and dropped his head back to the floor.

Unlike every other dog in the world, Hercules neither feared nor loathed her. He didn't love her either. Usually he ignored her completely. But today he seemed to recognize if anyone could save his balls—*literally*—it was her.

"Lucy," she asked, focusing on her pet. "Why are you doing that?"

The ferret managed to glare briefly at Shelley and continue her assault at the same time.

In that momentary bit of eye contact, another collage of images soared into Shelley's head. It took a moment for Shelley to assemble them into an order she could understand.

"Ah, Hercules, *the gaseous*, accidentally sat on you, again, after eating his breakfast. Now you want to put 'that upstart pup' in his place?" Shelley sighed. "All right, you had your revenge. It's not like he wants to be gassy. Next time, try to avoid him after he eats. Let's go." The ferret didn't budge. Shelley prayed for patience and for no blood to be drawn. "Lucy, let go right now. You can't gnaw off his leg. And if you could, he'd be three-legged, wobbly, and end up squashing you anyway. Then you'd be trapped and forced to breathe his stench all day."

Hercules let out a rumbling *woof* of assent and shifted his weight, as if threatening to fulfill Shelley's prediction.

Lucy leapt away from Hercules with a shriek. She raced up Shelley's arm and wrapped herself around Shelley's neck for comfort. "You're all right, girl. Why don't you snuggle with me for a bit, hmmm?"

She patted the ferret on the head and rose to her feet. Hercules immediately began intimately examining his body, reassuring himself that he was still fully intact.

"Wow, how do you do that?" Jacob appeared behind her. She turned to find his brown eyes rounded and his mouth agape. "Ferrets are more like cats than dogs. But yours actually seems to understand you. Oh! They could make a reality show out of you. It could be called 'The Ferret Whisperer.'"

Shelley swallowed a chuckle; no sense encouraging him. Instead, she spoke directly to the brown-and-white puppy behemoth still at her feet. "You're okay now, Hercules. It's safe to move again. Thanks for not eating her."

Hercules sprang to his paws and raced out of the room without so much as a backward glance.

And we're back to ignoring me. World order has returned. She chuckled and didn't try to disguise it this time.

"Don't laugh. I'm serious," Jacob said. "We could make some real money if Hollywood ever heard about you." He stood, arms akimbo, in the doorway. His shaggy black hair hung in his face. He jerked his head to the right, throwing the sideways bangs out of his eyes. "I swear, I went near her and that rat tried to munch on my fingers. But *you* . . . you walked in and talked to her like Dr. Freaking Dolittle. And don't think I haven't seen you do it before. Mr. Fuzzbutt, for example. Yep, your parents misnamed you. You should have been called John Dolittle."

"I'm a woman."

"Jane then."

She shook her head at him. Little did Jacob know, she was more like the fictional character than Hugh Lofting had ever dreamed possible. Except she didn't speak to animals in their own languages. Shelley simply communicated with them telepathically. All creatures were connected. Well, mostly.

Humans were an entirely different story. She often felt like an outsider. And she was a member of the species.

"Lucy's a ferret, not a rat. If you're going to be a vet, you should know that. And as for what happened in the spa, it wasn't hard to figure out what was going on. Look, she's a good ferret who normally gets along with everyone, animals and people alike. I figured she must have been upset with Hercules. You saw him sit on her last week. And let's face it; he hasn't adjusted to the new dog food well. It didn't take much of a mental leap to figure something like that might have happened again," Shelley said, leaving the back room and heading toward her office.

"Yeah, I suppose so." Jacob sounded disappointed, but he rallied. Hurrying down the hall, he reiterated his previous comment. "Still, I've seen you do that with other animals too. It's like you know what they're thinking. Is that how you skipped ahead in vet school? You read the minds of the animal patients. Hey, would that be cheating? Can I learn how to do it?"

"What are you talking about?" Shelley stopped and faced him. His dizzying barrage of questions too much to absorb. She instead focused on the first one. "You can't skip ahead in veterinary school. I graduated last year."

"You're not old enough to have gone all the way through." Jacob waved at her. "Hello, you're my age, and I'm just getting started. Next semester anyway."

"First, you're barely old enough to be carded, but I'm twenty-four. Second, I graduated from high school with my associate's degree."

"Seriously? You took college classes in high school?"

Something about the tone of his voice set her teeth on edge, but still she kept her voice light. "Yes, and you could have done it too. I went from there to the university, where I finished up my bachelor's in twenty-four months because I didn't take summers off. Then I enrolled in veterinary school. I didn't *skip* anything."

Jacob frowned at her, then gave her a very obvious once-over. "You're . . . you're a *nerd*? But you're . . . hot. For a vet who dresses like my grandmother."

Shelley glanced at her four-inch heels. "Did you just compare me to your *grandmother*? Does she walk around in ankle-breaking high heels too?"

Jacob just grinned.

Shelley's eyes were going to pop out of her head if she listened to this guy another second. Without responding, she spun on her heel and closed the distance to her office door. Once inside the tiny space, she propped up the wooden and plastic-mesh baby gate across her doorway, designed to keep Hercules from wandering in while she was out. Setting Lucy on the floor, Shelley gave her pet a stern frown, then added aloud for good measure, "Behave. I mean it."

Lucy shook her head, sneezed indignantly, and pranced beneath Shelley's desk where her small travel cage rested. After climbing inside, she curled up into a tight ball and did what ferrets do best. She went to sleep.

"What do you want me to do with the guinea pig?" Jacob asked. All questions about her age, her clothing, and her career seemingly forgotten. He leaned over the mesh gate rather than crossing into her sanctuary. Not that she could take refuge in it. The computer work she had to file needed to be done on the main computer out front. Her desktop had been crashing all week, and the repairman hadn't come yet.

"Leave him in the examination room until Beau's ready to take him home. I've already examined him. He's fine," she said, gathering her supplies and carefully stepping over the gate. "Look, I've got plenty of paperwork to finish before Dr. Kessler returns. So if you want to get started on Mrs. Hoffstedder's beagle, that'd be great."

"No problem," Jacob said and disappeared into the back.

The smell of cinnamon and pinecones permeated the receptionist area. The scent was an instant soother for her nerves. Now that the dogs in the spa had calmed down, all was quiet. Peaceful.

Settling into the chair, she pulled up the afternoon schedule on the computer. The muscles in her shoulders eased. At barely noon, she had an hour before the next animal . . . er, guest, was set to arrive. Fifty guaranteed, crazy-free minutes.

She exhaled a relieved sigh. A little more tension slipped away.

Breathe, relax. This Wednesday isn't that bad.

"Uh, excuse me . . . Dr. Morgan?" Jacob's voice sounded a little too tentative. A little too respectful.

She glanced up to find the young intern standing before her. His gaze bounced around the room. He looked everywhere but at her.

An icy sensation slithered into her stomach, making it shrink. "What did you do?"

"It wasn't my fault," he said, quickly. "I didn't realize you'd left the front door open. I certainly wouldn't have let Hercules wander through the clinic unattended if you'd told me that the place was open for business. Or that you had some kid carrying bags of food inside from the shed. I would have locked him up."

"Him, who?" The words were out of her mouth nanoseconds before the answer slammed into her.

Hercules. The dog. *The* dog.

"Are you telling me that Hercules, Dr. Kessler's prized St. Bernard . . ." Her voice pitched higher with each word. "The one he calls his *only true baby* is *missing*?"

"Not my fault." Jacob held up his hands.

From behind him came a sound of someone sniffing back tears. "I'm so sorry, Doc. I didn't see him by the door until after I'd opened it. I tried to stop him. I had him real good for about a minute."

Beau stepped out from behind Jacob. His blue shirt was torn from the shoulder to the wrist down one sleeve. Worse, he had an ugly patch of road rash on his upper left arm that disappeared up the ripped shirt. His glasses were askew and hanging by an arm.

She raced around Jacob and checked Beau's injuries. Pointing at the intern, she ordered, "You, chase after him."

"Yeah, see, I can't run. Remember, I tore my ACL doing that Mud Run with the Barbie Twins back in September?" He gestured to the brace on his knee. He wasn't on crutches anymore, but that didn't mean he was cleared to go chasing a dog all over town.

"Shoot, shack, shipwreck!" she cursed, kicking off her ridiculous heels. What she wouldn't give for a pair of sneakers and some jeans right now. "Jacob, help Beau get cleaned up. There's a sewing kit in my desk, get it out and we'll repair his shirt. See if you can fix his glasses. Make sure the rest of the dogs are locked up tight. Do *not* answer the phone for anyone. Let it go to voice mail. And for the love of that St. Bernard, if Dr. Kessler returns before I come back, do not tell him you let his dog escape."

"What do I say?"

"I don't know. Tell him I took Herc for a walk or something."

"Right, like he'll believe that one," Jacob scoffed. "Dogs hate you, remember? So maybe you aren't like Dr. Dolittle after all, huh?"

"Jacob! Focus." Shelley headed for the door, calling over her shoulder, "Let's hope Dr. Kessler doesn't beat me back here."

Shelley shoved open the door. Sunlight poured in, along with a blast of unseasonably warm November air, belying the sodden state of the area after last night's downpour of sleet and rain. At least she wasn't running in her stockings in the rain or snow. This time. Yeah, like that single bit of good news made up for the fact that it was a Wednesday, and she was about to run outside shoeless on the still wet and most likely muddy ground.

Hercules, come back before anyone in town sees you doing your Born Free *impression.*

That would just put the stale dog treat on top of her already rancid dog-food bowl of a day.

TIDEWATER POLICE DETECTIVE Devon Jones pulled his black Lexus into the parking lot of Elkridge Veterinary Clinic. He cut the engine, imagining what he'd say when he saw Shelley again.

Her email to him last week had been like a gift from God. He'd been searching for her for weeks. Even going so far as to track down her fiancé—his former roommate—and that was all kinds of a suckfest because Camden Figurelle, that rat bastard, was in Africa. In the *Peace Corps.* There was no way to get in touch with him, if it wasn't an absolute emergency.

What the hell was Cam doing in the Peace Corps anyway? They were supposed to be married by now.

Shells. Shelley Grace Morgan.

He'd spent the past few weeks searching for Figurelle because the wedding should have happened last summer. Cam's family had listed the engagement in the society section of the *Baltimore Sun.* Dev read it, marked the date, and noted, with some disappointment, he hadn't received an invitation. Not that he'd have gone. As much as he wanted Shells to be happy, he hadn't wanted to watch her marry the wrong man.

But she hadn't married Cam. Maybe Shelley had come to her senses and seen the prick for what he was and given him the old heave-ho. The thought brought a smile to Dev's face.

Still, wrong man or not, at least Cam had been a link to Shells. Without the connection, Dev had been stumped in the search for her. But then two days ago, she contacted him through an old email address he'd kept from his college days. And damn if that wasn't some good luck.

Dev pulled his phone from his inside jacket pocket and clicked to her saved email. He read it again, although he had it memorized.

Hey Dev,

It's me, Shelley Morgan. I know it's been a long time but I could use your help. I heard you're a police officer now but what I need is to use your puzzle-solving skills. Speaking of the police, I remember you wanted to be a detective. Did that ever happen?

Anyway, I was wondering if I could convince you to leave Tidewater for a few days and come to Elkridge. It's a little town on the border of Suffolk and Tidewater. Great place. Friendly people. Quiet community. Low crime. Sounds like heaven, right?

Well, something strange is going on. I think. See, there's this private zoo. Since I moved here last June there have been a number of unexplained disappearances of animals. I've tried contacting the USDA, but they're no help. It's hard to explain in an email but I just know something is wrong. I've tried investigating this on my own, but I can't piece it together. Plus, I have to be careful how much noise I make. People in small towns talk, you know.

If you could come and take a look around, I've got some papers, animal records, and old newspaper clippings. Maybe I'm paranoid and there's nothing really wrong here. But if I'm not, then your time could save the life of an animal. Or ten.

Email me back and I'll give you directions to the veterinary clinic where I work.

Hope to hear from you soon,
Shells

He darkened the screen and returned the phone to his pocket. Maybe he should have replied to her email or called first instead of just driving over. But what could he say?

"Hi, Shells, long time no see. Can you believe it's been three years since graduation? Time sure flies and all that. While I want to know about this mystery you've unearthed, I'm more interested in the fact that you and Cam aren't together anymore. I've been crazy about you since the first time you smiled at me. Had you not been Camden's girl in school, I would have moved heaven and earth to get you into my bed. I also have a big surprise for you. I've found something of yours. If you'll just come back to Tidewater with me, I'll show you."

Yeah, that would go over really well. He sounded like a stalker or like he was just hoping for a quick-and-dirty one-night stand. And a one-night stand was absolutely not what he wanted. Although, he'd settle for it if that's all he could have.

Dev gave himself a mental shake. He'd come to give her news she'd once told him she never thought she'd hear. Her older sister, Jules, was alive, well, happy, living in Tidewater, still seeing ghosts, and searching for Shelley.

The news of her long-lost sibling should be enough for Shelley to forgive his disappearance after graduation. But really, he hadn't known what to say. And Camden had made it pretty damned clear that Dev was not welcome in their lives. Plus, it wasn't like Shelley had called him, even once, in all that time.

Okay, so she'd been busy getting her veterinary license and building a happy life with Cam-the-sack. At least Dev had thought she'd been happy, until a few days ago. Although he couldn't quite ignore the pinch to his ego that she hadn't called him sooner. After all, they had been friends.

Christ, he was starting to sound like a freaking girl. First brooding over *feelings* and worrying about why she hadn't contacted him sooner. Next he'd want to start a knitting circle.

Okay, so his motives for coming here weren't completely altruistic. He was man enough to admit to himself that if a hint of the spark he'd felt for her back in college still ignited when he saw her again, he'd do it. He'd ask her out . . . This time, no one would stop him.

He'd use the next few days to let her really get to know him. Help her with her little zoo problem and take her to see her sister Jules. Maybe then, he'd have finally earned the right to spend time with the sexiest, most caring woman he'd ever met.

Dev shoved open the car door and stepped onto the damp cobblestone. His Ferragamos crunched over the wet, gritty street. He glanced around the nearly deserted road of the picturesque little town. Despite Elkridge's location on the scenic James River—with no elks or ridges in sight—the place lacked one key element Tidewater was known for.

Salt air.

This afternoon, the scent on the warm November wind was rife with apples and cinnamon from the local shops. Refreshing and sweet.

Just like Shelley. Assuming she was as perfect as he remembered. Right. Like she could be anything other than the sweet, shy girl he'd crushed on so long ago. She'd probably be so grateful he had come to help her solve her mystery and had found Jules on top of it that she'd ask him out.

Dream on, man!

While he and his partner had wrapped up the biggest case Tidewater had seen all year, there were others that still needed his attention. A few days were all he could afford to spend away from the office. He'd really only taken the five days because he'd foolishly hoped he'd what . . . see Shelley and she'd finally fall in love with him? They'd run off to Vegas and get married?

Right and we'll have a unicorn and Elvis stand up for us at the ceremony.

Exhaling hard, he started to make his way toward a whitewashed brick building with the Elkridge Veterinary Clinic sign hanging over the front door.

A huge, blurry mass appeared so quickly in front of him, it seemed to pop into existence from nowhere.

Blam!

It flew at his chest, knocking him to the ground. Dev's head smacked the pavement. Tiny stars burst to vibrant multicolored life in front of his eyes.

The something was large and furry and pinning him. Still he managed to get a hand free. He reached for his sidearm, which . . . shit! . . . he'd left locked in the trunk of his car.

The damned beast burrowed its muzzle against his cheek and rumbled a deep, throaty growl.

A bear?

Cold fear slid down his neck. Or that might have been the animal's bloodthirsty drool. He might be a city boy, but he'd heard all about bear attacks in small towns like this one. He held perfectly still, eyes closed, playing dead as he tried to get a sense of the animal's size. If it were a bear, it wasn't fully grown. A cub, maybe? But a big one.

Relief at the thought evaporated.

Where there's a cub, there's a mama bear somewhere. Dev couldn't just lie there; he needed to protect his vital organs before the animal figured out he was still warm enough to chew on. He rolled onto his side and into a ball, protecting his head, face, arms, and torso.

The bear seemed to tighten its hold on him. Its breath coming hot and nose hair curling against Dev's ear.

He was going to be eaten by a bear in the middle of this damned street while everyone in Elkridge was out to lunch. Trying to curl more tightly, he elbowed the beast in a front leg. It yelped.

Wait. Bears don't yelp. Plus, it wasn't trying to bite him. No, it was pawing at his arms, not painfully. *Playfully?*

A long, wet tongue slid across his hair, his ear, his *cheek*. And that growl he heard was followed by a deep *woof*. A dog, he was pinned by a dog. A great bear of a dog, but definitely the canine species as opposed to the Ursus americanus.

Dev slowly turned onto his back, then drew his arms away from his face only to throw them up again when a slobbery tongue swiped from one cheek across his nose to the other. "Ugh. Serious dog breath. You need a breath mint, Fido."

Shifting onto his side, he attempted to scoot out from beneath the beast, but the dog took it as a game and began licking him in earnest down the neck of his suit. If he hadn't needed a shower before the dog knocked him down, between rolling on the cobblestone and the sloppy dog kisses, he certainly needed one now.

Hoping not to hurt the animal that was clearly looking for a playmate, Dev pushed at the beast's midsection in an effort to make a break for it. He'd barely touched the dog when someone yelled, "Stop it, you big bear! You'll hurt him."

Okay, that wasn't the first time in his life he'd been called a bear. Still, the words stung his pride. The average person might consider him to be bearlike, due to his large size, but he wasn't an animal. He was a police detective. A cop. A friggin' hero.

Although, at the moment he was in the least heroic position. Ever.

"Hercules, stop before you hurt him. You bad puppy," the voice said, closer now. "I'm really sorry about Hercules. Are you okay down there? Give me a minute. I've almost got his leash on him."

Ah, Hercules was the *dog's* name. She was calling the dog a big bear.

The relief coursing through him at that knowledge was quickly overshadowed by a sickening realization. He knew that voice.

There was a distinctive clink of metal on metal and the dog was off him.

"I'm so sorry," she said, then she laughed. The sound more exhalation of air than joy. "I'm really, *really* sorry. He doesn't normally do this. But I guess all creatures crave freedom, right? Are you . . . are you hurt?"

His gut shrank at her melodic voice. Now? She had to show up and see him covered in dog drool and muck, lying on the ground, pinned there by a playful bear-dog.

Maybe if I'm lucky, she won't recognize me beneath the slobber?

"Dev?" Her voice was closer now. He could feel her breath against his chin as she leaned down to look at him. "Is that you?"

"Uh . . . yeah." Dev lay there for a moment. His arm still firmly over his eyes and his head throbbing. His luck was good for buckets of suck.

"Why, bless your heart. Devon Jones, it *is* you." She sounded positively gleeful. "What are you doing down there?"

"Playing possum with Fido." He tugged his arm away and blinked open his eyes. The starbursts were gone, but he'd have a nice knot on the back of his skull later. It was already coming up.

And there she was. Leaning over him, her hair a cloud of red curls around her face. Concern and confusion crowded into her sapphire-blue eyes. Her pink lips twitched. "Thank God, it was you Hercules tackled. How do you do it? You always manage to show up just when I need saving."

If only that were true.

LOVE

ROMANCE NOVELS?

For news on all your favorite romance authors, sneak peeks into the newest releases, book giveaways, and much more—

"Like" Love Always on Facebook!

LoveAlwaysBooks

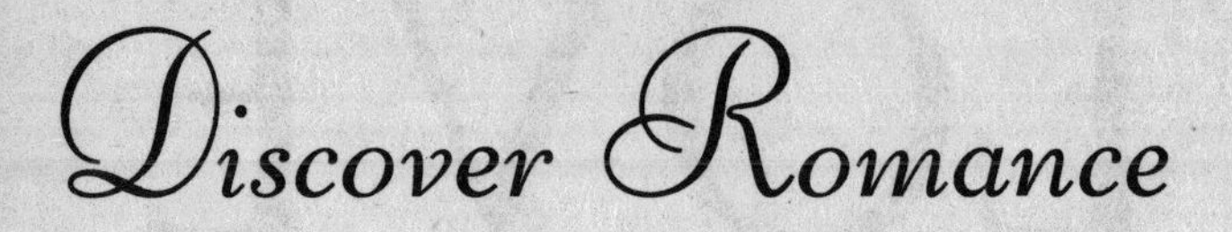

berkleyjoveauthors.com

See what's coming up next from your favorite romance authors and explore all the latest Berkley, Jove, and Sensation selections.

See what's new

~

Find author appearances

~

Win fantastic prizes

~

Get reading recommendations

~

Chat with authors and other fans

~

Read interviews with authors you love

berkleyjoveauthors.com

M1G0610